CELTIC LOVE KNOT TRILOGY

KRIS WELSH

Ordering Information:

Prime Seven Media
518 Landmann St.
Tomah City, WI 54660

Printed in the United States of America

TABLE OF CONTENTS

PART I

SCÁTHACH

I

Sepulchral yet beauteous,
the Otherworld, the isle of Hy Breasil, is my
fortress now -
I am forever young, my spirit looking down from Tír na nÓg,
with many a trained hero
by my side,
watching, waiting, willing, wanting, remembering...

I miss Alpae,
the Isle of Skyenorthwest,
her homecall, her voice, her *rúin adh*, silent secrets,
calling to me from the aeons,
calling me back.
I hear her gentle whispering, feel her soft, quiet tendrils
reaching to me, touching me,
both jeremiad and saudade,
enticing and evocative,
not so much maudlin as mournful,
as pining,
as yearning,
through the mists and veils of Time...

I miss the barefoot damp of Dún Scáith, my fortress of shadows,
for the ruins of Dún Scáthiag, another, later castle, stand on her now.
What once was cannot easily be forgotten,
nor should it be - partly vitrified, inhumed by the ravages of time,
even her beneficiary's fifteen foot high, five foot thick curtain walls,
now mostly fallen into the sea,
once standing summit-proud now only grass-covered foundations remaining,
that which never dies reestablishing dominance,
structural impermanence versus the indelible abattoir-taint of the detritus of the ages
(archaeological decline imbued with energetic resonance,
the haunted wailing and memories of blood)
verification of my tangible and intangible impact,
ephemeral in the scheme of things,
lingering, not quite sempiternal...
If you allow me the vanity of remembrance
enter my impossible web with me now:
assuming your puny animal skin *carrach* has not been swallowed whole
by Manannán mac Lir's raging waters,
nor drowned by surrounding treacherous waves and hidden undersea knives,
her next defence,
come into me, my indulgence: standing forty feet above the crashing turmoil,

her lime-mortared walls impregnable,
clinging to the cliff's edges like a hanging boulder,
a southside gate gives access for those of you
brave enough, foolhardy enough,
to come ashore to me, to surmount the bridge,
stone-walled, spanning the chasm below,
leading to the drawbridge, closed to all intruders,
opening to an entrance stairway up - it, too, flanked by walls of stone,
by where Úathach my daughter-love may refuse you -
then, further, beyond the well, the great hall, onto the stairs, into my tower,
my eyrie,
my seclusion,
my sanctuary,
my refuge...

I miss the nether roots of the *crann na haithne*,
the Tree of All Knowledge, Good and Evil,
and in its branches
crann-nathair, the tree-snake.

I hear, too, another calling - the clamours, the cacophonies, the sounds, the cries of battle,
muted whispers of the shuffle of feet, of the gasps of breath,
of the crash and clang of weapon,
of the soft moans and final gasps and morbid wails of the dying -
aah, *fanfaidh sé i mo chuimhne go deo*.
It, these, will abide in my memory forever.

Mothaím uaim thú, spin of sword in wrist, circling,
thud of blade in flesh,
thrust of spear inside...

I miss the grin of skull,
the grimace of wound,
the harshness of the slap and thwack of sword on shield.

I miss the redded pulse of desired action, the rusted colour of pain.

Beware the geyser blood as droplets of life essence spray outwards,
as they sprinkle into timelessness, into *síoraíocht*,
into life after death:
with this ring of steel ye are blood of my blood,
bone of my bone,
and your blood, like the honeycomb, will drip, tainted,
binding you to me,
tasting sweeter, if defiled, coming from my knife-plunged hand.
Beware my resting bitch face, beguiling...

It has been a long time since someone deigned to call me back...

It feeds me
It feeds me
It feeds me

You feed me,
claiomh of perfect steel, your shining point
honed to perfection,
your ice-like iron balm to my lips - *mothaím uaim thú, mo cuisle...*
Mo cuisle, mo chroi.

My pulse,
my heart.

At last, now that you have found me, *aoi oinigh*, guest of honour,
come hither into my defences, if you can.
But take care - the more sure you are the more wrong you will be:
trust none but me.

Do you trust me enough to be honoured enough to let me teach you?
I am the thief of hearts, of souls -
dare you trust to my honour?
Not every blade of mine is gilded, but
is there not honour among thieves?
Nach bhfuil aon onóir níos mó?

Ach, riddle me this: I have birthed children, killed men, rendered flesh
- none could stop the blood of my foes from feeding the land,
as none could stop my mother blood from feeding my daughters all,
Úathach, Lasair, Ingean Bhuidhe, Latiaran,
and my sons Cet and Cuar,
children of my pangs...
Aye, I know the pain of never surrender -
and yet, I know, too, that in ultimate surrender,
in *géilleadh deiridh*,
there is no pain:
is this not *claimhteoireacht* at its finest?

Do I need to spill your guts on the floor for you to keep your valour, your honour,
your *luach géilliúna*, or will you surrender unto me,
join my *Fejnnidh*, my band of warriors?
Dare you come?
Are you ready and brave enough to be reborn through me?

Or can you, too, draw back from the abyss of me?

Be wary of me: I trained even he - I the woman behind the Hound,
yet only with my deception could he take Aoife, my sister-twin.
He impaled of her, and broke my daughter's finger sparring, after bedding her, my Úathach,
even as she was offered - berserker, he,
fear fiáin,
ferocious and amoral.
Yet he became my, our, her, your success.

Because of me.

The rape was of my betrayal, Aoife, but whose fault the golden ring unseen?
I bear no guilt, no remorse, for even with your loving he made you promise
to never oppose me again - was it your wiles
or your jealous fears of me
that betrayed you to his arms?
From my arms...
I lose no sleep over you.

We made our peace over him,
but not quite with him -
he grew to have love from you, Aofie,
Connla came from your union, yet
the nefarious dog skulked back to Emer,
his spineless infidelity perfidious -
he was fool to be ruled by hubris,
blind to his own.
Ever a cuckold to some,
did not betrayal and death surround him like a dark shroud,
a narcissistic shadow-net woven from his own conceit cloak him
unto his own demise?

Or was it, o sister, a hexed fishnet web of mine that finally ensnared his fate,
a karmic debt, retribution for his pretension,
his *'Tá mé níos fearr ná tú, Is mise an ceann is mó'* posturing?

For in his arrogance he commanded me, so I faced him, to prove,
only the once, who was the better - even so,
t'was only with one daughter's betrayal he bested me,
and with another daughter's tears was our sparring appeased.

First rule of survival: use every advantage.
Rule two: win at all costs.

Who outlived who, Cú Chulainn, the shadow woman or the Hound?
Which of us had the last laugh when the final curtain closed?

A bhí ar an sotalach is mó?

How many died at your hand over your eros,
your ego?
Because of your vain, cocksure demands?

No man demands of me.

No one demands of me.

I made him bow to me, then, before taking him, too...
Then I released him from beneath me,
fully fledged at last,
a year and a day in the making,
and you all became servant to his spear.

Who shall be my next success?
Who shall feed me now?

II

Consider this: I rewrite all the stories' endings, I will not be servant to any,
ni bheidh mé i mo sheirbhíseach do dhuine ar bith - I,
Scáthach of the red hair and green eyes,
daughter once of Ard-Greimne of Lethra,
to whose judgements heroes oft deferred,
he who had power over seat, couch, and food,
bandraíodóir am I.
Now I choose my own form and my own designs.
I choose who entertains me - I am no *ainse saor,*
no chattel slave, possessed, no *sclábhaí airnéise.*
I lay down for no *ceann slea,*
let no love curse my pale flesh.
I who have known death,
I am no *scáthphuipéad,* no shadow puppet to your desires.
I may lend you the friendship of my thighs,
but am I not also
She Who Strikes Fear,
the Dark Goddess?
I am the shadow under all of your eyes,

the dark *línitheoir súl* that surrounds the window to your soul.
Like All Heal, parasite plant that sucks life from the living,
I can grow from nothing and yet appear everywhere -
draw swords with me at your peril,
for your world is neither my first nor my last,
and all weapons in my hand never fail to find their mark.
I am the Warrior Maid, the She-Witch,
enthralling, enticing, intoxicating.
I steal hearts to bleed and draw their essence - you think the strength of the
fallen
resides in the severed heads of your enemies, their 'seats of life',
their emotions, their souls,
but no, believe me, it's their hearts you want.

I want.

Remember this, those who cross swords with me: the son died of betrayal,
slave to his fate, with the belly spear I gave the father,
the ring of the father's father recognised too late,
for once released the shaft is inevitably fatal…
You slew your own yet saved mine, Cú Chulainn -
why is there often so little semblance between what is wanted
and what is gotten?
I do not owe you for Cet and Cuar,
rather consider it debt of gratitude for your modelling,
by my hands,
your sword-like tempering and forging,
dipped in the flames of hell,
in the crucible of initiation.

I made you who you are.

What was it you really wanted, Cú Chulainn?
Your sword between my breasts earned you my favour,
you became my champion,
my success.
I gave you Aoife's weakness, betrayed her to you,
yet were you not also betrayed by her requital,
Connla's sacred oath to her to always keep his true name a secret,
to never step aside for anyone, and to stand his ground when challenged to combat
the unravelling of her scornful vengeance?
But was it not betrayal of your own judgement that took her only-man from you,
the son betrayed in like manner by his mother"s own decrees?
Was sharing only with you the secrets of my spear
somehow not also a form of betrayal,
indirect, subtle, and cloak-and-dagger,

knowing, as prophetess,
that both your foster-brother and your boy would be subject to its barbs,
leaving only me to lick and bathe your wounds,
turning your eyes from my sister and my daughter,
my scornful vex repressed, it's volcanic fulminations latent,
awaiting remedy, atonement, execution?
Was it closure, was it cliche, or was it inevitable? -
maybe it was the only way the tedious human feelings of
pride, double-cross, abandonment, resentment, self-pity, insecurity and rejection
could truly work themselves out of me,
without evidence of influence, unrest, or anarchy stemming from bias
present during nor affecting my training of you,
without overt compromise holding sway upon my tutoring,
be it icy, dispassionate apathy, disgruntled torpidity, or a dangerous devil-may-care hostility
that fueled temptation to push you beyond all normal levels of acceptable risk,
my 'you're dead to me' scorn alive and cumulative,
destined to harden my heart to you even more so over time,
but, luckily for you, not instantaneously overly fanatic nor exorbitant,
my temperament and emotional control as precisely balanced and finely tuned as my blades in hand,
allowing my resentment to simmer below the surface,
my wrath poised, my scorpion-like stinger filled with spite on hold,
watching, waiting, willing?
Did I not betray you by forseeing your demise but nae warning you,
the last of your three wishes granted
after apprenticeship and Úathach with no bride-price were yours?
Was gifting you the secrets of my Gáe Bulg not, perhaps, the beginning of your ending,
the foreshadowing of the scarlet gushes of blood striking upon many variously-cloven shields,
alone in great hardship against the host,
a sick-bed awaiting thee after a wound of revenge at the final breach
in face of slaughters of great ferocity?

Did you betray Úathach, Aoife, Emer, myself,
by thrusting your naked sword into the fertile flesh of my, their, human weakness?
Did you betray Queen Medb by not?
Did I betray you in the allowing?
I taught all my charges thus -
did you feel betrayed by my polyandry?
Was your demeanour thereafter unconsciously sabotaged
by undercurrents of simple jealousy?

Ever it was betrayal that followed you unto your time,
wrapped itself around you like morbid, phantom, chiroptera-like membranous wings of woe -
even though at the last you died with a laugh in your mouth,
strapped to a standing-stone by your own innards,
unable to bear the thought of dying on the ground like the animal you were,
it was betrayal that took you down,

duplicity of your own and same of others the cause
of your death, your shame, the setting of your son.
Aye, betrayer to geasa, your own manifesto impaled and roasted upon a stick of rowan,
betrayed by the Mórrígan for spurning Her;
betrayed, thrice-bloodied, by the wine of Deichtre that would not unturn,
betrayed by the consequences of your own actions,
by your ríastrad -
a woman's scorn, a wife and mother's relentless pursuit
coming to fruition in Gleann na mBodhar,
when one of the daughters of the sorcerer's six,
in guise of Niamh with the lore of Old Night, convinced you to enter fray,
as darkness was all about and innocents were being slaughtered,
only to be spear-taken by Lugaid Cú Roi,
in league with the sons of Calatin,
events set in place by the long-smouldering wrath of Queen Medb of Connacht
for your slighting of her,
for undying is the ire of a queen...
Aye, betrayed by your own misplaced sense of honour,
betrayed by your own supercilious ego and arrogant pride
- where did the betrayals begin, Cú Chulainn?
With Forgall?
With you?
With me?
What carnal sin out of your antiquity
set up the energetic penchant
for these reoccurring threads of perfidy?
Or was it that the seeds of betrayal were lain down long ago,
when Breas betrayed the Children of Danu
and brought out his father's brood
to solidify his claims by force?

Whose back was the first to be stabbed by you?
Who did you first throw to the wolves?
Who did you first think to blame for your own deficiencies?
When did you realise everything you did was nothing more than self-aggrandizing,
that every life you took blackened your own soul,
betrayed your father's adherence to oath, truth, and law,
betrayed your inheritance of rightful kingship?

Betray me at your peril -
I do not forgive and I do not forget.
Should any attempt to thwart me
they will meet the fury of my blades.
If you cross me, prepare for your funeral...

While under me use your own judgement,
then do as I say -
do your best to satisfy me
is all I ask of everybody.
If you wish to learn more about things you're not supposed to,
learn from me - *spaewife* am I,
she who strikes dread,
mistress to heroes.
I lead the fallen, or any skilled and courageous enough to defeat me in mortal combat,
to the Land of Eternal Youth,
scouring battlefields for souls proved worthy,
even helping wandering souls simply lost upon the way
- wrong-doers, welcome in neither heaven nor hell nor even the Otherworld,
those contemptible, iniquitous, and malevolant enough to be rejected by others from my pantheon
more forgiving than I,
spat upon by the very earth itself,
they I leave on an island,
to pay for their crimes and learn what lessons they need,
to spend their eternities flying soul-less,
as *sluagh*, troublesome and destructive,
in groups like flocks of birds, coming from the west, disembodied spirits
thereafter slated to try to enter houses of the moribund via unlocked western windows
in effort to carry the dying souls away with them,
to help assuage and redeem the shattered pieces of their own...

What are the lessons you need to learn?
What is it that you want so badly you came to me, called to me,
willing to risk my rejection and the threat of
wandering aimlessly throughout the void,
guideless, for eternity?

If you trust unto me
I will be your morning light and your inner darkness,
your guide in the nightness,
behind the soft breath of steel.

III

Aye, I miss the grin of skull,
the grimace of wound,
the rusted colour of pain.
I miss the redded pulse of desired action,
the shadow walls of my fortress.

I miss the chthonian darkness,
and I miss the red scent.

I am Scáthach of the seven teachings - I suckled heroes at my breast,
the blood and bones of my adversaries either sang or screamed my name,
but I feasted on them, regardless -
I took their bodies and savoured their souls,
animalistic, cannibalistic, as carrion crow,
as frenzied shark,
for my blades and spears were perpetually thirsty,
and once I entered the fray
my blood-rage and skill set ensured none would be left alive.

The debates of bards and poets left me bored,
energetic, pragmatic, dynamic engagements kept my reflexes knife-edged,
my mind keen as an eagle's claw,
my stamina wolven,
my strength that of the untamed unicorn, the horned stag,
my ferocity unconquerable and unconquered.

I miss the sensations of the flesh of the world,
the articulations of the primacy of embodiment,
my lived body centre stage.
Did I feel pain? Aye, but I learnt to lean into it rather than fight it,
to melt into every searing stroke, untroubled and invigorated,
breathing in with each strike, each slash, each cut,
breathing out to release the pain and discomfort
to the point where the pain became tolerable,
where I'd enter a kind of solace that transported my essence into subspace,
a dreamlike frenzy of wildness and lust and channelled sword-point focus -
plummet so deeply inside myself I'd lose all sensation of pain,
lock in with the breath and just strike back, instinctually, instantly, right on point.

I miss the touch of cold iron,
the weight of spear and oaken shield,
the sweat stench of lathered, tattooed skin, blue with woad designs,
the tastes of fear and phlegm and blood,
limewashed bleached hair and my belt of skulls,
bloodcurdling yells, visages of flashing eyes and swelled necks,
the gnashing of teeth and blows mingled with kicks,
like shots discharged from the twisted cords of a catapult,
steeling oneself for victory…

Aye, I miss my time on your world, but watch from afar now with disdain,
reminiscent, some part of me sickened at
the deplorable ease with which your weaponry wounds from such distance - cowardice,

the lack of mettle and valour required to pull triggers,
as opposed to stampede, battle-raged, with sword, javelin, axe, dagger,
rushing headlong towards foes armed with same,
every nerve alive with consternation,
preparedness, both kinaesthetic and psychogenic,
knowing every step, every swing or slash or parry could be the last,
every breath a blessing as much a curse
as it meant either there was more to come or no more to be had.

Don't misjudge my meaning here - I know the bravery and grit required of every style of war game,
the nerve and daring and spine and fearlessness of every battlefront commando,
every piratical adversary, every fear-stricken warmonger, every cornered chevalier,
every wartime player on or off the stage, front or back of house - nae,
I refer only to the timorous and the poltroon,
those too spineless to front for the slaughterhouse of close-quarter engagement,
those not inoculated against tumult and turbulence more in their face than a fire-fight at distance,
armed not with blades for slicing and chopping meat and bone
but with ranged weapons beyond the comprehension of gladiators of my time,
with reaches of inferno beyond that of javelin, sling, or bow,
of ballistae, mangonel, or catapult,
the process of killing perverted, the ability to torpefy, cripple, massacre
no longer completely as tactile, as carnal, as visibly, audibly, smellably sensorial,
as tangible as face-to-face, hand-to-hand, blood-to-blood and sweat-sweat melee.
There may be more mangled and maimed and festering corse
littering your fields of carnage than e'er before,
and more bloodshed to satiate my one-time ravenous, vampiric thirst for grume,
but it is quality not quantity I desire - I lust for ichor,
lifeblood imbued with the golden sap of heroic attainment long lost,
of actions of barbarian-style berserker fervour transmuted to legendary status,
of talent, gift, aptitude, flair, expertise, and finesse at arms lionized,
saga-worthy and meritorious...

I miss the older styles and symbolisms of blatant bravado,
where to defeat a man with blade or axe or mace or fist was an act of highest devoutness,
and to eat his flesh was to secure the highest blessings of health,
where altars were stained with the blood of captives and deities consulted through human entrails,
where warriors in their prime fought either naked for intimidation,
heedless of consequence, adorned only with golden torcs and armlets,
reckless abandon and fearlessness born from knowing their souls eternal
and that a second life awaited them dead,
or in chainmail and gambeson for the priveleged,
more flexible than solid plate or *lamellar cuirass*,
highly effective at stopping slashes and most arrows,
better by far than unclothed flesh and faith alone,
but little protection against blunt force blocksplitter-style hits
or thin bladed skewer stabs,

where the manner of fighting most revered in large measure was that of wild beasts,
frenzied, and erratic, cacophonic and relentless,
where at one moment they would raise their swords aloft and smite after the manner of wild boars,
throwing the whole weight of their bodies into the blow like hewers of wood or men digging with mattocks,
and then they would deliver crosswise blows aimed at no target,
as if they intended to cut to pieces the entire bodies of their adversaries,
protective armour and all,
where to cut off the heads of enemies slain in battle, attach them to the necks of their horses
and hand over the blood-stained spoils to their attendants was commonplace,
where blood, shit, iron, and steel, ferity, verdure, fettle, and brawn dominated -
these I could understand, these I could train, these I could refine.

They are the ones I relate to, the ones I miss most...

IV

To come to me, then as now, was, is, perilous:
as drakania I train dragons,
but only those worthy,
those skilled and brave enough to penetrate me, my defences.
I will break you, wyrm-like, beneath me,
your blade sheathed inside,
my sword tip at your throat,
even if you find me in my shadows,
for few survive my training:
it's hard enough to reach my Isle, and harder still to return from it...

.Beware my wyvern tail sting, my second strike,
poisonous - I, too, come from behind, shadow-like, *mar scáth*, as silent assassin.
My hair and lips are red from the blood of men and women,
for I am the taker of hearts, bodies, souls, heads.
I am both mother and nurse to heroes:
I have secrets that will make you unstoppable.
Invincible.
Not the dead bodies of secrets that aren't quite secret,
nor invalid paradoxes that only serve to confuse and contradict,
but vibrant, living enigmas,
conundrums, questions and answers of defence and attack,
of melee and retaliation,
of preservation of self and poise amidst the tumult and catastrophe
of battle,
be it outright, guerilla, or discreet -
I teach the ferocious yell and the vaulting pole,
and if you come into the waters with me

I will teach you how to breathe,
beyond the ninth wave.

I taught him, them, to dance on the tips of their enemy's spears.
I will dance on the tip of yours - but do not watch me.
I teach the art of no distraction, of focus undivided:
if you think of me, it will be your undoing.
What's my best side? Every side is my best side, be warned -
your mind on my *cioch*, my *aoibh*; mine, your neck.
Beware the lusts of the flesh, your concupiscent satisfactions -
your *mian leis an bhfeoil,* your prurient indulgences - they are but distractions from your pain,
and the pain to come.

Distraction both undid and remade my sister rival -
by turning her head at mention of losing chariot was she first defeated,
after gifting her body to bear the son was perhaps distracted by portends of companionship,
opening herself too quickly to the son of god and mortal,
and, later, by the enduring sorrow of losing her only boy to same,
her vengeful machinations proving ruinous,
her given and taken love turned to the bitter hatred of a scorned and scarred woman,
her lust for revenge ending in tragedy;
as was distraction of spear and shield Ferdiad's labefaction,
the space between moments allowing the notched daemon to be cast,
piercing his unpierceable, chitinous armour from behind,
its thirty spicule coursing through the highways and byways of his body,
every single joint filled with barbs;
and, moreover, distraction caused the death of the son,
for surely with enough pause the ring would have been recognised,
the belly spear turned aside...
Distraction has been the cause of so many demises,
will it be cause of your demise, too?

Metal and silk, leather and lace, fear and rage and pain, punishment and reward to distract you...

Distraction wastes your energy, concentration restores it.
Be resilient - there are always more distractions, if you allow them.

Choices.
In the moment.
Again.
And again.
And again.

Strike parry feint swing twist stab turn slash thrust turn slice strike parry feint twist stab sting.
Strike parry feint swing twist stab turn slash thrust turn slice strike parry feint twist stab sting.
Strike parry feint swing twist stab turn slash thrust turn slice strike parry feint twist stab sting.

Strike parry feint swing twist stab turn slash thrust turn slice strike parry feint twist stab sting.
Engage, disengage, re-engage.
Again.
And again.
And again.
Impale, transpierce, penetrate, thrust, drill.
Again.
And again.
And again.

Learn to dance if you deign to best me,
for only the acrobatic and fleet of foot survive my training:
come from behind, wraith-like, as shadow, *mar scáth*, as I do, if you cannot meet head-on.

I come from behind - am always behind you, always before you, always attached to you, circling you...

Circles. Always circles - there are no straight lines in nature,
rather natural curves, more circles and bends, and wrapping, twisting branches.
My natural curves will beguile you, until
the unnatural lines of force of my hard, cold steel come unto their own,
sliding, effortlessly, across your exposed flesh...
My hair and lips are red from the blood of men and women,
for I draw strength from the fallen.

I, Scáthach ni Uanaind, am both teacher and switch to heroes.
I have secrets that will make you invincible.
Do you dare to trust me this day?
Do you dare to come to me?

Someday you will be with me...

Remember, though: tomorrow is promised to no-one,
so do not shirk your training,
and cling to the hope, however small,
that you will survive me, abay my *baintside*'s keening,
my cry mournful beyond all other sounds on your earth:
as today was yesterday's tomorrow,
but tomorrow never comes,
treat every day with me as your last, or your first.
Will I be your first?
Your last?

If you can find my castle on An t-Eilean Sgitheanach,
or, better, my castle in the sky, in Tir Tairngire,
the Land of Promise,
I will receive you.

If you call to me at Samhain and Beltane the expanse between us will be lessened,
the *sidhe*'s mounds open,
immrama summons enticing, intoxicating, calling you to
the golden path of the sun across the waters,
to where the horses of Lir have their pastures -
I offer you the silver branch and the drinking horn,
fortresses of precious metal and feather thatch,
poems, music, mirth and wine at the feast of Goibniu
- come to me, to where the sun meets the *sidhe*...
Our parting this world entwined will be as sweet as honey,
and forever.

Forever.

If proven worthy my secrets can be yours,
and you may enter into me:
I am both *cailleach feasa* and *cailleach piseog,*
wise woman, fortune-teller, sorceress, charm-worker.
I have the *imbas forosnai* of the most gifted *banfhili* - I trained even Fedelm
in the gift of all-knowledge, of illumination.
Through dancing wickersmoke shapes that curled around us,
I forewarned Setanta/Cú Chulainn of his ending to come -
with the Light of Foresight I spoke of plucking ravens, weeping women, the passing of a hero,
bloody events on the Plain of Muirtheimne,
but he felt only joy through his sorrow,
for through me he learned the further truth:
his name would never die so long as the world turned,
and instead of life it was his red soul that would be torn from him,
and with it the killing lust, the blood-colour veil before his eyes
that made him butcher and slaughter again and again and again...
Dying in his own blood at the foot of a tercentenary oak,
upright against the standing-stone his final indomitable bravado,
as life left him he felt his bloody madness leaving, too -
away the blood curse that made him both fearless
and the most miserable of men,
the worst of fathers,
the most shameful warrior...
No, Cú Chulainn did not only die at a young age, he died also to himself,
as he died to Aofie, as he died to me,
as he died as Setanta to become Culann's hound,
as Connla his son and Ferdiad his foster-brother
and hundreds unnamed died on bended knee before him, around him,
as Láeg, charioteer, and Liath Mach, king of horses, died defending him,
as even Cathbad had spoken unto the boy,
losing the taste for blood, the madness for war, and the pleasure for the lightning spear I gave him...

He died to me but he did not escape me.

Nothing escapes me.
No-one escapes me.

V

Hear me: always do I know the right thing to say, but only,
it seems, after the right time has passed - words were never my forte,
feats of arms and bedding mine...
While you are with me spare me the ghastly remembrances of your happinesses,
they are nothing but more distractions from your pain.
Pain is to be your comfort, your peer, your measure,
your only caress through *ceannlann* armour,
your scathes and bruises your trophies.

My hair and lips are the colour of your pain,
my comely visage the face of your *dúil eagla-bhunaithe*,
my tutelage neither blessing nor curse, rather invitation.
If you can find me beyond the Plain of Ill-Luck, the Glen of Peril,
if you can cross my Bridge of Leaping, then you may enter into me.
I will be both your reoccurring nightmare and your *dùil*
on my island rock.
Be wary, though, for if you believe in me, I exist,
in any and all of my three manifestations,
as interplanetary succubus, as mortal, as luminary,
and my training, as am I, are irresistible -
the only way to avoid being without me
is to be with me.
If you take me on, you take all of me:
I will be no man's *leannán cuileáilte*,
no *striapachas* -
I choose the manner of our coming together,
and I will release you from the breath of me, spent,
when there is nothing left of you but me:
I will illuminate the dark of your life with the light of death.

VI

As water is the gateway 'twixt your world and mine,
the veil permeable,

where there are tears 'tis ever more so -
to inherit the visage and wile of femme fatale,
to become succubi, as I, to inhabit fantasy and dream,
controlling, volatile,
seducing with earthy sensuality the hearts and minds of men,
simultaneously desirous and threatening
(no formal contract, but three times betrayal of thought, word, deed,
of succumbing to your chimeric indulgences, and your soul is *tiomnach* to me),
to wash your face in the faerie's waters
beneath Old Sligachan Bridge,
is not as simple as it sounds:
you must be on hand and knee,
supplicant, like fallen angel,
must dip face and head and hair, submerged, for count of seven,
neither bringing the waters up to nor washing them from your face,
but allowing for drying by wind and sun
- then, only then, can my daughter's tears gain for you
eternal beauty, *áilleacht síoraí*, faerie's gift, fey dryad's charm,
able to disarm and penetrate and seduce and persuade,
to choose to kiss or kill,
as the *claíomh órdhoirn* is to the warrior...

For 'twas with her tears she brought to me of how to defy and defeat him,
through chicanery and hospitality, through breaking bread and feast and song,
for no guest may strike the host.
Guile and artifice, shrewdly manoeuvred...

But beware, though, the price of faerie's beauty - the more beautiful the serpent,
the more fatal is its sting (oh yes, looks do kill) -
was not the snake symbol of the cult of Crom Cruaich, the old god of every folk of every clan,
considered a thing of beauty,
before your later Naomh Pádraig cast him, them, down,
toppling the massive golden megalithic standing-stone at Magh Slaecht,
the plain of adoration,
and its twelve subservient bronze pillars,
the air of mystery pervading the site the remnant taints of firstling and scion sacrifice,
the imprints of painful prostrations
- tops of foreheads, the gristle of noses, caps of knees and ends of elbows broken in supplication,
three fourths of the men of Ériu having perished at those misguided orison,
women and children, too?

And beware, also, the jealousies of the covetous -
your beauty may be your undoing,
for was not my well-endowed beauty
a bait
for those who had evil in their hearts,

why in my mortal ending I was violated and defiled,
violently raped to death and beyond?
Aye, my fey beauty was of legend known, but it helped me not in the end,
perhaps even somehow exacerbated the fervid atrocity of my persecution,
spurred my captors on in the depths of their depravity,
gave them more cause to excacerbatingly satiate their sadistic, sanguinary lusts
upon my bent and bruised and broken body...

Or perhaps it kind of did render me aid, for amidst the excruciation and wretchedness and the misery
and utter torment of my ending,
in the throes of my final unbearable, exquisite agonies, I called for, raged for, demanded

release
restitution
retribution
revenge

- against injustice, fallacious, illegitimate incarceration,
excessive torture both deplorable and scandalous,
false incrimination, not just for myself but for all those wrongly persecuted,
abused, defiled, gratuitously molested and victimised
by the heartless and vindictive.
- against my tormentors all, that they be eviscerated, gut-wrenchingly slowly,
or be mercilessly scourged then flayed alive,
every last one of them,
that the severity of their agonies be proportionate to the intensity of what I was forced to endure.

My hate burned like lightning strike until I passed beyond the wall of separation...

I called for and received release of the burdens of your world,
flew beyond the gravity of mortality,
not as retreat back to my previous preternatural, eldritch embodiment,
to dwell in and let fester the miasmic swamp of my enrage and vehement lust for revenge,
but rather to abide forever in the Otherworld,
servant to higher cause.
If you call to me I will come, shining,
will compress the edges of my being
to enter your atmospheric pressures once again,
to continue your learnings untimely forsaken,
if I judge you worthy of my ministrations,
whomsoever you may be.

VII

Countless animals fled before us, terrified,
the very earth itself shook as the Hound and I met,
our fomorian footprints formed the cumulous mountains and valleys of the sky -
we raged and clashed and sparred and fought,
until we didn't,
and he bowed before me,
guest to my hearth,
and then, and only then,
did I allow of him to be learned of my mysteries…

Cú Chulainn was my success once,
are you his successor now?
Will you succumb to me as did he?
I am the great initiator, deadly to approach.
I am the ultimate combatant and trainer of warriors.
I train the outer and the inner,
for it is not I, or 'they', but yourself who is your worst adversary.
I am those aspects of you that you
suppress
neglect
avoid
because of shame, guilt, fear, anger, and more.
I am those parts of you that you would rather not face,
nor admit, nor dare not ever identify with.

Once you capitulate to my mythos and *liopaí dearga fola* you are ready for my drills,
then can the process of dismantling and rebuilding you begin -
if I become your ego, infiltrate the part of your mind
that mediates between the conscious and the unconscious,
awake and dreaming,
responsible for reality testing and your sense of identity,
is not my greatest triumph to inveigle you into believing
my best interests are your best interests,
and even your very survival depends upon my whims?
I will infect you - where my shadow passes,
fey nightmares will slip loose of their slumbering shackles
and gnaw upon the edges of your dreams.

My sword will make you bleed and my beauty will lick your wounds
(in the space between lives I was human, too, remember,
after the dark shadow, before sublimity),
but only when you can lick your own wounds and die to who you were
will you join me in Tír na nÓg …

Ach, even so, if you can enter my fortress of silhouettes,
find inside me your greatest strength and wholeness of being,
you will succeed me,
for to come to Dún Scáith, then as now, takes *tiomantas, misneach,*
buanseasmhacht:
if you enter mine again, be wary.
I kill them with confidence,
those who make the mistake of underestimating me,
for my smile cuts sharper than any honed blade.
Let my feints and subtle passes seduce you closer,
my guard of the woman inveigle you,
my thigh gap's timelessness beckon,
our shedding blades be metaphor for nympholepsy - aye, but beware,
the more intricate and delicate and gossamer the seduction,
the stronger the web of me,
the more easy it is to take you as prey...
To be a temptress you don't have to be slinky and sensuous and disastrously beautiful
(it does help),
you just have to have the will to disturb.

Few survive my training - do my methods disturb you?
Do I move too fast for you,
give you naught to hold on to?

If you learn anything from me, learn this:
you cannot cling to anything in a changing world,
not the tail of my corslet of bull-hide leather,
my flowing blood-red bangs and waves beneath my *cathbharr,*
not even the hem of my diaphanous chiffon,
my tensioned whale-bone corset,
nor the pommel of my murder stroke, bludgeoning...

Strike parry feint swing twist stab turn slash thrust turn slice strike parry feint twist stab sting kiss kill...

Sorry if I just ruined your life with my riposte.
I take no prisoners and give no quarter, nor expect none.

VIII

Heroics be damned -
if you have eyes to see you will surpass me,
for believing is seeing.
If *fíor-fheiceáil* is within you,
see me through the veil of separation,

no perils will ignite fear in your heart,
and your warrior strength, your *neart laoch*,
will bring you to me,
and beyond.

You called me to serve you,
but do you trust me enough to let me teach you?
Like your psyche I can be both a beautiful servant
and a dangerous master, an unpredictable mistress -
I can either be a tool for your torture
or an instrument for your inspiration...

Draw from me what you will,
but I gift you this,
as *conradh anam*:
let your blade be as my blade,
your blood be as my blood,
your heart be as my heart
your mind be as my mind.
United in heart, mind, body, soul,
should silence rather than anger be needed,
you will blend with me,
will become as the shadows,
as *scáth*.
If it is to draw blade you need
let it be as silent and as swift,
as sure and as unerring as my own...

Fear me, as your preceptor,
for to be with me is to embrace both pain and delectation,
taking buttressed spine and impregnable fortitude
to persevere,
to allow my andragogy to sharpen your reflexes,
to erect your defences,
to whet your desirous, mercenary esurience,
to refine your edacity for blood-letting.

Fear me, for when fear ends life begins.

All fears left me after imprisoned rape, agonized torture, violent murder -
my soul's death song, that guttural, blood-choked cry for revenge,
died in my throat as my body was left behind,
my sentience transmuted
as I plunged the nether depths of my being and saw my plight for what it really was,
as provision, as opportunity.
The shattered fractions of my soul were regathered,

touched by the *Tuatha Dé Danann*,
a gift of grace usually only reserved for *sidhe*,
my ascension to demi-goddess status granted,
to take place beside the Turner Of The Wheel,
the moment I released the tentacles of my vitriol, my rancour,
retracted my venomous, maleficent, acerbic claws
of spite and pain and rage and hate,
all tendrils of both humanity and entity maliciousness metamorphosed, redirected,
values reconfigured, redefined.

My charge, then, became to seek to do all the wrongs right and to protect the innocent,
teaching women to fight and to read, write and learn,
not to be the weak sex or submissive to man, but the opposite and more
(in my time on your earth only women could teach men the arts of warfare,
no self-abasement or expectations of docile servitude then),
and to inspirit men to be faultless and resolute in their pursuit of impeccability and integrity,
courteous, gallant, deferential, and fastidious in their perfection of mastery of self;
why my role now is to protect, too, the plights of the down-trodden,
the ridiculed and the poorly,
just as much as the honourable and the mighty fallen in acts of virtuosity,
to lead them all through the dangers found on the path,
bringing them through to the Land of Eternal Youth.

Life hacks:
learn to have an impregnable inner strength and a strong will.
Let no foe passed your defences
nor think that it's easy to get
under your skin.
Be vigilant - err not, my blades are fast and sharp.
Commit as many mistakes as possible,
but do not make the same mistake twice -
don't avoid the pleasure to avoid the pain,
don't avoid but surrender to and transmute the pain,
do not avoid life to avoid death,
and know that death is just another beginning,
one of countless new beginnings before you...
Elude my blade, my subterfuge, my advantage,
but make no mistake - fear works in the short term
(hence the ferocious yell).

Perhaps it was always meant to happen,
our swords crossing over lifetimes,
our everlasting entanglement?

It takes courage to be with me,
for courage is a love affair with the unknown,

and the only way to best me and survive my inculcations
is to accept the cost of being yourself, whatsoever the cost -
to run the gauntlet of your asinine inner torments,
to drop the dark cloak, to unbuckle the corslet, the *lamellar cuirass*,
of your unknowables,
to know you are already paragon:
I cannot improve you, only perfect you,
your nous in duelling refine, your reactions sharpen,
your fastness indurate, make your grit temeritous and just that bit temerarious.
I will increase you, whetstone your rough edges,
knowing well your addictions, fears, bloodlusts are indirect fuels of your faculty,
your weaknesses your allies:
do not speak badly of yourself,
for the warrior within you hears your words and is lessened by them.
No need, either, to parade your epitome,
for pride comes before a fall -
you have only to come to it, to know it, to be it.
I teach the harnessing of power - acknowledgement of, right use of,
the execution and extirpation of. Not to gain such over others,
but over yourself:
to react or respond, that is the question.
Melee requires freedom of movement, freedom from distraction -
the greatest freedom, unsurpassed, is to be free of the distractions in your own mind,
free to dance and weave as whirlwind, dust devil, maelstrom,
mindless of the cathartic *stramash* surrounding you,
to strike parry feint swing twist stab turn slash thrust turn slice strike parry feint twist stab sting as instinct,
fearless but aware,
minding nothing.

And regret nothing, either, for concern will slow your strike -
be present to the moment only,
there is no space for error when every stroke could kill,
and though the past cannot be changed, the future is yet in your power -
the sword is the axis of the world and its power is absolute,
symbolically and existentially,
so pick up your sword, your shield, and fight for me.

You are a warrior - warriors don't give up and they don't back down,
If you will fight not for me, then for whom?
And if not you, then who?

Those who think you weak have yet to notice
the wolf hiding behind your eyes...
Let them think you're puny, enervated, but then do what wolves do best:
surprise them when they least expect it -
with action, mind, because our words are dead until we give them life with blood.

Wild, true hearts cannot be broken - look into my eyes and see how much I want it,
know that I will never back down.
Be as me.
And remember, too, it's not over when you lose,
it's only over when you quit:
that is the human dilemma,
for to be human is to love hurt bleed smile cry rage endure.
I came to your world not to play games but to be midwife to warriors,
those whose conquests would satiate my voracity,
my rapacious predilection for the pith and esse of souls;
natheless, in seeking ascendancy and sway amongst you
I had to become one of you,
infiltrate the intersection between the layers of existence,
embody somatically, corporeally,
had to disassemble my ineffable vastness
and engender it terrene;
had to incarnate as Scáthach, she-child,
beget her history, lineage, mythos, and legend,
as woman and cacodemon simultaneously,
tethered to the emotions and sensations of your species,
learn to navigate the choices and consequences required
to not only commingle amongst, but to excel, exceed, surpass, and transcend your humanesses,
your weaknesses, your cowardly propensities toward listless battlefront asthenia,
frozen anergia and hebetude when facing weapons raised against you in violent, apoplectic wroth,
to master situations minacious and radge,
and inculcate expertise of the same in others:
everything I have taught, I embodied.
Use my eyes as kindling, as fuel source for your inner fire,
as provocation, as afflatus, as fillip.
Never quit while you still draw breath - don't be like the weak of spirit,
colder by the hour, more dead than alive with every shallow, fearful chest breath they take -
use every advantage,
because if an enemy can't take you out, they will try to wear you out -
those who give in first die first.
If I have to I will breathe for you,
will breathe new life into you to keep you in the fray,
but 'tis better if it is of your own doing,
if it comes from you directly,
drawn deeply beyond the diaphragm, full body.
On your inhalation let my vitality, my vigour, and aye, even my vivacity, course through, enter into you,
fill those dormant spaces inside of you with aliveness,
with vim and flame and brio and resurgence;
on your outbreath, move, as liquid, as shadow,
mar scáth.

Leaving something to the imagination is part of your mystery, too -

your wolven eyes are your secret weapon,
they reveal your real soul and your next move,
show your hunger.

My hunger.

When it comes your time to die be not like those whose hearts are filled with fear of death,
be like the Hound, joyous - sing your death song loud,
and die like the hero going home,
or like myself, using the platform of pain as a springboard towards sanctity,
for Tír na nÓg awaits you,
if I deem you worthy.
Come with me.
Come beside me.
Come.

When all is said and done I did have fun on your world,
and remember it with fondness...
I yearn to return one more time - it calls me,
its quiet whispering pulling me like the drawing of a bow,
arrow nocked, the hand shock quivering, shaft held home,
lips poised on the kiss button, tensioned, auspicated,
awaiting shot.

It calls me.

You call me.

Ahh, to train *trodaithe, laoch* again, to draw sword, javelin, axe,
to lie in wait, wanting, hungry,
to love hurt bleed smile cry rage endure.
Mayhap even to feed again...

But, hold - where are the old-style killing fields?
Where are the rivers of blood and the ravens of death,
the goblins and sprites and daemons of the air who shrieked around battles,
once *Tuatha Dé* - are they now your drones and stringers,
beholders to the atrocoties,
but just as hungry, still as bloodthirsty,
for isn't the pen in your world now mightier than the sword?

Where lie the *laochra tar éis titim*, dead without issue,
under their forgotten cairns,
their *uaigheanna ársa dearmadta*,
their abandoned dolmens and cists and passage chambers?

Must needs I bleed the souls of departed children,
even though I draw no strength from them,
as children dead-born are considered, in law as well as in life, as if they had never been conceived;
or is it from the heart-weary and the aged I must syphon vestige of essence,
screwing from them every last drop of life like drawing thinned blood from old stone?

Aye, you call me, but to what end?
The aftermaths of carnage I once scoured are inside hearts and minds now,
memories body-bound, scripted into an endless web of networks of myofascial bondage,
impeding equilibrium,
pains and wounds internalised, chained and locked away in dreamscape, in soul
- there is no more real blood to spray,
no more need for the fashioned bone of the *Coinchenn*, *Curruid*-taken,
my belly spear, my *Gáe Bulg*, that only the Hound could wield.
Where are the *laochra láidre cróga* now,
if no longer standing victorious, exhausted, bloodied and proud,
decimated multitudes about them, creating fields of gore,
feeding grounds for the hungry soul-eater I once was?
Do they reside only in imaginings or portends of vitriol, of abuse,
of pique, rancour, vexation, of incessant, venomous rage?
Are my *ban-gaisgedaig*, my *ban-fejnnidh,* now only femme fatale,
intoxicating and of rapier-sharp wit, mistresses of deceit and wile,
my sibling enchantresses confined to legend and lost allure?
Or perhaps they are now aspects of all women determined and strong,
at least in those moments where their inner goddesses emerge,
be they Ana, Brigid, Epona, Eriu, Mórrígan,
I,
willing to do what it takes
to defend their honour, their virtue, their families, their children,
to deliver the *Cailleach*'s kiss when and if need be?

And my *Fejnnidh* - where are they now?
Where to find the men who know the secrets of the cutting edge,
who smirk at death and honour their pain, their scars, as trophies,
as spoils of war, as legacy of courage?
There is violence, still, in the people, but 'tis tempered, as compared to days of old -
few are they today not hyperalgesiac,
not frightened of their own blood,
not loathe to bruise and chafe and cut and slash and wound.

Everything is changed and yet everything looks the same.

I seek the authors of courage, fearlessness, champions resolute.
I long for and search for both paladin and perfected pagan,
trodaithe cumhachta of truth, august men and women of conviction,
arrowheads of astute acumen,

to join with me on the *Immrama na Anam,*
the Death Journey,
to merge their souls into mine,
to allow me to be their Otherworldly guide,
unto and through the final doorway.
But know this: I want no 'boy-men', no 'girl-women', no little-kid bullies in adult bodies,
no pretenders, *fear nó bean*, who flee and whimper and wet themselves with tears and piss and blood,
use others as their scape-goats, mock and abuse the down-trodden as masks for their own insecurity,
whose ferocious yells are but a mere mewing,
'what-about-me?' whimperings, whinings,
who push others to the vanguard and hide behind their valour
when faced with spearhead, stiletto, claymore, scimitar, scythe,
then deride their incidences of vicarious trauma out of jealousy and spite -
the petulant fears of these pretenders at once contemptible, reprehensible, piteous,
inexcusable, rebarbative, vomitous, and pathetic,
for actions speak louder than words
(they are the ones I will leave behind on an island on the way to Tír na nÓg).
I want *laochra misniúla, sciatháin na n-éin,*
courageous warriors and shieldmaidens both,
strong, passionate, chivalric in essence, honest, diligent, accountable -
the finest are not only those who do not know or show fear without just cause,
but those without unjustified, baseless anger, prejudice,
volatile projections stemming from their own redundancies,
but are committed to perfection of self,
ready to face enemies unknown, internal and external,
naimhde anaithnid,
ready to die to themselves
for me, with me, by me, in me.

If you believe in me, I exist,
and I will search for you and find you,
for we were bonded,
you and I.

The ancient portals direct to Hy Breasil are closed now,
the ancient doorways no more -
all that is needed in this age to summon me hither
is to call my name with earnest -
to solicit my presence in body or in soul,
to invoke the very essence of me,
to summon me with fervency, with longing,
in seance or in prayer,
call me.

Closed now, aye, are Dún Scáith and Oweynagat portals both,
the former once opening through me alone,

the other ofttimes Mórrígan's thoroughfare, *cath* cave and sunset cattle-rest,
her countenance dissembling prying eyes,
the souterrain and older, natural tunnels shrouding interplanar ginnel,
wynd-ing between worlds,
a two-way portal through which once ushered triple-headed Ellen Trechend,
rampaging and slaying until Amergin took it down,
flocks of small coppery-red wither-birds
whose very breath withered the plants themselves,
swine of disease and rot that could disappear and shed captured flesh,
and other hellish-spawned bastions of torment and disaster, necrotic and foul...

And before even them, Brú na Bóinne, river's bend portal for the *áes sídhe*,
the shining beings,
not the initial pioneers, but the first tendrils of the paradox to descend upon your world,
cast from the Light as clouds of mist,
burning their ships upon landing, settling - this embodiment's predecessors,
defeating but respecting Eochid son of Erc's Fir Bolg's battle prowess,
Nuada Airgeadlámh's pain of never surrender restored by Dian Cécht,
but his life the cost of ousting Breas and the Fomóire, bag men,
personifications of chaos, darkness, death, blight, drought,
the harmful, destructive powers of nature,
driven underdark and mound by the Milesian,
yet to this day arising to the surface at whim,
féth fíada-clad, unseen,
to torment, take lovers, to seduce or detach,
either as penance for their dereliction, their eventual failed conquering, or in spite of it;
their bloodied histories, skill at arms, their moxie in the face of belligerence,
their fey immortality - all this and more, my inspiration...

With all of this in mind,
now you are aware of some of the lineage of me,
now do you trust me enough to let me teach you?
Is the price of my love one you are willing to pay?
How much of my love is enough?
Are you ready and brave enough to be reborn through me,
or do I need to spill your guts on the floor to prove to you,
for you to put trust in me, *chun d'iontaobhas a chur i dom*, when I say to you,
that I believe in you more than you believe in yourself?
That nobody else can destroy you except you,
that nobody can save you except you,
that wherever you go, there you are,
that now all the stakes and chains are lifted,
the authentic unmasking of you can begin...

Is *this* not *claimhteoireacht* at its finest?

Are these not the dictates your *seanchaí*, bearers of old lore, should be learning you,
enthralling hearth-fire guests with tales of veracity
wherein characters of probity and wit
espouse wisdoms and pearls and such existential teaching gems,
cleverly word-crafted quests where the listeners become the central players,
the key figures?

You can garner much from me, if you dare.

I am Scáthach of the seven teachings,
and we are bonded, you and I.
I may now serve purposes no longer for self alone,
now of nature benevolent, sanctified, and pious,
but I remember your world with fondness -
I miss the grin of skull,
the grimace of wound,
the redded pulse of desired action,
the rusted colour of pain.
I miss the shadow walls of my fortress,
and I miss the red scent.
Your heart bleeds, and I miss the taste of blood.

Mothaím uaim thú, Anamchara.
Beidh cónaí ort i mo chuimhne croí go deo
(I miss you, Soul friend. You will abide in my heart memory forever).

PART II
AOIFE

- a sister's perspective and an existential crisis of being

And yes, I know you're still annoyed, o sister of mine, still rankled, still vexed
that my very name means beauty, radiant, joyful,
and yours, quite literally, the 'shadowy one'
(perhaps our parents knew something about our inherent natures that neither of us did?),
the wound of hurt still angry and infected and inflamed,
affecting your countenance and demeanour even as you were transmuted, sublimated,
that it irks your spirit still, it no longer corporeal but gaseous, as phosphoric wisp,
and that, despite what you think, it was never really love for the Hound that came between us,
that kept the flames of our rivalry ignited,
but jealousy of yours that burned all the brighter
knowing that I was always regarded as the hardest woman warrior in the world
and you a teacher of renown may be, but still only a teacher, nonetheless.
And let's go further - you were jealous of me,
because even though we were twins in beauty and allure
there must've been something about you that repelled suitors,
despite alleging that you would let no love curse your pale flesh,
and though you may have seduced your charges by way of initiation
I never needed the officiality of such an excuse to lure men to lay by my side,
to allow them the moistened sanctuary of my womanhood,
so much so that not even your pretentious lapdog could resist me
when he was so turned on by my pulchritude,
my elegant, lithesome artistry and skill at arms,
that he had to have me then and there,
that I took your golden madman's manhood and seed into me
between my outstretched, open lower limbs
before you had lent him yours
(admittedly 'twas at knife point - to begin with, at least,
but being violated by the son of a sun god was not the worst of experiences, I can tell you,
later many times inviting him closer with honeyed tongue:
"Imagine inside of me the pot of gold at the end of the rainbow
- find it, and when you find it,

don't just leave it there, but take the treacled sweetmeat of it for your own",
"As the sun follows its course, follow the seasons,
the rutting calls of our spring, our sunshine", and such forth,
even though he was still seemingly working for you then,
by making me promise to never oppose you again
- unless that, too, was part of his ruse, another one of his deceits,
overtaken as he was by my lusciousness?),
and begat the boy-child, the strong, green sapling branch of his own lifeblood
who would eventually prove to be the primary organ
of his melodramatic, filicide-induced emotional disintegration,
assuming the alexithymic asshole had any feelings
other than overbearing, condescending imperiousness to begin with anyway
- no, I haven't forgiven the mongrel yet,
for skulking back to his betrothed bitchslut
after the rampant beast-on-heat cocked his leg over me
and marked me as his territory,
both our bodies still warm with the slick and sweat of our canine-like coitus,
our later oft-times feisty, feral fornications,
the taste of his narcissism still fresh in my mouth,
his wanton, arrogant pride still trickling down my throat,
his smug, patronising sputum still dribbling out from between my thighs as he walked away
the beginning of his unravelling,
of the formulation of my apophyllitic revenge
(oh, sorry if I drew his eyes away from you, sis,
interrupted his 'special training' with you with my voluptuousness, my hypergamy,
my perfumed pheromones and cock-hungry eyes
- surely you're not still bitter over my winning him,
or had it brought up those repressed feelings of
pride, double-cross, abandonment, resentment, self-pity, insecurity and rejection
that I know had been festering inside you all those years,
despite your pathetic attempts to push them away
by pretending to be more than you really were,
by being 'Scáthach, the epic female warrior who trained the heroes of legend',
otherwise known as 'Scáthach, the pretentious bitch'?)
- and, even though it was seemingly my decrees that sealed his fate,
I sure as hell blame you for my boy's demise,
because you divulged the secrets of your horrid spear to that prick of a hound
who was so wrapped up in his own superciliousness that he ejaculated before thinking,
for once released the shaft was inevitably fatal
(I deplore the lying, opportunistic bastard now for what he did,
but do miss the constant ravishing...);
that it was from your fear of me licking him
(that came before the end, figuratively speaking, for a time...),
besting him, or, if he survived my trouncing,
my dogwhipping of the sleeveen, conceited cur back to his kindergarten kennel on your island rock,
in his timidity his thrashed tail tucked shamefully between his legs,

his head hung low, his ears drooping, his testicles retracted in humiliation;
that even after the rape of trade I became his lover for a time and not just his other tutor;
that the world didn't, doesn't, never has, and never will turn around only you, Scáthach,
alive or passed beyond,
but you around it, like as not,
and it's the lighted ones that people and history remember, not the dark,
those of radiance, not of shadow;
and that there has always been more baby girls bearing my name born than yours,
my darling 'Miss Shadow', then and now,
their mothers perhaps frightened of evoking your name
for fear their daughters would become like you,
would grow into adulthood revering you, want to be as you, invoke you
- aye, we were already rivals before him, remember, you and I,
and, yes, his and my skills were so well matched he may have toppled me,
felled me of his own accord,
but the shoe was nearly on the other backward-turned foot,
for without your blatant love-sick meddling
the dog would have, could have, should have, been quickly neutered,
your concern for your precious puppy well-founded as I would have killed him outright,
slit his torso from pubis to sternum with one deft upward slice without hesitancy,
and was on the verge of doing so,
your precious guard dog's heroic sword broken to the hilt
and he powerless to halt my strike
like a misbehaved mutt slunk into a corner, kicked for its insubordination,
before the arrogant son of a bitch
(and student to one - yes, you know who I mean)
threw his final, frenzied finagle,
your bitterness and spite towards me evidenced by your subterfuge.

Ostensibly we were reconciled after that, you and I,
the transition of power between us peaceful,
our acrimonious, resentment-filled eyes turned aside,
looking the other way,
our red bloodied and daggered nails of bitterness sheathed,
the whorls and bonds of our sisterhood re-entwined after years of discord and fire
sparked by seemingly trivial disagreements from our childhoods
neither of us could really remember anymore, the reason for the arguments long forgotten,
recalled only as lightning-strength flashes of fear
or rapid or sometimes slowly rising floods of rage,
depending on which one of us had been the aggressor or the victim
- I am more ashamed of the times when I dropped the sandbags of my guard and let you best me
(admittedly they were few in number)
than I am of the scale and atrocity of our escalated argufies,
because for me they were moments of weakness and imperfection
which I thereafter strove to expiate from my memory,
to lustrate and decisively exorcise as limbic responses of failure and abortion

from my nervous system
(I may not have been able to control how other people felt
or what they thought of me back then,
but I could control how they treated me) - ostensibly reconciled, aye, you and I,
but long smouldering are the deeply buried vexations of indignation:
I can still recall every moment
you ridiculed me, tried to better me, taunted me,
the burns inherent in every venomous glance of yours,
the scathing lacerations of your emphatic, vehement rage
wounding for a time, haunting me,
ofttimes deflected by my triumphant returns,
but serving in the end more to intensify my feelings of vitriol towards you,
to exacerbate my loathing and odium, than to subjugate or subdue me,
your bitchiness and brutality towards me catalytic,
spiralling me further from you, particularly as the longer I was with him
the more blatant and obvious and increasingly desperate
became the depths of your possessiveness,
the lengths to which you'd go to control him, me, us,
to keep his every move enslavable, enthrallable,
his very survival dependent upon your whims,
claiming it was a hexed fishnet web of yours that finally ensnared his fate
when it was actually internal alchemical choices I made that delivered unto him
definitive karmic retribution, turned what had become rotten into gold,
for when he seized me under my breast, threw me across his shoulders like a burden
and took me before his host he planted in me initial seeds of rancour,
hidden as they were amongst later earth-shaking, euphoric waves of ecstacy
and portends of companionship,
that blossomed into venomous thorns of spite and animosity
once his true nature was revealed after said promises of togetherness had coloured my eyes
- aye, I both relished him and hated him,
lusted after and afeard him even, until it came time to curse his perfidiousness
and destroy him as a father and a man -
he should've known better than to mess with the emotions of a hard ass bitch:
first rule of survival: use every advantage;
rule two: win at all costs.

I shared cramped birthing space with you but that is as far as our bond went,
for our enmity and animosity began even back then -
I swear I can still feel the pulsating, tightening cord around my larynx,
like the slipping, shortening knot of a hangman's noose, sensations of choking, breathlessness,
some part of the essence of me
beginning to be sucked free of my being,
senses, images of parts of my spirit being vacuumed through tunnels of ebony blackness,
hurtling out of control towards endless space,
like a drop of water being disembogued into the seemingly immeasurable expanse of the ocean,
only my resolution and pertinacious determination to live reversing the hurtling momentum,

my next memory the entering this world cocooned, ejected in a rush of blood,
our bodies entwined en caul, sharing amnion, chorion, allantois,
aware of your subtly baleful presence beside me,
our essences somehow also energetically, existentially co-joined,
like the one continuous line of a three-sided knot,
it usually representing the forces of nature, earth, water, fire,
even standing for unity and oneness of spirit,
for love and fidelity in love - it could've been the thread linking a mother and her daughters,
but not so for us - there was something veiled and sinisterly eldritch about you even then,
something that I never quite put my finger on
but that caused me to fear and disrelish you from the outset,
even our prenatal suite imbued with tomb-like ambience, catacombed,
meant I second guessed everything you did forever afterwards,
learned to live with a constant whirlpool of uncertainties within me,
a tangled mix of conflicted emotions over you,
a dichotomy of twisted sentimentalities versus prudent warinesses
(you were my twin sister, so I loved you, too, in a way, despite the unconscious, internal confusion)
- no-one told me I would suffer, no-one told me I would grieve the loss of you,
it happening slowly over time, feelings of sadness and tearing creeping worm-like into the guts of me,
writhing and contorting, mingling with the maggots of scepticism and disquiet
until their rot and stench had infested, infiltrated every part of me,
until all thoughts of you were acquainted with, permeated with, revulsion, distaste,
and unshakeable feelings of abomination -
despite extensive inner cerebration and meditative ponderings
I found no solution to the paradox of feelings within me,
coming to the conclusion that here was where I stood:
if you were not part of the solution you were part of the problem,
meaning you, Scáthach, were nodus to me, gremlin,
your very presence polluted with the virus of cruelty,
your social graces and etiquettes tainted beyond all manner of acceptance,
your relationships surreptitiously doomed to fail,
your moral compass affected by your bloodlust, your apparent hunger for gore
- you became dead to me early on, your very existence anathema, odious and repugnant,
a bloated corse-like obstacle to my endeavours to be removed as quickly and as messily as possible...

Father would have said that what we allow is what will continue,
that best is to forgive and forget, to not make more waves in already turbulent seas
- but I know you did neither, and, therefore,
nor would, nor could, I - there was too much water under Old Sligachan Bridge between us
and we were both too bloody-minded and obdurate, too attached to the scars we had accumulated,
too much each like sleeping drakania, requiring caution and wariness to be approached,
our talons and pigsticker wingtips resting, enfolded, latent yet vibrant, awaiting release,
prepared to strike and slash and slice flesh open upon immediate mental command,
to stream exhalations of ire across the fields,
incinerating foe in vengeful, wrathful, spiteful tongues of flame,
for 'tis true that a woman scorned and hurt has no equal in choler,

and we had both divvied out and received as much of either to be marked with cicatrice,
our weals and welts the stories of the battles we had fought and won and lost,
too contumacious to take heed of his discourse,
too stuck in our repititous propensities and inclinations
for either of us to really change our ways,
as old habits die hard if they die at all;
but perhaps my inability to exculpate you,
to allow you to acquit yourself from the role of daemoness I had cast you in,
that you seemed oh so willing and ready and able to oblige, mind you,
stemmed from my namesake's tortured restlessness,
her resentment at being given as consolation slow to build,
coming to fruition one night of dark decision even so,
her inability to forgive herself for planning to kill her stepchildren a direct result of her bitterness,
her vindictive, detestful animus,
even despite not being able to wield the blade to its apogee
and hexing the innocents instead,
and then being unable to reverse her sorcerous peccancy,
leaving them in new guise,
she banished to the four winds as demoness her damnation,
her sighing and sobbing faintly audible above the sound of the roaring winds on stormy nights
- aye, now I have eyes to see was there not semblance in our stories, hers and mine,
had not the tendrils and fire-like threads of remorse,
fueled by the acrid kindlings of jealousy and the hot oils of spite and discontent,
enmeshed our names and sex together,
somehow magically, energetically, created analogic parallels between us,
our emotional realities empathically transposed,
unaware yet aware of each other's feelings,
not unlike the phantom limb sensations of battle-torn amputees,
prone to seconds or even hours of tingling, itching, twisting, cramping, pins-and-needles, stabbing pains, pressure,
even a sense of fullness as if the limb was still there,
yet tangential, not fully realised,
our tales of wretchedness, deceit, torment, and despair unique yet not dissimilar,
both our histories soaked in the mephitic poultices of jealousy laced with scorn and anger,
of self-deprecation and disdain, of, like you once had,
the whole gamut of internal negatives, of conduits of self-doubt - aye, perhaps I couldn't forgive you
because she couldn't forgive herself, and she and I were, are, as one,
her feeling more like a sister to me than you ever did,
even though we had the same drillmasters, you and I,
were learnt and taught equivalent Sycthian skills,
me using my knowledge to prepare armies,
you only ever a select and priveleged, arrogant few
- those who served under and survived
your tutelage gained exceptional virtuosity, to be sure,
but so, too, did pupils of my own - my training methods were more customary than yours,
I may have produced more quantity than quality,
but there is inherent strength in mass,

particularly in the theatre of war - numbers always win, or at least are more likely to:
set our forces against each other on a field in murderous, violent contest
and without your precious lightning spear advantage, your cheating predilection,
your natural-born internal, external, eternal bitchiness,
the outcomes would have inevitably been favoured my way,
for no doubt your mercenaries would have fought valiantly beside you for a time,
impressed by your almost-Otherworldly abilities, but their loyalty would have faltered
as soon as they realised you were only there for you,
serving your own agenda, satiating your own desires;
mayhap we should have faced each other in single combat,
naked and raw, woman to woman, breast to breast, breath to breath,
without your champion puffed-up poodle in your stead,
affected an outcome so different from what came to be
- you were meant to be a prophetess,
so why did you let the rape of trade come to pass?
Did you hate me that much your betrayal was born of spite,
or was it just that the writhing constrictions of the snakes of your jealousy,
the lateral and sidewinding serpentine undulations of your fevers,
fed and nourished by some carnal sin out of your antiquity,
set up the penchant for the perversity of our sisterly partnership,
our on again/off again coexistence?

Epilog: :Where do we go from here, Scáth? What, who, comes next?
I never warmed to you in life,
but I grieved your torturous, vindictive decimation - when you passed beyond the wall
I felt you go, and part of me was glad you'd finally left, for both our sakes
- yours, because despite our lifelong estrangement you were my bloodsister, after all,
and no-one, particularly no female, deserved such vile persecution,
such atrocity and sadism rendered upon them no matter their origin or role in life,
to be repeatedly raped and beaten and violated for so long by so many
as you were forced to persevere,
and because of how you transcended such decrepit agonies
beyond even your sadomasochistic perversions,
how you were lifted higher in reciprocity when you let go the desire for revenge,
called to do battle in the realm of spirits, to serve higher cause,
to continue to teach and train warriors from the other side of the veil,
free of the trappings of embodiment but able to inhabit the hearts and minds of devotees,
those you deemed worthy of your ministrations, whomsoever they may be,
and to choose your own form as when and where and as what or whom you would
- perhaps you were hoping I'd've been awed by your ascendance,
found solace in your apotheosis, but no, I may have been relieved for you,
but I still thought, still think, part of you was awaiting the chance to depart this world,
eager to return to wherever it was you'd come from before this life,
and I'm yet to forgive you for the projections of your jealousies while you were here
- you carried yourself with an aura of disdain and indifference
that kept you detached and isolated on your island rock,

kept an austere, dour edge around your eyes that no amount of black berry juice could disguise,
only accentuate, exacerbate,
and gave you an aloofness and an unattainability, a standoffishness
that may've served its purpose for your warrior trainer persona
but marred the missing link - empathy, Scáth, that quality of being sensitive to others emotions
apart from those of fight or flight, agony or ecstacy, pain or delectation,
the ability to read their hearts and minds and synch with them,
to let the memories of your own wounds kindle the warmth of tenderness and vulnerability,
of compassion and commiseration within you - we were both implacable to a degree,
careful to always portray the image of indomitability,
knowing that a strong woman is one who can get up in the morning after wounding and defeat
and set her face determined, resolute, even smiling, like she wasn't crying the night before,
and that those of the weaker sex need the scent of strength and bravado to rally around
and ignite the infernos of their own,
but with you there was both something missing and something more, a knife-like hardness,
a narrow ridge-line of undemonstrativeness overhung with cornices of emotional frigidity,
where breaking through the upper crusted coldness of your attitude and disdain
was both unthinkable and unattainable, perhaps even unsought, unwanted, unwelcome,
coupled with an insatiable, esurient hunger in your wolven sniper eyes,
perpetually scoping prey, wary of the next slash and cutting stroke of steel, the next javelin's point,
of who would be your next victim or, perchance, your next champion;
and mine, because I was released from the cycle of psychological abuse,
of the imbrued, ensanguined residue and habitual vitriol of our dysfunctional relationship - we were like two wild
animals always circling each other, you and I,
grey wolf and wild cat, both hunters after similar prey,
after the same putrefied carrion, the same torn and rendered flesh,
sometimes even the same horned stag, destined to be forever on guard and resigned to difference,
to be rivals and bitter enemies in both conflict and in loving - I have pulled broken arrows
from my own heart and returned the bloodied points to their rightful owners,
and I know you have done the same to others,
to those unaware enough to mistake our feminine grace for vulnerability,
forgetting or not knowing it is women who teach men the skills of warfare and hardship,
that only those who have given birth know the depths of agony and surrender it is possible to withstand,
that capitulating to the pain is akin to befriending it,
to almost welcoming and even inviting it, not as forfeit or penance,
but, instead, as a springboard toward greater possibility, be it birth, expiration, or sanctity
- free of the paradoxical poralities of my feelings toward you at last...
But isn't it often said that freedom comes with a price,
that nothing comes for nothing,
that there is a price for everything,
that everyone must pay something, sometime?
You asked me once, after one of only the handful of times you bested me
and held sword point to my throat, one booted foot savagely pinned between my breasts,
how much of your love was enough,
and was I ready and brave enough to be reborn through you?,
both questions posed with our bodies still wet with the sweat of melee,

our breaths ragged and panting, our muscles wearied, blades bloodied,
our nipples hardened with the euphoria and intoxication of exertion
- pretentious, pseud slut, I thought you then,
your 'love' deemed metaphoric by the cuts and lacerations dealt me by your blades,
being 'reborn' through you nothing but trope, an analogy to the cutting stroke I awaited,
but, interestingly, surprisingly, was not forthcoming - you spat on me as upon the very earth itself,
globules of your splenetic, caustic rancour sprayed and expectorated in distaste,
asked me thus: "Why should I not spill your guts on the floor and take from you your pride?
Slash your stomach open but let you live
so you can crawl back to your brethren for sympathy, for solace,
or should I be done with you for good, rid these isles of your weakened flesh,
sever your seat of life from the neck of you,
and hear your death song scream my name
as your spirit gurgles and drowns in its own blood?"
I thought you conceited, egoistic, egocentric, melodramatic, vainglorious,
such scathing, sardonic verbal histrionics emetic, more for effect than for real,
but part of me also believed you capable of such sordid evisceration,
memories of repressed fears of you from childhood resurfacing,
the feeling that the moods of every day were dependent upon your whims,
and by extension my survival,
my persona and consciousness retreating inside myself as a result,
seeking safe harbour in face of storm,
refuge and rest before retaliation...
But therein lies my primary existential dilemma:
maybe none of my hypotheses were true?
Maybe you were only ever toying with me, humouring me,
playacting, pacifying my needs, my wants, my desires for infamy,
your dual roles of sister and rival made more complex by your questionable, ghoulish origin?
Who, what, were you under the light of the sun, shadow exposed?
I can accept pain as part of being warrioress - warriors don't give up and they don't back down,
breathing in with each strike, breathing out as release - I, too, have felt the agony and ecstasy
of bringing life into darkened spaces,
know only too well the levels of surrender both possible and necessary to enter subspace,
to still be able to cut and strike and slash free of oneself, putting on hold the sensations of hurt
until there was space to weep and grieve and bleed and rest and heal - no, it's not the perils of melee
that in any way daunt me - I do not fear mortal pain nor death itself,
I fear only two things: the weight of the sky falling and what comes after death - I fear you, Scáth,
in Death Goddess guise, immortal, omnipotent, with aeons of time on your side to pass judgement,
to hold me accountable to the flagellations of my curses towards you,
my pretence at reconciliation, the lime-mortar hardening of the walls of my heart
- should I be worried, Scáth, that when it's my time to meet the Turner of the Wheel at last,
whether I find my glorious ending on a field of gore or pass gently into the dreaming, star-lit void,
that you will not leave me on the island on the way, an eternal castaway,
will refuse to usher me forth through the house curtains of the Blessing Place,
seeing me as one of your 'wrong-doers'
because I refuse to forgive you your discontent and pique, your vex and blame and dudgeon,

force me to try find my own way along the Death Journey through the darkness,
leaving me guideless for eternity?
Or will you reject me outright, my second life destined to be as *sluagh*,
bound to the air of this earth of meat and dust, endlessly searching on the wing
for the shattered pieces of my soul, stripping others of their own as placation,
as a remedy for torment?
All warriors always have cracks in their hearts,
because that is how the enigmas and the paradoxes seep in,
but haven't the cracks in yours now been sealed,
now you've passed beyond? I mightn't be able to forgive you
your misdemeanours and shortcomings, might still harbour resentments and frustrations and pains,
but aren't you above all that now? Surely, now you have everything you ever wanted,
are free of the anguish of unfulfilled desires?
Can you forgive me my life-long uncertainties about you,
my emotional estrangement, my love affair with your hound dog?
If you really were - are - druidess, soothsayer, once sibyl, now godly, teller of auguries,
surely you knew beforehand of the troubles of our irregular, low-level sisterly war,
surely you knew - know - my fate - what are to be the tenets of my next soul life, my transmigration?
This is the crisis of my being to come: am I destined to live on the wing or will I be gravity-bound,
returning as wolf or stag or salmon or seal,
rock or mound or oak or bush,
or is my penance to be anchored to both lake and dirt, earth and wave,
to spend eternity as a mute swan pen - not one of the birds of the druids or the bards,
able to travel between realms to the Otherworld at will, but one wrapped in, born of,
jealousy, of vindication,
of remorse too late and the burning, inner, reprehensible self-loathing turned to rage because of it,
bringing my namesake's spell of shame and derision full circle,
left with human sense and reason, the golden chain around my neck sundered, losing its potency,
clutching still the stiletto of spite towards you, its needle-like tine reminder of my remorse and loss,
feathered wings never resting in their perpetual balletic beat, graceful yet suffering,
my lament to remain forever as a morbid, haunting squall above the wind
- will you receive me, or is too late to claw back your favour?
Can you, will you, let sleeping dogs lie?
What need I do to secure guided passage clinging to the hem of your skirt,
snatching at your heels as you walk away?
Will you lead me thither? Everything is changed and yet everything looks the same,
now you are out of mortal reach - we will always be twin-bonded, you and I, and yet I wonder,
who am I to you, Scáthach - am I your Aoife, daughter, too, of Ard-Greimne, sister to shadow, shieldmaiden,
grieving mother, spurned lover, delegator of retribution, rival, love-threat, nemesis,
or am I the other, victim of eternal, internal shame - have I not shaken free of the shackles
of the Aoife of beforetimes, or am I still slated, as was she,
to be banished to the four winds forever for her or my crimes,
not welcomed by you nor others from your pantheon, left to roam the nightness,
unguided, lost and defenceless?
I fear only the weight of the heavenless night sky falling and your decision of finality -
will you, can you, forgive and forget our lifelong turmoil?

Can you rewrite all of our stories' endings?
Have you?

It means nothing to you we were sisters, Scáth, despite our differences, our petty grievances?
Is this another one of your betrayals as a scathing, parting gift to me?

Scáthach?

Sister?

Scáth, please don't leave me guideless,
our vexes unresolved - work with me, now, on this one, I beg of you…

Sis?

I… I will forgive you, if I can, let you go,
not in pieces, but in peace...

Scáthach?

I'm sorry, Scáth.

Scáth?

Is it over, now? Are we done?
Will you take me with you?

Scáthach?

Scáth?

Scáth?

PART III
CÚ CHULAINN

Debunking the myths of manhood one bloodied corse at a time

Ruminations and reflections from the edge of the point of no return

Caught between two worlds, ne'er hath known I such grievous woundings,
such depths of torment and agony and chagrin and pain
- strapped upright to this pillar of stone by yards of my own intestines,
the still pulsating, lacerated guts of this self wrapped around the coldness of this menhir block,
it an erect phallus standing ten foot high looking down upon a bloodied green bed of slaughter,
highest place above a rolling swell of undulating fields,
its vantage point shrewd, allowing me to oversee the trembling creep of would-be executioners,
gombeens come to attempt to pick at my remains like birds of carrion, like *sluagh*,
to attempt the final stroke of cutting and claim the kill of me,
too frightened of open approach, knowing oh too well the slavering ferocity of a cornered beast
and that I wouldst die to save honour
(and rightly so, for who fears death when the nightness be already upon thee?),
it the most fitting site for my endgame,
my final ejaculation - 'twas not an attempted thief of honour after all, though, who took from me
my last exertion, rather *dobhar-chú*, ill fated water-hound, spurred from its holt by the red scent,
alerted to my plight by the sudden call of a raven stumbling amongst my gore,
an auspicious fetch, ferine, my first kill, its appearance fated for one of its kind to have the last laugh,
for what goes around comes around, and none are immune from the reverberations of the turning of the Wheel,
its muscular, stream-lined body and tail oscillating in rhythmic, humping gait,
webbed forefeet pulling, hind legs and tail surging its carnivorous animalism forward,
non-retractable claws pawing at the naked earth just as Scáthach's dark vampiric, blood-red fingernails
once scoured down my back in perverted, deviant, algolagnic initiation,
both it and her hungry and determined, voracious and insatiable,
thirsting for the titillating, salacious taste of blood,
the sadistic euphoria of the swallowing and relishing of raw meat and its juices,
of still-dripping flesh, creophagous and predatory
- the casting of my spear true, it tumbling backwards, impaled,
slipping again into the murky waters it crawled from only moments before,
same waters from didst I bid my

tormentors come for me if I couldst nae come myself,
not unlike some sort of miniature swamp creature out of prehistory emerging from the muck,
only to be driven back again by volcanic explosion, strafed by ash and fire-rain,
it succumbing to the clutches of the mere of dead things, back into the peat bog
- all this at stone's foot, its glans pointing to the sky, it and I both reaching upwards, imploring,
either as a plea for release from these wounds of mortality or as a damning curse to my father,
he of the daystar, for even allowing such an event to occur to one of his own in the first place,
for surely he could've waved the 'man down, fledgling deity in peril' flag, solicited the Dagda to intervene,
because I know He couldst slay or resurrect a man with his club, his *lorg mór*,
all that be needed just a touch from its handle to bring me back on point,
cleaving armours and bodies and limbs and heads from necks left, right, and centre again,
a running hound back in the race after stumbling…
From its summit overlooking An Breisleach Mor, the guts of I tied off to themselves,
a couple of half-hitches of horrific, dripping gore holding them together,
a fine example of emergency battlefront surgery though sufferance throbbing and intense,
worse than any incarcerated hernia, any embedded blade, any impaling javelin point, beyond enduring,
the final reserves of strength of will the last vestiges of indomitability
- this stone I name Clogh an Fear Mor in honour of my plight,
it slated to wear the belt of these innard's stains
that may take many seasons of rain and wind and sun to erase,
the energy and memory of evisceration and slow execution
bound ne'er to leave the Plain of Muirthemne again, haunting it beyond my passing,
three-legged bloodied motif marking my past, my present, my future,
for I refuse to die like a decrepit cur lying on the ground,
bruised, broken and bleeding from being kicked and beaten into submission,
ears dropped in wound and shame, tail tucked, shaking with fear and disgrace,
barking up the wrong tree in accusation, not accepting my own lot
- nae, I will face the ignominy of defeat on my feet, with open-eyed bravado,
face as pale as one night's snow regardless,
though drowning, unable to speak nor cry out in recalcitrance,
my own bile and gut-blood filling my throat,
vomiting fluid into the internal, mangled mess of me,
exposed and opened wounds a palette of coloured grume,
my refusal to die easily defiant, bellicose, irrefutable, saga-worthy, and meritorious,
knowing that in order to get from what was to what will be, needs must first I go through what is
- I might not have known exactly what I wanted in life beyond bloodshed, glory and women,
but, aye, prepared was I to fight to the death to get it,
my *roc catha* from above the fray only e'er 'I want what I want when I want it, now',
and, leaping into frenzied array amassed with swirling, hacking blades and fast slashes of steel,
vertigo naewithstanding, 'Give me what I want and no-one gets hurt",
and nothing or no-one would deign keep me from my envisioned prize:
'tis said better to be a coward for a minute than dead the rest of thy life,
but I say nae, glory be all and martyrdom superlative,
and if die thou must, die like a hero going home, for Tír na nÓg awaits thee on the other side of the veil,
and if thou turnest away in fear before the end, before the crashing weight of the concluding sunder,
thy future may be sadder than the happiest days of thy past,

so live for the now and go down fighting hard - use every advantage
('tis better to be poorly armed than unarmed),
because if an enemy can't take thee out they will try to wear thee out, and those who give in first die first,
and those who die first art forever shamed, dishonoured, spat upon by their victors,
globules of slag and spit and blood sprayed across their wretchedness as tangible penance for their fault
(note to self: ne'er step aside for anyone, and always stand ground when challenged in combat
- when facing such use this refrain: "Which bit of 'thou art about to die, slowly and very painfully'
wouldst thou like me to explain?"; follow with ferocious yell and *riastrad* - works every time);
and it seems 'fight to the death o' me' is exactly what I've done,
there be no coming back from this, no remedy or cure against this demise,
all that but left to me now my memories, my prosopography,
grudges and grievances of unfinished business matured into redundancy,
recollections of conquests and carnage and coitus my legacy, mine the chance to die
either a hero with a laugh in his throat and a smouldering, intense flame of dare in his eyes,
or a whimpering coward, gutted and wretched, crying tears of spite and woe,
discarded by history and legend, a forgettable fire doused with the eye-waters of remorse and shame
- ach, chooseth I the former, for 'tis easy to come and go unheeded,
passed o'er with scarcely a notice by the recorders of histories, the harder to remain,
the tales of one to be written into myth and song, immortalised, remembered for all of time
- nae, I take not the recreant's way,
staying at the rear of the charge in order to be in the vanguard of the retreat,
destined to vanish into the oblivion of the forgotten,
hidden and unremembered like a thief in the night, ashamed of my trade and my deeds,
I will remain standing, still as stone, fingers curled hard about the pommel of my blade,
and, as the dark clouds riseth, let any who come near to smell the death of me beware,
for he who takes my head shalt lose the hand of striking.

Úathach's usurping was one of my initial attainments, aye, my first footsteps upon the Shadow's hallowed stone
- after hurdling the fulcrum of the pivoting bridge,
three times failing and having to haul this self up off the ground,
floundering like a fish out of water thrashing itself around from lips to tail trying to submerge again,
other student's bemusement fuel for spleens,
next my salmon-leap of legend status, unforeseen and unrepeatable by others of like lithe;
she, though, a different kind of brilliant, with focus undivided,
the vacant timelessness of her eyes wide open mesmeric, their fathoming stillness paralysing,
despite her ne'er locking gaze with mine, instead luring this self closer with fluttering lashes,
coy sideways glances, downward-turned lids darkened rustic with half cut crease her mystery,
her fearlessness ramification of her autistic propensities,
her sperg making her resolute, uncompromising and steadfast in combat and in laying
- I'd detected more than the heat of exertion
and the smouldering coals of the shame of defeat in her rosacean cheeks,
and, after broketh I her finger *colg* sparring, so taken with her beauty was I didst forgetteth I my own strength,
despite her being of age but that of a girl to be wed, somewhere between childhood and womanhood,
a moment of enrapture distraction, and broketh, too, her challenger suitor twain,
one Cochar Croibne who quickly became one less,
cameth she to me and with me, a mother's pleasure,

charged was I by my own sense of virtue to take her ex-man's position,
my loving of her enacted both as tactless, egocentric satisfaction,
a kind of long-ranged sneer of humiliation aimed at Forgall,
punishment for his disallowing me the taking of his daughter's hand,
and as authentic affair, she her mother's daughter in more ways than one,
the friendship of her thighs and her prowess with blade and spear intoxicating and arousing,
capturing this mind's and body's attention for a time, gift without bride-price,
a prize demanded and extorted, until our fortunes turned
- messengers of portend brought news of Aofie's approach, and, aware of the sister's vitriolic rivalry,
and the other's reputation preceding her like dust clouds announcing her cavalries advance,
choseth I to meet her in my mistress's stead, Scáthach's vex at her sibling's arrogance and gall volcanic
- knowing lava always findeth the weak points in the bedrock, I feared for her against her sister,
thought the potential distraction of her eruptive, explosive anger a possible line of fault in her defences;
but 'tis said that a person's mouth canst break his nose, so, by voicing concern and then championing the Shadow,
didst I, perchance, play into the entanglement of a hexed fishnet web of the she-witch's own devise,
the varying, connecting threads of deceitful retribution that she as *bandraíodóir* manifested
to pacify her feelings of bitterness towards me, melioration for my daughter sister mother slightings;
or was it simply the birth of Aoife's own acrimonious redress,
her stolen and later found love of me turned to the contumelious wrath of a spurned, discarded woman,
left to single parent my her our only son, it proving ruinous in its own fortuitousness,
and must have needed I beware, for death sometimes takes the form of seduction,
and kneweth I not the depths of her enrage?
Further: the first inkling of betrayal and recrimination was laid down by Breas long afore times,
but the living energy of the initial seeds of destruction and hypocrisy
that gave rise to the fulmination of Aoife's scornful revenge and Scáthach's own of same,
that surrounded me unto my own demise, was planted even so within my own mother's womb,
the conception of this self as convoluted as it was contentious:
snow fall, birds of power, shelter sought, a host's wife's labour and birthing of an unnamed other boy,
Deichtre's midwifery her first touch of this soul albeit different form,
a mare delivering twin colts portent, the Ulaid king and men awaking at river's bend *sidhe*
with only the boy-child and colts beside them, she raising the *leanbh* as belonging to no avail,
the sickly young'un soon departing into the darkness;
enter come my father-of-light, Lugh, Ollamh Érenn,
claims was he the host, the maker of I, Sétanta,
his passive contribution scandalous - Conchobar king suspected,
she deemed 'virgin-whole' after abortion then lying with mortal betrothed, one Sualtam mac Róich,
he the donor of sperm, my father of flesh and blood, but the spark of the Light of the seed of me remaining,
buried in the heart of the boy, travelling from child to child, an invisible and twisted, energetic, embryonic conduit,
interlocking us in the infinite triskelion unity of father mother son,
an Otherwordly supply line of connection for this boy, numinous, awaiting fruition, growing, maturing, perfecting...
Under the shelter of each other people survive - a woman may birth the boy,
but it takes a community to turn such into a man, my coterie of foster fathers and their offerings thus:
Conchobar, himself promoted from boyhood to kingship after but one year of trial,
similar to the self-appointed rise of fame as I from Sétanta to Hound to Hero,
despite ne'er quite attaining the mantle proper of kingship from my father,
his adherence to oath, truth, and law my undoing, berserker-styled belligerence my recrimination,

(he taught rightful strength and rule, the use of both over self and subjects, in that order);
Sencha, his lore that of astuteness, shrewd choice, percipience;
Blaí Briugu, hostelier, charged to protect and provide,
his own demanding, selfish, pimpish inclination osmosic,
his personal *geasa* that required him to sleep with any unaccompanied woman who stayeth therein
eye-opening to the boy-me, it the foundation of my rampant proclivity,
the best lore any oversexed young pup could've e'er hoped for;
his lascivious learnings offset by those of Fergus mac Róich,
his to care for and combat train and instil championing the weak into this beating heart;
and, last but not least, bard Amergin and Findchóem, husband and wife, she sister to my mother,
hers to nurse and nurture, his to edify, alongside their boy Conall,
he of the wry neck, his vicarious gifting that of tenacity and resolve, of endurance and patience,
aliken to the spiral journey of the twining vines of woodbine, its leaves of merit but its berries toxic, misshapen,
yet used to prevent spirits nefarious and sinister from entering windows and doorways facing west,
both bringer of good fortune and as cure for the evil eye,
its benefits belied by its deformity - aye, I had nae licked my demeanour off a stone,
the shaping of the contours of my character begun even so,
trainings furthered by Dordmair, daughter of Domnall Maeltemel,
leaping aloft and balancing chest and breast on spear tip entry, a trifling matter,
hers the beginning domain of feats of valour and warfare:
the pierced flagstone with bellows blowing beneath, dancing and practising the warrior's arts
until blackened and hardened as granite was my footstep,
next the hero's coil on the spikes of spears without cause of my soles to bleed,
to smite after the manner of wild boars with relentless, erratic frenzy
and follow through with crosswise strokes of cutting, and more,
for behind all great men is a greater woman;
but lesser students draw lesser teachers, and behind the greatest of men is found the greatest of women,
and after year's end hadst I exhausted her scope and so sought I a better woman-knight, as charged,
my whittling and hammering, moulding and creating in the furnace of actuation continuing,
further tutoring in blood, blade, and swedge, in combat and in coitus,
the realm of she, *scáth dragan*, her drills relentless, her methods unconventional and unabating:
she taught the vaulting pole, to saltate over castle walls, the air of water, the yell of fear,
the dance of strike parry feint swing twist stab turn slash thrust turn slice,
without breath squandered, without cause for pause or distraction,
every decision perfected, every shift of weight exacting,
every movement of blade or spear or shield or fist precise, purposeful, powerful;
she taught the feats of the apple (juggling apples nine with ne'er more than one in my palm), thunder,
sword-edge and sloped shield, javelin and rope, the body-feat, the feat of the cat,
the pole-throw, the leap o'er poisoned stroke, the noble chariot-fighter's crouch, the spurt of speed,
the feat of the chariot-wheel thrown on high and the feat of the shield-rim,
the breath-feat, with golden apples blown up into the air, the snapping mouth and the hero's scream,
the stroke of precision, the stunning-shot and the cry-stroke,
stepping on a lance in flight and straightening erect upon its point,
the sickle chariot, the trussing of a warrior on the points of spears, and, aye, many, many more...
Before the refining touch of her hadst I the undaunted, primal ferocity of the wolfhound to be sure,
revelled in the delight of untrammelled fury and blades slick with blood,

my presence itself intimidation personified, reflexes and feats of strength uncanny,
able to fight on despite grievous woundings, unfeeling and uncaring,
this body alive with the rage-infused hero light of exorbitant, dynamic catharsis,
the transformation and distortion of my flesh painful and abhorrent,
an explosion of the untapped reservoir of life force within every cell, their source of energy infinite,
but my savagery and raging were unbridled, my fury unquenchable and unthinking,
as uncontainable as the furious turmoil of the violent ocean
pounding relentlessly against shingled beach and sea loch,
taking dunking in barrels of ice-cold waters three to extinguish, the first exploding,
Coire Goirath, its furnace heat my life force, archetype, and energy,
cauldron of warming and incubation, once upright but at touch of gelid wetness inverted,
my lifeblood spilling, erupting, molten, and so, too, my soundness and my manoeuvre,
the second boiling over, *Coire Emmae*, cauldron of vocation, my heart seethed and steeped in sudden febricity,
the mystery of the cauldron's brew turning utter darkness into chimaeras of light,
only the third cooling the heat of me, *Coire Sois*, cauldron of inspiration and knowledge,
the waters cold dulling my mind's ferocity,
cooling, too, my longing and my grief, my father-wounding, the sorrows of my jealousies
and my yearning for to visit places of mine own making, crusades of remembering, *riastrad* abating,
culminating in the depleted, exhausted aftermath of energy spent both with and without the breath of air,
the sleep of the dead after having been oh so very much alive, beyond this form's capacity
- but to rue the dichotomic characterisation of me, my natural comeliness, three heads of hair, brown at the skin,
blood-red in the middle, thatched with golden-yellow crown, smooth as though a cow hadst licked it,
the unabashed beauty of my form that caused the men of Ulaid to mind their women's eyes,
offset by the abomination of my low, arrogant shape of magic,
would be to spit in the face of Lugh - I bemoaned his phantasmic gift until seeneth I a man with nae feet,
remembering in that moment truthes taught I by Amergin,
that opportunity oft comes disguised in misfortune's form,
and, knowing well fortune follows the brave, tooketh I not the craven's way of playing the victim,
blaming the world for my deformity, but choseth I instead taking the bull by its horns and embracing my mutation,
firm in resolution that kneweth my soul the geography of its destiny,
that it alone holds the map of my future, and to put trust in that indirect, oblique side of myself,
as it wouldst take me where I needs most go and help me relax into the rhythm of who I am,
for who among us can predict the machinations of the Turner of the Wheel?
I know we live amongst two worlds, the world within which we're born and the Otherworld,
born within us, that, depending on choices made, both may be either affliction or boon,
that cursing one's allotted incarnation be as futile as wishing 'twere in another,
that we may well be deathless living in these bodies of death,
and glad am I there dost be another world, because I'll definitely need another life to understand this one...
Aye, she harnessed my virile potency, moulded my manliness from maquette to formulation,
her vision of the splendour of my becoming, my eventual eclosion,
equalled only by her tenaciousness as despotic martinet,
as unrelenting dominatrix in the heat of her chrysalid furnace of repeated drills,
of tutelage relentless and exhaustive, of gruelling challenges of melee and retaliation,
requiring extreme fortitude and full mind and body commitment to o'ercome,
her moderating and perfecting of my form culminating amongst the shadows of Dún Scáith
- she taught discernment and right action, when involved in argufies not to make rash judgement,

but to be responsive to the moment on hand exclusively,
to separate persons from their behaviours, reactions from catalysts,
to be always mindful of who's agenda I or they were serving in any given moment,
which of us the perpetrator or the victim, the culprit or the casualty, then, regardless,
to separate their seats of life from their necks, heedless of consequence,
the only agenda worth serving mine the causality, for forgetting a debt didnae mean it was paid,
and blood was worth more to me than any coin, any cattle,
the settling of accounts in arrears demanding real sacrifice, my penchant for massacre naewithstanding,
for discourse and parley may well be worthy forms of communication
but they will ne'er replace osculation, coupling, or the cold, hard kiss of steel;
but a man manages only what he must, be he son of deity or mortal or both,
and woman what he canst not - aye, charged to tame me, was she,
to hone my rabid, maniacal, violent, extremist bents,
to whetstone the roughened edges of my facilities,
my predilections for rape, rodomontade, and heroic attainment mindless of out-turn,
for he who acts like and lies down with dogs gets up with fleas,
and Forgall would shun any mangy cur nae matter his dowry,
be it of gold, silver, or brass, of cattle, clothes, horses, bridles, or land,
of allegiance, fealty, steel, or bond,
nae matter the amount his posturing and pretence at bravado,
as 'tis true that an empty sack dost not stand,
and any hound would need more than princely sums and theatrical gestures to convince him to relent,
and I wouldst have Emer as mine, come what may - one has to do their own growing,
no matter who or how tall, how illustrious their father,
and yae, left her nest didst I fully fledged, relied on naught but my own faculties
to persevere and survive her measures, her disturbances, her secrets of invincibility,
having attained dominion over her poisonous predictions of my weaknesses,
used her daughter, her sister, and her, all three, the dreadful, the handsome, the modest,
as steps upon the ladder of expansion, as tools for my graduation, my success...

Completely stuck in the radiant, liquid doorway atwixt Aoife's thighs for some time was I, though,
thoughts of former whispers of union or vows of betrothal lost in euphoric releases
impassioned and all-consuming, her offerings of her very own treacled sweetmeat irresistible
- our first togetherness began as sour spoliation,
the pains and tears of my defilement of her exacerbated by the length and width and size of my thrusts,
until she succumbed to my relentlessness and relaxed into resolve,
her body losing its fighting tension against such befouling desecration,
her capacities for converting pain into pleasure a learned, exquisite skill,
useful in rape, bedlust, battle, for fierceness is oft hidden under beauty - until they weren't,
and, ach, 'twas time for leaving, to fulfil my oath to Emer, despite or because of her father,
my contumelious perfidy premeditated, perhaps ordained (ask the prophetess)...
Connla came from our union, but my plea to hath him sent
when the ring of marking fit his finger became the ruin of her, of him, of me,
her requital, Connla's sacred oath to her to always keep his true name a secret,
to ne'er step aside for anyone, and to stand his ground when challenged to combat,
the unravelling of her scornful vengeance, rendered all the more vindictive by the pain of her seconding

- wouldst taketh she the air from a dying man in her desire for revenge,
even her boy realising such when he saw me enter *riastrad*, battle light upon this brow,
my berserker disfigurement unrelenting and unstoppable,
my honour at stake because for the sake of Ulaid I wouldst stand against even my only son;
but one knoweth not what one knoweth not,
he knowing in that moment I his father, turning his cast spear aside and announcing thus,
yet the action of awareness and my recognition of his gifted ring too late,
nor even of seeing Aoife's face and hair and my seven-coloured eyes in his,
for once released the shaft was inevitably fatal,
and none couldst survive the inverted hooks and spurs of the *Gáe Bulg*,
set in a stream and cast from between my toes, its one dart entry point seemingly subtle,
belying its thirty crustacean-formed barbs sharp and abrasive,
serrating and lacerating organs, muscle, tissue, and flesh upon withdrawal,
tearing and maiming from the inside out,
its retrieval opening the body of its target like ritual disembowelment as its hooks tore backwards,
the casting of the shadow-witch's cursed belly spear, the one feat she taught not to the boy,
and that even Ferdiad succumbed to despite his unpierceable armoured plates of chitin,
the beginnings of my remorse and torment and grief: no father should outlive his son, nor his foster-brother,
let alone wield the weapon of their untimely demise - spare me thy sympathies, though,
for if 'tis drowning thou seekest don't torment thyself with shallow water but dive, as didst I,
headlong into the darkest, deepest maelstrom of disconsolance,
cephalopodic squid-like tentacles of grief reaching up from within its rotating vortex,
pulling my natural senses of fervidness and alacrity beyond its whirlpooling point of nae return,
cutting and boring a heart-wound of depression into the yawning, cavernous, blackened centre of me
the moment recognition of my filicide and repent of my sibling's murder ensued
- just as the souls of the dead depart westwards o'er the sea into the setting sun,
so, too, didst the very heart of me, ashamed and aggrieved anti-hero, plunge itself
into the very depths of the wetness, the pain of the despair driving this self mad,
indiscriminate slaughter and spraying of gore the result of my desire for release from the torment,
only Cathbad's spell of illusion liberation,
causing me to see the very waves themselves as targets of my vengeance,
exhausting myself in rage-filled exorcism and deliverance against the wild horses of Manannán mac Lir,
knowing well Connla's soul was being tide-dragged towards Tech Duinn, the house of the dark one,
driven onwards beyond the ninth wave by phantom horsemen upon steeds of white,
to await final passage to either Hy Breasil or to come again in another life, same soul, different form,
for 'tis always darkest before the dawn and sunshine always follows rain
- even the Dagda cried tears of blood o'er the death of one of His sons,
one Cermait taken by my father's thirst for revenge, his filing for adultery such;
but, alas, there our stories diverge, for I holdeth not His staff of resurrection, my only heir my legacy,
His later reviving of His boy a rubbing of salt into the wounds of honour and redress,
for already was my father Otherworld-bound, he taken by sons three, forty years of ruling done,
speared through the foot and forced to breathe water in loch nearby navel of province and realm...

Hope you were right, Scáthach, when you made your prophecies of me,
when through the *imbas forosnai* you spoke of my future and my end,
the same light of illumination Fedelm spoke unto Medb when she saw the host crimson and red,

and of the striking, magnificent figure who wouldst bring death and destruction to her forces, this self truly,
knowing that as *banfhili* her and thy verses and visions hid nothing,
spoke to truthes that duly came to pass
- aye, t'was thee who taught of I the higher truth, that not only this self but none of us will truly die
as long as the world turneth, I destined to lose the addiction of the lust for the red scent,
the predilection for rampant warmongering and heroic bravado that singled I out among men,
my ability to put mind o'er matter amongst the turbulence and slaughterhouse of battle
(if I didn't mind, the bloodshed and killing didnae matter,
the means justified by the finality, the causes by the effect,
the accolades and admirations of others satisfactory mitigation for my malfeasances),
that 'tis only my skin and bone and guts and blood that will endeth here,
the meat of this form destined to return unto the dirt from whence it came,
once again becoming the dust of stars, the fourfold cloaks worn upon the circle of life,
the breath of me destined to alight unto the stellar wind,
joining my father and his ilk in their Otherworld abodes where believing is seeing,
this soul to sublimate but this oft-times barbarian body of grotesqueness to extinguish,
and with it my madness and berserker-styled penchant for slaughter
that guided and o'ertook my sensations of the desires of the flesh of this world,
my hungers for wounding and wenching as insatiable as a dragon's thirst for raw meat and gold,
rivers of underfoot cruor and mounds of those grievously torn asunder
hallmarks of this body's mortal apogee,
my own blood a red plague amongst slaughters of great ferocity,
my straight sword dyed red in darkened gatherings of claret its swansong of black portent,
I destined to die young yet live forever in story and in tale,
the suggestion of immortality preordained to somehow keep these sensations of excruciation at bay,
to see me through this pain to the culminating shudders of my spirit's ultimate finality,
its last, irreversible discharge before leaving the indefatigable securing of my intestinal waist belt
and the casted spear at the accursed water-hound - thou taught to play every game as if 'twere to be the last,
but to play well enough so that it were not - so far so good, but here I findeth myself at the last, at the endgame,
the final breach of the crenellated walls around my soul, having played this game of life to its fullest,
relished its bloodsheds and its glories, its wanton proclivities, its attentions and its acclamations...
Had thou no sense of guilt, Scáthach, no flickers of remorse, no penitence, no inklings of contrition,
that thou were harbinger of my catastrophe from the moment I entered thy darkened domain
and sprayed my manly seed upon thy gathering of bitches - daughter, sister, eventually even thee,
vampress of umbra? Thou were a stern disciplinarian from the outset,
thy words of introduction, "Hither wilt thou assure all my consistency, for I will make thee or break thee,
dependent upon my whims and thou submission", onerous invitation and irresistible provocation both.
I was taught to ne'er forgive and ne'er forget,
that if I crossed thee I wouldst meet the reckless fury of thy blades,
that as drakania thou trained dragons, that thou hadst secrets that would make of myself invincibility,
that only if were I worthy wouldst I, couldst I, find and come to thee
- 'tis said that when the student is ready the master or mistress appears,
and so was I led to thee by fortunes and dictates not all of this Cú Chulainn's choosing,
my own actions and disparate circumstances and decisions made by others leading me thus;
or is it that students will only appear once the master or mistress themselves are primed,
steeled and braced in preparedness, summoning pupils towards them,

magnetising searchers, mesmerising them as moths before a flame,
he she they fully equipped to impart their knowledge upon faithful recipients,
to enter into codependence closer than any bond of loving,
one of apprenticeship, discipleship, of surrender and re-creation, remodelling and reforging,
only those who have what it takes to persevere surviving, metaphorically and even literally,
abaying thou *baintside*'s keening whilst engaging in union similar in essence to that of slave and mistress,
dominant and submissive, headmistress of impenetrable darkness and obsequious sycophant,
thou the ultimate initiator and maker of champions,
having o'ercome everything and everyone e'er meant to destroy thee,
a ruthless, exotic seductress who's deadly measures those searching fame flocked to be near,
only a handful few ever reaching thy halls of shadowed stone, let alone enduring thy devices?
There be always great desirability in the veins of someone a bit dangerous, awake and dreaming,
thou deadlier than most men, an unforgettable virago, thy very presence arresting,
infiltrating hearts and minds like a living fey nightmare that gnaws upon the edges of cognisance,
the only woman possessed of the power to take her charges to the very edge of the land of the dead,
scarred and bleeding and beyond exhaustion, and return them to their chambers at session's end,
craving, hankering, wanting for more of the same, hypnotising with thy *suire's* ecstasy,
thy training and thy methods enticing and addictive, salacious even,
thy vixen's allure both experiential and visceral: wardrobe part armour, smouldering eyes as warpaint,
the magnetic attraction of thy corslet or sometimes corset-clad bosom the epitome of torment,
brandishing edges of sharpened steel that severed flesh, reflexes highly acuminated,
thy mien such that thy very words could both wound like wolves howling from the darkest pits of woe
or engender an ache to become merged with the very flame of thee, owning both worlds at once
- thou represented the core truth in us all in that thy lessons taught that to engage in combat
undistracted and free of constraints, one must need face one's inauthentic self,
embrace one's desires, eroticisms, mutations, tenebrosity, wounds, perversions, and shames,
must refuse to hide or live a life of abashment,
but, rather, one of daring, unbridled passion, irrepressibility,
knowing that fame dost be better than triumph. repose better than bitterness,
that, though timidity be the catalyst for fear, fear itself dost be the leaven of death,
that when one embraces one's fears they become as weapons,
that 'tis better strength than boasting, better to be a slave than slain, better control than chaos,
that intelligence o'ercomes fury, an attack is an inducement to a counter-attack,
that force arouses hostility, and that hostility creates an offender; knowing, too, that one
must embrace life, death, loving, challenge, adventure, and heroic attainment fearlessly
whilst being true to one's own self and morals, must live life to its plethoric culmination,
vacillating between the shadows and the light,
attuned to the natural and sacred rhythms and cycles of *dòigh nàdair*,
the gratifications, raptures, glees and sombred realisations of expansion and contraction,
of consequence of action, of restitution, responsibility, retaliation,
their counterparts antithetical to accomplishment,
must understand that, whether one said one couldst or couldst not, either way was one right,
be it to master or even survive thy training, to perfect a feat, or rupture thy defences,
for form follows thought and what one dost think about one dost bring about,
that trepidation is ne'er justified even though mistakes would be severely punished by thee,
and to use every advantage and to win at all cost,

knowing that once thy nestlings came of age, wings fully matured,
they would either fain leap or, if apprehensive, need expelling from their island rock cocoons,
thine imago of thy charges not so much as butterflies but rather fully-fledged birds of prey,
golden eagles, hen harriers, kestrels, red kites, peregrine falcons, osprey, owls, raptors and scavengers both,
taking hunt on the wing and scouring fields of gore for bloodied, mangled sinew,
their survival nae longer dictated by thy vagaries and caprices,
their very breath nae longer dependent upon thy desires...
Didst trust thee I enough to be honoured enough to let thou teach me?
Aye, 'twas as so: learnings undertaken by thee, shadow vamp of Dún Scáith,
both thy blades and thighs relentless, thy tutoring impeccable and addictive,
honed my skills with sharpened edge 'till couldst cut I a hair on the water,
or the hair off the head or the beard off a chin w'out touching the skin,
or cut a man in two so that the one half of him wouldst not miss the other for some time after,
and filled thou in gaps in my knowledge ne'er known hadst I
- thy blades were fast and sharp and there was a wolf behind thine eyes,
but did thy prophecies tell thee this: behind mine were the ferocity of the wolfhound,
hunters of wolves, and mayhap I gaveth thee and thine all more than thou'd e'er hadst before,
including from thine once precious Duncan, father to thy litter,
he who gaveth thine eggs the sperm of being,
and somehow the delicious taste of my glamour infected thee all,
and secretly didst thou yearn for my recoming,
making my swaggering back to Emer all the more scandalous in all thy vexed women's eyes,
for who amongst thy weaker sex liked to be put aside for another?
As teller of auguries, as sayer of sooth, thou must have foreseen such an outcome,
must have been prepared to taste the bitterness of rejection, come what may, or, if not swallow it,
at least let the warm, salty, mucous taste of it linger upon thy fellatrix's tongue
before spitting it out as thy forewarning of my demise,
for I belonged to thee once but would ne'er belong to thee again,
the act itself nothing more than a preemptive, impaling stab of retribution for thy collective slightings,
delivered afore their unfolding - thou predicted my ending,
bloodied events to befall upon the Plain of Muirthemne, it to become fields of mourning thereafter,
but hadst I as Setanta listened further to Cathbad's specious prophecy of same,
hearing not only what I desired, that any pupil who took up arms that day wouldst have fame everlasting,
but in the eagerness of the boy remarking not his final words, those of destiny short-lived,
words assumed solecistic but that bore weight of import (if I'd known better I'd've taken heed,
for where the tongue slips it speaks truth), mayhap my escapades wouldst other turns hath taken,
fomented other outcomes, created new sets of fated events, and I'd've come not unto thy darkened halls of shade,
lain not with the daughter nor sisters twain, begat not the sapling youth, presage of disintegration,
learned not the secrets of thy harpoon of mortal pain and death,
stolen not the lives of my foster brother nor my whelp;
but 'tis only afterwards that everything be understood,
and one can relax into knowing that everything will be alright in the end,
and if 'tis not alright, 'tis not the end - here I be facing mortality's last vestiges,
and, if thy prognostications were words of veracity, Scáthach,
'tis fated not to be this embodiment's final endgame...
Aye, thou sayeth thou saluted me, weary after triumph,

after my stunning destruction of Medb's forces, her lackeys after being killed,
five tear-sodden days of hardship and a long sigh, one against many,
the field of slaughter growing red, chopped flesh for craven raven's hunger abound,
and with thy penetrating, far-seeing, *cailleach piseog* eyes hadst saluted my retaking the hand of Emer,
it alone a feat against all odds - temper broken after twelve month siege at Lulochta Logo,
her father's stronghold, alone again against a host, chariot charge and thunder leap the result,
three hundred and nine corse left in my wake as breached I outer rampart and inner wall,
fish of flying, sword of slaying, this rabid Hound unstoppable,
three groups of nine cut down save brothers to my beloved, Scibor, Ibor, Cat,
her sister Fial having been sent away and so spared the ignominy,
Forgall, most coward father of fear and fraud, fleeing the hall, falling o'er the rath,
suicided victim of his own deceit and sleight,
for he hadst promised me she upon return and there be nae greater fraud than promise unkept;
saluted, too, one hundred men dead at every ford from Ath Scenmenn at Ailbine to the Boann at Breg,
every blow a mortal wound, pursuers all cut twain upon Rae Bán, the Plain of White,
renamed from that on by I, Crufoit, the Sod of Blood, saluted my not accepting first forcing lawful due,
my passion cooled after gathering in all the herds of all the beasts around Sliab Fuait naewithstanding,
saluted the worriment of my wrath in the hearts and minds of men,
saluted my final, fatal paroxysm against the sons of Calatin,
saluted my career full of triumph and women's lusts, what matter how short,
for the dog that's always on the go 'tis better than the one that's always curled up,
my cleverest trick destined not to be to become older and older and to fade into nothingness
- what say you of your Cú Chulainn now, strapped to his dolmen with his lifeblood draining?
Am I worthy of thy prophecy still, as was once I worthy of the friendship of thy thighs,
thy sedulous tutoring, thy favours?
'Tis said '*Maireann croí éadrom i bhfad*', a light heart lives long - ach, well, my heart is to both weights,
light with the promise of martyrdom and yet heavy with the dolour and angst of torment,
the severity of these agonies threatening to tear my capacities asunder
- thou taught *claimhteoireacht* at its finest,
that where there be surrender there be naught pain,
that mastery be nae about what happens to us but what we dost when something doth
- well, here be my happening now, and, while there may be nae remedy or cure against this death,
in these endmost throes grant my eyes the gift of discernment,
that I may find the pearls in the legacy of me,
may meet my father's gaze unabashed and unashamed,
proud son of Lugh of the Long Arm, His judgement often swift and without mercy,
that I may surrender unto fate with nae friend for sorrow but memory,
remembrances of virgin women deflowered and heroes cleaved asunder,
of wounds won, treasures and approbations gained and lost,
of blades bloodied and shields splintered - aye, life hurts a lot more than death, it seems,
and I feel worthy of and ready now to embrace thy prophecies of me, mistress of shade,
ready to embrace thy foretold gift of eternal milk and honey,
for, though he that will nae bear adversity for a while deserveth nae prosperity,
'tis true hath seen I my fair share of affliction and tribulation,
and, whilst mortal death be both an end and a beginning, if what thou sayest be truth, Scáthach,
our expiration 'tis not the greatest loss of our lives,

but 'tis, rather, what dies inside us whilst we live our most prodigious loss,
for thou sayeth our bodies will die but our souls and spirits ne'er, that, unless we embrace life,
wholeheartedly and with fervent reflection,
something dies within us and the deepest parts of us fail to come alive,
and that there be profound tragedy in this failure: we want to experience the fullness of life,
the authenticity of every moment, true capitulation to its ebbs and flows - why else art we here?
Aye, this, then, be my prosperity: I hath lived my life to its ambrosial fullest like a mug of o'erflowing mead,
and am ready now to follow Connla beyond the ninth wave, to reconcile the wounds of my heart
left by his parting at this hand, to make peace with his expired essence, to plead for his forgiveness:
if immortality in tale is to be my affluence, my mastery, then, aye, let it come to be,
surrounded by and surrendered to my sorrow - I am nae afraid of the thought of death,
as was I nae afraid whilst living.

Understanding of such naewithstanding, what of the role of Medb in the reconfiguring of my saga,
the Dark Queen of Connacht's insidious intermeddlings,
her words of poison and deceit, her intentions devious, promiscuous, and sadistic,
she who thought nothing of causing entire wars to gain possessions for reassurance of her power,
of exploiting Macha's labour-pain curse against the men of Uliad just to prove a point,
though through my youth and my chin was her deceit undone,
the excellence of her form such that two-thirds of his valour was quelled in every man who beheldest her,
falling in paroxysms of desire at her feet and he struck impotent before her,
her demeanour both fierce and libidinous? She could be dangerous or fanciful,
vulgar or quietly alluring, an innocent *suire* both glamorous and ferocious,
she wallowing in sybaritic splendour, coveting without guilt or committing evil with a light heart,
depending on the nature of her aims - by no means was she ordinary, for even black hens lay white eggs,
and she was of both beauty and persuasion renowned as well a terrible, unrelenting enemy,
as the cat is always dignified until the dog cometh by, she both feline and raven interwoven,
the Mórrígan her icon and insignia, her idol and her veneration, her muse,
both of them fast and strong, sensuous, hypnotic, intoxicating, powerful women,
both promiscuous and lustful, self-centred, prostitutive harlots, both battle-hardened mistresses of woe,
Medb well known for sleeping with her best warriors,
itself a habit that ignited ire, challenge, machismo, combat,
her very presence on the battlefield making her armies feel righteous and invincible,
men going against their wills to serve her, ofttimes even her own Ailill,
himself risen to kingship by her self-serving nymphomania, he her man of service,
for any man dare marry her must've he been without fear or meanness or jealousy,
or suffered he the consequences of conditions put upon her, as befell many another husband;
and was she not coquette and quean personified, alike the darkened Queen of witches,
malicious enough to murder another from resent and jealousy,
yet still hold court o'er the desires and lusts for power and coition of men,
as true maleficence is, above all things, seductive, and blood is the desire of the raven
- 'tis difficult enough to trust a woman,
and nobody really knows how lecherous or capricious these sovereign ladies are?
When I watched said ebon scavenger stumble on my innards I thought of her,
laughed out loud at the analogy, the similitude almost caricature: in blackened corvid of carrion guise,
appearing so confident, so smug, its borrowed deep, throaty, croaking caw a mockery, imitation of my pains,

volucrine stare hypnotic, the unfathomable depths of its emotionless eyes a deep pit of nothingness,
strutting about this death-dolmen like a pompous, arrogant, conceited, supercilious cock of black,
the femininity of she who intoxicates balanced by her certitude of her role in my downfall,
as evidenced in her familiar's very swagger, its large curved beak pecking at my cruor,
having broken away from its unkindness to peck at these remains,
to murderously stab at the very flesh of I, dripping mangled sinew from its hook,
my guffaw the best of revenge to her witchery machinations,
her antithesis of order, it turpitude incarnate, yet in that moment rendered incompetent,
all her execrable, fiendish designs coming to naught, if Scáthach's predictions prove forthcoming,
for I will remain in some form to slight the bitch, to make her pay for her unwelcome intrusions, come what may,
because, as demoness, she is not entitled to forgiveness and I curse her,
serenade the rest of her reign with maledictions and condemnations thus:
may she have an itch and nae nails to scratch for eternity,
may the consequences of her cozenage devour her, may disease without cure be upon her,
may she be burned and scorched and bad ending be upon her, too,
may the first drop of water she takes boil in her bowels,
may her living flesh rot off her bones and fall away putrid before her eyes,
may her limbs wither and the stench of her rotten carcass be too horrible for hungry dogs,
may she fade into nothingness like snow in summer, and leave this earth without returning.
You taught, mistress of shadow, to ne'er forgive and ne'er forget, and so be it:
I cannot forget her ruinations, and I will not on my life's blood give her the honour of forgiveness,
for a friend's eye is a good looking-glass, and, when faced I Ferdiad, didst bear I witness to her interfering,
saw how with her words of wile obtaineth she easy surety of oath and challenge atween us,
as didst I witness close ruse when later pact with Fergus madeth she,
his shame of sword of wood and sex the cause,
though as foster-father and foster-son hadst we already made concord,
,he to yield at time of choosing mine, as didst I so yold to him
- but, aye, we were heart-companions once, comrades in the woods, Ferdiad and I,
men that shared a bed when we slept the heavy sleep after hard days and weary fights,
valiant brothers who sallied forth as strangers in many a strange land,
ranged the woodlands through side by side when with Scáthach we learned arms,
yet how cometh he forced to fight his comrade sworn if not at woman's hest?
Medb's wonted fashion of stirring up disunion and dissension,
taunts of thy honour and the curse of drink seductively poured the catalyst,
for days of three didst we champions match our tempers,
all the while engaged in the civil discourse of comradeship
- clotted gore in this brave heart and near to be parted from my soul t'was to fight with thee,
foster brother, blade brother, friend of years and deeds and blood and bruise and jest,
but each man is fated constrained to go 'neath the sod that hides his grave,
and thou deemethed it better to fall by the shafts of valour and bravery and skill
than to fall by the shafts of satire, abuse and reproach,
the blisters three of blame, blemish, and disgrace upon thy countenance,
accursed set by the druids and poets, lampoonists and hard-attackers of Medb,
as went thou nae with them to her persuasion, to promise of reward and lay
- ach, Ferdiad, had you but nae heeded her guiles mayhap the ending of thee would hadst nae come to pass,
and comrades in arms against the slut we could've been, repelling her armies back-to-back,

for good care takes the head off bad luck; but, alas, there is naught sharper than a woman's tongue,
and her mockeries of thy valour were the ruin of thee,
her whorish, devious, seductive whisperings thou temptation,
for an evil tongue begets treachery, and she, like her mentor Goddess, was as evil incarnate
- 'tis said temptation will ne'er leave one but rather one will leave temptation,
so I ask of thy spirit now, either on its way still across furious seas to Teach Duinn,
to abide awhile in the keeping of Donn en route on its journey to the Otherworld,
or already there, in the flowery meadows and forested wilds of Tír na nÓg,
thy bird-like voice mingling in beautiful music with other souls of warriors dead,
my clan and my kinsman thee, whom ne'er found I one dearer, thy loss the sadder for,
why didst thou nae say to her nae, I will nae go to engage in ford-feats face to face with this Cú Chulainn,
knowing how hard the toil, for, though any stick may be used to beat a dog, nae light thing was I to subdue,
strong as hundreds, brave as mien,
as even, yae, didst I plead thee to break nae oaths of friendship made, nor word, nor promise, to come nae nigh me,
and knowing, too, of thine own fall foretold by she of all shadows, Scáthach ni Uanaind herself,
my fall at thy hand wrongly augured so by fey dark queen and husband,
itself retaliation for revulsion at her menses, wrong blood for a battlefield,
what of thine asking was enough to turn thy fealty and allegiance
to she of wealth and cunning whom nae spouse could e'er bridle,
what bond of earth's fair treasures were to be given thee,
what great rewards in arm-rings, shares of plain and forest,
what freedoms for thy children till the end of nights and days,
what fine pied satin, ringed brooches, apparels, gold, silver, fame and power were proferred thee,
what reins and splendid horses, cloths of every colour were given thee as pledge to thwart thy mind,
what, or who, was promised thee once thou hadst slain the Smith's Hound,
what lover as beautiful snare free of cain was thou temptation - nae only Findabair of the champions,
Queen of western Ériu, daughter of Ailill and Medb, white phantom she, oft prostituted
- ach, Ferdiad, one might well hath tried tie sand with rope as secureth her provision,
her charms and beauty driving force behind deaths of hundreds, herself once proffered, too, to this self,
brought thus by a fool dressed as king in pester, pillars of standing two left in bait's wake,
her muliebrity first accepted then spurned by my hand - was it not also promise of the queen of Cruachan herself,
the lure of the philtre of her venom irresistible,
invite into the earthy, moist sensuality of the cave of her womanhood too tantalising to oppose,
she disastrously beautiful but of callous, cruel, cold, darkened heart,
her allure cutting sharper than any honed knife's edge,
her words of enticement as finely balanced as her blades in hand,
able to either invigorate or bludgeon thine ego to death at megrim,
her proffering of more than thou couldst hope for cataclysmically efficacious,
her apparent penchant for causing others to leave trails of gore in their wake voyeuristic,
a disturbing blend of sadistic violence and eroticism that appealed to thy want,
causing thee to acquiesce despite protest, perturbation of enforced combat mine,
my word and vow that 'tis I as would conquer the son of Daman mac Darè, nae thee the Hound,
that Cruachan's heroes all 'tis I who wouldst destroy, they broken-necked and stained with grume
after red battle's distant roar, cruel club's hard edge and hewn raw flesh my battle's badge,
for thou to die and I to remain, thou to liest in thy bed of cruor?
Ach, Ferdiad, because of youth and littleness was once I thou serving-man and didst I so much for thee,

arming thy spear and dressing thy bed, but this by nae means remained my mood after thy treachery,
for 'twas even thee who sayeth treason hath o'ercome our love,
and I proffer thou this as tocsin: when thy hand is in the mouth of a dog, withdraw it gently,
for then it was didst cameth I, cutting, feat-performing, battle-winning, red-sworded perfect hero of legend,
Hound from Emain Macha, Hound formed of all colours, Hound of Culann,
the Border-hound, the War-hound, amount chariot mine under sky bloodied red,
as around shrieked goblins and fiends, the sprites of the glens and the demons of the air,
for the *Tuatha Dé Danann* were wont to set up their cries around me,
to the end that the dread and the fear and the fright and the terror of my countenance
might be so much the greater in every battle and on every field, in every fight and in every combat wherein I went,
and 'twas nae so long hadst thou postured when heardest thou something of my approach,
in all a rush and a crash and a hurtling sound, a din and a thunder and a clatter and a clash,
the shield-cry of feat-shields, the jangle of javelins, the deed-striking of my *claideb*,
the thud of my helmet, the ring of my spears, the striking of my arms, the fury of my feats,
the straining of ropes and the whirr of wheels, the creaking of chariot and the trampling of horses' hoofs,
the deep voice of this hero and battle-warrior on his way to the ford for blood-letting of thy quarrel,
my coming like water down high cliff or peal of thunder depicting heraldry unrivalled
- our torment raged with sword and dart and spear and lance, from chariot faced and then on foot,
'till with heavy smiting blades thou and I didst make our final stands:
thrice didst thou strike down this Hound, and yet thrice didst I arise with the speed of wind,
into the clouds of the air, with the swiftness of the swallow, the dash of the dragon, the strength of the lion,
'till alighted I on the boss of thy shield, seeking for to reach thy head and striketh it from above,
yet thrice was I shaken from thee as a fond woman shakes her child,
washed from thee as cup is washed in tub, returnethed I to the middle of the ford,
the same as if hath nae sprung I at all - 'twas then my twisting-fit took shape,
a swelling and inflating as with breath in a bladder until madest I of myself hideousness,
fashioned alike a dreadful, terrible, many-coloured bow as big as a giant or a man of the sea,
and, though was I then the hugely-brave warrior towering directly o'er thee, Ferdiad,
yet still such was the closeness of combat madeth we,
our heads encountered above, feet below, hands in the middle o'er the rims and bosses of our shields,
our shields themselves didst burst and split from rims to centres,
our spears bent and turned and shivered from their tips to their rivets,
and forced we the river from its bed and from its course, so much so that
there couldst've been a reclining place for a king or a queen in the middle of the ford,
nary a drop of water left in it but what fell therein with the trampling and slipping of our heroes feet,
and rude were our woundings of flesh and blood hacked, of skin and body hewn,
and the *boccanach* and the *bananach* and the sprites of the glens and the eldritch beings of the air
screamed from the rims of their shields, the guards of their swords, and from the tips of their spears,
as, in similar vein to my defeat of Aoife thanks to the treachery of the shadowed sister,
causing her distraction with cleverly-worded diversion and avert her thus the killing stroke of I,
so, too, after caught was I in unguarded moment at the edge-feat of swords and wounded so,
didst distraction of succour by faery cause thee moments pause,
and were it nae for Dolb and Indolb, *Danann* mine with cowls unseen,
with I together smiting thrice upon shattered shield against thee to draw all thy care and attention thereto
after gaveth thou to this self thrust of tusk-hilted blade to bury in my chest,
my own blood to fall unto my belt and the ford become crimsoned with clotted spill of it

as endured I not under death-bringing, heavy blows, long strokes and mighty, middle slashes,
nae recourse wouldst hath I to o'ercome further strike and cleave,
as each of us took from shoulders, thighs, torsos of the other
lump and cut as large as the head of month-old child, as to slay and undo his fellow each sought we;
but more worthy opponent than she were thee, for matched in lore hard won were thou and I,
and thou called my deceit and I thine armoured advantage and sharethed we each other hence,
and no secret was harboured atween us kept save the *Gae Bulg* when returneth us to the fray;
wounded found was I by faery, so three heavy woundings upon thee inflicted they apiece,
yet such was, aye, the vigour of Ferdiad son of Daman son of Darè, stalwart friend and formidable foe alike,
great and valiant warrior of the men of Domnann, that rallied thou anon, and fitting 'twas for thou to go thither,
for well-matched and alike was our manner of fight and of combat, of our strength and of our skills,
and thereafter gaveth thee two blows to my one,
and with casteth spear right and left both *Danann* mine didst thou fell,
and sorely pressed was I upon the sward at foot of ford till Láeg's rebukes of revive,
his torment such: "Nae more hast thou right or title or claim to valour or skill in arms
till the very day of doom and of life, thou little imp of an elf-man!", and enraged so became I thus,
in such that a swelling and an inflation filled I top to ground as the wind fills a spread, open banner,
and madeth I a dreadful, wonderful bow of myself like a skybow in shower of rain,
and madeth I for thee, Ferdiad, with the violence of the serpent and strength of a blood-hound in my smite;
yet thrice again thrown from shield to ford was I, and woundings severe becameth my lot.
Aye, thou hadst of this hound bested, yet one more game hadst yet I to play,
nae unlike the entrapment of finality unfigured on a board of *fidchell*, druidic deviousness mine,
my father's wood wisdom gift itself oft used as settler of contempts, of fortunes won or lost,
for this was nae to be Cú Chulainn's final reckoning - thou heard my call for the spear of mortal pain and death,
prepared thou for the feat thus: thou thrust thy shield down to protect thy lower half,
looked at thy Cú Chulainn, I,
saw only the hero's light in my eyes and all my various, venomous feats madeth ready,
and kneweth thou nae to which thou shouldst first giveth answer, whether to the 'fist's breast-spear',
the 'wild shield's broad-spear', the 'short spear from the middle of the palm',
or to the white *Gáe Bulg* cast from fair, watery river;
gripped I a shorter spear and ushered it forth off the palm of my hand,
o'er the rim of thy broken shield and o'er the edge of thy corslet and horned-skin,
its farther half made visible from piercing thy heart in thy bosom,
once I associate and companion now of thee nemesis, for treachery always returns to the betrayer;
gaveth thou thrust of shield upwards to protect thine upper parts,
but 'twas of help that cometh late, for my Láeg set the fiendish belly spear down the stream,
and, this Cú Chulainn nae longer of thy comradeship, caughteth I said spear in the fork of my foot
and casteth I the Shadow's gift as far as couldst I cast, underneath and straight and true,
and passeth it through strong, thick apron of iron wrought thine,
its impetus such it broke in three the huge, goodly stone the size of a millstone thou didst wear,
piercethed it thy chitinous shell and cutteth its way into thee,
'till every joint and every limb of thee was filled with its barbs,
Medb's snaked tongue and Scáthach's cursed gift now thou bane...
For the causing of I to cause harm and finish to thee, my foster friend and brother in arms,
I curse much her, for the bitch was above her station - the cock grows but the hen should lay the eggs,
nae engage in the war-games of the hosts, of sleights of hand and fate's intrusion,

for 'tis mockery of the gods to intervene: Ferdiad, thy fight was hard yet thou didst fall,
pierced from behind like a dog on a spit, thy ribs' armour burst, anas defiled,
thy heart all gore, body sworded sore, thy bloom all gone, I oppressed with rage and grief beyond compare,
for if 'tis true discretion the better part of valour and honour be, then aye,
valiant and prestigious I may be in other's eyes but nae so in my own,
for nae madeth I the perfect of choices - it may have becometh me to nae weep then,
rather to exult, but tears of salt and blood dost I shed for thee now, Ferdiad,
and pleased would this heart be if thou were stood beside me here, nae matter our plight, my comrade…
I can forgive thee thy discretions, but of this hound's self I have naught such sentiment,
for the taking of thy life was of roguishness contempt, if of guile and artifice shrewdly manoeuvred
- ach, you taught me well, Scáthach ni Uanaind, modelled all you had to share with aplomb,
thy mastery resplendent, thy dexterity and play with *colg* and *claideb* inimitable,
thy bullseye javelin's hurl unsurpassable,
thy catwalk the dust and dirt of the squared circle of Dún Scáith's training grounds,
thy very message loud and clear: use every advantage and win at all cost.
But cost of sundered heart ne'er figured I - unfairly was Ferdiad slain, aye,
and 'tis my own guilt clingeth still to he, remorse and bitter mine for the taking,
and with the blood of he is my soul fore'er stained,
and may my curses o'ertake the Connacht queen bitch
and their enactment be her undoing,
for I will pursue her even from the other side of the veil tenaciously, liken a wolf against a bone,
for I will nae forgive and I will nae forget, and, though 'tis hard to kill a bad thing,
as complicit was she in the ruin of he may her downfall be my upbringing,
and may her demise bring consolation to my soul, for justice delayed is justice denied,
and every dog will get his day, sometime.

Lingering in the back of my thoughts, too, though, art glimmers, hints, snippets, whispers,
of memories of shame, of remorse, of confusion and seethe, of another's comeuppance,
intermingled with scattered recollections of rapture, of sickness, of lust, of brightness,
these sensations of hurt in this pain-wracked form sparking flashes of secrets long forgotten,
like streaks of lightning, shower-clouds of fire, illuminating momentarily darkened, shadowed recesses,
half-remembered fragments, snatches and impressions of conversations and moments
barely recognisable through the haze and fog of forgetfulness, glimpses of other parts of my past,
like haunting ghost lights of remembrance barely visible through thick, amnesiac brume,
vague undertones and murmurs, whisperings on the edge of perception, anamnesis forthcoming,
flirting with exposure across the frost-bitten, rain-sodden marshes and bog lands of my awareness,
their record ingrained in the consciousness of my very cells,
engraved like ogam on the walls of the nucleus of the meat of me,
for the heart knows everything about everything all of the time, more so than e'er the workings of my mind,
and, even though these disparate recollections art stored in the sentience of my very own somatica,
'tis through the vehicle of said primary organ dost I sense them:
through the lour sparks of recollection strobe my awareness,
recall of the haunting lingua-touch of a drink of oblivion preceding impenetrable darkness,
yet through the murk come disjointed images: flock of white birds, their cries enticing,
a hurled sword in parabolic arc stunning but nae killing,
feathered friends falling a ladies' desire, yet Emer has … nought?; nae, flashes of two more winging in,

linked by red gold chain, a warning - fae magic, the Otherworld?; stone slung wide - I missed?;
my spear then clipping one's wing in flight; next image knowing nightness, maidens twain approaching,
beauteous and dignified yet one weeping - dreamspace?,
both smiling in titillating tease, yet - flashes of - a whip?; sensations of pain, relentlessly scourged, more of the whip,
watching their heels as they walk away - abandoned, more dead than alive?; images of sickbed, stillness - time?
I remember the balm of Emer's touch, her voice pithy, pulling me back into my body;
follows next a sequence of images, moments captured and exhibited upon my consciousness like a long fresco
viewed at rapid pace, only just enough to ascertain their import, their coherence:
the bird-women, one *suire*, wife to… the sea, but waves face away (unclear) from her?,
the other faerie - ach, 'twas they put the cursed sickness into me!; a plea for my sword, my strength,
whispers of healing and betrothal; Láeg reporting confirmation of -?; overwhelming brightness;
sword upon sword, yet again alone against a host, sword against thunder, a king and champions toppled;
snatches of naked skin, lustrous, natural curves beguiling, soft and gentle feathered kisses,
of descending, returning, of clandestine bigamy by tree of yew at strand of Baile,
of a horde of fierce, pale women, knives abound, thwarting elope and absconding rapture, led by - Emer?;
of woman and *suire* face-to-face, enraged, of my plea of intervention,
of words of derision and hurt, of recognition, of bond, of matrimony fueled by amatory,
of a wail of lament smothered by wave of shaken sea-sprayed cloak,
of discord and woundedness drowned in lethen liquid - 'tis oft said that a drink precedes a story,
but here, surely, the story preceded the sup, for 'tis only now this unravelling is revealed,
as the cells and fluids of this profusely bleeding form disgorge their secrets,
vomiting up instances long forgotten or erased from the depths of the memories of me,
and, as I travail in pain, as these bowels are unravelled about this unfeeling stone,
it seems I cannae escape my destiny nor fail to become accountable for my actions,
nae even those hidden by anomalous delusion caused by said drink of hallucination,
for 'tis his own wound is what everyone feels soonest:
I am recalling other draughts of poisoned liquids and tastes of affected meats
that have passed beyond these lips, some to more avail than others - ach,
as the life of me is abating must needs I draw deeper breath,
and, as the very air inhales into my tender organs, the inverted trees of my lungs,
evaporates from the bloodied mess of my exposed, mangled flesh,
as the final vestiges of waters licked from nearby loch bring some cleanse to my broth,
diffused art the remnant venoms from their cellular imprisonment,
and so, too, art their memory traces released into my awareness, and, ecce,
more echoes of remembrance infiltrate my consciousness: a tincture of drowsiness, shadow-laced,
imbued with the liquid scent of fear, remnants of lethargy in the matrix of me,
its effect but a hint of torpor, nae keeping me from the sister's provocations and of the bedding of her,
an attempt at skulduggery come to naught, for I bested her and took her radiant beauty with my thrust,
begat the boy-child, he a father's only pride, albeit he, too, the source of my regret;
the brush of bloodied wine upon these lips, burning thrice like scalding, molten kisses,
tongue intumescent with the curse of the taste of foreboding unattended, violently spat,
a mother's plea ignored; the piquancy of roasted meat familiar yet turned rancid in my mouth,
half-chewed flesh of manifesto mine inadvertently bit, debilitating my prowess despite abnegation,
both hand and thigh torpefied, halved was my might, the weakening of me thus,
cursed by the *geasa* of hags three, the Mórrígan in tripled form, revenge for my slighting of Her,
and ne'er returnethed I to capacity hence - hath I but, these innard's stains upon this dolmen

wouldst nae be the epitaph of me, for how else to account for this predicament: I hath killed more warriors,
routed more armies, surpassed more feats, escaped from more stresses wherein I was
than any other, living or passed, and yet taken was I by Lugaid Cú Roí, son of a different dog,
in league with the sons and daughters of Calatin and their king-felling spear,
my own last cast plucked from another dropped, twitching foe then cast true,
piercing the guts of me to shame mine, hero's light upon this brow waning,
my breast full of fierce hate, sharp sword mine above my shoulder ready to strike in retaliation
- so how cometh this to pass if this Cú Chulainn was not dwindled?

Ach, nae always hath known I the right thing to say, even after the time hadst passed,
feats of bravado, brawn, and bedding more my forte than the debates of druids and bards and satirists,
their attempts at wooing my favours with panegyric paeans, encomiums and accolades fruitless,
yet ne'er reviled because of niggardliness or churlishness without swift retort hadst been I,
as knewest I the value of loyalty, honour, and respect, of constancy when due,
for where the battle rages there one's fealty and true mind be revealed,
and I would have none save Láeg my charioteer deride me thereof,
nae if any other wished to live to tell the tale, his taunts of my merit but fuel to enkindle my ferocity,
nae slights on my rectitude, my apodeictic acclimation, nor my very character
- nae, I wouldst let nae slur go unchallenged nor unheeded,
not since as Sétanta hadst verified I my strength against gibes and goading from boys at play of *iománaíocht*,
provethed myself against them with clash of ash, bas, heel and toe,
and with same *camán* and *sliothar* against Culann's watch-hound,
hadst proffered myself in replace of its service to gain recognition of convictions and ethos mine,
thus alerting all to my oath keeping, they learning that, aye, my word was my troth,
be it promise of *geasa* fulfilled, respect acknowledged where due, adherence to laws, feats executed,
slaughters undertaken - I wouldst hold fast to my words of bond, expected of others the same,
as didst Fergus hold to his to Medb's resent, turning his forces aside, causing her to affect retreat,
and as didst I to my own by sparing said dark queen when with woman's pangs I didst findeth her,
easy prey to my blade; but nae wouldst I a woman striketh, nae matter she the scourge,
the inciter and fomenter of ruinations - aye, even unto the death of me,
for but once and once alone didst knowingly woundeth I single woman,
she beauteous beyond believing but spurneth love from her didst I,
for I hadst nae the time for women's backsides nor their games,
She the corvid queen of *bodachs*, more eidolon than human, the Mórrígan, daughter of Aed Ernmas,
direct from faery dwellings come unto myself whilst in sore distress and combat locked was I,
o'er our heads a shrieking, lean hag in raven-shape, quickly hopping o'er the points of our weapons and shields,
She then in form of heifer white, horn-less and red eared, led sorcerous stampede against I,
a silvered bronze-chained cattle charge of witchery till struck once I Her with stone from casted stick of sling,
putting out one eye, stumbling She and one shank riving and splintering Her pain,
then as greasy water-worm entangled She my crus thus,
as blows of strike and piercing tooketh I crosswise through the chest,
my newly-bearded form thought worthy of hurting by Lóch, son of Mofemis,
and She the torment worsening 'till raged incited smote I my heel through ribs and head Hers,
it, She, momentarily stunned and lamed until morphed did She into bitch-wolf form, rough and grey-red,
wolfess versus Hound, She sinking slavering, rabid canine bite into my arm,
puncturing and shredding as She thrashed and ravaged upon my flesh, all the while gesturing, spell-casting,

driving forth Her bovine charge as against my hurtling javelin pierceth Her soul's window again didst I,
shattering same orbit, She blinded half but savage still, distraction enough Lóch the advantage took,
impaled he my loins anon - bloodied and enraged employest I the *Gáe Bulg* upon him in my pains,
it passing through his heart in his breast, he mortally skewered and severed,
yet a boon didst he make of me, to lay his broken face to the east so as to illustrate his gallantry,
and, though full of hateful wounds was I and showers of blood rainethed upon my arms,
granted didst I thus his true warrior's prayer, my engagement in said task only barely done
when appearethed She as *cailleach* and as cow, bearing woundings same as given,
thrice pourest She cup of teated milk, repentant, thrice of blessed healing Hers then mine to give,
atonement for my shame, my self-degradation;
other words of promise unbroken didst see me lay this neck bare for the stroke of churl's axe,
to wit the cutting steel of Cú Roí, settlement for the spread,
recompense for his departing headless thrice the goad,
his the voice of taunt at tongue-poisoned feast, my topping of feats refuted,
my later taking of his salmon-appled head recompense for his plucking the wrong flower,
redress for his shaming of I milkstreamed betokening, the lopping stroke of he forthcoming,
though her ending hidden by spell of illusion nae caused by these hands but by that damned poet's thwarting,
the *bachlach*'s revenge a blight left in memory's wake, natheless
- aye, what cruel twist of fate 'twas for his son to cast my final piercing;
and one time found I sucking from another woman's woundedness shot slung from my own hand,
she guised, too, as swan, a philanderess seeking this self with the pursuit of one besotted,
her amative designs aroused after rescue from not-so deserted beach,
she discarded, Fomorii-bound in lieu of tribute, myself white knight narcissist slayest he,
my act of deliverance her enchantment, blood-touch on my lips her impediment,
yet my heroics provest naught when she was later of women's envy cut upon,
organs of her senses mutilated, she disfigured beyond repair,
thorns in her heart and blood upon her breast - torn between revenge and *geasa*,
redress choseth I, and thrice fifty bitches burned at my hand that day,
incineration brought to them as karmic retribution for their maliciousness borne of jealousy,
nae traces of honour left in their charred and blackened wakes,
unlike the exultant glorification of Áine, her sacrifice significant,
she who knowingly stepped into impending conflagration without consternation
so as to avenge her man and promote her boy, her very actions saga-worthy and meritorious,
inspirational and poignant, the results of the heat of both infernos similarly unforgettable yet contrasting,
their deserved deaths not counted within my reckoning
- aye, 'tis a fine line between fame and infamy,
but only shallow men believe in luck and the strong in cause and effect,
and where some wouldst curse my name others extol and laud it,
hosts decimated, battles won, and feats of valour triumphed ne'er by luck alone
but by my thew and my skillset, by my steely determination to win at all cost,
my course to champion the weak and avenge those wronged,
my penchant for self-aggrandising naewithstanding,
my hero's scream oft enough to cause challengers to quail,
my berserker rage so great 'twas enough to boil water thrice,
for some of the things which I now wish I'd ne'er performed took much courage;
and, aye, there be bitter wounds to bear, and some exertions and exclamations wouldst I retract if I couldst,

but by accepting who I am and what I've done I do not abandon all hope of improving,
the perfecting of myself relentless, my quest for mastery peregrination,
my seeking of acknowledged, rightful kingship resolute and fastidious,
even from upon this death's bed of stone,
westward my glance craving such from Lugh, a gesture from my godly father's hand be enough;
and, aye, to retract and remedy split fatal stone, my plea for it to roar under my own trod lifelong desideratum,
it burst asunder under a sky bloodied red in misdirected rage not my proudest moment,
a blow of pent purgation like ritual violence spent against it for nae recognising the true king of the time,
one Lugaid Riab nDerg, my protégé, husband to Derbforgaill, said tortured beauty
- 'tis said a father expects his son to be a better man than he e'er be,
or at least as good a man as he once purposed, quick to respond to the exigencies of the fray,
dutiful and honour-bound in action and in deed, superlative in reaction and response,
knowing that change is better than destruction, and to always expect the unexpected
- look how often the unexpected happened to this man yet still I ne'er expected it,
despite the Shadow's prophecies of I, had naught but my own faculties to steer my course,
to navigate the oceans of happenings, the maelstroms of the consequences of my choices...
I grieve for my Connla still, dare look not my fathers in the eye,
repercussion for shame, unanswered my question thus:
is it harder to parent a child or be the child of a parent, be a father to a son or the son himself,
to be the perfect, tri-colour haired hero of legend or the beastial, turpitudinous villain of fey nightmare?
My mentors were many, my learnings multifaceted, but it nae matters who my fathers were,
rather how I remember they were, and, the closer to my ending cometh I,
the smarter and softer and wiser dost they become,
and despite my bravado and my biography I see but sorrow for my plight in their eyes,
their heart strings like rays of equinox and solstice sun streaming through precise passage chambers,
alighting subterranean altars at souterrain ends nae so much for sacrifice, prostration, or oblation,
but for acknowledgement, for endorsement, for welcome, embrace, release, and, aye, perhaps final restitution...
Ach, it comes to this at last, then: that so hungry for assent was, am, I,
from the peoples of this land and from those of the realms above sky and below mound,
hankering for applause from audiences of mortals and deities both,
accolades and adulations from men and sighs and satisfactions from ladies,
that my mindsets of 'it's nae about how but that one wins that matters',
and that 'it's nary so much I dost nae win but rather that I cannae let mineself lose, nae matter how hard the toil'
art paramount to stability, fortitude, my being worthy of (his? her?) salute,
because once the battering ram of doubt of myself breaches the inner ramparts of my defences,
once my belief of who I am be overcome by the fathomless pit of grief that I nae can shaketh free of,
what becomes of this Cú Chulainn then, still but a whelp,
pleading with my pantheon to be hurried to Tír Tairngire, for he who waits thinks the time long,
and I but a snivelling, pain-wracked dog with his guts unravelled about him am fast running out of time?
Aye, what use these hard, stern arms with stubborn edge, this notched spear gifted,
what use that I the mighty champion hath stood against the crashing waves of hosts,
heroic in my acts, and with harsh scream and cruel heart
built walls of many a severed corse about me,
hath vaulted castle walls with the salmon's leap and turned bog and field to bloodied sod,
hath extracted myself from the shadow queen's hexed fishnet web of retribution,
karmic entanglements she as *bandraíodóir* manifested in league with the sister, augmenters of strife,

and my only-man and foster brother both the victims of her their complots, like as nae,
guile and artifice subtly employed; aye, what use I shake off weakness and neglect and arise once more,
what use men in Alba know my name and in the winter night pity my wail,
what use I retain sharp valour and harsh force, that my career was full of triumph and women's love,
nae matter how short, that I cannae add another year and bed of death's sickness lies in wait,
for there art three things only canst I cling to on this journey:
belief in myself, whomsoever I be, Cú Chulainn, Sétanta, the Shadow's man-bitch, or some other cur;
belief in a higher self, be it the sparks of the sun-splendoured godlight of my father Lugh within me,
or those of An Dagda, He the good god, all-father of the pantheon Himself, many-skilled man of the peaks,
wise beyond measure, chief of the *Tuatha Dé*, tribe of the gods;
and belief in a 'higher self' ingrained into the neural network of the thinking physiology of my architecture,
the infiltration and imprinting upon my very consciousness lessons and learnings of her devise,
Scáthach, my vixen tutor herself, she who taught of blade and bedding, endless hours of repetition of
engage, disengage, re-engage, impale, transpierce, penetrate, thrust, drill,
to circle and blend with shadow, to come from behind or to meet head-on,
to strike parry feint swing twist stab turn slash thrust turn slice strike parry feint twist stab sting,
to dance and vault and gill-breathe, to focus on and to prioritise reaction and right response,
again, and again, and again, before spite and acrimony turned her sour, vindictive even,
for gaveth she birth to this Cú Chulainn in her crucible of initiation,
created habits and patterns of melee and retaliation I cannae and nae dare erase,
reprogrammed my very foundations, the essence of my truest self,
turned me from uncontrollable *fáelán,* too big and strong for my own good, into the War Hound,
bane of the enemies of morals and engagers of uncharitable behaviours,
for I dost nae forgive and I dost nae forget;
and, too, belief in the truth, both the higher and the worldly,
light and physicality blended thus, nary unlike the double beams of golden sun
illuminating earthen floor and upright stone in the womb of the moon,
conception-place of this self, and final mortal resting place for my father of the long arm after drowning,
that wisdom begets respect, foolishness results in crudity, and risk and arrogance produce disfavour,
that better than afterthought be forethought, that honour opens out to prowess,
yet to be humble is to be exalted and 'tis an eminent person who promotes harmony,
that desire engenders perseverance and good habits lead to piety, because pride dost be the catalyst for evil,
that complacency marks the edge of decline and weariness the beginning of misery,
that confrontation leads to injury, so better diligence than audacity as courage hath a brutal core,
and, whereas exultation after victory be surely the most mellifluous of sounds,
battles result in lamentations? Aye, life dost be better than triumphs, and woe to him who leads the martial life,
unless through it great repentance and ataraxis he achieve, for inner repose be better than bitterness,
cordiality better than fomenting discord, knowledge better than aggressiveness,
and dignity better than ruthlessness... Ach, is this my time for penitence, then, for the gaining of elder's wisdom,
time to make a wiser person of this fool, to lift me from the miry clay of violent retaliation and recrimination,
for absolution of my lot through the vehicle of this entropic succumbing to these persistent agonies?
As I am strapped here, sword raised above my shoulder, staring at, glaring at,
daring any and all to try their luck upon my apparent helplessness,
now dost I know, as I feel descending upon my heart like a tangible, blackened curse,
the heaviness of the weight of the souls of all those slain by this hand...
And, aye, knoweth I, too, now, the further truth,

that 'tis better forgiveness than vengeance and better wisdom than weapons,
and though it may be good in the beginning 'tis all the more better in the end,
for knowledge leads to an answer - but, ach,
what use art my histories, legacies, tales of myself as the swollen wave that wrecks like doom,
accounts of braveries, slaughters, wooings, feats, knowings,
lessons and learnings, what use my avenging the preys, the evillings and the wrongs,
what use that ne'er sprang from sea or land a King's son that hadst larger fame than I,
if I hath been at silent, secret war with parts of myself for so long as the deliverer of my own ruin,
for isn't the real question nae so much that there be truly life after passing,
albeit in different aspect, different form,
but, rather, was I e'er truly alive before this death that is upon me,
for if a man may well still live even after losing his life, may he after losing his honour?
Ach, Ferdiad, were it that I saw thy fall amidst Scáthach's foretelling I'd've nae lived on after thee,
but together we'd've parted our souls from flesh and blood, brothers in the brume of *immrama*,
rowed out beyond the ninth wave, destination unknown,
the white horses of Manannán mac Lir momentarily spancilled, allowing easy passage,
skirted the savage, rocky coast of Tech Duinn en route to Hy Breasil,
believing we needs but nae pay visit for on *echtrae* we be, feigning death,
destined to return anon after hero's outing, though longer the years in the making;
and hadst I nae heard tell of and hadst nae my fated course been to wield her shadow-cursed spear
I'd"ve nae faced Connla, he'd've nae come hither to Ulaid in his bronzed skiff with gilten oars,
harrying birds of the sea with slinged stone and tuned song until challenged met,
his mockery of the host and his challenge to my honour his reckoning,
the unravelling of Aoife's revenge of me so, the Shadow's tidings hard - hath I but stayed my pique,
heeded my woman's sooth, nae sought the brightened victory of triumph in deeds,
but with cry of "*Agus crosaim thú*" rebounded their curses, returned unto them any trace of futured reckoning,
together we could've vanquished the men of the world before us on every side, thou and I,
the gore of thy body nary a vapour upon my flesh - but, hold,
here the excruciation of my predicament distorts even my own perceptivity,
for I forget Amergin's teachings and my own proclamation,
that opportunity oft comes disguised in misfortune's form, and that cursing one's allotted incarnation be futile,
for, surely, now is time for acknowledging that upon myself hath brought I this ruin,
for pride goeth before destruction and a haughty spirit before a fall, and in seeking my father's nod of homage didst I
seek such from other men and create burdens to o'ercome, burgeoning thus my hubris:
everything that happened to this Cú was only what on some level hadst I'd asked for, looked for,
everything that hadst or hadst nae but the same,
for my soul hadst known the geography of my destiny before I,
hadst, unbeknownst to my own temperament, chosen these entanglements such,
and, with hope for ascendance forthwith, now canst I die without grimace,
this moment a boon to a dying hound, recollections and conscience cleared of spite and spat,
remembrances of loves and loss and cuts and feats vivid still in my mind and feeling,
for while young and virile 'tis all dreams and when old or dying 'tis all memories...
But better one good thing that is than two good things that were, or three good things that might ne'er come to pass,
for, even though imminent is my last breath, and allowing that he who falls today may well rise tomorrow,
even ostensibly knowing my fame may well outlive this life of skin and bone and blood,
my span and triumphs having been already determined,

that yet nae will I for the world's lying vanities forsake prestige and battle-virtues,
seeing that from the day first didst I a full-grown warrior's weapons take in these hands
ne'er hadst shirked I fight nor fray, and now, therefore, still less wouldst I so, although tremulous,
for the actuality of passing is as yet but promise and envisioned theory only,
and mayhap all my braveries and warmongerings hath just been cocksure posturing after all,
for one nae knows what one nae knows despite preparedness and prophecy,
and, while in concept I may nae fear to die, the reality of the reality becomes increasingly daunting
- before entering the sea even a river trembles with fear... Aye,
why wouldst I want to pass beyond the veil while there be life in me still,
albeit its continuation speculative, pain-racked and distorted?
Couldst I avoid the slow death of me but still take the fame if forceth I myself from this world first,
bypass this body's sufferings and last shudderings by sheer force of will alone,
my last and greatest feat nae longer that of surrender to foretold predictions but one of defiance to destiny,
having my ending be of choice o'er circumstance, taking prophecies of me by the horns
and forcing bend the hands of fate - is it even possible to outrun one's preordained lot?
I know that as long as one is breathing 'tis ne'er too late to start a new beginning,
but if one holds their breath for long enough wouldst one nae just sleep forever?
Dying here wouldst easy be, disembowelled thus against this dolmen, drowning in my own bile and blood,
stuck between hard place and stone, neither yet fully dead nor having e'er been fully alive,
'tis living through this excruciation for longer that scares me to death
- I, who hadst ne'er been scared of anyone nor anything,
nary a feat too onerous, a task too daunting, an enemy too dark, a host too great, nor challenge unmeetable,
canst I nae feel the breath of my lifeforce dissipating upon the whispering wind?
And, aye, 'tis nae shame to tell the truth, and what I'm afraid to hear I'd best say first to myself:
if I am destined to die regardless, what matters whose hand deals the death blow?
My wounds are red, my cuts deep, my flesh sworded sore,
and I see nae end to these stabbing agonies and I tremble, this faltering a stigma upon my resilience...
Isn't it said that death be surely better than lasting blemish, certainty better than doubt,
and that life entails anxiety? To be freed of constant consternation and deformity appeals, aye, to be sure,
and if life and anxiety art twin-bonded, what dost thou sayest of thy Cú Chulainn now, Scáthach?
Thou urged me once to go where I wouldst find comfort still,
but what comfort comes with most speed, with most urgency,
if nae matter where I taketh stand dire danger is e'er at hand, this body is to wasted be,
and grief and sorrow follow wherein dost I roam? Where'er I go, there art I, and there my torment and misery follow
- what becomes of thy Cú Chulainn if thou wilt nae add another year nor tell more of my career?
Tell me true, o *banfhili*, through the wickersmoke of thine *imbas forosnai*,
why for Cruachan's heroes to render Cú Chulainn 's dogflesh open upon bloodied sod it be fitting,
but nae so for this man to alter the course of a few ounces of his own blood?

Canst this truly be my life, or hadst there nae been some mistake?

There be nought to stop me enacting thus except what's inside myself,
my own integrity, my own moral code,
and it comes to now I must weigh up my choices, the aftermath of whatsoe'er path chooseth I,
be prepared to face the repercussions of decisions made - so, dost I cut through myself,
reduce these agonies with one deft downward slice upon the very guts of me without hesitancy,

fall upon my sword and let thy prophecies dissipate into the timeless void, Scáthach ni Uanaind,
forego, p'haps, the elevation thou hast promised me, put my ascension potentially aside,
disappear into my own twilight and end this game of life by my own hand,
let every day hereafter be a day without one more selfish mutt to prowl,
or dost I hold to my allotted course, wake up from this idea of felony upon this self,
step aside from fears and, though in twain torn asunder, become again Cú Chulainn of brave mein,
perfected hero of legend, peerless champion, afraid of naught upon this world,
esteemable, virtuous, honourable, indefatigable, cocksure, haughty, proud son of the sun,
fully prepared to meet death face to face so as to live on in song and myth and legend,
to fulfil the auguries of myself, to be the true Hound of Ulaid in full glory,
master of my own reactions and responses, choosing prestige and honour amaranthine,
nae more a dog being wagged by its own tail, thrown this way and that by the vagaries of life, victim to fate,
knowing it's nae over till it's over, and one ne'er knows of what one be capable until one tries?
Ach, thou win some, thou lose some...

[pause]

I hath set my resolve, and so mote it be, my choice madeth thus:
the only way to win this war upon this self must needs be I lose it
- I must set free myself to become my true self,
must let the prophecies and predictions unravel as they may, cometh what may,
must loosen the stakes and chains that bindeth me to this form,
must nae waste final inhalations hanging on to that which will be taken away,
for that which ne'er dies inhabits both my past and my future and is itself the absence of suffering and sorrow,
and surrendering unto its embrace is as medicine to these pains, beyond even waters drawn from the Well of Sláine,
for, though they but once restored life to the fallen so as to get them back onto the battlefield,
ne'er didst they imbue their charges with essence of *síoraíocht*,
nor brought them to the *géilleadh deiridh*, the surrender of their soul unto the ninefold elements,
the strength of Tír na nÓg itself, the light of sun, radiance of moon, splendour of fire, speed of lightning,
swiftness of wind, depth of sea, stability of earth, firmness of rock, themselves enduring witnesses of promises made,
of oath, *geasa*, vow, and bond. 'Tis oft said if one digs a grave for others one might fall into it oneself,
and, as hadst dug I many a grave for and made quick work of the men of Ériu,
seemeth it only fitting now what 'tis to come,
for my plying of weapons hath scattered reddened bones across the loam
and broadcast grey the fields with heads and skulls and hands and feet halved,
left numbers liken to the sands of the sea and leaves in the forest in onslaught's wake,
and now on chopped flesh doth ravens feed and crow scour the ploughed ground,
surrounded as I am by the butchery and slaughter of my foe. Aye, 'twas for them to comply or die,
to succumb unto my will or consequence pay - and consequence pay they didst, to detriment theirs...
My best course now must surely be to heed the various foretellings of my lot,
to wit the dusky blood tears on my Liam Macha's cheeks and his nae coming to meet his bridle nor his master,
the candour of Niamh, she who to refuse most irked was I,
herself undoing my exacted troth empowering her licence to bid warring upon the men of Ériu,
that nae for the globe's gold nor the whole world's wealth had she e'er given I that leave,
but that it was one Badb, daughter of thrice-cursed Calatin, in shape of she that deceivethed I thus,
the entreats of Cathbad and Emer-mine, to share feast jovial with the women and the poets, so far their doings,

the warnings of cloak and bodkin, friend and foe, my countenance red for shame,
a yellow-haired fairy woman washing my spoils upon Emania's green,
the roasted deceit of crones three, embodiments of Her, the Morrigna, Badb, Macha, Nemain,
beautiful seductresses and red-maned, frenzied crows alike, She, they, augurs of woe,
the thrice-bloodied wine of mother's cup, and the *imbas forosnai* of the hooded shadow witch herself,
for surely didst some part of I knowest of my sad and lamentable ending in the onset to come,
I but an accident waiting to happen?

I hath made my choice.

Ne'er let it be said that any couldst encounter a warrior harder to deal with,
nor a spear-point sharper or keener or quicker, nor a hero fiercer,
nor a hound more voracious for bloodied foe,
nor one of my age to equal a third of my valour than I, Sétanta-come-Cú Chulainn,
for here, aye, nae will taketh I the recreant's way,
and even in my final throes upon this gut-soiled monolith dost I stare down the darkness of my fears,
nae will succumbeth I to their chthonian depths, but reignite the bone-fire of my sharp pluck and my force,
regather these bowels into this breast, save these girdle strands around this unfeeling stone,
hear again in the spaces between ragged breaths my heart boom loud in this bosom,
it a clarion call like the baying of a watch-dog at its feed or the sound of a ravenous wolf among boars,
for he who nae everyday be conquering some fear hath nae learned the secret of living,
that life begins where fear endeth - aye, nearly didst I forget everything and run, skulking,
into the belly of my doubts, tail tucked in submission and defeat, ears drooping,
but nary a man be the worse for knowing the worst of himself,
and now chooseth I to face everything and rise, resplendant,
hero light upon my brow nae longer waning, for I am the actual architect of my destiny,
malignant mists and spurts of fire flickering red in vaporous clouds that riseth boiling above my head
so fierce my fury - at myself, for near succumbing to such weakness,
for 'tis an ugly sight, a man afraid, and was I nae born knowing my soul eternal,
that a second life awaited I dead, and that death be but the middle of a long life?;
and fury unmatched at my very king, for nae cameth Conchobar out with help in this fight, nae troops of his,
and, whereas 'tis hard to say which suffers worse, my right side or my left, my heart or my flesh,
I am worn from each day's eke of bloody toil as I alone these cattle guard,
because he who hath kine upon the hill nary sleeps easy, and, as the best means of defence be to attack, to be sure,
fight on fight it hath been, though as much I vowed and hath kept my word in all,
and whilst for pure honour's sake itself didst I draw blade, 'twas too much to stand alone,
for one sole log burns nae so well as when one doth burn by its side,
one single log gives forth nae flame,
and one alone e'er is vulnerable to guile that canst be employed, nae matter how stalwart be he
- the single mill-stone doth nae grind, and ill 'tis my plight, there's nary a hope for I,
for it nae be the size of the dog in a fight that counts but the size of the fight in the dog,
and I cannae last these fights, still and all the scale of my ferocity
- mournful cries of woe are heard for on Muirtheimne's plain is grief,
yet I hath made my choice: ofttimes is nae the best way to be useful to get out of the way,
for how canst I fail when my purpose be to let the Wheel's turning continue,
to let the foretellings of my outcomes become delivered unto their own,

from Cathbad's call to take arms and have everlasting fame though shortened span,
to Scáthach's hex of dark gatherings of blood and grief and sorrow upon the sod,
of plucking ravens, weeping women, the passing of this hero on the Plain of Muirtheimne,
my enemies kept for thirty years yet only the meat of me destined to return unto the dirt,
my name ne'er to die, only my red soul and killing lust, so long as the world turneth?
There be nae need now to wait for said deliverance, for the shining beings to come up from under their mounds
and touch upon my brow and there to be nary more blood nor pain, these woundings salved,
my expired self reforged, either by the Dagda and His shaft or Dian Cécht and Airmed,
Lord of the Heavens or swift healer, great grandfather mine and his daughter left,
one who could've reinvented me with His *lorg mór*, if choseth my fate such hadst He,
the other to secure fashioned girdle of silver for my organs, as didst once he so silvered hand for Núadu,
maimed first king of the children of Danu whose death paved for my father the way,
though prefereth I guts rewove of flesh and sinew if 'twas my story to tell;
but beggars can't be choosers, Miach of his father's spite nae more, fourth cut of jealousy the cause,
my only recourse for natural antidote, then, the daughter, she of incant and herb, Awen-blessed,
her fingertips and soft voice alive with flow and essence,
only with her plant and song the reknitting of my form the possibility,
her melody of bone and vein and balm and sap, of skin and tissue, blood, and flesh,
of sinew, marrow, pith, and fat, of membrane, fibre, and moisture a healing bath of sound,
she able, too, to tender wounds of heart-blemishing, for didst nae her tears of grieving herbs produce,
grown upon her brother's grave, remedies that, though scattered, when gathered and thrown in well,
mixed with verse and herb under water, revived men struck down and mortally-wounded,
others more poorly, more grievous sláine than I, salve their griefs of soul and story?
But, ach, I doth ramble, for nae need hath I of such devices, alchemical nor magical,
for my path 'tis chosen and Tír na nÓg awaits, all that be needed my surrendering,
the essence of I to depart this form,
because unless I move from here this place where I am is where my spirit will always be,
my co-walker bound to the cold, hard stone of this deathly dolmen,
it only a shaded simulacrum of this beasted form, he, it, still connected even after the death of me,
my side bored and my body mangled yet it able to inhabit both sides of the veil,
if to embrace *síoraíocht* nae be my spirit's destiny,
remnants and vibrations of my essence destined to linger long upon the very dirt of this plain itself,
mingled with great spoil of arms, of armour and of gear that which by my sword and my spear
lie there drenched in blood, in streams and pools of curdled gore,
mesmerising passersby, enticing them closer, in league with my family's *bean-sidhe*,
itself birthed into being and attached to my bloodline as payback ages past by Clíodhna, queen of *sidheog*,
once she goddess of love and comeliness, indifferent to human affairs, voyeuristic witnessing her pleasure,
yet turneth her beauty sour didst she and redress becometh her satisfaction from loss of sport and swain,
she vexed at Dian Cécht's thwarting of the promise of the forthcoming fell filth of Méiche, thrice-hearted snake child,
scion of the juice of the Mórrígan and the spunk of the Dadga, its countenance heinous, its prediction deathly,
it to've wasted by its nature all the kine of the indolent hosts of ancient Ériu,
all beasts of field and woodland ne'er more longer to draw breath, consumed utterly,
hath the killing of it nae come to pass, burning its fate, ashes scattered in silent river,
neither barrow nor mound safety, tomb without walls nor roof-tree its watery grave,
seething and boiling to rags all things living therein,
bitter reminder of her loss, creation of said *bean-sidhe* venom's slur at the fertile Father and His raven bitch,

disregard for venery's consequence the bedrock of her grudge;
she, too, still enraged at Manannán Mac Lir
for his taking of her from her Ciabhán's side with incantation of the ninth wave,
she swept by wild horses white, their salt water kisses her saturation, luscious lips parted in drowning her doom,
her vitriol still heard in every breaking wave thundering from the sea,
and in the final, gasping breath of every drowned sailor lured towards her lovesong,
and, too, for his harbouring of my blood-line, Dal Duana-come-Lugh,
the sun who held the light of this Cú Chulainn in his Otherworldly seed,
kinsman of Dian Cécht, until in woman's care his fostering, she the tree-cutter, field-maker,
Tailtiu, last queen of the Fir Bolg,
whom my father's spirit laments still, his mourning gift the Áenach Tailteann,
harvest festival and funeral games, contests of strength and skill and endurance,
in honour of and challenge to match her onerous exhaustion, her heart and body broken upon clearings end,
himself the issue of Cían and Eithne, he my father's father, she the daughter of one whose name meant death,
father of evil eye, Fomor king, Balor of the Mighty Blows, he bested thus:
Cían's serving-girl employment on desolate bandit isle where eaten meat uncooked his artifice,
held counsel with ocean's master by night his guile, Eithne's liberation from lifelong loneliness his shrewd manoeuvre,
my dream-seen grandfather's face her deliverance,
their tryst in crystal tower atop Túr Mór pregnant with consequence,
attempted drowning of *leanbh* three at Balor's behest further cause of this family's darkened fortune,
fear of druidic prophecy his argument, fear of druidic devices borne from smoke plumed spell of death the fuel,
yet they to nae avail, his covet his undoing, one child thus surviving and dousing his cycloptic heat,
putting out said orb with fiery stone of sling, his own grandson both his ruination and swoll for Clíodhna's spite,
father mine, Lugh of the long arm, revenge brought from beyond thought grave, prophecy so unravelled,
my bloodline's surviving of filicide unforgiven us by Clíodhna still, her disdain and malice grim and unwavering,
a long-smouldering coal enkindled, p'haps, by undercurrents of simple jealousy,
her envy of Biróg's claim of *leannán sídhe* over Cían another reminder of her grievous loss,
exacerbating her vehemence, the only remedy for her malison my demise, I the last of the line,
my only heir extinguished by my own hand her delight,
her overseeing of corses following my family's footsteps relentless, sedulous,
her keening wails harbringing deaths imminent nae from benevolence benign but from bloodlust,
for in her lament of beauty taken abhorreth she the living and wished she all things fallen,
as hadst fallen she so far from shapely, comely allure and status,
beyond e'en her own birds' curing calls, kingfisher, blue tit, bullfinch,
their trills and warblings lost in the fathomless briny,
her very presence upon the plain drawing victims towards her like will o' wisp o'er marsh-land,
her trailing ragged, gossamer tendrils of white and flashes of moments of seductive beauty
nary belying her hate-filled, blood red eyes that when beheld at length delivered instant demise,
foci for her haunting *caoine* her rotted mouth e'er opened,
tormenting living souls with her perpetual, piercing scream, this self included,
it presenting in their minds upon commencement more as direful, mental torture than audible affliction,
she become a twisted, tormented hag whose incessant, baleful wailing heard internally drove sufferers insane,
she inherited penance for the deceits and failed filicides of my antecedents, the carnal sins of my antiquity,
her business unfinished until either my mayhap coming expansion or my demise,
whiche'er cometh the sooner, her interminable viscous mockeries the epitome of vengeance,
voicing in my mind and ear when at each day's end my head resteth I, splenetic premonitions of dark unfoldings,

nightmarish visions of my very fall by Medb's great hosting and by incantations of Calatin's children,
their king-slayer spear to be hurled by the son of the battlefield hound destined to strike monarch's three,
one Láeg mac Riangabra, king of charioteers, one Grey of Macha, king of horses,
and this king, I, though mantle proper ne'er taken
- her forecast of my ending hath proved veracious,
yet if dost I not accept such as to be my fated course, including the dorning of crowned horns upon my brow,
surrender not to my lot but, instead, hold tight to the reins of my bile and spite and questioning of my dole,
invite I thus said revenant extra to stand alongside the morbid slattern and join its wails with hers,
her rancour's longevity so...

Nae, ne'er let it be said that I bared my teeth where couldst I nae take bite,
for, even though sorely wounded here art I, any who come too near will feel the rake of my claw
and meet with the diplomacy of my sword - I nary fear the cold steel of cowards,
for we who art born to die yet know our souls immortal art nae afraid of bloodshed,
death robbed of all its terrors and the entering of flesh again invitation,
and, if the head of my spear cast in my weakness can burst the head of the *dobhar-chú* asunder,
surely in my strength canst I split the veil betwixt the worlds,
can seek and find Scáthach's ferly prophecies of immortality in tale and promise of another life recreated,
because if there be a chance to be the bull of seven battles, the eagle on the rock,
the strong wild boar, the salmon in the water, or the perfected hero of legend come again,
why wouldst I nae take it? Aye, always hadst been I the point of the spear in battle,
first to the fields of slaughter and most oft last man left standing,
my commitment to fulfilling oaths of vengeance purposeful and unrelenting,
I, Conchobar's champion of the Red Branch Knights, willing to battle even my own boy for Uliad's honour,
the only warrior exempted from the birth-pang curse of she of the speed of wind,
cradling bloodied stillborns her malediction their downfall in the hour of their greatest need,
only my beardlessness my saviour, yet I proven as much man and more as any who'd e'er taken arms,
for without my holding of Medb's forces at bay many wouldst hath met with death in birthing faux;
but rarely is a fight continued when the chief hast fallen,
and mayhap with this death of me there will be a retiring of blades upon their racks by the men of Ériu,
a ceasing of the wailing and lamentations by the thrice fifty queens of Emain Macha,
nae more their shedding tears of blood and hands smote in great cry,
nae more the spurious batting of their eyes, licking of their lips, their coy flirtations, breasts thrust in titillation,
nae more the provoking of their husband's wrath, for wounded by iron and scarred by spear and sword art I,
and oft hast seen I battle for the very heart of both women and prestige,
yet, now in this predicament, the guts of me splayed out about this stone like a sickened dog's breakfast,
tired art I of fighting - I, War Hound of mightiest deeds,
irresistible in hardness of combat, my spirit like an unquenchable ball of fire every day and every night,
I an indestructible fortress, an unassailable rock that yet can move like mountain mist upon the plain,
with the speed of a hill-hind, my step fast and oft joyful like snow hewing the slopes,
becoming doused now is my heat, cooled by the waters of my own unexpected tears of pain,
for hard-edged steel honed by blacksmith's hammers hath constantly attacked this self,
and each time I am knocked about and bitten once again awaiteth I something else, something worse,
the *colg* and *claideb* gashes upon my flesh growing bigger day and night - aye,
warrior's deeds canst perform I nae longer as men have almost worn this self out in these single-handed fights,
for they love the war until hadst seen they too much of it, and witness hath I been to more than any's fair share,

and may I ne'er forget what is worth remembering nor remember what be best forgotten,
and may I honour the space atwixt 'nae yet' and 'nae longer', for holdeth still I to my pledge,
that their dead shouldst be more than their living, and yet nae yet art I nae longer, my sundering fallacious,
my prophecy as yet unfulfilled, despite that my plying of weapons hath scattered red bones
and broadcast grey the fields with heads and skulls and hands and feet halved
in numbers as to the sands of the sea left in my onslaught's wake, choking the plain,
each wave of this reddened sea a straggling line of the fallen
- dost I stay present to these agonies in this soon-to-be lifeless form,
purge these sensations of excruciation from within me with one final dynamic, cathartic thrust,
one last ferocious scream becoming this dog's death-agony's howl,
spray pus, spit, and blood from these lacerated innards and grume-filled lungs upon the men of Ériu,
inflict upon them with vomitous excrements curses and promises of swedge and rammy in this life and the next,
or, as there is little of my own time remaining, dost I surrender unto my fated course,
affect retreat from this mortal shell and alight unto the stellar void,
my voice and my breath becoming but remembered whisperings,
for, even though life may be better than triumphs, fame doth be better than deeds,
and the ingredient of my success may well be to turn this premortem humiliation into honour,
this torment into exultation, this guietus into new life? Aye, reputations last longer than lives,
and howe'er long this descent will be 'tis true my evening cometh,
and truth stands when everything else falls - must needs I nae borrow more trouble,
nor bite off more than canst I chew, for I hath made my choice:
I hear the voice of my father inviting me, imploring me, beseeching me to release the canine claws of my *riastrad*,
to look nae longer out through my soul's windows with veils of vengeance, vitriol, nor vexation foremost in mind,
but to cast my gaze inwards and upwards,
to let the pinprick lights of the welkin ignite new desire in my cauldrons' bellies,
enkindle unto my soul fires of new proclivities of awakening and elevation, of accession and enlightenment,
to finally accept the mantle of his blessing - sovereignty, at last, my humility my diadem,
to embrace a new freedom, a new sublimity, a transcendence of heart, mind, soul, spirit,
release from the vagaries of my desires, rages, fixations, prides, fervours, lusts, and pains,
the attachment points, origins, and insertions of my sentimentalities loosening and relaxing,
their final capitulations forcing from my throat one last, bellowing lamentation, a ferocious finale,
a gutting scream, death-knell of the totality of aloneness that hadst become my loneliness,
my emotional disintegration thus: "My father, why hadst thou abandoned I?
Why didst thou relinquish thy favours, impart such bestiality upon me?
Wherefore art thou now in my dourest hour of need?",
it nae unlike the very roar of agony and excruciation of Macha's final exertion,
or Aine's last whispered prayer before her martyred immolation,
though my pains nae be those of birthing nor of burning but of extrication, disencumbering,
leading hopefully to liberation and release from torment,
they a literal disembowelment of the temperaments and obstacles within the very depths of the guts of I,
allowing thus my ability, my will, and my acts to become those of *géilleadh deiridh*,
of becoming nothing to find... everything.
I was taught to ne'er forgive and ne'er forget, but aye, now it be the time for release from all teachings,
to let the fervour of my convictions dissipate unto the nightened sky of stars,
to let my blood-pacts of amity extend to all players, self included, for I see now through all thine eyes,
ancestors, brethren, tormentors, satirists, enemies, compatriots, mistresses, lovers, fellow men and women of war,

revealed to my cognisance now their deceits and wiles and artistries, their manoeuvres, expedients, and complots,
their chicaneries and contrivances, their hearts and their guts and their hurts, what was and what is,
from the guiles and artifices of Forgall, Úathach's spats of shame and grief and confusion,
the unravelling, embittered revenge of Aoife, borne of hurt, she scarred from our once-love and my spurn,
so vindictive she wouldst taketh she the air from a dying man, yet shareth my very breath with her wouldst I now,
for yae, 'tis only now I see the gravitas of our union and understand why her nemesis didst I become,
Scáthach's lust for dominance and her hidden, voracious thirst for grume, tendrils to her pre-life,
she, too, hurt by my betrayal, though foresaweth she the script of my sharp valour and my force,
saluted she such as fated, certain course, her poetic illuminations shining true,
knewest she oh too well both Ferdiad and Connla wouldst fall victim to her gifted barb,
and that, aye, in part, within her crucible of initiations, she madeth who I am,
through Emer's fidelity, she the root cause of my gaiety, my loving prior lawless as the wild tides of the sea,
as cruel as the north wind blowing o'er barren rocks, any port in a storm to do,
yet with she 'twas like storm-ravaged ship coming home to safe haven,
for a good wife be the beginning of good fortune, and, though better good fortune than a consort,
to have blessing of one in the other be surely a gift of abundance, boon and guerdon from the very island itself,
for part of the beating heart of Ériu art I, of all that She was and all that She is, land and goddess combined,
fullness and and bounty personified, one of sisters three to stare down the Milesians 'til 'twas clear victory theirs,
the *Tuatha Dè* fading, so passing the fifth age of the world, their queen's names inshrined upon the very sod itself,
Banba, Fódla, Ériu, their husbands grandsons of the Dadga, sons of sun, hazel, and plough,
though Ériu hath more the mantle worn, for 'twas with calm utterance she words of power and *draíocht* spake,
gaveth she injury for the insult to one Donn mac Miled for his slur, sentence of death enacted, he drowning his due,
Medb's designs of cruelty and vengeance, their fuel her arrogance and vanity, consequences naewithstanding,
Connla's longing for this vanishing father's embrace, his yearning for my nod akin to my once pining for same,
his concepts skewed from his mother's and aunt's wounds of hurt, his true self-worth elusive,
my shadow a dark cloud above, his only recourse contest, blow for blow, strike for strike,
'till released I her water spear, too late to recognise the ring,
his worth proven to my eyes but by my mouth ne'er known in the heart of he my shame,
to this vanquished father's despair and desolation, for a man should nae outlive nor bequeath to his own son,
let alone wield the weapon of his demise, my thirst for honour my remorse and my regret, my very grave itself,
my own exoneration hardest - 'tis easier to forgive others than to forgive myself, but, even so, it must be done,
for there is nae further West to flee, my departing this form more renascence than escape, transcendence,
for now dost I have what I need inside to embark upon the voyage into the mists of my true self:
aye, everything is sacred when one takes the time to notice,
and, just as every eye forms its own fancy, now I have eyes to see, there nae be absence of pleasantness,
only firming of my resolution that yea, didst I depart this sentence naturally, gracefully, my facilities sundered,
following the eternal cycles of *dòigh nàdair*, of the seasons of man and the rise and set of the son,
and nae longer now dost I question if thy tributes hadst fallen on this self's deafened ears, mistress of shade,
or if my own sense of honour, my felicity, my fervour, hadst themselves abandoned I,
victim to my own traumas, my own plights,
for Scáthach's salute and my father's satisfaction of this Sétanta hath overcome my inner torment,
and, yea, now, surely, canst I, dost I, come to Thee, Turner of the Wheel, to where the sun meets the *sidhe*,
to the joining place of earth and sky, beyond the western horizon,
towards the beckoning firmament of my father's chain,
towards my pantheon's and my family's enfold, to be embosomed by Danu, mother of us all,
to be hailed and welcomed by my kin and proclaimed worthy of the hero's portions for my feats;

beyond the passage chambers and portals, floating in my spirit-chariot above Emain Macha, dost I come,
to be cosseted and coddled amongst the stars, bundled up in the fourfold cloaks worn upon the circuit of our lives,
to Reul Near, star of the east, the spring star, bringer of wind and kindly birth, dost I come,
to Reul Deas, star of the south, the summer star, bringer of fire and hearth, dost I come,
to Reul Niar, star of the west, the autumnal star, bringer of water and quiet age, dost I come,
and to Reul Tuath, star of the north, the winter star, bringer of wisdom, silence, and death, too, dost I come,
the seasons and carriage of the ether intertwined, interconnected, never ending in infinite embrace,
permanently woven into I as the knotted triad leaves of the trinities, the three-legged whorls of triskelion alchemy,
earth air water, battle death nativity, mind body spirit, father mother child, life death rebirth,
and casteth myself now into the molten core of that which ne'er dies dost I,
my spirit reverberating with the pure potential of a future nae set yet in stone,
for the past is the past and what will ensue is yet to happen, tomorrow promise to none, nae the least to this self,
is as yet nae more than rays of light in the darkness, 'twill come when it comes and 'twill be what it be,
for nothing is too common to be exalted and nothing is so exalted that it canst not be made common,
and death makes beggars and paupers of us all - the craven may die many times before their death,
the valiant but once, but both in time will succumb to their embodiment's erosion,
it but a necessary finality that will come when the gods decree, for only the gods know what they know,
the places where the sun sets and the ages of the moon,
though it be but nae more than a new beginning, either another form's accouchement
or amelioration of one's soul - naught can come between me and full prospect of my hopes,
the shades of men like I nae seek the dismal darkness of death's pale kingdoms but the very breath of life itself,
be it life in saga. legend, myth, or song, or as same soul, different form, same dog, different day,
and with nae fear of that which frights all others didst I with hands and heart undaunted
headlong rush upon my foes and scorn to spare this life that will return,
for plied I axe, sword, javelin affearing not bloodied defeat of myself, neither earthquake nor wave,
thunder nor roil, slash nor cut nor piercing, this body mere encumbrance to my fortitude,
for 'twas the very promise of death that madeth my life worth the living
- there was always straight course if I couldst feel hilt or shaft in my hand, if my courage was coupled with desire,
for what worth threats of kisses of steel without heart's force behind their wielding?
Aye, this dog's days are near over,
for days of three hath I hung in this balance, my spirit neither there nor here, sore wounded, red with blood,
actively dying, my own torn heart the only anchor to the inevitability of release from this affliction,
for ne'er since the shadow witch's prophecy of me, of how 'twas thirst for the red scent shalt I lose
and not my esteem, the underpinning of this life only but not the very essence of my legacy,
didst my nub truly falter, and close came, my chagrin my blemish, and, here at the endgame,
as I draw closer to thee now, my father, as I tie my wrath with grace and benevolence,
as I let the battling wolfhound of white inside me overpower the wolfhound of darkness and ruination,
knowing that the one who wins the day is the one whom which hadst I most fed,
and it be bearer of charity, moral, empathy, compassion, ethic, poesy, living, laughter, dance, and mirth,
said other dog of deaths and despair but nae,
didst I send skulking the arrogant, rage-filled, envious, aggrieved anti-hero of my wounded past,
thank the gods by whom my people swear,
for to believe in the heroic makes of us heroes, in thoughts and words and deeds and action,
and 'tis thy voice I hear now in my mind o'er the roaring beat of my fast depleting redness,
o'er the bellowed grief of their mothers that fills the land as calves no longer suckle in deference to my plight,
o'er the quickening pulse of my inner heart salivating my forthcoming, thine invitation to constancy thus:

"Let my blood's taste be thine upon thy tongue as thou drawest near to the point of nae return, my son,
let thy footsteps be firm upon the sod and thy sword-hand gripped tight about the hilt with my gift of perpetuity:
let thy flesh and blood and bone and marrow in every morsel of meat thou takest be our merging,
and let my blade be thy blade and my blood be thy blood,
as my heart and mind be thine in sacremental bond, united together as father and son in mind and body and spirit,
in present and past and future,
and as one shalt we defeat and vanquish all thy nemeses and destroy all thy foes before thee,
and none shall stop the blood of their severing from feeding the land,
for if thou dost believeth in me and my tenets I will hereby exist within thee, with all my strength, my brawn,
my vigilance, my honour, my force, and my thew thine to draw upon in times of need,
for as I walk between the worlds I gift thee this, my son: there is nary a reason to doubt, flesh of my heart,
thee with heart of steel, that thou cannae lustrate and sanctify thyself this day, this moment, it be but thy choice,
for if thou comest to me kicking with aliveness like a newborn lamb, thine only defence thine innocence,
though trouble and pain be plenteous about thee, yea, canst I bring thee home to where the crucial magic arises,
as promised miracle, direct to Hy Breasil, even as foretold by thy mistress of shade herself,
that thy career be to seek nae longer thou the crimson stains of gore and glory, nae matter how short the span,
but to take thy rightful kingship by the horns, to let thy wound that ne'er bleeds be cauterised,
and the shattered pieces left inside of thee face the final knowing
- in short, thou needst nae feel this as pain, my Cú,
and, though thy vision be bloodshot and thou be blemished sworded sore,
and though words cannae seldom convey what only the heart canst express, know this in thy final torture:
in thy defencelessness lies thy true power,
and, though thou hadst valiantly defended against the forces of Medb,
and other evils sordid and foul, hadst p'haps outwit even She,
darkest raven of death's despair and blood's foreboding, the Morrígu Herself,
'tis not thy prowess that paves thee now the way but thy choice just made
- of thy surrender, of thine abdication of unworthiness,
of thy willingness to let the prophecies of thyself ring true,
to let thine adamant need to prove thyself acquiesce, to become as but dust amongst the blackened night of stars,
and to listen and hear me with all thy conviction when I say to thee that yea, I am proud of thee, my only-man,
son of my bosom, more than thou canst e'er fathom, and I hath longed for thee as thou hath longed for me,
and I offer thee now ease of all torment and suffering, for thine ending is nigh
- I have watched thee from afar with both awe at thy capacity and with heaviness in my heart at thy slog,
and, aye, thou hath travailed enough and thou hath paid for thy honour thrice over in my eyes,
and 'twas kings three didst fall by the spear which Lugaid Cú Roi long since cast this day:
one Láeg mac Riangabra, king of charioteers, one Gray of Macha, king of horses,
and one Sétanta-come-Cú Chulainn, child of my Light,
for I dub thee now King amongst men, and I am calling thee home."

Endgame

Ach, 'twas a long time coming, my father's words of praise and assent,
and sought such hath I as tenaciously as a dog against a bone o'er my time,
through the plaudits and tributes of many named and unnamed others,
always at the forefront of the fray, always steadfast in my troth, beholden to my word and pledge unbroken,
relentless in my duty to serve my king and follow my own logic, to be the perfect hero of legend in real time,

exercising real feats and real quests, inflicting real wounds and spilling and shedding real blood, cleaving real flesh,
yet with the silent, discrete parts of myself always seeking to salve that primal wound,
the quality of my acts and quantity of corses left in my wake both recognition of the intricacies of my pain
and soothe for such, salutations of others naewithstanding; but, aye, better late than ne'er, as 'tis said,
níos fearr déanach ná riamh, and with those endmost words of Lugh resounding in my innermost mind, 'tis over
- I feel the gravity of the abyss where this boy-become-man shalt exist in form nae longer pulling me hither,
and I liken a dog w' two tails leave this dolmen with guffaw in my throat and remedy for my fracturing both,
let the utter darkness of my plight give way to the light of the sun within me and above me,
draw me away from these plains of sorrow and grume and halls of darkness towards Tír na nÓg,
land where believing be seeing and time standeth still, and help me let go of what I'd thought was my life,
ne'er to set foot upon the turf and grasses and rocks and mounds of Ériu again,
for w'out the burden of this tortured frame dost now I turn to face Thee, Turner of the Wheel,
my father's accolades and embrace the doorway,
to add my valour to Thy valour and to let Thy realm become mine,
bringing to a close the knotted circles of life and death and new life,
my rebirth into that of *síoraíocht*, my gaze now above the loch,
entwined in the branches and reaching night sky of the tracks of the snow-killed calf across the raven blackness,
these blood-stained lips left parted from their final exclamation, this body as helpless as a ewe between two rams,
my beauteous form nae longer the cause of trouble and strife between the women and men of Uliad,
'tis Cú Chulainn's head now the prize - and I laugh out loud in these final throws,
for he who seeks my seat of life whilst my blood nae but cold upon the earth shalt lose his hand in the taking;
and yet nary a care hath I, my death song of silence joyous and resplendent regardless:
nae matter I a jewel above all others deemed yet how short the span, and, too, braggart with cageling's heart,
nae matter vision of ravens of the sky and the flakes of snow flecking the plain in commiseration for my loss
be but sods of dirt hoof-kicked and foam of bridle spat by my coming creditor's steed,
nae matter the slitting of my only-man's throat to ease the pain of his passing the burgeoning fruition of my own,
the ring recognised too late and my Connla taken by the spear of fear my forever-shame,
nae matter my lament o'er Ferdiad's bed of blood, the rude wound, the grievous strike, his body pierced thus,
nae matter my betrayal to lust and Aoife's scorn, her rape, her revival, her redress even so,
nae matter my spurns of Mórrígan and Medb, luna wolven raven queens both,
nae matter losing the teardrop of beauty nor drinking not from my mother's cups,
nae matter Emer's six gifts so suitable, her beauty, voice, sweet speech, needlework, wisdom, chastity,
her womanhood esteemed so, my swift falling and plighted troth, my weapon rested in sweet country hers,
nae matter she whose cause for spite her steadfast dignity engendered,
nae matter I knew her first and last, but oh, nae the least,
nae matter the friendship of the Shadow's thighs and the thrust of spear inside relentless and addictive,
nae matter her tutoring nor her predictions of my pains, nae matter her drills and her devices,
nae matter Forgall's broken bond, nae matter the straight swords dyed red nor the dark gatherings of blood,
nae matter Bláthnat's fall forced, nae matter the burning of the jealous bitches, nae matter the death of the hound,
my only desire now my spirit to leap the Beltane fires and be freed of ire by their heat and smoke,
my heart's cleanse and prep for the entering of Thy halls
- everything hath I been and everything I am dost I join now with Thee, Turner of the Wheel,
nae longer to wear these cuts and scars and blemishes and agonies writ upon my skin as mediums for remorse,
but, rather, as a full life's trophies, every woundedness a laurel, its remembrance honoured,
this expiration more a change of priority than a demise,
focus nae longer exclusively upon myself, my feats, my pains and hurts and woes,

but upon merging with Thine all-seeing, all-knowing foci, a heartshift unparalleled in my career;
and, as the levee of my resistance and, aye, real fear, is broken,
I am flooded with the sense of grace, its celestial pith permeating every part of me,
this heart ne'er again to be unsatisfied as a torrent of blessedness washes o'er and through my wracked spirit,
as if the divisions of sorrows of grief, jealousy, and longing for *echtrai* upend nor nary invert the cauldrons inside of I,
their contents spilling out to be lost forever amongst my internal self-condemnation,
my vitriolic, philippic diatribe, the lusts for revenge, glory, and accolade,
stemming from lack, that fuelled and sourced my rampant proclivities,
but, instead, o'erflow with Ériu's abundance,
their esoteric potage cultivating and maturing as they heat and boil and brew,
spilling o'er their brims to enter and glut my life-stream as tangible revelations of unmerited mercy and salvation,
their mysteries plumbed, their sources of nourishment, quest, and transformation nae longer out of reach,
instead invigorating the health of my inner heart, my mind, and my psyche,
and, too, as if the Eochaid Ollathair had upended His *Coire Ansic*'s undried oatmeal broth upon my broken self,
its contents food for both my next body and this soul to last for a day and a night unending,
its sustenance such that in times of desperate need, in the harshest and toughest of times,
all those of valiant heart whom henceforth call upon this Hound
shalt forthwith have my sharp valour and my force to draw upon, as didst my father gift myself as much,
and, too, so shalt the bestowed skill sets and hard-eyed mettle of my peerless tutor of shade herself be theirs,
Scáthach ni Uanaind, Warrior Maid, She-Witch, trainer of heroes of legend, she of irrepressible thrust and lust,
the empowering and silent, swift, sure, unerring fury of her very blade-craft and uncompromising wrath,
her meticulous methods and devices, fuelled by her pre-life's esurience, ingrained into my very muscle-memory,
my every thought and my every exhalation, my every movement and my every combat,
my every strike and parry, feint and swing, twist and stab and turn and slash sourced by her drakanian shadow
- none shall stop the blood of their foes from feeding the land, those who call upon this Hound with earnest appeal,
if trial by combat o'er lenience 'tis to be their lot,
and they will succumb all the swifter to my ghost-whispered persuasions and Scáthach's vicarious words of wile,
brought together in the cold, hard kiss of steel and the clash and tramash of blood spilt in great flood,
ensuring restitution, retribution, reprisal, for none of us can escape our destinies, be they what they may,
though some of us will continue on for longer than others, in sagas, myths, and memories, tales and tunes and lore,
in the minds and hearts of all those facing troubles, nae just those whose penchant nae be for discourse and counsel,
but for attainment of mighty deeds with reddened spears and beds of blood,
with hard-headed blades made slick with grume and gore,
but all those, too, of demeanour calm and steady, of stillness in the face of crashing waves of sword and spear,
of firmness of conviction before tumult, those who still thirst for vengeance
yet who's inner strength means their control of mind o'er matter be virtuous in essence,
able to hold back the strike, howe'er worthy felt, to remain steadfast in their stance that mercy begets merit,
that it nary matters if tidings of defamation thereafter precede their coming if valour and honour theirs hadst prevailed,
that though they may be judged by others for their actions only they knoweth why they made the choices they made,
and only they canst claim the right of appraisal or discard, nae other's opinions worth their salt
- aye, if I am to continue on as source of strength for the worthy, so mote it be.

And now, looking back, as I start to quit this earthly form, bosom no longer pained slowly fading,
beating anew with different pulse, the gentle, rhythmic waves of *na cruinne ar fad*, of *síoraíocht*,
the heart's beat of the *Díadacht* roaring through my veins, encompassing all,
a dragon eating its own tail it's power and essence, its *dòigh nàdair* and immortality, an inverted, twisted knot its form,

now my blood be dried up and my sinews hath hardened,
this last vision dost I see: lit upon my corse's shoulder black corvid of carrion,
the Mórrígan in *scald-crow* guise, Badb Catha, *spaewife* of doom and death or victory in battle, mistress to ghosts,
come to check the death o' me, Her peck at my neck the closest touch of Her lips to my flesh She e'er hadst,
vestige of revenge for my slightings of Her; but, ach, cometh She too late,
for, even as She asked I once how wouldst I survive this Táin w'out Her,
that She be guardian of my death-bed and guarding it henceforth,
Her eye-brows red and crimson mantle around Her sweeping bloodied ground behind Her morbid chariot,
dream or enchanted vision upon Grellach Dolluid nae kneweth I,
kneweth I then Her hankering for my ending be born of pique,
Her certainty of claim to power o'er myself spat from parted lips thus abortive,
pregnant with the delirium of the intoxication of control in situation beyond even Her gods-feared command,
Her foretelling and Her moving of souls through the cycles of birth and and life and death,
by blood, bone, and blade, by the darkness, horror, and miseries of war,
She who held sway o'er light and darkness, ofttimes only e'er seen through the eyes of frightened men
- if knewethed I 'twas She in form of hag wi' tripple-teated cow I'd nae hath healed Her, ever,
rather left Her wounds to fester, let the blood of Her heart and the kidneys of Her valour mould and rot unseemly,
knowing She, the one I refused and denied, who lusted after my prowess and loved me for my reputation,
coveted the taste of my blood and only gained my favour through guile and artifice,
She is mighty enough to destroy all I am - Scáthach may have forged this Hound in her crucible of initiation,
but She who hath always been, who came to this isle with the *áes sídhe*, the shining ones,
who in the battles of Maige Tuired stood fast, pursued what was watched, destroyed those subdued,
who cried portends of doom and rained down fire and blood upon the Fir Bolg on behalf of Her own,
who watched o'er the fields of Formorian gore and slaughter with volucrine, hungry eyes,
breasts heaving with the sweat-dripped passion of lust-filled maleficence,
She who sees the birth of every bloody battle, red-wombed, the points of every fierce and enraged sword or spear,
who delights in every reddened shame and plucks the very harp strings of our mortalities, then and now,
gatekeeper of souls, harbinger of calamities, watcher of the cauldron of regeneration in the Otherworld,
of adherence to the circles of life and death and rebirth, of the decrees of Her own unfathomable whimsy,
She who slept once even with the Dagda, one foot either side of the Unius as She took Him inside Her,
their juices later mixed with two handfuls of Indech's blood, groaning struck incitement at the Ford of Destruction,
Her cries of fulfilment promise of spellcraft, Fomorian forces cast into the sea Her climax,
Méiche's snakes Her abortion, She who controls destinies,
who spins the gossamer threads of the tangled, morbid webs of our fates,
even the most stout of men cowering, dying in fear before Her shrieking, unhuman cries,
more potent, more grave, more frightening than any of Clíodhna's heart-gutting wails, and,
as She could harvest severed masts of Macha from ploughed fields of carnage and replant such upon their necks,
revive Her wounded warriors thus, bodies theirs split asunder but souls theirs undisturbed with the rising of the sun,
even bloodied sod and battle-torn plains declared sacrosanct in carnage's wake to allow for Her scavenging,
Her picking o'er of bones, She, too, hath the power to end even I
- mayhap all of this Táin and my demise hadst been of Her design from the outset,
renderings of Her meddlings in the stories and histories of Ériu
through Her venomous frenzies and whisperings in the depths of midnight,
through re-creation from the ruins of all that She destroys,
from being taken into the deepest, darkest caverns of ourselves to be lifted up upon Her wings
- who can guess of Her desires in the movements of our souls? But, ach, She is cometh too late:

the moment was I born started I to die, nary a need Her phantom meddling, and I am now nae afraid,
for though this body may nae longer shake off weakness and neglect from its bed of sickness,
nor revive from its plight upon this gut-strapped stone and arise once more and seek arms,
its blood dripping through cracks in the floor of time,
I will live on within thy hearts, within thy *bairdne* tales, within thy recollections and thine evocations
as the spear that spoils and wages battle, the boar of valour, the powerful ox, the war-hound of Culann,
and with every new breath thou takest my gift to thee be access to my pure, unadulterated force and fire,
every breath released an invitation to join with me in my surrendering, to wash the blood of all thy pains away,
for 'tis true the merits of thy futures lie in the comity of thy pasts and reputations last longer than lives,
and, aye, truly dost we suffer deaths three,
the first when our vessels cease to function and our cauldrons tippeth over,
the second when our bodies art consigned to grave or mound, to bog, dirt or pyre,
the third that moment sometime in future unknowable when our names art spoken for the very last time
- aye, there is only one thing worse than being talked about, and that is nae being talked about,
so remember me, and think of me where e'er thou art, corvid crow-woman,
Emer mine, Aoife, Scáthach, Connla son, Ferdiad, Úathach, my Deichtre, Bláthnat, Cathbad,
my fathers all, fostered and true, and those fostered or tutored by these hands, cuffed by these paws,
my adversaries, forgiven but nae forgotten, my compatriots, courteous and so remembered,
my brethren and sistren, my ancestors, my featured other players all - remember me, and remember this:
none of ye shalt die as long as the worlds turneth,
and as long as thy feet touch neither sod nor bog nor stone nor barrow nor plain nor hill of blessed Ériu e'er again
we shalt meet once more upon the strands and swards and grasses of Tír Na nÓg,
and remain young, beauteous, potent, fertile, relevant, and renewable forever,
timeless-locked in the land of eternal youth where aeons pass in a whisper,
until I bid you come to me, call to me, if I cannae come myself,
my sweet, shape-changing bright body stretched in sleep nobly broken,
bound to the *sidhe* mounds of the Fae, awaiting revival in times of hardship,
when the men and women of Ulaid hath in grave danger's gap fallen
and this Hound, his heroes, and the old gods, art called to champion and fight for them again...

Ach, it is finished: ne'er let it be said that I nae fulfilled the auguries of myself,
that my career of three and thirty full years was nae filled with triumphs and women's love, what matter how short,
this body wasted in its final bed of sickness, for now dost I succumb to Thy calling, Turner Of The Wheel,
to salmon-leap o'er the fortress walls around my inner heart, nexus to sorrows,
to die to myself to be reborn anew, to come again in legend, myth, saga, dream, vision, story, song,
for into the ale-washed odes of the myriad turners of wheels of chariots of flesh and blood I place my legacy,
and into Thy hands now dost I commend my spirit, Thou now guarding my bed of death and new life,
the blood in my veins soon but the space between the shining links of my father's chain,
my essence scattering, becoming the dust beneath the white cow's hooves spanning the darkening sky,
because here, at the last, after five tear-sodden days of hardship and a long sigh,
nae more years hath I to add: alone against the hosts,
spear-taken by Lugaid Cú Roi, in league with the sons and daughters of Calatin,
recompense for shames and sorrows yet unwashed from my soul,
pierced by fierce hate's reddened nails, lacerated with gore,
my valour an angry strife, my hero's light but a shade,
my fierce battle's roar nae longer making blood blanch in the veins of men,

the sickness of death be upon me...
I was taught artifice and guile and shrewd manoeuvre,
to play at the stabbing game with harsh scream and cruel heart,
versed with bloody spike and feats overweening,
to win at all costs, consequences natheless,
yet to be victorious in this endmost fight against my predicted fate must needs now I lose it:
I cannae outrun my destiny, and every victory is a defeat of sorts thereafter
- I hath had nae sleep in peace since e'er in pursuit of this great Táin,
and woe what I befell therefrom, much ill-luck hath been upon me,
but better a good retreat than a bad stand, and we who face the sun must turneth our backs to the storm,
for the wind doth not blow in the same direction every day
- weary after triumph, I am fallen, and I acquiesce, for my hour 'tis now at hand,
and I hath already paid for my honour with debts of blood and flesh this day,
I naught but a fair man facing his foes in the starlit ford of night...
Aye, casteth I my eyes westwards and beholdeth I the great mering,
as, finally, at last, Turner Of The Wheel,
my Father, An Dagda,
gods of my people all,
sundered yet supplicant,
here at the end of this dog's days,
I come to Thee.

ADDENDUM I
CONNLA

Connla's deathbed stream of consciousness

Apparently I'm the child of the child of light, the son of a son of the sun god,
my grandfather Lugh of the Long Arm, my mother she of radiant joy and beauty,
my father the dastard mutt in between
- his name was not mentioned by the light of day in my home above the sea,
and spat upon in the dark of night, cursed as to be worthy only of redress and requital,
his memory lambasted in my presence, all mention of him disparaging, scurrilous even,
he cast as a scoundrel mongrel, the root cause catalyst of Mother's bitterness and hurt,
any talk of him addressing only the harm he'd caused
and his exploitation of her ardour and her want,
his rampant ego and his arrogant pride the subjects of disdain and derision and spite,
rambling embittered curses and disgruntled mumblings of irk and vex oft her conversation,
a sentiment of spleen and fret surrounding her like a perpetual, subtle, foetid perfume,
her demeanour dour, her countenance contemptuous,
recall of his time with her justifyingly sullied,
except for occasional moments of overheard wistfulness,
hushed reminiscences of his earlier days before absconding,
fonder remembrances of his prowess with feats of sword and bedding,
snatches of hints of awe and admiration at his skill
- Aoife loved him once, for a time, I'm sure,
or at least grew to love him as a matter of course,
even if their first togetherness began as a rape of trade,
a life for a life, as it were, his seed forced into the fertile soil of her my begetting,
I to become heir to his dog's breakfast of a legacy - my father, the Hound,
hero to Conchobar's people but not so to us,
for, despite her acquiescence, the cur bolted before I was born,
tucked his tail between his legs and left her spoiled and childing,
the coming of me attended only by her sister, Aunt Scáth,
she pulling me from within her feet first in a rush of blood and cruor,
both women the epitome of spunk and pluck,
both with hands upon the dagger that severed my still pulsating cord,
knuckles gripped tight about the pommel of the blade,

white with the intensity and portent of the moment,
a few brief seconds of sisterly unity augmenting both the knotted strength of our triad
and the depth of their vindictiveness,
their desire for revenge upon my father, their wanting for to bite the dog that had once bit them,
neither able to forgive nor forget his slighting, his scorn, his spurn,
his haughtiness and his conceit,
their eyes meeting in solidarity across the fluid mess of my afterbirth
- a nod of assent and the pact was made,
I to become the primary vehicle of their vitriol,
the vigilante vanguard of their vengeance,
the carefully crafted deliverer of their dissent,
a pawn and outlier of their maleficence moulded to, for, and by their caprice and fancies
- by candlelight in the shadowed recesses of the halls of Dún Scáith
I listened to whispered conversations of their guileful scheming,
their predictions of my fated course, the string-pulling of their strategies and manoeuvres,
I a tangled puppet at the mercy of their desires,
destined to be the enabler and enacter of the endgame of their enmity.
As a babe in arms I absorbed their rancour and their malice,
my boyhood's freedoms stripped from me early after only a handful of years of play
- on the cobbled stones of the Dún Scáith training grounds I knew naught else
but anger and pain and hurt as they prepared me for my fate,
endless disciplined repetitions of melee and retaliation,
Scáthach's tutoring relentless, and somewhat frightening, too,
for, though she allowed fumblings in the learning of skills,
once attained, the making of mistakes would be severely punished by her,
and to cross her or go against her will
was to meet the fury of her redress and her blades, she a malignant narcissist,
her sense of superiority such that it was her way only or no way at all,
her distinction of friend turned enemy black and white
(a friend could become her enemy, but no enemy could ever attain her friendship),
both it and her lack of remorse and empathy egocentric,
keeping her distant and aloof in her island home,
she doing anything and everything to win the point,
even the use of the point of her blades and finely honed stratagems of punishment and reward,
her sadism offset by her deviousness,
her sense of reaction and response acumen to the moment only,
any accountability for decisions made and actions undertaken skewed,
she always portraying the victim as the transgressor, both the foment and the cause,
her will and whim paramount, her loyalty only ever to herself only,
her oft spouted belittlements born of envy and derision, her feeling like the world owed her,
yet her smile such that it could dismantle any and all pretence of retaliation or defence,
her seductive capabilities addictive, disarming, unsurpassable even,
cause for confusion in the heart of the boy,
bait for the loins of lesser men.
And it was as if she knew my very mind,
for she could gaze clearly into the most direful, hidden corners of me,

and, as the full moon could light up the blackness of the curtain of the night sky,
and send its illumination into my best forgotten darknesses,
the souterrain and passage chambers of my unknowables,
could bear witness to my next move, my next defence,
my every covet, my every hunger,
could read the very pages of my thoughts before they were even written,
anticipate my every motivation,
my every strike, parry, feint, and swing, thrust, turn, slice, and slash,
before my weight had shifted in preparation,
before my very inhalations of preparedness
- she taught the art of no distraction, of focus undivided,
no matter the temptation, pain, nor pleasure,
of guile and artifice and shrewd maneouvre, that all warfare was based on deception,
that supremacy and excellence meant not that one must need fight and conquer in all engagements,
but to break an opponent's resistance with least amount of effort be the goal,
and those who hearkened to her counsel were victorius, and those who did not were not,
the mainstay of her teaching thus: use every advantage and win at all cost,
for victory was all and martyrdom superlative - if one had to go down,
then 'twas best to go down fighting hard until the final stroke of cutting,
for to succumb to hurt was weakness reserved for the dearth of backbone, nerve, and spirit,
those who knew not the art of subspace and that affliction nourished courage,
were opposite sides of the same coin, parallel steel of a double-edged blade,
and that there was nothing so bad it couldn't be worse,
so to treat every day as both their first and their last,
for tomorrow was promise to none - this do I know now only oh too well,
for who but Scáthach in *cailleach feasa* guise and mayhap the very Turner of the Wheel
knew my lamentable ending was forthcoming this day,
my rising with the sun's light this morning the beginning of the setting of my own?
Aye, she could bring me to the edge of the point of no return,
dripping sweat and blood and tears of frustration,
until in blind fury or cathartic rage would I summon second wind and accept not defeat as an option,
would meet her face to face and steel on steel - then, and only then, would she call halt,
and then, and only then, would I gain her praise and her smile,
it alone enough to ease the wounds of each day's hurts and leave me hankering for more,
she the top dog mistress bitch and I her deferent whelp,
the stars of my grandfather's chain alight in my eyes in veneration of her skills
- aye, she was tough, unrelenting, and I both afeared her and loved her all the same…
And Mother, too, had hardened edge, had learned the same Scythian skills,
was Scáthach's equal in swedge and rammy, perhaps even her better,
yet hers was also to edify and improve me,
to inculcate and impress upon me views of the world,
views of her world, if tainted, I now her only man,
the dust trails of my father's footsteps a darkened shroud about her lenity and tone,
she cloaked by a cape of capricious contrition,
of sentiment scathing and embittered - aye, she both relished him and hated him,
lusted after and loathed him even, until it came time to curse his perfidiousness

and destroy him as a father and a man.
At times they would work with me together, sisters of the sword,
despite their odium and the oft glimpsed glances of distaste and mistrust between them,
creating challenges of combat like no other, both their whirling blades fast and sharp,
two wild cats side by side with skills unsurpassed,
able to put aside their grudges and their vex in service to my drills,
no single warrior ever there equal or their better - except, of course, my father,
but, if the tales be true, their bladecraft outshone, outclassed, and eclipsed even his,
his besting of them both thanks to trickery and subterfuge adroitly employed,
opportunities taken and distractions exploited
- he fought to win, used any and every advantage,
for there are no rules in bloodsport, it's either kill or be killed,
hence Aunt Scáth's dogged insistence on the art of focus undivided;
yet we who know our souls immortal fear not the cold, hard kiss of steel,
can meet provocation and trial by combat undaunted,
know that only shallow men believe in luck and the strong in cause and effect,
and that the exultation of victory must surely be the most mellifluous of sounds
- I'd always dreamt of having my very own belt of skulls adorn my hip,
garnered from seats of life I'd taken in frays directed either by my mother or my aunt,
but, alas, it seems that is not fated so to be,
both my youth and lifeblood quickly fading,
impaled as I am by the one feat she taught not to this boy,
this cursed belly-spear her weapon of legacy,
harbinger of the completion of the machinations of her and mother's vengeance,
the fatal finale of their cosenage,
only my father's blade across my throat merciful deliverance…

Longing to know the intricacies of my ancestry led me to him,
his behest for me to be sent to him when his signet ring fit this thumb mother's detest,
yet for reasons why did she follow his decree, he whom my mother despises still?
Aye, my father may've been long gone when I entered this world, but he'd served his purpose:
sometimes it seems a man's presence in a woman's life
is naught but to help her become a better woman without him, and mother was all that and more
- she needed no pretentious guard dog to protect her from her foe,
no man to control or subjugate her, to have her be his token bitch,
decorative apparel for his viewing pleasure,
to reduce her to the subservience of many another woman,
slave to domination and a husband's humour.
No, she was a hardened shieldmaiden in her own right,
the hardest woman warrior in the known world, her craft with steel and javelin of master's edge,
the foci of her demeanour as her sister's: to use every advantage and to win at all cost,
to show no mercy yet remain impassive, sedulous,
to lose not her hard won control of thoughts, words, feats, and actions,
no matter the scale of the atrocities she'd both inflicted and averted,
the blood she'd both spilled and shed,
no matter she'd conquered her *deamhans* and wore her scars like wings,

no matter how many times she'd thought the bloodletting was over
yet had had to find strength to carry on,
her blades, though heavy, fast and sharp and splashed with gore,
she weakened with fatigue but resolute,
nothing and no-one able to quell her ire once she'd ignited the fire of the cauldron in her belly, *coire goirath*,
harnessed its potential with her breath and blood and mind,
used its vitality not for life-giving but for life-taking,
the warmth of it reinvigorating exhausted thew, she shaken off of weakness and neglect,
arising once more to seize arms, rising again with renewed force, seasoned in the crafts of war,
no matter the number of her victories, accolades and ovations of others,
trophies and spoils of war attained, pleasures appropriated,
her past an armour she could not nor would not ever remove,
knowing life is a long road that has no turning,
and one never knows what one is capable of until the bitter end
- aye, she was formidable in her time, an inspiration, as was her sister,
both setting standards I could only dream of attaining…
But what the child sees, the child does, and what the child does, the child is:
I watched and learned from the vixen twins, I a wolf hidden in the garb of boyhood,
deceptive and dangerous, though cautious, prudent,
ever vigilant to the vagaries of their vexations and their vitriols,
the changing nature of their desires
- aye, the wind doesn't blow in the same direction every day,
and some days there were zephyrs, others storms of fury,
but did she really know what I was capable of even after all those years of preparation?
Did she trust in her sense of righteousness so much that she never saw the glitch in her subterfuge,
that my yearning for to know my father surpassed even the powers of her persuasion and pretence of love,
that by shielding me from knowledge of him she succeeded only in increasing my hunger for him,
my need for searching for the answers to my questions, I estranged even unto my own self,
some part of me placing the weight of the burden of the cause of his leaving upon my very own shoulders,
I forever seeking his, her, my own forgiveness, it the fuel for the furnace of my ferocity,
the absence of him the underpinning of the turmoiled *stramash* of uncertainty within me,
stillness in my restlessness desideratum?
Ach, If I don't end these wars inside of myself, they will end me:
I have both cursed him and craved him, wanted him beside me and wished the seat of his life severed,
prayed to the gods of our people for both his deliverance and his demise, his reconfiguring of our destinies,
the reforging of the bonds of the triad of our unity, the retying of the knot of our beginnings, father, mother, son,
he to return to us of his own volition, or be damned to spend eternity on the wing, as *sluagh*,
a cursed, restless soul seeking satiation his injury if not
- ach, if only wishing had made it so…
But would she have had him back after his spurn of her, even if he had?
No woman likes to be put aside for another, and rightly so,
but maybe all her posturing was all just pretence, amelioration for her discomfiture,
because, deep down, she, too, was unable to forgive herself, somehow blamed herself,
just like the Aoife of legend and myth before her who laments her own jealousies still,
she who became so jealous of Lir's affections for his children she sought their demise to thwart him,
yet, even though she was as impotence when it came to the final strokes of cutting,

her remorse come too late, for, despite the pleas of Fionnuala,
she was unable to reverse her sorcerous peccancy,
they turned into swans her compensation,
she banished to the four winds as demoness her damnation,
cursed for eternity her incarceration,
her sighing and sobbing faintly audible above the sound of the roaring winds on stormy nights her perpetual torture.
Aye, was there not semblance in their stories, Mother and the other Aoife,
both unwilling victims of their own execrable natures,
my Aoife somehow blaming herself for his absconding, she, too, a consoling 'second wife',
her newly-found lust and love for him having gone to the dogs,
jealousy of the devotion and attention he lavished unto her sister also cause,
inviting shoulder cold and passion spurned,
she seeking solace in the sword, her training of my bladecraft exacerbated by her tempers,
the culmination of circumstances wrought by and upon her,
she no longer holder of his hearth, his place of rest and ease after days of hard toil,
his sword to be sheathed in her no more?

No, I can't, won't, fully love him - not now, not yet,
for even though part of me wanted to know him, needed to know him,
I want to hear from his mouth why he'd left, what it was they couldn't give him, do for him,
neither Mother nor Scáthach, nor even Úathach,
despite all three offering him the friendship of their thighs,
their open palms, their hearts, their blood, their very womanhoods?
He broke Úathach's finger sparring, split her suitor twain, took his position as her man,
such was his sense of honour - but, it, too, was distorted even so,
for, even after she was promised him as gift without bride-price,
Aunt Scách's attempt to pacify him and keep him beholden to her,
he broke any whispered pledges made with Úathach as soon as Aoife appeared,
his wandering eye and rampant lust greater even than his probity, Mother's beauty notwithstanding…
His sword between Scáthach's breasts earned him her favour,
but Mother's intimate amity with him was not so easily forthcoming after that initial violation,
he first having to prove himself a better man to her before her animosity reconfigured,
before she could let herself learn to warm to him and nestle in his embrace.
And, as she lowered her defences and slowly settled into him, so had he into hers - or had he?
How much of their togetherness was simply sly concord, a liaison of opportunity,
a deception of coitus-laced comity placating to her lust and need for comfort and control,
he the guileful sham, stringing her along for purpose of his own,
his chicanery exposed when he skulked back to Emer, his perfidy spineless and contumelious,
premeditated, blatant and uncaring, particularly after she'd forgiven him of the rape of trade,
it the beginning of the unravelling of her revengeance, Scáthach's pique, the outcome of my lot?
Aye, some part of me wonders if he'd been playing them for fools all along,
if he had never truly fallen for my mother but used her and cast her aside once he'd grown tired of her,
had enjoyed her as amusement whilst under Scáthach's tutelage, played her like an eel on a line,
just as he'd used Úathach for a time, just as he'd used Scáthach's knowledge and teachings to further his own cause,
his memory mendacious, tainted with hubris - he used every advantage in his determination to win at all cost,
but a lie is the truth guarded, and, though gallant may be the search for truth,

if you say nothing when you have something to say, are you not really telling a lie?
It's as if his whole time at Dún Scáith was naught but one extended untruth guarding his duplicity,
adulterous in essence, his cocksure posturing drawing Mother towards him as a moth is drawn to flame,
his sweaty allure primal and provocative, salacious and low, appealing to her want and yearn,
she unaware of his plighted troth, though it seemingly only a token handfast,
the very reason for his entering Aunt Scáth's darkened domain in the first place
- lie upon lie upon lie, all lies, and, in the seeking for one thing I found another,
for in searching for supremacy with sword and shield I found the lie, aye,
but I also found the disdain, the contempt, the loathing, the anger, the hurt,
maybe not so deeply rooted as Mother's rancour, to be sure,
her once-love for him turned into the bitter hatred of a scorned and scarred woman,
but the hurt and rage and pain, natheless: first I found the sadness of his going, then came the questioning,
then the anger and frustration, then the disappointment and disillusionment,
and then, finally, the wellspring of life in the deadened parts of me, fuel to my ferocity, the rage.
The dog left before I was born, tucked his tail between his legs, back bent over like a whipped cur,
left my mother childing but with naught else save memories needing exorcising,
the signet ring, and his one decree to have me sent to him once it fit my thumb
- well, it fit my thumb and wear it I did, yet to no avail, for he saw it too late, even after I had curved my throw,
known him for who he was, itself only just a breath of recognition amidst exhalations of exertion,
an act of shocked compassion belying not my underling ire - this, then, the other lie uncovered:
as much as I have cursed and spat upon the learned tales of his biography
and considered traces of him within me tainted staines upon my countenance,
when he cut my throat to ease my pains and with eye waters of remorse presented me to his fellows,
I saw another side of him long hidden from me: my father is not the boggart as painted,
the man of dark convictions self-serving and unsavoury, an overly aggressive barbarian,
a rabid dog off its leash harrying any and all who stood in his way,
an aggrieved anti-hero bent on bloodletting and violence for violence's sake,
relishing in the grume and cruor left in his wake upon fields of slaughtered foe
- nae, he may have made his mistakes, but he is, moreover, a man of steadfast principles and conviction,
true to the tenets of his own moral code,
his passions great, his sorrows deep, his feats overweening,
a king amongst lesser men.
So, was it my fault, then, that he left? Or, with his planting of the seed of me in the soil of Mother's womanhood,
had he bitten off more than he was willing to chew, realised not the ramifications of his rampant thrust and lust,
the thought of having to teach and train and edify his own progeny a blight on his autonomy?
His sense of honour meant he must return to his Emer, yet it did leave us, me, in quandary:
what was Mother to him? What, or who, were Scáthach and Uathach to him,
beyond mere mistresses and daughters of shadow, sword and swedge?
Where amongst such convolution did the edges of his moralities begin and end - whose rule did he truly serve?
What was the thought of this boy incoming to him?
If he can remember what it was like to be a son, what did it mean to him to be a father, to have now a son of his own?
What was it I meant to him?
What was I to him?
Who am I to him?
Who is he to me?
Who, what, is he?

Questions.
Serious questions.
Serious questions worthy of serious answers.

[pause]

Natheless, life is too important to take seriously,
and mayhap it is I don't really want to know the answers to my questions, even so…
And yet, mayhap it is I do,
for, despite or because of our biography,
even though I've yet to find space for him in the depth of my bosom,
there is a sense of duty running through the veins of me I cannot now ignore,
and it falls to me I must defend his reputation, his rectitude:
never let it be said my father was not a man of honour and pride,
bound to his own uncompromising creed,
willing to forego the appraisals and accolades of others to fulfil his oaths of promise,
for, though he may have fought me for the sake of the prestige of the men of Ulaid,
may have employed guile and artifice and shrewd manoeuvre in his besting of me,
he also slit my throat to ease my hurt, knowing me now of his heritage,
I to arise no more and seek arms against him,
the very slice across the naked flesh of the neck of me a dagger piercing the very heart of him,
both the act itself and the bloodied tears following born of wanting for to spare me further pain,
and for some part of him to know me as his boy,
though grief and sorrow seems to follow us like a red plague,
shame and guilt and penitence left in misery's wake my epitaph,
remorse and torment turned cathartic his…
Aye, if Cú Chulainn had only bitterness and spite about him he'd've regretted not the strike,
and it means not naught that in my final, gasping moments he shed eye waters of not disdain and acrimony,
but of real emotion, knowing that to be a father was to love, hurt, bleed, smile, cry, rage, and endure,
and, witnessing such, I absolve him of all grievance, my grudges against him now redundant,
his choices made and actions undertaken understood, my forgiveness of him both resolute and absolute,
both of us of new ken as to the depth of the sister's malice, spite, and scorn,
of the length and depth and strength of Mother's thirst for the bittersweet taste of blood shed to appease her hurting.
I had been looking for him in all of the wrong places, had spent my childhood fearful of his legacy in me,
thought I an unwitting and unwanted spoil of his loins,
had been a fool to myself and a foil to my own growing,
had invested too much time in becoming who I am not rather than accepting who I actually am,
Mother's bitterness keeping secret from me the truth of my parentage until it was too late,
the revolutions of the Wheel turning with seeming, unwavering, unfeeling, revelatory certainty,
we all naught but spokes on its unfathomable, directed course;
but here, cradle-held in the strength and warmth of my father's hands,
though my body be broken and my spirit sworded sore,
being beside him is as philtre to my spilt cauldron's broth, situation natheless,
our separation reconciled, our blood and sweat and tears commingled,
both of like mind and like knowledge, bonded in canine courage,
the celebration of sacrifice and the cerebration of new consciousness, newly kindled awareness.

Though for one to gain freedom another must lose it,
it was never meant to be the death of the boy by the hand of the man,
so my question to the omens of druid and fae, to the tellers of fortunes and tales,
to the vate and the *spae* (I'm looking at you, Aunt Scáth), is this:
is it not possible to outrun the predilections of one's envisioned lot?
Could I have turned the attentions of the Wheel aside, just as I turned aside my javelin at the last?
If I had first known 'twas he I'd have not have faced him, ever,
would've altered the course of both our histories, would've rewritten the auguries of both our tales
- ach, Father, had but I have heeded not her guiles mayhap the ending of myself would have come not so to pass,
and comrades in arms we could've been, repelling armies back-to-back, for good care takes the head off bad luck,
and fighting with and alongside you we would've been good and we would've taken care...
But, alas, there be nothing sharper than a woman's tongue,
and Mother's mockeries of your valour and repeated lambasting of your name has led to the ruin of me,
for an evil tongue begets treachery, and she and her sister had become as evil incarnate,
the thirst for the titillating blood-touch of revenge upon you turning them so.

Oh, I used to love them, Mother and my aunt, used to revere their teachings and their tenacities,
was awed by their swordcraft and other weapon skills, their drills and their devices,
coveted their attentions and their accolades, though scant the latter were in coming,
reprimand and scold more oft the case - I learnt to garner an impregnable inner strength,
for there was no room for error when every harsh word could wound and every blade could kill, their lessons such.
Few survived Aunt Scáth's teachings as it was, but in league the sisters were formidable,
and at times it seemed only the burning heat of their pursuit of revenge upon my father shielded me from harm,
though whether from attempt at acceleration of my learning or angers only held in check just in time
when they remembered their enmity's goal, I know not.
I know there was once warmth between us, Mother,
my first gaze yours, my last to be his, yours one of adoration and acknowledgement,
of pride of both the progeny of your pregnancy and the wonderment of your womanhood,
those initial moments free of later anguish and spite, connecting me to the continuum of your breast,
his not forthcoming until this death of me, the windows to his soul fathomless pits unreadable, imploring and dolorous,
in each eye his seven pupils captivating, mesmeric, pulling me towards him even as I drain,
his accolade and honouring come late, but better late than never,
though knew I not it was the missing ingredient of my cauldron's brew,
salve to a hidden sadness in the very pit of the guts of me:
I am the son of both Cú Chulainn and you, Mother,
the Hound of Ulaid and the Aoife of radiance, beauty, and joy,
both warriors of eminent renown, both assured of your places in history and legend,
estranged lovers turned traducers, your vengeful machinations having proven ruinous,
your lust for revenge ending in tragedy - *my* tragedy, my life a comedy of errors leading to this cursed belly spear,
the one feat Scáthach taught not to this boy, worthy though I may have been,
I woefully wounded and stained with my own gore,
the scent of my own blood unlocking a tenebrous clarity of purpose rarely afforded
that only my own mindfulness can overcome,
every part of me screaming kill *and* be killed,
this last stand to have been my finest hour, the ferity of my father's *riastrad* a latent force within me,
threatening to overtake my training and my senses, my every action and my very demeanour,

it like an unexploded, internal volcano unable to vent its heat and steam,
its torrents of lava having sought weaknesses in the bedrock of my cognisance,
the blood rage having infused the cells of me with all the malice and torment of a ravenous, rabid wolfhound,
I my father's son whether I liked or knew it not, his character traits and fortitude mine,
his bravado and his brawn, his allure and his provocation, his parentages mortal and divine,
his predilections for rape, rodomontade, and heroics mindless of out-turn,
his swiftness of retaliation and his pertinacious adherence to his virtues by way of javelin and of blade
only able to be held at bay by the learned artistry of your and Scáthach's mentoring,
his berserker-calling treated as distraction, a burden to overcome, I to find my own self amongst such inheritance
- too young, too bold, too lovely to remain bound by the chains of bitterness and spite,
no matter how long this day may seem to be my evening is coming,
and I've had to do my own growing, no matter how tall and infamous was my father,
no matter the reputation of your prowess and poise in swordplay and in bedding, Mother,
Aunt Scáth's secrets of invincibility and sorcery,
so choose I instead to let not the circumstances of your and her lives dictate my sentiments,
your spurious distortions of the annals of my father's biography,
nor will I succumb to his temptations of choler and catastrophe within me,
I no more to be aliken a dog being wagged by the tail of fate and the sway of others,
nor the automacy of my ancestry.
Nae, instead do I choose now to be the architecture of my own destiny,
master of my own time, fomenter of the chronicle of my own tale
- I've never escaped rumours of his feats and deeds,
have always awoken with him both inside me and ana of him around me everywhere,
either as a fuel for the force and foci of my training
as I tried to exorcise him from both our minds with repeated feats and mighty acts,
my own blood splashed on many a smashed shield as I played at the stabbing game,
or as a haunting questioning over where my facilities and faculties arose from,
my almost Otherworldly comely visage and capacity for *iománaíocht* and finesse at arms,
when the thirst in me to swing and thrust *colg* and *claideb* first issued,
where my unsurpassable skill with *camán* and sling, *sparra*, *scian* and javelin derived,
the smouldering fires in my guts and in my loins, my predilection for the lust for the red scent
- must needs now I accept my plate, take the good and the bad of both his and your gifts of inheritance,
blood-soaked as they may be, for my roots follow a sorry trail awash with gore,
of feats overweening, of unconquerable fears and doubts conquered natheless,
of cuts and scars and slashes, scratches and scrapes and sunderings,
of the feral inclinations and ferocities of you and Aunt Scáth, veritable she-wolves yourselves,
of gifts of swedge and rammy handed down from Ard-Greimne, maternal grandfather mine,
yet perfected and refined by you both, for better and for worse,
for, though it is true the youngest thorns are the sharpest,
my erratic, youthful wildness did need taming,
as did the primal, sanguinary force of the wolfhound latent within me,
his tempering and forging in the crucible of Aunt Scáth's initiations and the ardent flame of Mother's affection,
mine by birthright and situation even so
- can this really be my lot or has there been some mistake?
A mother's doting turned sour, a father's pride found in the moments of his boy's demise,
the sonsetting of me at the dawning of my prime, at the burgeoning of my becoming

- ach, sometimes years change nothing but one day changes everything.
If this is all my life was meant to be I'm sorry it wasn't better, but I'm sure glad it wasn't worse.

Caught between the two worlds, the guts of me splayed out upon the cruel, cold strand,
never have I known the depths of such agony and chagrin and pain - I am torn , literally, torn almost in two,
sundered and cleaved both by the dubiety of my upbringing and the *Gae Bulg*'s impaling stab,
only my mind's escaping the wretchedness of my plight and the agonies of my wounds
allowing me these mere moments of recollection and understanding,
awareness of how things were and how things are exploding into my consciousness with a suddenness of clarity
aliken the instantaneous take of a funeral pyre built of faggots dry,
the pain of the flames of transformation igniting and inviting a shift of perspective,
a recognition of not only how deep the wounds of Mother's hurt and pique had reached,
but of the lengths she'd been willing to go to in her incessant desire for revenge,
her distorted affinity with the Aoife of beforetimes,
both ladies so affected by their jealousies they'd lost all sense of prudence and right action
- sometimes I'd awake at night to find her no more beside my bed of rushes,
would search the shadows of Dún Scáith to no avail,
a small, frightened waif stealing along corridors of wave-echoed stone,
thickened, mortared walls muffling the frequent furore of a raging tempest beyond,
lashing rain and pounding seas creating a crescendoing, cathartic cacophony,
and, as I'd breach the outer ramparts, I'd see her,
a forlorn figure standing ever alone, head bowed,
silhouetted against the pounding, foam-flecked froth of Manannán's wild herd,
wind-swept braids trailing behind her like a torn flag fluttering or the branches of an aged oak bent before the tumult,
or, worse, on particular shadowy nights of thick, blackened brume overseen by thunderheads nefarious and grim,
nights better left for *sluagh* on the hunt for wretched souls and other beasts and bastions of purpose foul,
like spilling strands of gralloched innards streaming not from the belly of a deer but from cloven head or helm,
unkempt and dishevelled, rain as blood extravasate, her seat of life's centre so unravelled,
she harkening to a wailing, demonic sighing and sobbing only faintly heard above the sound of the four winds,
her namesake's perpetual keening for revenge sullied with remorse come too late her malison and meditation.
My life in its entirety has been sculpted, moulded, and formed to serve nothing more than purpose hers, like as not
- did I mean so little to her or her sister? Until this very moment I thought I'd been her, their, everything,
harbinger of their hopes for redress for sure, I their burgeoning champion in training,
prepped to become the prime new kid on the block, destined to fight for them alongside Cet and Cuar,
my secret and elusive cousins training solely under Scáthach's tutelage, venue undisclosed,
they rarely seen but oft alluded to as yardsticks of my improvement, benchmarks for my tutoring,
goal posts for my tuition, theirs the standard to strive for, albeit unseen and unknowable,
all the while thinking the persistent attention to my schooling was secondary to her, their, affections for me
- perhaps all of my life has been no more than a long preparation for the leaving of it,
for once released the shaft was inevitably fatal, and both ladies knew Culann's Hound wielded such,
it slated to be the culmination of Mother's and Aunt Scáth's thirst for satisfaction…
But I shouldn't ask the question if I don't want to hear the answer, and it may well be I do not
- I belonged to you once, Mother, but I will never belong to you again.
Though defiant and principled in my own right, I will always love the false image I had of you,
but I must now call it as it is: you deceived me, Mother,
crushed the childhood of me in the acerbic claws of the bitterness of your hurting,

tried to twist and bend the hands of fate to force my father from this world through the manipulation of my sentiments,
let the passion of your pains override your senses of right judgement, right action,
heard not through the cacophony of your callous vituperation the whisperings in the deeper reaches of your heart
the clamouring and crying out for you of my own, my calling for you, if unknowingly,
to see me for who I am and not for who you wanted me to be,
that I was more than just the assassin bred to fulfil your virulent desire for revenge,
a tool to be utilised, ultimately nugatory, tossed aside and discarded once my duty fulfilled,
I was of your flesh and blood - I was the child of your womb, your one and only son, your Connla!
Ach, my father may have discarded you, like as not, but you discarded me in essence,
as amelioration, as placation, as compensation for your scars
- or was it simply you following in your sister's footsteps,
just as Aunt Scáth discarded Duncan, father to her brood, once she'd tired of him and he'd served his purpose,
skullduggery to win her favour and sow the seeds of the threads of solidarity in your sisterhood?
Where was the real you inside the maelstrom, Mother?
Where are you for me now as he and I lie in the sands soiled by my own bleeding,
as my hindsight becomes my insight, my foresight forsaken,
relegated to the annals of a future yet unknowable,
as my eyes fill with redness and my life's blood slowly fades away?
Do you grieve for me, Mother, as I leave this world,
or do you more rue the issue of whilom love unrequited and the father's outfoxing of his son,
the ruination of your machinations, your schemes of villainy having been brought to naught?
Some recollections may be best forgotten, aye, but I do not forget your treachery
- if you and Aunt Scáth taught me one thing, you taught me to never forget and never forgive,
and who'd've thought that that lesson would come back round to bite you, the circle turning full wheel,
the cause and effect unravelled so, the boy become the man embittered,
unwilling and unable to forgive your ruination of my lot?

And, so, in the last, as I turn my gaze westward I behold a great mering,
and I feel myself drawn to it like nothing before,
feel myself leaving this sordid mess of flesh,
the guts of me in bloodied, wave-splashed pool about me,
the breath of my father's sorrow upon my brow, his tears upon my very cheek,
the scars of Aunt Scáth's sundering and the mendaciousness of my mother within,
and I remark upon the strand the hungry, volucrine stare of a black corvid of carrion,
having broken away from its murder,
silently, intently attending the fall of the son,
remarking my ending, bearing witness to the final atrocity of me,
watching, waiting, willing, wanting, remembering
- who's eyes do you have on, raven mistress?
I know you venerated the queen of crows, Mother, your muse such,
Aunt Scath's homage but casual and cursory,
a coven of one and occasionally two before Her altar
- has She come at your beckoning, then,
to be the recorder of stories, ominous and uncaring observer of the final stroke of cutting,
silent spectator seeing the seat of my life rived and severed,
only to return to you with tidings of my ending,

though you hankered for it to be his?
Who's eyes do you have on, Mother?
How do I reconcile these pangs of uncertainty within me,
fathom the twisted sentimentalities of my unfolding?
I loved you and trusted you, until I didn't,
until the boy became the man only to fall at the feet of the father, my patrimony - what?
Am I to be remembered only out of pity, as the youngster hero who could've been,
if only life and death and vindication hadn't gotten in the way,
if only there'd been new beginnings and different endings, if only -?
My hope that I'd live long enough to learn to face my own death has been granted,
but it seems all of my life has been nothing more than preparation for the leaving of it
- aye, sometimes the years change nothing but one day changes everything!
Who am I to be in the annals of Èirinn?
Will I be remembered simply as a scapegoat of spite,
a discard of destiny, the best-forgotten failure of the fruits of a father's furore,
a continuum of the carnage of collateral damage left in Cú Chulainn's wake,
a mere ripple in the wake of his legacy,
or will I be remembered for my own account,
for the lightness and joy and spring oft my jaunt,
for the youthful vigour of my activity and narrative, my alacrity and ardour,
the ease of my breath, and gait,
for my breaking free of the shackles of the ties that held me bound to the whims of Mother and Aunt Scáth,
for my conquering of the Red Branch champions and the near besting of the Hound?
Ah, but, ach, it matters not, for some questions simply have no answers,
and, as a dog owns nothing yet is seldom dissatisfied,
and here, at the end of this pup's frolic and adventure,
even the wind of my pant no more to be my own,
I am free of constraint: I have met my Father face to face upon the strand,
seen both sides of the veil of the pretence of motherhood,
have tasted the salty tang of the flesh of fear and have mocked and spat in defiance to its temptation,
seen all my ambitions thwarted by this one spear embedded in the belly of me,
for ambition is only as good as the success it brings, and, if this is to be my success, I want no more of it.
Aye, together we would've carried the flag of Ulaid to the gates of Rome and beyond, Father,
you and I, and yet I am not dissatisfied, for I am the son of the both of you,
the Hound of Ulaid and she of radiance, beauty, and joy, albeit turned sour,
nephew of Scáthach ni Uanaind,
grandson of Ard-Greimne of Lethra,
and I stand proud of my ancestry, no matter it be of tales awash with gore,
of deceits and ire and slanders,
of honour and regret and a light upon a hero's brow waxing and waning,
of lives cut too short and others bolstered by defiance to destiny,
of sharp valour and the coming of age of sapling youths, of initiations in crucibles of fire,
of straight swords dyed red, the gristle of bones broken by the spear and breasts full of fierce hate,
of the cruel club's hard edge and feats overweening.
Aunt Scách, you taught the art of no distraction, that there be no room for error when every stroke could kill
- I lie here awash with my own foulness guilty of heeding not your didactics,

for, aye, in the last did I let distraction overtake my foci,
my seeking for to fill the void of him within me now my malediction,
yet I am not dissatisfied.
To get to a good place sometimes one must go through numbers of bad places,
and, in order to get from what was to what will be, must first go through what is
- I have been in many bad places both inside of myself and out,
been taken to the very edge of the plane of despair, battle weary, slashed, bruised, and bleeding,
whimpering and crawling in the dust, blood and tears mingled with the sweat and bile and erection of exertion,
yet brought back from the brink by Mother and your taunts and ministrations,
both of your devices hard and unrelenting, purposeful and practical, void of sentiment,
yet I have known none more grievous than in these dying moments,
stepping aside of myself beyond the 'what is' the only recourse to this pain…
Where I go now few can follow - I dissolve myself of all teachings and believings,
and, in my final apostasy and acquiescence, I whisper his name and our gazes lock,
and our spirits merge as do our bloods and juices, and in that moment I am released,
released from this sordid mess of myself,
released from the entrapments of the stakes and chains that had bound me to these pains,
this body's wounds of viscera and sinew, these cursed barbs, beyond retrieval,
released from the entanglements of the hexed fishnet web of deceits that has led to this demise of me,
released from the need for swedge and rammy, javelin and sword, sling, *sparra*, chariot and shield,
released from the acerbic claws of Mother's bitterness and spite,
from Aunt Scách's maleficence, aloof and torturous even so,
released from all memories of wounds of the flesh and a boy's searching for the man,
searching for to numb the pain of the loss of him,
to fill the void in me with the fullness of him.
With curses for her subterfuge and spite upon both our lips,
her damnation near my final, gasping, blood-gurgled whisper,
the hour that I have longed for has at last come:
cradle-held in the arms of his indomitable, iron will,
the breath of his pertinacious, indefatigable honour upon me,
the very scent of him a pheromonic philtre to my mixed cauldron's broth,
his acknowledgement of me to his fellows auspicious
("Here is my son for you, men of Ulaid"),
I am carried content towards the opening in the wall between the worlds,
westward toward the setting sun,
toward this lifetime's endpoint, toward Tech Duinn,
to take peace and draw breath awhile,
ar an tslí to the Otherworld,
beyond Mother's spite and acrimony and Aunt Scáth's bitter accord,
beyond their spurious predictions of my fated course,
beyond the devastation of this very death of me,
beyond the boundaries of the spirit of the body of me,
beyond the blood-drenched and tear-soaked sands of my final stand upon the strand,
beyond my father-wounds and my Father's woundings,
beyond the threshold of despair of a king amongst men lamenting his murdered son,
beyond all his and my unforsaken sufferings,

beyond all torment and all anger, all remorse and all spleen,
beyond recovery,
beyond the ninth wave.

ADDENDUM II
ÚATHACH

*A daughter's reminiscence of the pain of discipline and the pain of regret,
lament for loves lost and ascent into womanhood*

Unabating, unassailable, uncompromising, unconventional
- how else to describe your teachings, Máthair,
the standards of expertise you demanded from all your charges,
benchmarks and touchstones set purposefully beyond their scope and frustratingly out of reach,
yardsticks for advancement and improvement nothing less than perfection,
ultimately unattainable, beyond the capacity of most all of those who came to you,
yet their egos so fragile, so nebulous, they'd do anything and everything to win a hint of your appraisal,
take any chastisement, suffer any hurt, any scar upon their flesh and reputation
to gain even a ghost of a smile from you,
not knowing that you were about to push them far beyond their every limit,
to the very edge of the point of no return itself,
so far they'd taste the salty tang of their own bile vomited into their mouths from exertion,
feel the very breath of fear and the kiss of death upon their cheeks,
before you'd drag them back from the edge at session's end,
beyond exhaustion, weakened, wracked with pain and bereft of spirit,
searching your face for any acknowledgement, any suggestion of recognition of their efforts,
one almost imperceptible smirk of disapproval their undoing,
it alone enough to dismantle any and all pretence of bravado,
yet one mere glance of acknowledgement their way such that it could ease their wounds of each day's hurt,
salve their lacerated prides and leave them hankering for more,
engender in them an addiction to the liquid agony of their own spilt, sanguine fluid,
a lust and desire for the red scent, no matter who's was being shed
- they had no idea of who it was they were training under,
poor, pathetic, pertinacious puppies,
just who the mistress of Dún Scáith really was, and what you were capable of,
Scathach ni Uanaind, trainer of warriors of legends,
cailleach feasa, cailleach piseog, cailleach an chlaíomh,
both drakania and *bandraíodóir*, gorgeously gynic,
fatally seductive and facinorous,
able to eviscerate all traces of cocksure posturing and *bród sotalach iomarcach*
with no more than a warning glance or a slight, coy curl of your *liopaí dearga fola*,

that you'd birthed children, killed men, rendered flesh,
tasted the delectable, exquisite agonies of subspace,
had learnt the erotic thrill of the transcendence of pain and knew how to use it to your advantage,
and that you would use it to introduce to them *géilleadh deiridh*,
the ultimate surrender, where there was no pain anymore, only capitulation -
claimhteoireacht at its finest.
       Ach, if only they'd known such before coming...
       Oh, you were narcissistic, too, Máthair, sure,
the top dog mistress bitch surrounded by a pack of piddling poodles,
thriving on the verisimilitude of their fear of you masqueraded as adoration,
they all so eager to please they were easy to train from the outset,
the thinning of the ranks of those who'd survive in the long run itself telling,
the rate of involuntary attrition caused by death or grievous wounding misery's penance.
       And weren't their little battles of dominance amongst themselves so cute to watch,
wee boys pretending to be men, toy soldiers shaking their big sticks and swaggering about in their *ceannlann* armour,
playing at stabbing games and challenging each other with feats of strength and daring,
each one of them thinking he was the man,
so valorous, so macho, so virile, so heroic, so andric,
parading about the training grounds like pompous, conceited cocks, unknowingly capon,
so sure of themselves in their self-centred worlds of arrogant fantasy,
I felt both bemused by and sorry for them at the same time,
for every cock crows loudly in his own farmyard, and they were unaware, poor dears,
of how relentless and frightening the tutoring they were about to enter into really was,
for, though you allowed fumblings in the learning of skills,
once attained the making of mistakes would be severely punished by you,
and to cross you or go against your will was to meet the fury of your redress and your blades
- you taught the art of no distraction, be it pain or pleasure,
that distraction wasted energy but concentration restored it,
that there was no room for error when every stroke could kill,
and it was ne'er by luck alone that some survived under you and others didn't,
there is no luck where there is discipline, the mainstays of your teaching thus:
use every advantage and win at all cost.
       Oh, aye, 'twas the same you taught to me, Máthair,
drilled unwavering courage into me with endless, repetitive drills of defence and danger,
challenges of retaliation and combat that would make even the bravest hero quail,
incessant and relentless, our blades oft slick with blood, both beyond exhaustion,
breasts heaving as we gasped for air to refuel muscles laced lactic,
nipples erect with the excitement of exertion and exhalations of assiduity,
all our energies expended yet somehow feeling invigorated, intoxicated, aroused even
- I may not have had the smarts and wiles nor virtuous esteems of my sisters,
Lasair, Ingean Bhuidhe, Latiaran, the six gifts of womanhood theirs,
beauty, voice, sweet speech, needlework, wisdom, and chastity (especially not the chastity),
nor were deemed deserving of the doting attention you lavished on Cet and Cuar,
brothers whom I saw rarely but for sparring or for *iomaíocht*
(I'd felt alone growing up, unseen and unheard, estranged even unto my own blood,
my very demeanour and countenance isolating me from my siblings,

their quick-witted, easy banter beyond my casual comprehension,
the directions of my conversations oft beyond their fields of understanding,
recognition of my worth forthcoming only once my bladecraft and dexterity outshone all of theirs),
but I had your skill at arms and your looks,
inherited your addiction for *mian leis an bhfeoil*,
perhaps was not so terrible and dreadful after all,
and, having grown up adoring you, comparing myself to and emulating you,
Warrior Maid, She-Witch, She Who Strikes Fear,
the she-wolf of shadow all men desired and all men feared,
no man was ever skilled enough to unarm me,
nor fool enough to forsake the friendship of my thighs,
for those who came to you knew of your skill in both swordplay and in bedding,
the finer arts of both you'd taught to me,
how to dance on the tip of their spears as distract and provocation,
my downward-turned lids darkened rustic with half cut crease magnetic mystery,
my eyes wide open sultry and alluring, mesmeric,
softening even the hardest of hearts, drawing them to me like moths towards a flame,
their minds on the natural curves of my *cioch*, my disarming *aoibh* and *súile suirí,*
mine the exposed reddening flesh of their engorged, waxing, tumescent necks…

And then came Cú Chulainn, the Hound of Uliad.
        He looked like, felt like, tasted like both a dog on heat and a man after sunset,
glands exuding pheromones of potency, nobility, courage, daring, and valour,
a warrior, a paladin, a *flah* and an espouser, stubborn, uncompromising, and unyielding to his own convictions
- I wanted him the instant I saw him, from the moment he hurdled our Bridge of Leaping,
magnificent in flight as he all but ran through the air,
arms pedalling wildly to help him gain the height and distance, defying gravity,
even after three times floundering, fuel for spleen and mirth,
an ungraceful fish out of water tossed to the side only to aright himself again,
determination as dogged as a disperser at the kill or a salmon leaping the linns,
a *lasair náire* then upon him, his visage red with rage,
seven hero-lights in each eye ablaze with ire,
a seven-pleated cloak of crimson about him,
held in place with a brooch of purest gold,
his sweat a sheen of gloss on muscles taut with tension,
his swole and pluck and spunk cause for swoon,
an *áer* of cutting satire, declarations, and taunts of bravado his habit,
his coming amongst us unknowingly a catalyst for catastrophe,
the beginning of a barrage of burgeoning, unfolding betrayals,
of a fury of failures of fidelity neither forgiven nor forgotten
- but, oh, he'd won me from the exertion and exultation of that initial victory,
that exquisite entrance unforeseen and unrepeatable by others of like lithe,
no need I be offered as gift without bride-price, no matter I a suitor already had,
I knew he was to be mine, and I always got what I wanted,
I my mother's daughter in more ways than one…
        I could have refused him entry yet I let him pass, gave him food and drink,

told him where you lay, Máthair, and to set his blade across your breasts,
for his desirous eyes ignited fervour in the cauldron of my loin,
and I knew he wanted me as much as I wanted him,
to nourish and enliven the inside of me,
to awaken the depths of my *coire goirath* that few had ever plumbed,
my need to have him in me paramount, renitent and resolute,
and you know that once my sights were set on something, or someone,
I was unstoppable, my focus unwavering, my attention obstinate,
and I would have him in my bed of rushes, though the sky fall and crush us …
      He found you and demanded of you, Máthair, and you fought,
for no man commanded you and ever lived to tell the tale,
or, at the very least, wished he ever had, and was rightly afeared to do so again,
rebuke and reprimand of swift retaliation…
      Aye, you fought, for days and weeks unending,
and 'twas tears of fear I shed in faerie's waters to gain you both respite,
through breaking bread and feast and song,
guile and artifice shrewdly manoeuvred, for no guest may strike the host
- I feared to lose him to you, Máthair, not so much you to him,
knowing your adroitness and your skills with blade unsurpassed,
and could not allow such to occur,
for I would have him cock his leg upon me, come what may.

Try as he might, Cochar Croibne couldn't even come close to him,
had lasted long enough in my thrall only to satiate my needs of the night
- I'd already tired of his fumbling attempts at venery, my womanhood rapacious,
his manhood maybe virile but his mannerisms those of a stripling youth,
lubricious and oft ludicrous, my *suire*'s song seduction itself,
my proclivity incessant, wanton, demanding even
- I needed more than he could deign to muster,
at times would drag him back out to the training grounds unsatisfied,
would force resurgence upon him with taunts and tease and threats of blood and dripping sweat,
willing his sword to hold steady, his steel to remain upright held against my vex,
no more coy flirtations and subtleties of posture meant to beguile, entice, and tease,
the birr of my blades slicing through the air as loud as a howling wolf encouragement,
the froth and lather of my lech increasing with every cut and slash of his flesh,
he none the wiser for my disdain and rising, aching hunger…
      Aye, 'twas high time sought I a better knight,
and 'twas as if I bended forced the hands of fate and I got my wish, as I always did,
for when one door closes another opens,
and he should've been grateful for what he'd already had of me and let sleeping dogs lie,
known that a good run be better than a bad stand,
and to stand against the potency of my new want was an endeavour fraught with failure,
Cochar split asunder for his foolishness
- he should've known better than to challenge the son of a sun god,
no matter how justified thought he his cause, there was only ever going to be one outcome,
Cochar so blinded by his rage he couldn't hit a hole in a ladder with his blade,

the bravado of the boy bested by the might of a real man…
        And so became I Cú Chulainn's moll for a time, leman to his libido,
both his satisfaction and his sycophant,
the perfect partner in swordplay and in bedding,
welcoming his desires of the dark and the predawn
- aye, we were a tight unit, he and I,
his rampant thrust and lust the only satiation to my paraphilia,
the sweat of his exertion and a lick of his bloodied steel glut for the needs of my longing,
I an eager, willing toy for his concupiscent, prurient bents…
        And yet, we can only know what we know in the heat of the moment,
and we don't know what we don't know,
so how does one know when enough is enough for another?
        Had his want for me soured, despite my being freely offered,
a gorgeous, desirous gift without bride price,
neither *in cenaind n-gárechtig* nor *In míarlig míepertaig*,
Mathair's attempt to keep him beholden to her,
a wish of my own wanting fulfilled
- oh, to have been his first and foremost,
no longer his *sclábhaí airnéise* but his serious line,
I his only woman, he my only man
- ach, if only wishing had made it so,
for it seemed I'd burnt my coal but had not warmed myself…

Here must I take breath a moment, though, must pause in this maudlin monologue,
must use the light of a looking-glass before my eyes for illumination and reflection,
for questioning and accountability - had I learnt nothing from you, Máthair,
heeded not your insistence on the art of no distraction,
be it either pain or pleasure? You taught all your charges such,
impressed upon them the import of indomitability and initiation,
to use every advantage and to win at all cost,
yet to ne'er forget and to ne'er forgive downward strokes of cutting,
be they of those that rendered flesh and bone or scathing tones that wounded reputations,
for reputations last longer than lives,
lives severed nothing more than new beginnings, anyway;
and, aye, the dog may have deserted me,
even after lifting his leg upon me and spraying me with his scent and with his spunk,
his fault of misplaced loyalty and rampant musth the cause,
but, ach, if I'd been searching for a man without a fault I'd've been searching for one forever,
and it seemed my dreams of having a real man by my side and in my bed were just that,
dreams and imaginings after all, he certainly living up to his reputation,
a hearth and a home with the Hound reduced to naught but a distant yearning,
seeds of togetherness planted in me but ne'er watered, instead left to rot,
seasons of dry discontent and damnation upon us,
destined not to see the spring growth of our coupled natures fulfilled,
the blossoming of my bosom and the life-giving harmony of my hormones,
the expression of his manliness within the womb of me untimely neutered,

I nothing but his *leannán cuileáilte*, chewed and spat out like a piece of rotted meat
- for his discard of me I do not forget,
his disdain I do not and will not forgive,
and for his burn I promise him this, as *mallacht*:
his betrayal of my longing for him will be his undoing,
for no man desires of me then turns from me with his next breath and walks away unscathed,
no matter his lineage or his libido,
no matter how tall and brave may his father be,
no matter the unravelling of my revenge be convoluted and cloak and dagger,
no matter the comings and goings of others bound for his bed,
no matter the turnings of the tides of fortune nor the revolutions of the Wheel,
for I shall not be injured by bevvies of bitches nor pitied by the taunts of lesser men,
those not worthy of even being spat upon by the Hound at his height,
before his eyes and shaft had wandered
- there be nothing sharper than a spurned woman's tongue,
nor the *claideb* edge held tight in her hand that thirsts for revenge,
and let any who tempt my resolutions beware,
I am my mother's daughter in many more ways than one,
and I will use any opportunity without fail to see the dog suffer his due,
as will all those who try to protect him or deign to stand in my way
- aye, he should've known better than to mess with a woman out for revenge,
for there be no more years yet to give and time is on my side…

All is fair in love and war, she'd said, Auntie Aoife, the pompous, arrogant, spiteful, rancid witch,
thinking herself so cocksure, so self-assured, so holier-than-thou,
but two can play at that game
- sister and rival to your shadow, Máthair,
nemesis ours, she nothing but an emotionally shallow, insecure, somatic narcissist,
a malignant, self-centred, promiscuous hellcat permanently in oestrus,
ever the bitch on heat, craving and demanding attention and admiration,
wanting only accolades and adulation,
overly concerned about her appearance and salving her fear of being ordinary,
her criticisms and supercilious vanity her autobiography,
her very demeanour imbued with the air of self importance tinged with libertine righteousness,
the extent of her mindset explained thus:
 I don't care what you think unless it is about me.
 He was caught in the charm of her, succumbed to her sex as he almost succumbed to her steel
- why do men find contemptuous carriage and the perfume of pretension so attractive?
 I lost him to her, his eye and his desire diverted
- she thought she'd bested me, taken my charge and wooed him with her wiles,
but I take your teachings to heart, Máthair, made pretence of peace with her,
used the compulsion of her fixation upon herself to my advantage,
played the part of the perfect, adoring niece to distract her,
to throw her off her guard while I systematically, surreptitiously dismantled her self-proclaimed aura of righteousness,
let him continue his exploration of the cavern of my womanhood the while
- she may have secured the latest attention of his wandering eye,

but I'd unravelled his needs of the night before she'd come on the scene,
and no man could resist open invitation to the friendship of my thighs,
no oversexed dog the chance to bury his bone in the warmth of the moist soil of me,
the moment his mistress's back was turned.
Aye, I took my revenge upon her intrusions even so, for, if you look into the windows of my soul,
you'll see I've neither forgiven nor forgotten she was an opportunistic rogue,
am yet to let go the spite and bitterness she engendered by taking my only man from me
- you can choose your enemies but you can't choose your family, more's the pity...
Nae, I can't, won't, forgive you, Aunt, for, if not for you and the so-called 'rape of trade',
I'd still openly be getting the ride, would still be nightly sheath to his sword,
instead of stealing moments of immorality like a brazen, wanton thief in the night.
I could've been, should've been, his sole satisfaction, gave him everything he desired of me,
thinking everything I gave him was everything he wanted, but, ach, 'twas not so,
for, though, in truth, everything we have is everything we want, and everything we don't have the same,
as our souls know the geography of our destinies more than we ever will,
he wanted what he didn't have, was so turned on by her pulchritude and her allure he had to have her then and there,
then found himself entangled, ensnared by her fishnet hex, caught like a fly in the mantrap of her web,
enslaved by the salaciousness of her seduction...

Crucibles of initiation, challenge, and combat, of confrontation and catharsis,
of choices of conviction made moment to moment - these were my constant companions,
all I knew from sunup to sundown, year in and year out,
cobblestone and sand and blades slick with blood my childhood,
to turn swedge to finesse and be deemed equalled you my dream
- instead of frivolous friendships and the girl gossip of bletherers I learnt to love the kiss of steel,
instead of trite, inauthentic conversations I listened to the exhalations of my exertion,
the complexities of the wisdom of my musculature, inhaled the sweet-smelling. seductive scent of my sweat,
my attention on naught but supremacy, of mastering mendacity and subterfuge,
of how to strike parry feint swing twist stab turn slash thrust turn slice strike parry feint twist stab sting kiss kill,
again, and again, and again, dawn to dusk, and ofttimes even 'neath the darkening night sky
- was this not pathway to *claimhteoireacht* at its finest?
Every skill I have I learned from you, Máthair, you made me who I am,
just as we thought you'd made Cú Chulainn who he was behind our walls of shadowed stone,
but 'tis true 'tis hard to twine old rod, and that dog may have appeared to learn a bundle of new tricks, *mar dhea*,
but seems he was stringing us all along like eels on lines the while,
we the unwitting victims of his choosings and calculations,
collateral damage left behind in the catastrophe of his cunning, conniving, canine wake
- he'd never planned to stay, the cur, used us all three,
for far away kine have long horns and her udders must've been full, her milk sweet,
she must've been quick in body and in mind to have snared him so,
so what matter he mastered feats of melee and retaliation beyond any come before,
what matter he was learned the gift of your *Gáe Bulga*, despite or because of prophecy of shortened span,
what matter he partook of the friendship of all of our thighs,
promoted himself as my only man yet followed wandering eye and left Aunt Aoife spoiled and childing,
what matter he surpassed the Bridge of Leaping, was o'ercome not by the Glenn of Peril, the taunts of detractors,
what matter I drank the faerie's waters and he placed his blade upon the flesh of your breast,

demanded discipleship from you, though, with hindsight, undeserved and unworthy,
we were all just tools to be used and discarded by the arrogant mutt,
chunks of sinew and meat chewed and spat out once we'd served our purpose,
once he'd sucked our marrows dry of all juices and extracted all he could from the each of us,
drained us of all resistance to his charisma
- or had he, because, even though there are days I don't recognize myself without him,
as at times do neither you nor your sister, the crater left by his parting a difficult hole to fill,
there be no doubt I, we, will have the last laugh, Mathair, *caellich piseog*, *banfilli* of renown,
the machinations of the unfolding of our revenge upon him soon to fulfil your prophecy of the failure of kings three,
of the dog's untimely demise, indirect consequence of his own actions
- I can smell it on the wind and taste it in the air,
have seen the omen of flocking ravens, the gatherings of the triple hags, the coming of storms and a dark tide:
Cú Chulainn is to falter soon, victim to his own pretentious vanity,
his persistent and pathetic, dogged pride his undoing:
he will suffer wounds of vengeance when he does battle at the last wall,
there will be bloody events amongst the standing stones upon the Plain of Muirtheimne,
the air fouled with the fetor of a hero's passing will draw forth the *dobhar-chú*,
the remnants of his embodiment a co-walker will be,
though he who takes his seat of life shall lose the hand of striking.

Had I known his coming amongst us would have caused such tedious dolour and been the catalyst for such change,
would I still have taken him, still have watched him dispatch my suitor with titillating lechery even so,
or would I have given Cochar Croibne my favour and championed his rightful cause against the dog,
helped bolster his defence of my honour against split pointer and sundered shame,
lain not with the son of the sun god nor surrendered my wantings to his craven desires?
Or, fate and prophecy and destiny aside, was the Hound's discipleship inevitable,
in part due to his enticing scent and beguiling allure, even more so directed course of the turning of the Wheel?
I don't know if we could have avoided the catastrophe of him even if we'd tried
- what had you foreseen from amongst the dancing wickersmoke shapes as they curled about you, Máthair?
Were we all just clansmen of white bronze or yellow gold disputing approaches on the far sides,
unwitting players neither unable to decipher the strategies required to surround Meath,
ruling manse of the High King upon the Hill of Tara,
nor stop the defending monarch from retreating to the board of life's edge,
unaware that our souls knew the geography of our destinies and that the outcomes had already been determined,
our courses fated so to be?
What had your gift of *imbas forosnai* revealed to you, Máthair?
Had you known all along the machinations of the unravelling of our revenges,
played us all along just as he later played us like eels on a line in service to your prophecies?
Were you a director of the fates that came to pass, or merely their messenger?
And that whore, the Mórrígan, was she your muse or your mentor,
your inspiration, even? You both lusted after the dog, as did I, of course
- was your prophecy of shortened span borne of jealousy of Her desire for your prize poodle,
retaliation for that which you wanted but had to wait to get?
You know I would've allowed you entry into our bedchamber if you had demanded it,
would've willingly shared the delight of him if it meant we could've kept him in our thrall,
for, as *bandraíodóir* with the gift of *imbas forosnai*, as *spaewife* of renown,

surely you knew he was bound to enter your vulgar gossip at some point,
would be unable to escape the lure of your finesse, regardless of the temptations of others?
What had you foreseen beforehand, Máthair?
Normally hindsight is the best insight to foresight,
but you had the inspired illumination of the most gifted *banfhili*,
had trained even Fedelm in the gift of all-knowledge
- what had you chosen not to reveal, and why, and for what , or whose, benefit?
Your penetrating, prudent, prospicient, *cailleach piseog* eyes had you saluting his retaking the hand of Emer,
augured events set in place by the long-smouldering wrath of Queen Medb for his slighting of her,
and for same of the Phantom Queen, royal, deific, surveyor of our histories, for undying is the wrath of queens,
had you vicariously abet the rising and the setting of Aoife's only son by the father,
the ring of the father's father recognised too late, for once released your gifted shaft was inevitably fatal
- surely you'd known Connla's lamentable ending was forthcoming, the boy bound to his fate,
the moment you first held the bone of the *Coinchenn* in your wrath-filled hands,
that both he and Ferdiad would be subject to its barbs, *riastrad* cast by the rabid Hound, himself,
the loss of his foster-brother he to be the sadder for,
the setting of his son dragging him into a maelstrom of disconsolance,
the pain of the despair driving his self near mad?
The mainstay of your teachings is to use every advantage and win at all costs
- what better advantage could there be than prescience?
Aye, I'm only beginning to understand the depths and lengths to which you'd taken your doctrine,
the savvy and adroit intricacies of your contrivances and manoeuvres,
the extensive network of your insidious, unscrupulous tentacles of deceit and control,
the extent of your subtle, covert exploitation of others egos and desires,
only to maintain domination over their decisions, their very thoughts, words, deeds, and actions,
manipulating them over time to enact your inclinations,
ofttimes placing *geasa* upon them through the potency of your persuasion,
even from within the shadowed walls of Dún Scáith, lime-mortared and impregnable to outside force,
tendrils of mental command emanating from you like a fishnet web of coercion and despair,
unseen yet somehow blackened with the charred bone powder of all those who had fallen victim to your blades,
abattoir-tainted with the memories of sweat and fear and blood,
the phronetic energy of kill or be killed, your ferocity unconquered and unconquerable
- you were a formidable foe, both on the battlefield and from behind closed doors,
teaching no quarter and no mercy, your judgement oft swift and terrible, your blades fast and sharp,
for all weapons in your hands never failed to find their marks
- if any dropped their defences against you, no matter how dog-tired and debilitated they deemed themselves to be,
they would meet the fury of your redress and the edges of quickened, sharpened steel,
for there is no space for error when every stroke can kill,
the vehemence of your onslaught unabating and sustained, their every breath a curse as much a blessing,
as it meant either there was more to come or no more to be had, your remedy for restitution relentless...
Few ever found you on your island rock, were honoured enough to let you teach them,
and fewer still graduated from your academy - it took courage to be with you, Máthair,
courage itself nothing more than a love affair with the unknown
- you taught all your charges as much,
that courage without conscience was a wild beast needing taming,
hence your insistence that while distraction wasted one's energy, concentration restored it,

that there'd always be more distractions, if they allowed them,
and I watched many a potential prodigy falter,
unable to maintain their temerity when pushed beyond the point of no return and left enervated,
lying in plash of their own blood and shit and sweat and grume,
only to be dragged back to the training grounds to once more face the temper of your tempered blade,
requiring ferity, verdure, fettle, and brawn beyond measure to endure...
    To me you were not only mother in my eyes, in your fullness you were Ban-righinn Scáthach,
queen of shadows and the dark, queen of melee and retaliation,
queen of augury and divination, of prophecy and illumination,
of red battle's distant roar and bitter wounds to bear,
of the grin of skulls and the grimace of wounds,
the thud of blades in flesh and the thrust of spears inside,
harbinger of ignominy and ruiner of reputations, for reputations last longer than lives,
and to be lambasted in tale and song is to be mocked and taunted forever,
a torture upon one's legacy longer lasting than the futile, dying expiration of the lung's of any bloodied eagle...
    Aye, though I have idolised and craved to be as you in every way, Máthair,
'tis true the student can never surpass the teacher, only hope to emulate their skills and devices
- so, then, did you knowingly step aside, allow yourself to be violated, persecuted beyond enduring,
solely to facilitate the passing of the mantle of your doctrine and your dogma into my hands?
    Is that the gift you gave to me, gracefully withdrawing,
    stepping back into the shadows you came from after labour of my preparation was complete in your eyes,
the golden sheath that held and protected me broken open,
whether or not I felt ready to actuate such a charge,
to be able to stand in your stead amidst *stramash* and tumult,
expedited eclosing allowing me to be birthed, primed and poised and ready for action?
    If it is true that when the student is ready the master or mistress disappears, then unworthiness be damned
- you made me who I am, Máthair, through you I have found my greatest strengths and wholeness of being,
embraced both pain and delectation, refined my edacity for blood-letting,
learnt to maintain an impregnable inner strength and a strong will,
learnt to use every advantage and to win at all cost, and, aye, if now it is I will succeed you,
and, in time, hope even to surpass you, it is to you I dedicate my service:
I will not betray the memory of you wallowing in self-pity and regret,
being distracted by sorrow's lament, will not let such concerns slow my strikes,
for there is no room for error when every stroke could kill
- rather, I will pick up my sword and fight for you, Ban-righinn Scáthach,
midwife to heros, you who have birthed children, killed men, rendered flesh,
suckled warriors at your breast and tasted the delectable agonies of subspace,
you who knew the pain of never surrender and the painlessness of *géilleadh deiridh*,
for if I don't, who will?
    I will sanctify the legacy of you with my own thirst for the red scent,
will let the wolf behind my own eyes run free, will let nothing or no-one escape me,
will come from behind, wraith-like, as shadow, *mar scáth,* as you taught me,
if I cannot meet foe head-on, will become both teacher and switch to heroes in your stead,
and will put aside my heart's aching to escape the pain of losing you, my hankering for

     release
     restitution
     retribution
     revenge…

     How long until I can avenge you, Máthair?
     Are you watching and waiting for me to act from beyond the isle of Hy Breasil,
willing me and wanting me to begin their slow executions,
their ritualised flensing and dismembering, the removing of their seats of life, dilatory and deleterious,
to celebrate the serendipity of retribution with a sup of their sanguine fluids,
enough to satiate both our pangs?
     I do not forget and I do not forgive your persecutors,
will enact onerous retribution upon them swift as may,
will repay their violence with brisk violence so they are quickly dealt with,
repay their rudeness with the kindness of the cold, hard kiss of steel and a slow, painful demise,
spill their guts on the floor and make them call out your name as they beg for clemency,
strip them of every shred of their faux valour, their so-called honour,
and let them bleed out, watch rivulets of claret spilling out of them,
strands of their gralloched innards splaying out upon the ground, capillaries of contrition
- I curse them as cowards, and may danger and violent death follow them all,
and know that I will not relent upon my pursuit of felony upon them until my blade is slick with their grume,
because our words are dead until we give them life with blood,
and they need not bother praying to their gods for mercy when they're about to meet them -
aye, I pity their mothers, for it took nine months of effort to bring them into this world,
and it'll take only a few moments for me to remove them from it.…

Mothaím uaim thú, Máthair…

     I can still hear your voice in the dead of night, not so much maudlin as mournful,
whispering me your *rúin adh* from the other side of the veil,
reminding me of you before they took you,
of how it used to be before violation of your body and your spirit,
before the excruciation and wretchedness, the misery and utter torment of your ending…
     I can still feel the last touch of your fingers on my cheek,
can still hear you cuss and curse and spit and rage as they stole you from your bed of rushes,
naked but not helpless, your unarmed strikes themselves feats of fierce finality, warlike, cruel and besting,
can still hear the crunch of broken noses and the harshness of the slap and thwack of sword on shield,
can still see the trail of your ichor as they dragged you away, my cries of

     'Lig di, a mahdraí!',
     'Fognad dúib ág is embas!',
     'Marhadh fáisg ort!', and
     'Narab marthain duit!',

mirroring *mallachts* of your own as your bones were broken by their spears,
as you fought against the cruel club's hard edge,
your own blood spilled in great flood, a red plague,
raw flesh, gore, and gristle your glory, your battle's badge...

      Ah, Máthair, you were my mainstay, my muse, my mentor,
my manager, even, moving me towards mastery, mother of my metamorphosis,
refining my nous in duelling, sharpening my reactions, indurating my fastness,
making my grit temeritous and just that bit temerarious,
inviting brash disdain and oft foolhardy contempt for danger,
bordering on recklessness, when caught in the bedlam and cacophony of rammy and swedge,
your manipulations mesmeric and methodic, mendacity only meant to mould me,
to monitor my becoming a mistress of both mindfulness and mindlessness during massacre and melee,
acumen to the moment on hand only
- without you beside me I feel an emptiness, a whirlpooling void,
a temporary hole in my reality that threatens to suck my self control into it,
a one-way portal into despondency that I dare not enter for fear of losing my way...

      Ach, why so morbid, Úathach? She is gone, aye, and everything about you is changed,
and yet, although everything looks the same, the barefoot damp of Dún Scáith,
her curtain walls and ramparts of precipitous stone, the indelible abattoir-taint of memories of blood and fester,
everything is different, and what once was cannot easily be forgotten, nor should it be, and nor will I let it be
- I do not forgive and I do not forget your abusers and will duly hunt them down,
enact revengeance upon them, and have their reputations ruined
- I will not, can not, forget your legacy, Máthair,
for you trained even he in the crucibles of initiation, you the woman behind the Hound,
mistress to heroes and trainer of warriors of legend, you made him who he was...

      You made me who I am.

      Who am I without you?

      Mothaím uaim thú, Máthair, and there are times alone I suffer the weight of loneliness, to be sure,
a heaviness of loss and grief about my heart sacks of shattered stone,
but through you I have garnered impregnable inner strength and strong will,
developed backbone, temerity, grit, nerve, and steel,
and know that to surrender to and transmute the pain of losing you is to mature,
that my capacity to be alone became the capacity to adore and honour you outright,
that to not try to be you but to be wholly myself, with everything I learned from you honed to perfection,
is to whetstone my rough edges and live in to who I am, to become Úathach the Unassailable,
unsurpassable assailant to be feared, irresistible and vixen temptress both,
daughter and successor of Ban-righinn Scáthach ni Uanaind, queen of shadows,
grand daughter of Ard-Greimne of Lethra, to whose judgements heroes oft deferred, my lineage straight and true,
I my mother's daughter in many more ways than one: clad about my waist my own belt of skulls,
my arms adorned blue with woad designs, limewashed bleached hair matted with the blood of others,
sheathed by my side a blade of brightest steel, it once held by He of the Silver Hand,

but lifted from the cache of the people of Danu by your own subterfuge,
the Sword of Light, *Claíomh Solais*, the *Gáe Bulg*'s twin in fierceness and in fury,
for once unsheathed no enemy could survive its wrath, let alone not find its sun-bright sheen irresistible...
   Though you are now exalted and seek paladins and perfected pagans,
trodaithe cumhachta of truth, august men and women of conviction, authors of courage and fearlessness,
champions resolute, arrowheads of astute acumen to take as your charges even from beyond the veil,
I am not yet set apart from this form of flesh and blood, am still bound to its wantings and its needings,
still yearn for blood spilled in great floods about me and for men to fall at my feet in paroxysms of desire,
still strive for supremacy of steel to bring heel to justice, to take those dogs down one by one,
and have them meet the heated ire of my revenge before they meet the darkness of yours,
for they, no doubt, will remain guideless in the void as penance for their atrocities,
wrong-doers welcome in neither heaven nor hell nor even the Otherworld,
their contempt, iniquity, and malevolence branding them as reprobates,
destined to be rejected by others from our pantheon more forgiving than yourself,
spat upon by the very earth itself, to be left on an island somewhere beyond the setting sun to fend for themselves
- and, aye, should any attempt to thwart me or stand in my way they will meet the fury of my swift and unerring blade,
for we are bonded, you and I, Máthair, and I will blend with you as umbra, our souls and silhouettes converging
- your blood is my blood, your heart is my heart, our minds fused together, not just figuratively, but literally,
and I draw from you now what I need, what I will, and use it to my advantage,
for you once declared that greater feats than you shall your charges bring forward,
that if they believe in the calibre of your *claimhteoireacht* you will exist inside them,
a wellspring of warrior's ways ignited alive within them,
largesse uncharacteristic to your somatic persona,
obvious evidence of your farseeing predictions of you now serving higher cause,
for, though 'tis only our bodies that will die, we destined to come again as the same soul in different forms,
to live without belief is a fate more terrible than dying, be it belief in oneself, belief in a higher self,
belief in hearts of valour and of feats of lithe and daring, unconquerable and unconquered,
belief in one's *roc catha*, the fear-provoking sight of spears upon spears, of *enech* gained upon fields of slaughter,
belief in resurgence and new life beyond the final strokes of cutting,
of Airmed's herbs and her healing bath of sound,
the sun-splendoured godlight of Lugh of the Long Arm overseeing the rising and falling of sons,
belief in the raven queen's overseeing of wars and fate, of Her foretelling of doom or death or victory in battle,
belief in him, whomsoever he really was, Cú Chulainn, Sétanta, Máthair's, my, Aoife's man-bitch,
or some other lowly cur too full of himself to know better, the hero's light in his eyes but the smell of death about him,
belief in the uncompromising, unabating, unwavering revolutions of the turning of the Wheel,
belief in *echtrae* and *immrama* and the breaching of the mering wall beyond the ninth wave,
belief in the Summerland, the ageless nature of the Otherworld of wonders that surrounds us all but many fail to see,
belief in the redded pulse of desired action, the rusted colour of pain, in *claiomhs* of perfect steel,
belief in guile and artifice smoothly manoeuvred, belief in salmon leaps and the vaulting pole,
in resurgence with one's in-breath when seemingly brought to one's knees with steel pressed against one's neck
- belief, Ban-righinn Scáthach, Máthair, my first friend, my best friend, my forever friend, in you,
and belief in all you taught us, belief that all shall cower before your great Wrath,
and belief that, though your death has left a heartache in me not even the hands of Dian Cécht could heal,
my adoration and awe of you leaves memories none could alter or steal,
of you who taught me how to love and hate, how to kiss and kill,
of the secrets and paradoxes of both blade and bedding you inculcated and impressed upon me,

of the endless hours of repetition of engage, disengage, re-engage, impale, transpierce, penetrate, thrust, drill,
breasts heaving and nipples erect with the titillation of exhaustion,
of how to circle and blend with shadow, to come from behind or to meet head-on,
to dance on the tips of spears as provocation, of the art of no distraction and focus undivided,
of how to perfect the perfection of imperfection through discipline and perseverance, through pain and delectation
- if you had known such pain was coming yet did not baulk at your preordained lot,
did not deign to twist and bend the hands of fate,
rather awaited its deliverance steadfast in resolve and resolution,
your death to be your ultimate climax, your beginning and your ending,
somehow knowing that your life, itself, only ever existed, was only ever made possible, for death,
that it was not you that would die, just your bruised and broken body, like as not,
your life a happening between, your death even closer than your own shadow ever was,
that you could only really live when the shadow of your death had disappeared forever,
that to lose the fear of death was paramount to the way you lived moment to moment,
for life begIns when fear ends, you used to say,
then your new life, sanctified, is blessed even more so in my eyes,
makes me even more determined to enact revenge upon those offending offal,
to ensure the severity of their agonies be proportionate to the intensity of what you were forced to endure,
comparable to their own levels of depraved cruelty and beyond,
to let them taste and smell and feel the fear of death before they learn of its falsity.

       Though you implored me to know your spirit is released without the burden of your wracked form,
dreams and visions alerting me to your new exalted status, never to speak of you in the past tense again,
still I will fight for you, Máthair, for if not me, then whom,
for I will not have your memory reviled and besmirched in *bairdne* tales,
lampooned and discredited by those not worthy to have even been spat upon by you in your prime,
bletherers and drunkards drowned in drink yet destined soon to be drowned in their own blood
- oh, they stabbed themselves in the foot and dug their own graves when they came for you, Máthair,
forgetting about the daughter, the progeny assassin you left behind, heir to your fortress and your ministrations,
the tip of my tongue touching my top lip in anticipation of the tip of my *claiomh* piercing their lungs,
each sac madefied with their own liquid agony, shattering their frightened and trembling minds,
and, with gashes on their foreheads and with limbs slashed asunder,
as they will lie gurgling out your name, drowning in their own bile and cruor,
pleading for release from their wretchedness,
it is to each in turn I will whisper, 'Filleann an feall ar an bhfeallaire',
and listen to them squeal and wet themselves with blood and fear and tears of chagrin,
taunts and chiding and ridicule theirs as I prepare to slake my sword in them
- dying for them will be the easy part, for there is no light awaiting them on the other side of the veil,
only your shadow and your retribution, depending on their atonement and repentance,
though better the trouble following their deaths than the trouble theirs following shame.

       I know this image of envisioned executions and ruined reputations pleases you as much as it pleases me,
that you hold it near your Otherwordly heart, for I feel upon my skin a zephyr of freshness in response to my reverie,
the touch of that which never dies from beyond the veil of death by the Goddess of Death, Herself,
Ban-righinn Scáthach, She Who Strikes Fear, the Dark Goddess, the Warrior Maid, the She Witch,
teacher, nurse and switch to heroes of legend, *cailleach feasa*, *cailleach piseog*, *cailleach an chlaíomh*,
both drakania and *bandraíodóir*, wise woman, fortune-teller, sorceress, charm-worker,

seductress and stern disciplinarian both, shadow-laced enforcer and teacher of indomitability,
preceptor of the seven teachings, hot in anger and cold in revenge,
she who gave birth to battlers and champions of acclaim,
and she who gave birth to me both from within her womb and the cauldrons heated by the crucible of initiations,
my Máthair, she whose breast I suckled and whose guiding hands ushered me forward towards superiority with steel,
servant now to higher cause, your spirit looking down from Tír na nÓg, reminiscent,
glowering or glowing depending on your mood and the initiatives of your charges,
watching, waiting, willing, wanting, remembering…

It is only now, though, do I feel ready and able to carry on your vision, your acumen, your argutness
- should silence rather than anger be needed, I will merge with you,
will become not just your favoured daughter but also a sister to your shadows, *mar scáth*,
rising with renewed vigour and conviction from the ashes of the bonefire I lit for you like Áine's exultant soul,
though it only the syndrome of my imposter incinerated through ritual and not the flesh of my form,
for there is strength in unity and bonds of togetherness beyond the beef of lesser men,
and, if it is to draw blade I need, it will be as swift, as sure, and as unerring as your own,
for we are united, you and I, all that separates us a mering wall and the consciousness of delusion
- you are with me this very moment, and will be so always, and, though I miss you being here beside me,
some part of me knows you are ever with me, you always have and always will have my back,
that the true power that coursed through you and that you gifted me, even more so than to your other students,
was not just that of domination and control nor that mastery was not about what happened to us,
but what we chose to do when something did happen to us,
of whether to strike or parry or feint or swing or twist or stab or turn and slash, kiss or kill, regardless,
of how to leave eyes without life, sundered heads, and bloodied, festering corse in our wakes,
but of freedom from distraction and focus undivided, of being attentive to the moment only,
a depth of awareness that slowly shed light on all our fears and limitations and freed us,
opening our perceptions to the vastness of all that which surrounded us,
allowing us to be as stillness amongst the catastrophic fracas and *stramash* of warfare,
as unseen as shadows even in the full light of day,
able to catch opponents off guard with sly sneak attacks,
not for us to entertain superiority or delusions of grandeur but to arouse and activate energies of satiety,
a fullness of being and credo earned through endless drills and repetitions of melee and retaliation,
of being taken beyond exhaustion to the very edge of the point of no return and brought back at sessions ends,
only to be thrust back onto the blood-stained arena of the training grounds, all pleas ignored,
to face whirlwind attacks and flurries of blows and the cold comfort of pain, again, and again, and again,
it becoming so ingrained in us we'd lose all concern about the sensation of wounding and fear of expiration,
no longer wielding the dulled blades of indifference, but become able to lock in with our breaths and strike back,
instinctually, instantly, right on point, to use every advantage and win at all cost,
for there be no room for errors when every stroke could kill
- was *this* not *claimhteoireacht* at its finest?

You made me who I am, Máthair, gave me both my esse and my *enech*,
raised my dowry and my *sarhaed*, impressed indomitability upon me,
gave me both reason to live and reason to no longer fear the loss of you nor even my own death,
witnessed and acknowledged the potential of me, sculpted and moulded me in crucibles of intimacy and initiation,
your investement in me inspired and intense, with unceasing, relentless invitations to be learned of your mysteries,

I more like a doting devotee before her mistress than your very own daughter, you the quintessential matriarch,
commanding, demanding respect, and even reverence, suffering no fools, giving no quarter nor expecting none,
and for that I owe you bonds of affection and a debt of gratitude everlasting,
am heartfelt beholden and bonded to you with an adoration that knows no bounds,
for I know somewhat of the lineage that sings in my veins, too, corporeal and esoteric,
and, yes, I loved you and trusted you enough to let you teach me, parent me,
be my morning light in my inner darkness and my guide in the nightness of my growing,
but, ach, many a sudden change takes place on an unlikely day,
and, though it seemed a long time coming, my maturation has come faster than e'er I thought it could,
forced upon me by circumstances beyond my control and domination,
and it is now I am ready and brave enough to be reborn both through and from you,
the glowing *gríosach* of my benefaction easily rekindled,
ready to release the cording of my reliance on you and stand free of the misery and pain of remembrance,
free of the calamity left behind in Cú Chulainn's wake poisoning my very bones and blood and marrow,
free of concern for the past and free of the fear of the future, a new life evolving as all fears end,
my ascent into womanhood and prowess as a *sciath mhaighdean* in my own right beginning,
free to become fierceness and formidable of my own volition,
free to shake off my vary troubles and follow you into the firmament while still of flesh and form,
to wear leafy crown upon my head and become Úathach the Terrible,
having vanquished fate, my birthright, inheritance, and destiny leading me from the unreal to the real,
calling me to become the iconic, enigmatic warrior-princess born of the mistress of shade,
my precepts now those of protection, strength, and war,
of vigilance in combat to master situations minacious and radge,
of dominion over indelible strokes of cutting with blades for slicing and chopping meat and bone,
of strength and valour to rival that of even the mightiest of heroes,
forever the Maiden Goddess, for no seed shall be planted in the womb of me that survives beyond the morning after,
all praise to woman's ways and heart kissed gold without measure sprung from Airmed's tears of grief,
our lineage ending but our legacy continuing, I your daughter in many more ways than one,
for here is where I surpass you, the dream of every parent realised, I to become an even better version of you
- whereas you had to literally die to be reborn, I need but die to myself with each outgoing breath to do same,
as 'tis true that though my fears couldn't prevent me dying in the space between breaths, they could stop me living,
keeping my attention ever so slightly distracted, wasting precious energy needed for precision and control,
only determined concentration and focus undivided restoration,
coupled with the ongoing small deaths of every exhalation and my convictions renewing with every breath drawn,
each inhalation opportunity to reinvigorate, reorientate, recreate myself anew,
to rebirth myself, again, and again, and again, ongoingly freeing myself from limitations and conditionings,
consciously dying and returning, perpetual palingenesis, each new birth and death both the first and the last,
the fleeting moment between both breaths serenity itself, an interval of expansion and paradox,
a momentary stillness wherein zero seconds pass and even arrows pause in their flight,
the cage of my bones, muscles, blood, and skin no longer prepotent,
each suspended moment a crack in the veil of time, a temporary hole in reality,
a portal between worlds and dimensions beyond even the starlit void of the darkening night sky,
entry into the way of nature and the circle of birth, life, death neverending, itself,
dòigh nàdair taken to its highest,
my inner soul freeing itself of all bondage and uniting with all that is,
even time itself momentarily ceasing, even amidst the crash and clang of weapon and shield,

the soft moans, final gasps, and morbid wails of the dying fading into the muted silence of revelation,
the eternal quietude reverberating in my mind, the very essence of my being,
not as noiselessness but as a soundless music, transcendence from all that is mortal and all that is momentary,
even as I melt into every searing stroke, untroubled and invigorated,
breathing in with each strike, each slash, each cut, each inhalation filling me with aliveness, vim, and vigour,
breathing out to release the pain and discomfort, our breath the most powerful tool we have,
itself the vehicle which parts the veil between the world of spirits and our world of matter,
using expansive breaths deep into the belly to eliminate pains and transcend the vibrations of mortality,
superseding the chaotic, gasping, chest breaths of combat and separation,
plummet so deeply inside myself I'd lose all sensation of fear or pain or fatigue,
enter into a dreamlike frenzy of wildness and bloodlust and channelled sword-point focus,
my awareness exponentially heightened, opponents very thoughts and desires laid bare before them,
unable to defend themselves against my percipience, my whirring blades fast and sharp, my blows irresistible,
the dynamic but controlled catharsis of my dexterity belying the composure and stillness within me,
using the redded pulse of desired action amidst *stramash* as a springboard toward sanctity,
my consciousness travelling beyond the mering wall while my figure and form fight on,
attentive to the vibrant, living uncertainties of melee and retaliation all about,
inherited skills and abilities salient and divine passed on from you my protection,
the chains and shackles that held me a prisoner of gravitas and gravity releasing,
taking my mind towards Tír na nÓg, the land of the young,
where time doesn't exist and wounds close as orison,
towards totality, the voidscape of *síoraíocht* and the no pain of *géilleadh deiridh*,
claimhteoireacht at its finest in the space between breaths,
retreating from this mortal shell to witness the birth of death,
of becoming nothing to find... everything,
taking me towards the beat between pulses of heartblood and lung air within me,
towards the living enigma amongst flashes of steel of that which never dies,
towards Hy Breasil beyond the mering wall, and tranquillity beyond the ninth wave,
towards the nether roots of the *crann na haithne*, and in its branches, the *crann-nathair*,
towards both your shadow and your light,
towards you.

Mothaím uaim thú, Máthair. Beidh cónaí ort i mo chuimhne croí go deo,
(I miss you, Mother. You will abide in my heart memory forever.)

ADDENDUM III
EMER

A keening for a husband lost

I

E'er have I loved thee, my husband,
thou wert e'er the beat of this pulse, and e'er shalt it be so,
for, even as thy lifeblood dries upon the binding stone from whence departed thee this isle,
splattered with gore, thou ne'er a Hound of weakness,
heroic even in thy dark-stained collapse,
a drop of blood upon thy spear-shaft,
a froth of blood upon thy sword,
wounds upon thy splendid skin reddened with blood,
gashes on thy side,
weary after triumph, thy seat of life severed,
the gravitas of sundering redress for the felony of defilement,
bloodied blade and appendage rived evidence of arrogance and audacity,
for he who took thy head was doomed to lose the hand of striking,
even as I lay wreaths of holly beneath thy feet to keep the *sluagh* at bay,
to allow thee safe passage beyond the setting, western sun,
to come unto the welcoming embrace of thy father's long arm,
He who holds the light of the day star,
the very span of the *Bealach na Bó Finne*,
the tenets of oath, truth, law, and the regality of rightful kingship itself in His upraised, open palm,
tears of grief for thy passing mix with the remnants of thy fluids,
anointing the very sod of the Plain of Muirthemne with eye waters of remorse and pain,
mine and those of all those red-eyed in the guise of cows and oxen and horses,
for what pains the heart must needs be washed away with tears,
our combined salted liquids as Airmed's,
daughter blessed of incant and herb,
my sorrow's keening akin her melody and healing bath of sound,
p'haps not so much reknitting form but enough to help thee pass and keep thy co-walker at bay…
Just as the druids of the *Tuatha Dé Danann* stood motionless with arms upraised

and poured forth dreadful imprecations upon their foes in the battles of Mag Tuired,
exposed to wounds,
their dogma their shields,
their defenceless their armour,
so, too, my husband, didst thou expose thyself upright stood against girdled stone,
daring any to attempt the final stroke of cutting and claim the kill of thee,
for ne'er didst thou take the recreant's way
- when dire danger was e'er at hand,
for five tear sodden days alone didst stood thee against armies,
thy breast filled with fierce hate and ringed with envy,
raw flesh thy battle's badge,
blood spilt in a great flood thine epitah,
for there be nae remedy nor cure against thy disease of death,
battalions smashed in bloody combats,
nae other man e'er to be found thine equal,
herds broken up in wrath by great hosts broken upon thy hero's stance,
thunderous waves pounding against thy shield of defiance as if against shingled beach, cliff, or loch,
thy frenzy, thy swiftness, thy violence poured forth as *riastrad*,
thou nae caring whose sacred cow thou gored,
thy refusal to die easily bellicose, saga-worthy, and meritorious,
for refused didst thee to die lying on the sod like an animal,
rather to face thy mortal ending with temerity and aplomb,
a fearlessness unfathomable, beyond comprehension
- thou art the epitome *laoch misniúil* in my eyes of adoration,
as art thee so considered in the hearts and minds of all Uliad
- all men in Alba and in Ériu know thy name,
and virgin women red-eyed pity thy wail,
one eye oft exsected in likeness of thy deformity evince of their love for thee…
What once was cannot easily be forgotten, my husband,
nor should it be,
our union forged despite my father's wiles and guile,
and 'tis only now canst I bear witness the inevitable truth, that, aye,
though I shouldst look beyond the gloom of my grieving,
and remember misty winters oft bring a pleasant spring,
and nae matter how tall nor lofty was thy father,
neither noble or lowly but up for a while and down for a while,
'tis true there be nae more years to give,
and, after hardship and a long sigh,
thy blessed dog's days be truly over.
Barely canst I look upon thy tortured, crimsoned, once beautiful skin,
for, though thy name will ne'er die so long as the world turneth,
it only thy red soul, the killing lust, and the blood-covered veil before thine eyes thou hast lost,
to envision thy soul's illumination I dare not look at thy viscous wounds directly,
lest my vision be altered by my nausea and my sentiment
- to truly see thy light through the *féth fíada* must needs I nae be trying to see,
must catch glimmer of thy radiance by displacement and deception, indirect,

penetrating the illusion of mortality with true sight only,
for, just as an eye cannot see itself nor my mind perceive its echt authenticity,
to pierce the veil between worlds for one brief moment,
enough to dispel the illusion of separation that threatens my mind's perception,
to eviscerate my very sense of this world of sweat and tears and flesh and blood,
to tear asunder my heart's knowing from my mind's convictions within myself,
I must let only the light of thy divine parentage shine upon the darkness of my despair,
the ravages of thine agonies a blade in the *coire emmae* of this woman,
thy illumination salve to the grief in my heart and in my breast...

II

Mayhap it behooved thee to nae acknowledge my prohibition of counsel,
the weight of this bosom the voice of reason ignored by thee blinded by the falsity of pride,
for 'twas I, alone, who knew Connla for who he was,
my conviction resolute and unwavering that, aye,
'twas truly Aoife's only son upon the strand,
a fair, wee javelin, as was once thee Sétanta,
the scion of the father aliken thee in many ways,
though lacking thy distortion and thy *roc catha*,
yet he well-versed in the bloody spike beyond his age of years,
learned of every feat as taught thee and Ferdiad by Scáthach, herself, bar one,
the fashioned bone of the *Coinchenn*, *Curruid*-taken,
her belly spear, the *Gáe Bulg*, that only the Hound could wield,
it the ruin of both foster brother and the son of the son of the sun, more's the pity...
Nae father should outlive the product of his loins,
nor his brother of milk and bond,
let alone wield the weapon of their untimely demise
- once a mountain he, Ferdiad naught but a shadow became,
play and pleasure betwixt ye comrades of choice and consequence rescinded,
as all was game and sport until met thee with Ferdiad at the ford,
the crown of tragedy upon his bed of blood left slick with grume after thee,
anas defiled, his loss thee the sadder for,
though ne'er hadst thee tormented one's self in grief and loss and hurt and rage and ruth,
until witnessed thee the death of thine only son by thine own hand,
tentacles of grief and lamentation having then arisen,
pulling thine own self into a wave-splashed maelstrom of disconsolance,
only Cathbad's spell of illusion liberation,
causing thee to see the very wild horses of Manannán mac Lir as targets of thy revengeance,
exhausting thyself in rage-filled catharsis and deliverance,
knowing well Connla's soul was being tide-dragged towards Tech Duinn, the house of the dark one,
driven onwards beyond the ninth wave by phantom horsemen upon steeds of white,
free of the burden of his father-wounding and mortality,
to await final passage to either Hy Breasil,

or to come again in another life, same soul, different form...
And yet, laws and their sanctions must need be adhered to, lest lawlessness abound
- *fingal* exacted, though thee deemed innocent in the garb of the guilty,
misdeeds of misfortune and malice the mainstay of thy defence,
salt in thy wound of regret half the *corpdíre* Conchobar due,
he thy nearest kin, kin-slayers exempted from receiving meed,
as if the death of the boy by thine own spear weren't wound enough
- ach, nae heeding propositional knowledge of my own,
if only thou hadst recognised the ring thee hadst gifted him and nae fought him,
as had Elatha of the Otherworld when he knew Bres as his own and averted such a course,
thy fortunes displaced by misplaced sense of honour and pride,
thee the worse of, therefore,
for days of three the bawling of calves not allowed their cows Connla's only death lament,
nae women left for keening,
the shadows of both Aoife and Scáthach notable by their absence,
I the only lady possessed of the verity, that, aye,
hadst thou but listened to thy beloved wife
an heir to Cú Chulainn's bloodline wouldst have thee retained,
women's wiles and women's words voices of culture and nous embodied in rebukes of indictment,
my voice weak and dead to thine emotion,
the deathblow of both thy fates rendered forthwith,
conceit and arrogant vanity the cause,
for nae woman wouldst kill her only son for naught but the esteem of others...
Ach, Cú Chulainn, though I loved thee greatly and treasured thy *eagna na laochra*,
applying such thine attainment of power beyond reckoning,
thou straight sword stabbing behind thee and before thee,
bones broken by thy spear, others lying broken necked,
fields of slaughter growing red about thee,
for all thy bravado and surety that glory be all and martyrdom superlative,
that if to die thou must than 'twas better to die like a hero going home,
to go down fighting hard, using every advantage thou couldst,
for Tír na nÓg awaited thee on the other side of the veil,
thou were but as a child in matters of heart and empathy,
prone to trysts of temptation and the wasting sickness of limerence,
impartial or indifferent to the shame of seconding,
behaviour juvenile and impetuous, driven by libido,
oft tactless, hurtful, grief to this heart and to this breast,
indiscretions demanding restitution and resolve,
even at knife point, if such demanded it,
above and beyond the legal dictates of the day...
But nothing would deign keep me from my handfast,
our courses fated so to be
- I would marry the man I loved, come what may,
but would not have my worth undervalued,
I his equal in eloquence and age and shape and race,
I, a sprig then untaken, only e'er to be his *cétmuinter,*

ne'er just the silent object of his desire,
rather one well versed in the barter and exchange of men,
though oft hemmed in by custom, the power of my parents, and the jealousy of my father...
Beyond good triumphs of tender youth, my only man,
you were bound to me, our contract irrevocable
- told I Lugaid Mac Nois, son of Nos, son of Alamac, as much when refused I his hand,
so as to secure from thee provision and protection
- steadfast and resolute in thy spoken betrothal, my husband,
prepared was I to await thy return, though timespan unknowing,
trust and faith in thine adoration and thy promise aspiration, almost dogma,
music to my soul and my conviction...

III

Everything looks the same yet everything is different, now thou hast fallen
- everything familiar is bitter, the sod upon Murtheinne's Plain bloody underfoot,
thy gralloched gore strapped about this morbid menhir standing sombre above a field of slaughter,
dried and still dripping rivulets of thy lifeblood stains upon thy battle-girdle,
mockeries of thy valour and thy violence,
thy splendid body oft reddened with *riastrad* now coloured same with curdled grume,
thy tunics, apron, and *cathchriss* of tanned and hardened leather having failed thee at the last,
thy delusions of invincibility pierced and torn asunder,
thou humbled by the spear, broken by thy bravado...
What is absent is honoured, what is known is neglected, until everything is known,
and 'tis with thy passing dost remembrance of thy deeds dominate,
thy body sorely wasted, thy persona now absent,
yet ne'er let it be said that any couldst encounter a warrior harder to deal with,
nor a spear-point sharper or keener or quicker, nor a hero fiercer,
nor a hound more voracious for bloodied foe,
nor one of thine age to equal a third of thy valour, than thee, my husband,
for, aye, ne'er didst taketh thou the recreant's way
- Scáthach may have betrayed thee by forseeing thy demise but nae warning thee,
but didst thou not shake off weakness and neglect and take Medb's bulls by their horns,
despite prophecy of shortened span and nae more years to give,
droplets of thine own blood splashed on many a smashed shield?
And, ach, even in thy final throes upon this gut-soiled monolith of unfeeling stone,
though thy vision was bloodshot and thou blemished sworded sore,
didst thee not stare down the darkness of thine augured fate and thine own fears?
E'er was thy spirit restless, thy breast full of fierce hate,
premonition, p'haps, of a sick-bed awaiting thee after a wound of revenge,
thou dwindling after the final breach in face of slaughters of great ferocity,
of thine inexorable, deplorable, pain-wracked ending to come,
agonies beyond enduring accelerating the lifting of the blood-coloured veil before thine eyes,
thy sundering platform for thy deliverance,

thy surrender and thy supplication fated so to be...
But from what perpetual anguish were thou fleeing,Sétanta-come-Cú Chulainn,
from what wound that ne'er bled didst thou seek salve,
e'er since as but a child sought thee recognition and appraisal,
oft by way of bettering thy peers with fists or with *sliotar* cast for wounding,
later through tests of *claimhteoireacht* among warriors of the Red Branch,
later still by standing alone, one against an army,
thine own blood a red plague, thy straight sword dyed red,
acknowledgement for thy skill at arms and prowess the only measure of thy worth?
Wast thou running from prophecy of thy shortened span and the yawning void of sorrow's lamentation,
or wast thou running towards life, towards thy sharp valour and thy berserker fury,
towards the glory of martyrdom and inheritance of thy rightful kingship,
towards the long, loving arms of thy Father's embrace,
the boy now man returning from whence he came, dog-tired,
worn down by the vagaries of a life lived by the sword,
thou homecoming triumphant,
though the cost be greater than e'er thou fathomed?
But hadst thou gone too far, my husband,
died needlessly in thy search for recognition,
for one need nae end thine embodiment to cast thy heart and mind beyond the veil,
one need only die to oneself to become thy true self,
to release oneself from the distractions of mortality,
sever its tentacles of temptation,
turn one's attention from the lacerations upon thy flesh and the lamentations of women,
ignore the morbid wails and keening about thee,
must plummet so deeply inside oneself one loses all sensations of pain,
just as every birthing mother comes to know as she capitulates,
as she puts her very self aside to make way for new life...

IV

Red the belt of innard's stains upon this stone of thy last standing,
red the battle's distant roar now faded,
an echo of the catastrophe and tumult of thy defense of defiance,
red the sky above bloodied in sympathy to thy pains,
red the gore dripped from flocks of scald crows beaks,
Mórrígan's scavengers of corse and the dying alike,
flesh torn from open wounds Her delight,
windows to souls plucked from faces fouled with wrack and ruin Her relish,
red the field of slaughter grown, smeared with an army's own stain,
thy strong, shafted, curved spear and straight sword dyed red in dark gatherings of blood,
crimson red thine eyes, full-red thy chariot bearings, deep red thy chariot rug
- aye, men in Alba knew thy name and in the winter's night now pity thy wail,
but that alone bears nae comfort to this heart a bed of sickness,
for what comfort came with most speed, with most urgency

when nae matter where thou didst stand dire danger was e'er at hand,
and thee alone those cattle didst guard,
great hosts driving the herds, one against armies,
thine own blood a red plague splashed on many a smashed shield
- aye, go where thou may find comfort still, my husband,
here there be nae more years to give,
and nae more shalt thee shake off weakness and neglect
and arise once more and seize thine arms, seasoned in the craft of war,
to come with valour sharp, versed in the bloodied spike,
to lay waste thine enemies, murderous on Muirthemne Plain,
and with long, sweeping, strong strokes Cruachan's heroes destroy,
for now, surely, as spirit disembodied, canst thee shake off thy darkened shroud of betrayal,
finally disentangle thyself from the hexed fishnet web of Scáthach's own devising,
forgive thyself the slaying of thine only son,
he to whom a mother I could have, should have, been,
his own too conceited and self-centred to have loved him for his own sake,
he more than a mere pawn to be used and discarded in the unravelling of sisterly revenge,
her enmity and animosity towards thee catalyst for the untimely setting of thy son,
dictated by a discourse of violence to which there was alternative,
hadst thee but heeded thine own wife's counsel, headstrong husband of mine,
for implored I thee to turn away from the words of She of Shadow,
severe against the skin-torture of the only sapling youth of thy tree,
her revengeance and redress even so...
Ach, though nothing is e'er lost, just buried,
'tis now must I bury the memory of thee inside myself,
to draw upon as grief and sorrow to follow wherein dost I roam,
thy breast once filled with fierce hate,
mine fore'ermore a bed of sickness and regret,
I wishing upon myself to be anywhere else but here,
perpetually pleading with the Dagda to resurrect thy broken form with His *lorg mór*,
one touch from its handle all that be needed to bring thee back on point,
cleaving armours and bodies and limbs and heads from necks left, right, and centre again,
for, just as Aoife and Úathach pity thy sweet, shape-changing, bright body nobly broken,
so, too, dost I, for there be bitter wounds to bear beyond those of evisceration and slow execution,
blemishes upon thy body, thy seat of life rived and severed,
this sorrow to last though there be no more more years to give thy form of flesh and blood...
And yet, ach, none bear the power to deny thee what the Dagda, Himself, hadst deemed be thine,
neither the sons and daughters of Calatin, Lugaid Cú Roi, the mighty wave of Medb's armies,
nor even the Scald Crow, Herself, the Mórrígan, overseer of the fates of all of corporeal form,
She who lit upon thy shoulder and pecked thy neck to attest the death of thee,
it the closest touch of Her lips to thy flesh She e'er hadst,
vestige of revenge for thy slightings of Her,
jealousy of his woman's betrothal to thee Her dominion,
for, nae matter Her meddlings,
thou hast earned thy honour with debts of blood and steel this day,
thy sublimation the zenith of thy potential,

itself both thine inheritance and thy destiny
- 'twas in the moment of thy surrender to the inevitable didst thou truly come unto thine own,
took thy rightful place beside thy father, become crowned and blessed so…

And yet, though thee as a new king may well be dead,
I as thy queen say long live the king,
for thy legacy and thy spirit shall live on in the wake of *bairdne* tales,
dictates of *seanchaí*, bearers of old lore,
and in ale-washed odes of reverie fore'ermore…

And yet, ach, I miss thee beside myself, my husband,
this bed of rushes cold and lonely without thee
- why didst thou play into the hands of fate and the prophecy of martyrdom?
Didst thou nae love this woman enough to rewrite the auguries of thyself,
to circumvent the designs of the Turner of the Wheel and the meddlings of the Shadow?
I fought for thee and oft with thee,
yet always within the confines of the thrall of thine adoration,
loyalty to our union paramount, above even loyalty unto my own self,
my adulation of thee greatest,
deference to thy wants and needs paramount,
saw even my very father and thine only son fall before thee,
so, how couldst thou deign leave thy *cétmuinter* behind?
In part I feel betrayed by thy selfishness,
betrayed by thine own supercilious ego and arrogant pride,
thy narcissistic fascination with honour and esteem from others,
thy commitment to follow through on prophecy of shortened span itself, too, a betrayal of sorts,
for didnae betrayal and death surround thee like a darkened shroud unto thine own demise?
Thought thee not to advise thine only woman of such,
or was thou somehow ashamed to admit as much,
for fear of chastisement and ridicule,
thy need for commendation from thy father the cause,
approval of thyself balanced delicately on the tip of sharpened blade,
loss of face and *enech* threatening?

I would nae have chastised thee, my husband, for I loved thee…

Red the chopped flesh left for raven's feed about thee,
red the blood tears of sadness in the windows of the souls of all the virgin women of Ériu,
red the stain of shame of the illgotten outcome of the rape of trade,
red the gut-blood that filled thy throat issuing forthwith before thy vorpal sundering,
capillaries of contrition spilt upon thy chest witness to thine ignominy,
fluids vomited from within the internal, tangled mess of thyself,
opened wounds palettes of coloured grume,
red the thrice-bloodied wine of Deichtre that would nae unturn,
a mother's premonition, a woman's knowing,
prospicience of thy lamentable ending to come,

red the sods of blood left in thy hero's wake,
red the voracious maw of the *dobhar-chú*,
the auspicious fetch ferine,
spurred from its holt by the red scent,
alerted to thy plight by the sudden call of a raven stumbling amongst thy gore,
scouring the plowed ground for remnants of thy cruor,
said water hound fated for one of its kind to have the last laugh,
for what goes around comes around,
one of its kind thy first kill,
for none are immune from the reverberations of the turning of the Wheel
- sometimes even when thou wins, thou loses,
nae matter vision of ravens of the sky and the flakes of snow flecking the plain in commiseration for thy loss
were but sods of hoof-kicked dirt and foam of bridle spat by thy forthcoming creditor's steed,
nae matter the slitting of thine only-man's throat to ease the pain of his passing the burgeoning fruition of thine own,
the ring recognised too late and Connla taken by the spear of fear thy forever shame,
nae matter thy lament o'er Ferdiad's bed of blood, the rude wound, the grievous strike, his body sorely pierced,
nae matter thy betrayal to lust and Aoife's scorn, her rape, her revival, her redress even so,
nae matter thy spurns of Mórrígan and Medb, luna wolven raven queens both,
nae matter losing the teardrop of beauty nor drinking not from thy mother's cups,
nae matter this Emer's six gifts so suitable, this beauty, voice, sweet speech, needlework, wisdom, chastity,
the bosom of my womanhood esteemed so,
nae matter thy swift falling and plighted troth,
thy weapon rested in sweet country mine,
nae matter this self whose cause for spite my steadfast dignity engendered,
nae matter thou knewest I first and last, but oh, nae the least,
nae matter the friendship of the Shadow's thighs and the thrust of spear inside relentless and addictive,
nae matter her tutoring nor her predictions of thy pains,
nae matter her drills and her devices,
nae matter Forgall my father's broken bond,
nae matter the straight swords dyed red nor the dark gatherings of blood about thee,
nae matter Bláthnat's fall forced,
nae matter the burning of the jealous bitches,
nae matter the death of the hound,
my only desire now my spirit to leap the red Beltane fires and be freed of ire by their heat and smoke,
my heart's cleanse and prep for the entering of the Dagda's halls beside thee...

Red this woman's mien and demeanour,
red the malison upon this woman's oft berating tongue,
red the colour of my lust and thou desire,
the lure of the gap of my thighs,
and red, too, the blood of my menses that marked my life-giving womanhood,
that could've, should've, borne thee thine only son,
red the smear of viscid grume upon my cheek,
the inadvertant design of my dole,
as pressed I lips and face against thy mangled, bloodied integument,
sorrow's lament of forced separation and untimely, unsought for divorce

- red be the wound of my heart without thee,
every waking moment the cruelest of deaths ne'erending,
for most all places where dost I look invokes memories of our togetherness,
evocations of our entanglements,
longing for our liaison now severed by violent rending,
only salve to the wound of my heart that believeth I the tenets of that which ne'er dies,
dóigh nádair, the way of nature,
steadfast held by these hands still shaking with remorse and rage at thy passing,
a breath of fresh air amidst such this widow's keening song of sorrow,
thy body to return to the sod from whence it came,
thy soul haloed about thine aura destined to ebb and flow through the aeons,
to alight upon the stellar wind and engender thy light terrene in some other time from now,
to come again, same soul, p'haps same form, thy divine immortality dominant,
to refill thy cauldron's broth and pour thine essence into being,
refreshed and renewed anew, to arise from thy bed of sleep nobly broken,
to embody once again the mantle of thy destiny as king among men,
and, perchance, my only man,
to meet and merge thy soul with mine one last time,
for us to join together, and thee fore'er be my man of service,
and I thy *cétmuinter,* for the rest of all the ages,
in spirit and in essence,
both tangible and ethereal,
though here there be nae more years to give…

Mothaím uaim thú, Anamchara.
Beidh cónaí ort i mo chuimhne croí go deo
(I miss you, Soul friend. You will abide in my heart memory fore'er).

RETROSPECTIVE
SCÁTHACH REVISITED

Ah, Scáthach, my sweetest angel of small death, one question still remains:
did I find you or create you,
remember you or conceive you,
disentomb your essence and exhume remnants of your persona and psyche
from the nether depths of my beginnings,
resurrect your lifeblood
into the systemic drift of my liquids,
rediscover your pulse and heart in mine,
or were you forged in the crucible of my creativity,
written into being upon the platform of my poetry,
a figment of the flesh and blood of my imagination made whole?

Ah, Scáthach, I gave you life within me,
reconceived the intertwining strands of your fishnet web of tensegrity
into my own network of patterns and responses, integrated your whims and desires into mine
- sometimes when I look at the world I see through your Otherworldly eyes,
the salt dried tears of memories best forgotten and the crow's feet of a life half-lived in hidden shadows
replaced with the visceral sensation of perpetual pencilled outline directing focus,
smouldering eyes as war paint wide open and resolute yet with softened gaze,
harshness and tendrils of woundedness gone,
now all-seeing and resolute, fixed upon a greater prize,
your soft-kissed blade's point ever ready to shred and dismantle other's words of derision and sabotage,
as well as projections and mindless reactivity stemming from loss of my own,
its edges honed with an unsurpassable clarity of connective cellular conviction
- everything you and I espoused in the literary bed of your saga we're in the process of embodying,
the word brought to life in the beating hearts of both you and I together, as one.

I've been on a wide orbit outside of myself for too long,
the circumstances of the turnings of the Wheel keeping me disconnected and distracted
from the search for my resilience within the heated cauldrons of my very core
- aye, I'd lost touch with the stillness and the timelessness behind the windows to my soul,
been battered and buffeted by the exigencies of life and the agents of agendas of forced change,
had let the vagaries of others affect my warrior's guile.
There's been many a time I've wished I could've just faded away,

forgetting some of your words of veracity, Scáthach, words that I wrote myself:
that it's not over when we lose, it's only over when we quit,
and that to rue the geography of my destiny is to spit in the face of fate,
and to put my trust into that oblique side of myself
- fuck, I've known that for ever, there's nothing like lying on the ground staring at bone and blood and shattered limb
and knowing - knowing! - that yep, I will find my way through this to visit again your land of milk and honey,
but, as then and as now, I just needed to both hang on and let go,
to trust that you didn't come to me or for me to chaperone me to the other side of the veil,
that your soft midnight breath brings not the cold, hard kiss of steel,
but the promise of the presence of you within the centre of my being as continuation of your teaching,
as furthering of our eternal bond...

When I found myself being increasingly drawn towards you,
succumbing to the gravity of the whirlpool of you,
had I simply unlocked some deeply hidden existential doorway inside myself,
raised the strong, heavy grating of the portcullis barring entrance into you and your devices?
I've wanted to be as you forever, can almost remember when once I was,
or if not was then at the very least was around you,
apprenticed under you, subject to your tutelage and your prurience;
but now I've woken up with you alive inside me,
your freedom from distraction and your harnessing and right execution of power mine,
inheritor of your shadows and your light,
resumed my training with you, your whetting of my stone heart recommencing
- when I first found you (heard your call?) and wrote you into being
who was to know I'd found parts of myself aeons old awaiting release,
that the unlocking of you and untangling the net of the Celtic Love Knot Trilogy
would be akin to remembrance, a reawakening, a rebirthing,
a rekindling of the same phoenixed fires that took Aine's sacrifice and elevated her memory into legend,
or the burning pain of muscle and membrane torn asunder as Macha's body broke upon her sprint's climax,
both their vessels shattered yet their spirits ablaze with the preternatural flames of transformation,
just as you were once exalted through the vehicle of transcending violent rape and desecration
to take place alongside the Dagda and His ilk, welcomed into their pantheon,
and, too, through the delicateness of my rewriting of your saga and your mythos,
feeling the warmth of your aura help form the very words that brought you closer to me
- you became part of my artistry, forged upon the anvil of my initiation in the crucible of you,
compressed the edges of your being to enter the atmospheric pressures of my consciousness,
became my affair with the unknown, my creation, my obsession, my muse, my tutor...

Ah, Scáthach, what was it you really wanted?
What was it that I was searching for, reaching for, whenever it was we first crossed paths,
when our bond of connection began, when our elicit entanglement first manifested?
My soul has always known the geography of my destiny since long before the aforetimes,
as, likewise, has yours of your own, so perhaps we were always destined to be together, as one,
no matter distances of time nor place
- who am I, are we, to question the machinations of the Turner Of The Wheel?
Who am I now with you residing in me?

Who am I without you?

Do you even exist without our bond of connection keeping you vibrant inside of me?
Do I, can I, exist without you?

Envisioning my sword between your breasts earned you my favour,
you became my champion, my apostle, my success - your weaknesses betrayed to me,
as were same of your sister and your lapdog,
as were, too, your perfections and your inclinations,
your natural curves and your hardened edges,
your secrets, your vivacities, your nuances, your wiles...
If I believe in you do you not exist within me, in any and/or all of your manifestations,
as interplanetary succubi, as mortal betrothed, as luminary?
Where do our bodies of light converge, our desires enmesh, our minds blend together?
At what point am I you and you me?

Aye, for all intents and purposes I wrote you into being,
but what if it was actually the other way around?
Did I summon you, or did I answer your call, come on bended knee at your beckoning,
head bowed, neck exposed, awaiting the stroke of cutting that would sever my connection to any other than you,
entangle our essences in universal bond?
Am I a manifestation of your reentering of our world,
the physical endpoint of a game of embodiment played from your Otherworldly domain?
Did you come through me to train me or to be with me,
to allow me access to you or to inhabit and overtake me?
I am a performer by trade and to create you I had to become you for a time,
so as to think like you, to know every inch of you, both inside and out,
had to wear the skin of you and move as you, walk in your shoes and feel the thrust and bosom of you,
penetrate your defences and scale the outer ramparts of you, taste the moistness of your blood red lips
and feel the hungry slice of your hardened steel upon my flesh,
had to envisage your shadow and your light,
had to let myself both be seduced by and seduce you,
had to incarnate as you, had to beget your history, lineage, tales, legend,
had to engender you terrene and tether your emotions and sensations to mine,
just as I had to become, had to embody, every aspect of, Aoife, of Cú Chulainn, of Connla, of Úathach,
let the conceptual seeds of you, them, burst into fruition, let their blood and natures be mine,
just as I've had to live into every character from every poem I've ever written,
fully inhabit every imagined milieu, every envisioned event, every fanciful notion put to paper,
for the pen in this world is more powerful than your sword ever was,
can bring shape and colour and texture, can embrace dimensions and other worlds,
can draw blood or satisfy appetites voracious and radge,
can midwife life and death and birth and rebirth with one, fell swoop,
one final stroke of disconnecting or one swift swirl of deliverance,
can bring both shower clouds of fire or sunshine after rain,
breaths of gold or dawns of darkness, whispers of steadfastness or the bitterness of betrayal,
the pangs of seconding or the friendship of your thighs,

lips that curl in perpetual pleasure or the crushing, scarred weight of cratered tears,
the grimace of wound or the delight of victory,
can strike, parry, feint, swing, twist, stab, turn, and slash language to suit,
can mould and devise, create and develop characters, plots, histories, legends, and sagas,
can give shape - life, even - to suggestions or subtle hints of half-grasped imagery,
to fractures of moments frozen in time - aye, I wrote you into being,
but I know not where the idea of you and the words I used to sculpt you came from…

And what of this 'pre-life' I gave you - where did its inspiration come from? I'm a woman with a history, aye,
but I'm also a being with an even more atavistic chronicle, ancient and bridging both time and space.
I have played many roles and worn many a different guise over the ages,
been farmer, king, maiden,and knight, peasant, hunter, slave, and druid, a sword for hire and a caster of spells,
a thief in the dark and a champion in splendour, a skinwalker, a merchant, a hermit,
owned and frequented brothels and guilds, houses noble and haunted, both taverns and dungeons,
taken empires, butchered and slain,
and been butchered and slain,
been both a being of light and a sordid, foul creature of fey nightmares,
and many more besides, same soul, different forms
- was your original eldritch embodiment drawn from the darkened waters of the well of my memory,
or have I simply read too many stories of faerie and wild, seen too many films of fancy and fantasy,
their narratives seeds for my imaginings, the conception of my creativity?

Only you and I know the real truth.

So, Scáthach, where do we go from here? What happens next in the unravelling of the mystery of you?
It is said, '*Ar scáth a chéile a mhaireann na daoine,*'
meaning, literally, 'people live in each other's shadows'
- not that we hide behind or within each other,
but that we rely on each other for shelter,
shield each other from the burning heat of the sun, help, nurture, support each other in times of hardship and woe
- well, my delectable mistress of shade, somehow we have come to rely on each other for fortification,
for understanding and solace in the maelstrom of circumstance and situation
- aye, we need each other, you and I,
are hilt to each other's swords, salve to each other's wounds of hurt,
each others caress through *ceannlann* armour, our scathes and bruises our trophies
- it seems the only way to avoid being without you is to be with you.

To be as you.

To be you.

Still, nothing comes from nothing and there is a price to be paid for everything,
so what price is it you would have me pay?
What further sacrifice does having you embody inside me demand?
What other blood do I need shed to gain your admiration, your veneration?
I have spent lifetimes seeking such from myself,

the yearning to see myself as paragon desideratum,
the releasing of the stakes and chains that bind me the beginning of the returning of myself to myself by myself,
the reigniting of my light beyond light.
I, too, have learnt to taste the delectation of the other side of pain,
learnt to lean into it and transform it into subspace
- did I learn that from you sometime in the distant past whilst under your tutelage,
or was it a skill I cultivated of my own accord,
garnered from a lifetime's disparate collection of endeavours and adventures,
either sought practice or accident, best of intentions turned sour,
most of which have involved recovering from injury and varying amounts of pain?
You were a great model, Scáthach ni Uanaind, taught all your charges thus,
took us to the edge of the point of no return, scarred and bloodied and exhausted beyond recovery,
yet returned us to our chambers at session's end
- I have lived such in real life, spilled real blood, broken real bones, come back to tell the tales
- is this not *claimhteoireacht* at its finest?

You said - I wrote - that even without the formality of contract
after three times betrayal of thought, word, deed, of succumbing to my chimeric indulgences,
my soul would be *tiomnach* to you - I stand guilty as charged,
for we are bonded, you and I, and there are no secrets harboured kept between us:
nothing and no-one can escape you,
not even I as either your creator or your servant,
just as you will never elude the tendrils of my fixation, my covet, my desire...

So, another question still remains:
I know that you in any any and all of your manifestations were but part of the whole, my whole,
but it's the hole left by our parting that opened in me a wound of sadness, feelings of loss,
the sense of something being just not quite right with you not guiding me,
my hand not upon your corslet or corset, your comely visage or your belt of skulls not my waking vision,
you no longer flickering on the edge of sight as wanton temptation
- we may have parted ways once lifetimes, aeons, ago,
you the irrepressible warrior woman and trainer of heroes of legends risen to divinity,
me but a fledgling harrier destined to re-enter the turnings of the Wheel once again,
but, if it was that you were always part of me, how did such fracturing occur?
Was I ready and brave enough to be reborn through you, or did I draw back from the abyss of you,
reverse the hurtling momentum of your vortex
and separate my being from yours before it was too late, before our, your transformation was complete?
Did it even happen, or, as you represent those parts of me I've hidden and repressed, neglected and avoided,
was it just that I couldn't face you in your Otherworldly guise,
could only avert my gaze and turn away in fear and shame from your newly realised mantle of acceptance,
you servant to higher cause?
Were you, are you, just a part of my asinine deficiencies I must need acknowledge,
those parts of me that I resist, suppress, fear because of shame, guilt, remorse, anger, and more,
manifestations of those intricate and multifaceted indirect fuels for my capacities?
Or are you slated to be my guide, my endgame escort to the castle in the sky, adjudicator of my histories,
my hand held in yours my spirit's final capitulation, its last surrender to destiny?

You've been part of me forever, it seems, but these things you have taught me, Scáthach,
have they not just been skills lying dormant inside myself, awaiting release?
Aye, united in heart, mind, body, and soul, we are bonded, you and I,
and I fear you no longer - and when fear ends, life begins,
and when we embrace our fears they become as weapons:
you said if I have eyes to see I will surpass you, and if I can't, won't, fight for you, than for whom?
You could've turned kings into heroes and ruined empires as courtesan, but no,
you chose the way of courage, the shieldmaiden's way, the mentor's way
- well, it took courage to do some of the things I've done, and some I would retract if I could,
but I have faced many fears, internal and external, including facing and coming to know the 'you' in me,
the beautiful servant and the dangerous, unpredictable mistress,
fought both for and against you with the weapons of my guile and artifice and shrewd manoeuvres,
walked the fine line of life-affirming fear, felt the perfect balance of your blades in my hand,
knowing that there is no space for error when the wrong move could kill
- I have not always avoided the pleasure to avoid the pain, have learnt to surrender to and transmute the pain,
used you as both an instrument for my inspiration and for degradation of my tortured self,
a mirror for reflection and meditation, as both a facility and a pawn,
and in so doing have usurped and released many of the daemons of my mind,
freed myself from the cathartic, cacophonic *stramash* surrounding me,
found stillness with my caprice and whim, made peace with my distractions
- I have dropped the dark cloak of my unknowables and found the spokes of the Turner of the Wheel inside me,
seen my footprints alongside those of the snow-killed calf across the raven blackness of the nightened sky of stars,
reconciled and regathered the shattered and fractured elements of my soul...
I know mistakes would be severely punished by you yet you urged us to commit as many as possible,
though not to make the same mistake twice - I have made multitudes of mistakes in my time,
and more often the same ones over and over,
but I know, too, that to be human is to love, hurt, bleed, smile, cry, rage, and endure,
that in life there will be slips, blunders, oversights, faux pas, flaws, and fuck ups,
and, though you may be watching and guiding and reckoning my lot from your abode in Tír na nÓg,
it is in me where the judge and jurist truly reside - aye, I am both my own worst enemy and my own best friend,
and only when I can lick and bathe my own wounds can I join you in your Otherwordly domain,
stand by your side and scan the horizon of existence for lost souls searching,
relax into the rhythm of endless potential, the calmness of eternity,
the very question of who created whom having become invalid, an unsolvable, useless paradox,
meaningless in the scheme of things, both realities coexisting as plausible possibilities
- again, only you and I know the real truth...

But, aye, as the finishing pages of the tome of our time together on these lands are turned,
as the last chapter comes to a close and we embrace a new beginning,
know that we will always be connected, you and I, no matter distance of time nor space
- the day I've written my final lines and exhausted the wellspring of my creativity
and it is my time to sing both my literary and literal death-songs loud,
to sheath my blood-soaked pen, put down the sword of my discontent
and discard the armoured plates about my heart,
for us to embark upon our endgame saga, our swansong of timelessness,
to disassemble the meat and bone and blood and dirt and dust of my being and blend with your shadow,

when you have finally released me from the breath of you, spent, and taken my hand so as to lead me home,
I will join you gladly, to come to the land beyond the great mering where time passes in a whisper,
to share endless mead and feast and song in perpetual abundance, to drink the health of all that has befell,
to remain vibrant, young, and radiant ever more, my writings relevant as tribute to our legacy,
all inquiry and cogitating matured into redundancy,
all my questions and queries answered,
our parting this world destined to be as sweet as honey.

Ah, Scáthach ni Uanaind, soul friend, tutor, mistress, confidant, conspirator,
we made each other who we are, and I thank you, and I miss you
- you abide in my heart-memory forever,
and when the time is right I will see you on the other side of the veil,
for Tír na nÓg awaits us,
beyond the ninth wave.

GLOSSARIES

Old Irish unless stated otherwise.

Scáthach

Glossary (in order of appearance)

Scáthach   Scáthach ni Uanaind, or Sgathaich, is a figure in the Ulster Cycle of Irish mythology. She is a legendary Scottish warrior woman and martial arts teacher who trains the famous Ulster hero, Cú Chulainn, in the arts of combat. Historical texts describe her homeland as Scotland (Alpeach); she is especially associated with the Isle of Skye, where her residence, Dún Scáith ("Fortress of Shadows"), stands. She is called "the Shadow" and "Warrior Maid" and is the rival and sister of Aoífe, both of whom were daughters of Árd-Greimne of Lethra. She is known as the warrior-woman risen to divinity, and became the Gaelic goddess of the dead, assisting those slain in battle on the passage of the dead to Tir Nan Og (in her duties, she is similar to the Valkyrie of the Norse). In this poem I refer to three aspects of her (different 'incarnations', same soul): she is speaking as the deity, remembering her time as the mortal woman warrior teacher, Scáthach - her connection to that life is still quite vivid for her, and she still trains warriors, though more as a spiritual guide; I also refer to her embodiment before that where I envisioned her as a massive, nebulae-like, interplanetary being that fed on the hearts and souls of the deceased, before choosing to incarnate as Scáthach in order to gain more readily available prey, while still somehow remaining connected to that other part of her; and, of course, as the warrior trainer of legendary status. Upon her mortal death she became deified, transcending (but still fondly remembering) the base desires of her two previous embodiments.

the Otherworld, Hy Breasil   the "*Otherworld*", was a domain of Celtic deities or supernatural beings such as the "Fairy People" (cf, *sidhe*). The Otherworld was considered to be the Celtic version of heaven (or even hell to most Christian writers). Hidden from mortal eyes by strong Otherworld magic, portals to the Otherworld, known as *Sidhe* (*síd* or *sídh*) were situated in all sorts of places, including islands, the dunes, dun-hills, forests, rivers, and lakes - a grand castle or even humble cottage could be the Otherworld, too, which would appear at night for mortals, but would probably vanish in the morning. Normal rule does not apply in the Otherworld: a year may seem to pass there, but in the real world centuries may have passed, time would have seemed to have stood still. Nor do the people who live there age like mortals, they seemed to remain forever young. The Otherworld also seemed to be able to move from one location to another. Or there may be only one Otherworld, but it exists everywhere - in another word, the Otherworld is a paradox. An entrance to the enchanted place may be close by or it could be a place far away. Imagination merges with reality where the island of Hy-Breasil is remembered in both travellers' records and ancient Irish legends.

Tír na nÓg   in the Irish myth cycles, the land of Tír na nÓg is the realm of the Otherworld, the place where the Fae lived and heroes visited on quests. It was a place just outside the realm of man, off to the west, where there was no illness or death or time, but only happiness and beauty.

Alpae   "the Alps", in this case refers to Scotland (otherwise 'Albu', in Irish).

Skyenorthwest   Scáthach's castle reportedly sat on the Isle of Skye, northwest of Scotland.

Dún Scáith   'Fortress of Shadows'. Scáthach's castle.

Dun Scathiag   Dun Sgáthaich Castle, also known as Dunscáith, Dun Scáich, Dun Sgáthaich Castle and Tokavaig, is a ruined castle on the coast of the Isle of Skye, in the north-west of Scotland, said to stand on the ruins of Scáthach's Dún Scáith itself.

carrach   a type of Irish boat with a wooden frame, over which animal skins or hides were once stretched, though now canvas is more usual. It is sometimes anglicised as "curragh".

Manannán mac Lir   ("son of the sea") known as Manannán or Manann, also known as Manannán mac Lir ("son of the sea"),[3] is a warrior and king of the Otherworld in Irish mythology who is associated with the sea and often interpreted as a sea god, usually as member of the Tuatha Dé Danann. He is seen as the ruler and guardian of the Otherworld, and his dominion is referred to by such names as Emain Ablach, Mag Mell (Plain of Delights), or Tír Tairngire (Land of Promise). He is described as over-king of the surviving Tuatha Dé after the advent of humans (Milesians), and uses the mist of invisibility (*féth fíada*) to cloak the whereabouts of his home as well as the sidh dwellings of the others.

Úathach   one of Scáthach's daughters, and thus the niece of her rival and sister, Aoífe. Cú Chulainn, who had recently arrived at Scáthach's fortress-home Dún Scáith (Fortress of Shadows) to be her pupil, accidentally broke one of Úathach's fingers, and Úathach's suitor, Cochar Croibhe, challenged him to single combat despite Úathach's protests. Cú Chulainn killed him and became Uathach's lover. 'Uathach' is the Irish word for autistic.

crann na haithne   Tree of All Knowledge, Good and Evil.

crann-nathair   black tree-snake.

fanfaidh sé i mo chuimhne go deo   it will remain in my memory forever.

Mothaím uaim thú   I miss you.

síoraíocht   eternity.

claiomh   sword.

mo cuisle   my pulse.

mo chroi   my heart.

aoi oinigh   honorary guest.

Nach bhfuil aon onóir níos mó?   'Is there no honour anymore?'

Ach   'but'.

Lasair, Ingean Bhuidhe, Latiaran   other daughters of Scáthach.

Cet and Cuar   Scáthach's two sons who she secretly trains in a sacred yew tree.

géilleadh deiridh   final surrender.

claimhteoireacht   swordsmanship.

luach géilliúna   literally, 'surrender value.'

Fejnnidh   band of warriors.

the Hound   refers to Cú Chulainn, known as the Hound of Ulster. Cú Chulainn was an Irish mythological demigod who appears in the stories of the Ulster Cycle, as well as in Scottish and Manx mythology. He is believed to be an incarnation of the Irish god Lugh, who is also his father. His mother is the mortal Deichtre, sister of Conchobar mac Nessa. Born Sétanta (cf), he gained his better-known name as a child, after killing Culann's fierce guard dog in self defence and offered to take its place until a replacement could be reared. At the age of seventeen he defended Ulaid single-handedly against the armies of queen Medb of Connacht in the famous Táin Bó Cúailnge ("Cattle Raid of Cooley"). It was prophesied that his great deeds would give him everlasting fame, but his life would be a short one. He is known for his terrifying battle frenzy, or ríastrad ("warp spasm"[] or "torque"), in which he became an unrecognisable monster who knew neither friend nor foe. He fights from his chariot, driven by his loyal charioteer Láeg and drawn by his horses, Liath Macha and Dub Sainglend.

Aoife   Aoife, the modern spelling of Aífe (Old Irish), is a feminine given name. The name is probably derived from the Gaelic aoibh, which means "beauty" or "radiance". In Irish mythology she was another daughter of Ard-Giemne, sister and rival to Scáthach, a fierce warrior woman in her own right, beloved of Cú Chulainn for a time, and mother to Connla.

fear fiáin   wild man.

Connla   son of Cú Chulainn and Aoife. He is later killed by Cú Chulainn himself, a death that could have been avoided - when his father left Aoife he handed her a golden thumb-ring with instructions to give it to Connla when he was old enough to wear it, and at that time to send him to him in Ireland. Some sources claim that the thumb-ring was given to Cú Chulainn by his spiritual father, Lugh (hence the line *the ring of the father's father recognised too late*).

Emer   daughter of Forgall Monach, eventual wife of Cú Chulainn. Forgall sends Cú Chulainn to train under Scáthach, secretly hoping he will not return.

'Tá mé níos fearr ná tú.'   'I'm better than you.'

'Is mise an ceann is mó.'   'I'm the greatest.'

Cú Chulainn   (cf., the Hound.)

a bhí ar an sotalach is mó   who was the most arrogant?

Ní bheidh mé i mo sheirbhíseach do dhuine ar bith   'I will not be a servant to anyone'.

Ard-Greimne of Lethra   father to both Scáthach and Aoife, his name translates to "High Fort of Lethra", a site commonly identified as Lejre near Roskilde, seat of the ancient Danish kings and a centre for heathen sacrifice. In Irish mythology, Lethra is also known as the place of red brightness, and is the dwelling place of the Irish Fomorian triple god known by such names as Buain, Buinni Buanainech, Buinne Mac Goll (Eternal One, Reaper, Wave, Rush of Water) Iall o'Buidhne (Of the Yellow Grain) Árd-Greimne (High Power) Cichol Grinchenghos (The Footless) Gabur. Father of the goddesses Aeb (Fire), Aoife-Scáthach: (Shadowy Queen/s), Mórrígan (Great Queen). He is referred to as the King of Scythia in one story.

bandraíodóir   from *ban-* ("female") + *draíodóir* ("magician"). Literally, 'enchantress'.

ainse saor   cheap whore.

sclábhaí airnéise   sexual slave.

ceann slea   spear head.

scáthphuipéad   shadow puppet.

friendship of my thighs   ie, initiate sexually.

línitheoir súl   eye liner.

All Heal   *Prunella vulgaris* (known as common self-heal, heal-all, woundwort, heart-of-the-earth, carpenter's herb, brownwort and blue curls) is a herbaceous plant in the genus *Prunella*. It is edible: the young leaves and stems can be eaten raw in salads; the plant in whole can be boiled and eaten as a potherb; and the aerial parts of the plant can be powdered and brewed in a cold infusion to make a beverage. It also can be boiled in water, which is used to wash and bathe in order to relieve muscle pain. It is a Parasitic plant, ie. it obtains all or part of its nutrition from another plant (the host) without contributing to the benefit of the host and, in some cases, causing extreme damage to the host.

... the belly spear...   the Gáe Bulg (also Gáe Bulga, Gáe Bolg, Gáe Bolga), meaning "spear of mortal pain/death", "gapped/notched spear", or "belly spear", was the name of the spear of Cú Chulainn in the Ulster Cycle of Irish mythology. It was given to him by Scáthach, his martial arts teacher and warrior woman, and its technique was taught only to him. It was made from the bone of a sea monster, the *Coinchenn*, that had died while fighting another sea monster, the *Curruid*. It had to be made ready for use on a stream and cast from the fork of the toes. It entered a man's body with a single wound, like a javelin, then opened into thirty barbs. Only by cutting away the flesh could it be taken from that man's body.

Cet and Cuar   Scáthach's sons from an ex unnamed man, trained in secret within a secret yew tree.

Gáe Bulg   (cf).

... scarlet gushes of blood striking upon many variously-cloven shields, alone in great hardship against the host, a sick-bed awaiting thee after a wound of revenge at the final breach in face of slaughters of great ferocity?   pieces of this section of text are taken from The Words of Scáthach; Verba Scáthaige; Rawlinson B 512; Egerton 1782; Egerton 88; Royal Irish Academy 23 N 10; Trans. P. L. Henry.

Queen Medb   ruled from Cruachan (now Rathcroghan, County Roscommon). She is the enemy (and former wife) of Conchobar mac Nessa, king of Ulaid, and is best known for starting the *Táin Bó Cúailnge* ("The Cattle Raid of Cooley") to steal Ulster's prize stud bull, Donn Cúailnge. Medb is strong-willed, ambitious, cunning, and promiscuous, and is an archetypal warrior queen and sovereignty goddess.

geasa   spells, or sacred prohibitions. Specifically, a geas can be compared with a curse or, paradoxically, a gift. If someone under a geas violates the associated taboo, the infractor will suffer dishonor or even death. On the other hand, the observing of one's geas is believed to bring power. Often it is women who place geasa upon men. In some cases the woman turns out to be a goddess or other sovereignty figure. Cú Chulainn's geasa that he broke was to never taste the meat of a hound.

Mórrígan   the Mórrígan is the term given to Goddess Mórrígan, one of the triple Goddesses in Celtic mythology. She represented the circle of life and was associated with both birth and death. Her name translates to "great queen" or "phantom queen". She was a shape-shifter and looked over the rivers, fresh water and lakes. She is also described as being the patroness of revenge, magic, priestesses, night, prophecy and witches.

betrayed by thrice bloodied wine of Deichtre that would not unturn...   Deichtre was Cú Chulainn's mortal mother. As he approached his final fight she offered him a farewell cup, full of wine to give him her blessing, but as he lifted the cup to his lips, the wine turned into blood. He threw it away, and Deichtre refilled the cup with wine, but again it turned to blood. Determined that her son would not go into battle without her blessing to protect him, Deichtre filled the cup again, and offered it again, but the wine turned into blood a third time, and Cuchulainn could not drink from it.

ríastrad   warp spasm or torque of Cú Chulainn.

...a woman's scorn, a wife and mother's relentless pursuit, coming to fruition in Gleann na mBodhar, by one of the daughters of the sorcerer's six, in guise of Niamh...   one of the daughters of Catalan magically disguised herself as Niamh, a friend of Cuchulainn's, and went into Gleann na mBodhar. She told him he was needed in battle, to pick up his arms and enter the fray. Cuchulainn, of course, leapt at the challenge, leading to his demise.

Gleann na mBodhar   Gleann na mBodhar; the Valley of the Deaf. It was called this because no sound from outside could enter the valley, so no matter what magical noises the children of Calatin brewed up, Cú Chulainn would not hear them there.

Niamh   woman friend of Cú Chulainn.

lore of the Old Night   ancient druidic wisdom and old magics taught to Calatin's six children by Mórrígan and/or Queen Medb..

Lugaid Cú Roi, in league with the sons of Calatin   warrior/s who defeated Cú Chulainn (Lugaid, son of Cú Roí, threw the fatal spear.)

Calatin   (also spelt Calatan) one of the men Cú Chulainn struck down was Calatin, a great sorcerer. He left behind a pregnant wife, who gave birth to sextuplets: three girls and three boys. She raised all of her children with all the arts of druidry and sorcery, and instilled in them that they were to avenge their father's death as soon as they were old enough. Cú Chulainn knew nothing of this, carried on with his life for many years, but when the time was ripe, the sons and daughters of Calatin set out to take their revenge on the man who had killed their father.

events set in place by the long-smouldering wrath of Queen Madb of Connacht for your slighting of her, for undying is the wrath of a queen...   Cúchulainn had made many powerful enemies, but none more bitter and dark than Queen Medb of

Connacht, whose armies he had routed and whose ambitions he'd thwarted. Year after year she brooded on the humiliations visited upon her, holding council with the families of those he'd slain, commiserating with their tears, but the only ones that were of any use to her schemes were the three sons and, in particular, three daughters of Calatin, whom she trained in the arts of dark magic. Medb, or Maeve, was queen of Connaught in the Ulster Cycle of Irish mythology.

Forgall   Forgall Monach or Manach is a character in the Ulster Cycle of Irish mythology. He lives at Luglochta Loga (the gardens of Lugh) in Lusk, County Dublin. Cúchulainn falls in love with his younger daughter, Emer, but Forgall is opposed to the match, ostensibly because his older daughter, Fial, is not yet married. He suggests that Cúchulainn should go to Alba (Scotland) to train in arms under the warrior-woman Scáthach, hoping the ordeal will lead to his death. While he was away he offers Emer to Lugaid mac Nóis, a king of Munster, but when he hears that Emer loves Cúchulainn, Lugaid refuses her hand. When Cúchulainn returns from Scotland fully trained, Forgall still refuses to let him marry Emer. Cúchulainn storms Forgall's fortress, killing twenty-four of Forgall's men, abducts Emer and steals Forgall's treasure. Forgall himself falls from the ramparts to his death.

Breas   the original leader of the Tuatha was Nuada (cf) but, having lost an arm in battle, it was decreed that he could not rightly be king. That honour went to Breas, a tribesman of Fomorian descent. His seven year rule was not a happy one however, and he was ousted by his people who had become disenchanted with hunger and dissent. Nuada was installed as King, resplendent with his replacement arm made from silver.

Children of Danu   term used for the Tuatha Dé Danann, which translates as "people of the goddess Danu," a primordial mother goddess.the Tuath(a) Dé Danann (meaning "the folk of the goddess Danu"), also known by the earlier name Tuath Dé ("tribe of the gods"), were a supernatural race in Irish mythology.They are thought to represent the main deities of pre-Christian Gaelic Ireland.The Tuatha Dé Danann constitute a pantheon whose attributes appeared in a number of forms throughout the Celtic world.The Tuath Dé dwell in the Otherworld but interact with humans and the human world. They are associated with ancient passage tombs, such as Brú na Bóinne, which were seen as portals to the Otherworld.

betrayed your father's adherence to oath, truth, and law...   Cú Chulainn is Lugh's son, and sometimes said or believed to be an incarnation of Him. Lugh, or Lug, was one of the most prominent gods in Irish mythology. A member of the Tuatha Dé Danann, Lugh is portrayed as a warrior, a king, a master craftsman and a saviour. He is associated with skill and mastery in multiple disciplines, including the arts. He is also associated with oaths, truth and the law, and therefore with rightful kingship. Lugh is linked with the harvest festival of Lughnasadh, which bears his name. His most common epithets are Lámfada, "of the long arm", possibly for his skill with a spear or his ability as a ruler, and Samildánach ("equally skilled in many arts").

spaewife   (Scottish) a woman who is believed to be able to predict the future.

Land of Eternal Youth   (cf.,Tír na nÓg).

sluagh   spirits of the restless dead.

woad   a yellow-flowered European plant of the cabbage family. It was formerly widely grown in the UK as a source of blue dye, which was extracted from the leaves after they had been dried, powdered, and fermented. It was used as war paint for intimidation by Celtic warriors.

where warriors in their prime fought either naked for intimidation   the typical Celtic warrior appears to have fought bare chested with a cloak. Roman triumphs typically show warriors with trousers, cloak and shoes, which was akin to being naked when compared to being clad in armour.

lamellar cuirass   leather cuirass designed to protect the torso with a reinforced leather breastplate and stiff backplate. Made from overlapping, vegetable-tanned, full-grain leather, shaped to deflect blows while still offering great flexibility.

drakania   a female serpent or dragon, sometimes with humanlike features.

mar scáth   literally, 'as shadow'.

... beyond the ninth wave   in Irish mythology, the Ninth Wave is the barrier that separates the Earthly world from the *Hy Breasil,* or 'otherworld'. The legends told of a mystical place that lay beyond the West Coast of Ireland, far out across the sea. This island was invisible to the naked human eye and only accessible if you managed to survive the mighty onslaught of the ninth wave. The 'ninth wave' may simply be an old seafarer's term for the phenomenon of the 'giant wave' – a rare occurrence, described as a huge wall of water that seemed to come out of nowhere on the back of a series of smaller waves. This wave would have had deadly consequences for a flimsy fishing vessel, hence the fear that such a wave could carry its victim off of the mortal plane. (The bodies of those lost at sea were very rarely recovered, so it's possible that the idea that they had been swept away to some mysterious island would have provided comfort for families left behind.)

cioch   Scottish Gaelic for breast or mammary gland.

aoibh   smile.

mian leis an bhfeoil   literally, 'desires of the flesh'.

Ferdiad   son of Damán, son of Dáire, of the Fir Domnann, is a warrior of Connacht in the Ulster Cycle of Irish mythology. In the Táin Bó Cúailnge, Ferdiad finds himself on opposite sides of the war to his best friend and foster-brother, Cú Chulainn, with whom he had trained in arms under the renowned warrior woman Scáthach. He and Cú Chulainn are equal in all martial feats, with two exceptions: the Gáe Bulg, a barbed spear which Scáthach has taught only Cuchulainn to use; and Ferdiad's horny skin, which no weapon can pierce. When Ailill and Medb, king and queen of Connacht, invade Ulaid (Ulster) to steal the bull Donn Cúailnge, their progress is held up by Cú Chulainn, who demands single combat. After Cuchulainn has defeated a series of Connacht champions, Medb sends for Ferdiad, but he only agrees to fight Cuchulainn after Findabair, Ailill and Medb's daughter, has seductively plied him with alcohol,and Medb has variously bribed, shamed and goaded him to do so. They fight in the ford for three days, first fighting with 8 swords, darts, and spears, then fighting with "throwing-spears" and lances, and finally moving on to "heavy, hard-smiting swords." It is on the third day that Ferdiad starts to gain the upper hand. At this point, Cú Chulainn calls to his charioteer, Laeg, for the Gáe Bulg, which he floats down the river to him. Cú Chulainn throws a light spear at Ferdiad's chest, causing him to raise his shield, and then picks up the Gáe Bolga between his toes and thrusts it through his anus upon which the barbs spread throughout his body, killing him. The Gáe Bulg is then removed from Ferdiad's body by Laeg, and Cú Chulainn mourns Ferdiad's death, praising his strength and bravery: "Ah, Ferdiad, betrayed to death./Our last meeting, oh, how sad!/Thou to die I to remain./Ever sad our long farewell!" Ferdiad's name has been interpreted as meaning "man of smoke", "man of the pair" or "man of two feet".

mar scáth   as shadow.

Scáthach ni Uanaind   (cf).

baintside   (also spelt *bean-sidhe*) 'woman of the fairy', the *baintside* or banshee is a harbinger of death. According to legend, she appears to members of certain Irish families to warn them of impending death. Banshee are often described as a woman in white with a ghastly pale complexion and white hair. She appears as a wailing spirit and sometimes wears the bloodstained clothing of the person about to die.Banshee is said to be a fairy in Irish legend and her scream is believed to be an omen of death. The scream is also called 'caoine' which means 'keening' and is a warning that there will be an imminent death in the family. Other Irish mythology stories relating to the Banshee say that she is the ghost of a young girl that suffered a brutal death and her spirit remains to warn family members that a violent death is imminent. It is said that this Banshee appears as an old woman with rotten teeth and long fingernails. She wears rags and has blood red eyes that are so filled with hate that looking directly into them will cause immediate death! This Banshee's mouth is always open as her piercing scream torments the souls of the living.

An t-Eilean Sgitheanach   Isle of Skye.

Tír Tairngire   other Old Irish names for the Otherworld include Tír Tairngire (Land of Promise/Promised Land), Tír fo Thuinn (Land under the Wave), Mag Mell (Plain of Delight/Delightful Plain), Ildathach (Multicoloured Place), and Emain Ablach (the Isle of Apple Trees).

Samhain   Samhain is a pagan religious festival originating from an ancient Celtic spiritual tradition. In modern times, Samhain (a Gaelic word pronounced "sow-win") is usually celebrated from October 31 to November 1 to welcome in the harvest and usher in "the dark half of the year."

Beltane   on the cusp between spring and summer, Beltane is a fire festival that celebrates the fertility of the coming year. Introduction. Beltane. Beltane is a Celtic word which means 'fires of Bel' (Bel was a Celtic deity). It is a fire festival that celebrates the coming of summer and the fertility of the coming year.

sidhe   sidhe (*shee*) are considered to be a distinct race, quite separate from human beings yet who have had much contact with mortals over the centuries. The Gaelic word Sidhe has three meanings: "Barrow" or "tumulus": ancient burial mounds often filled with treasure; "Fairy" or "Fairies" (the word is singular and plural); and, as the sidhe that are Fairies often live within the sidhe that are barrows, sidhe also means "Fairy mound." In this text the use of the word sidhe refers to a portal or gateway to the Otherworld.

immrama   an immram is a class of Old Irish tales concerning a hero's sea journey to the Otherworld (ie, Tír na nÓg and Mag Mell).The immrama are identifiable by their focus on the exploits of the heroes during their search for the Otherworld, usually located in these cases in the islands far to the west of Ireland. The hero sets out on his voyage for the sake of adventure or to fulfill his destiny, and generally stops on other fantastic islands before reaching his destination. He may or may not be able to return home again.

Lir   Lir, or Ler, is a sea god in Irish mythology. His name suggests that he is a personification of the sea, rather than a distinct deity. He is named Allód in early genealogies, and corresponds to the Llŷr of Welsh mythology. Lir is chiefly an ancestor figure, and is the father of the god Manannán mac Lir, who appears frequently in medieval Irish literature. Lir appears as the titular king in the tale The Children of Lir. In this poem 'the horses of Lir' refer to the endless expanse of the waves of the sea, as well as referencing the myth itself.

feast of Goibniu   the feast of Goibniu was bestowed on the warriors of the Tuatha Dé by Manannán to protect them from sickness and decay. Goibniu is said to be owner of the Glas Gaibhnenn, the magical cow of abundance, and in surviving folklore also has a magical bridle for the cow.

cailleach feasa   witch of knowledge.

cailleach piseog   witch of superstition.

imbas forosnai   a gift of clairvoyance or visionary ability practised by the gifted poets of ancient Ireland. In Old Irish, Imbas imeans "inspiration," and specifically refers to the sacred poetic inspiration believed to be possessed by the fili (Old Irish: inspired, visionary poets) in Early Ireland. Forosnai means "illuminated" or "that which illuminates". Imbas forosnai involved the practitioner engaging in sensory deprivation techniques in order to enter a trance and receive answers or prophecy.

banfhili   "woman-poet".

Fedelm   Fedelm is a female prophet and *fili*, or learned poet, in the Ulster Cycle of Irish mythology.

Plain of Muirtheimne   site of *Cú Chulainn*'s death, also where he grew up as Setanta.

Setanta   Cú Chulainn's birth name.

Culann's hound   in the Ulster Cycle of Irish mythology, Culann was a smith whose house was protected by a ferocious watchdog, most like;ly a type of Celtic hound (they were a breed of dogs in Gaelic Ireland described in Irish legend They may have corresponded to the Greyhound, Scottish Deerhound, Irish Wolfhound, or ancestors of all of these breeds.). Culann invited Conchobar mac Nessa, king of Ulster, and his retinue to a feast at his house. On the way Conchobar saw his young nephew Sétanta playing hurling, and was so impressed he invited the boy to join him at the feast. Sétanta told him he would catch him up once the game was over. The feast got underway, and Culann asked Conchobar if he was expecting anyone else. Conchobar, who had forgotten about Sétanta, answered no, and Culann unleashed his watchdog. When Sétanta arrived he was forced to kill the dog in self-defence, and out of obligation offered to take its place until a replacement could be reared (for this he was renamed *Cú Chulainn* – "Culann's hound")

Láeg   Láeg mac Riangabra - Cú Chulainn's charioteer.

Liath Macha   sometimes referred to as the 'Gray of Macha' - one of Cú Chulainn's horses, referred to as the 'king of horses'.

Cathbad   the chief druid in the court of King Conchobar mac Nessa in the Ulster Cycle of Irish Mythology, also said to be his father..

ceannlann armour   worn by Celtic warriors, it is a layer of metal scales sewn onto linen, which is, in turn, sewn onto chain armour, creating a very effective multi-layer armour that could cover the entire body.

dúil eagla-bhunaithe   fear-based desire.

Plain of Ill-Luck, Glen of Peril, Bridge of Leaping   obstacles on the way to Dun Scaith.

dùil   Scottish-Gaelic feminine noun for person or thing that is a source of hope, belief that something wished for can happen, that which is expected or looked for, also the act or state of expecting.

leannán cuileáilte   discarded lover.

striapachas   prostitute, prostitution.

tiomnach   dedicated, or testamentary.

Old Sligachan Bridge   The legend of Sligachan states that if you dip your face in the river water by the Sligachan Bridge, you will be granted eternal beauty. It is where Cú Chulainn and Scáthach first met and fought. Reference: https://www.wingingtheworld.com/sligachan-bridge-isle-of-skye/

áilleacht síoraí   eternal beauty.

claíomh órdhoirn   golden sword, gold-spine sword, sword with a golden hilt.

Crom Cruaich   pagan god of pre-Christian Ireland. According to Christian writers, he was propitiated with human sacrifice and his worship was ended by Saint Patrick.

Naomh Pádraig   St Patrick.

Magh Slaecht   In Pre-Christian times the small area where the Crom Cruaich idol stood at Kilnavert was originally named Fossa Slécht or Rath Slécht and it is from this small location that the wider Magh Slécht area received its name. In 1911 BC during the reign of Fodbgen, the Firbolg High-King of Ireland, the name Magh Senaig was changed to Magh Slécht (*The plain of prostrations*) as it became the nationwide centre of the cult of the god Crom Cruaich.

Ériu   Old Irish term for Ireland.

formorian   the Fomorians (Old Irish: Fomóire, Modern Irish: Fomhóraigh or Fomhóire) are a supernatural race in Irish mythology. They are often portrayed as hostile and monstrous beings who come from under the sea or the earth. Later, they were portrayed as giants and sea raiders. In this context used to describe the scale of the battle between Scáthach and Cuchulainn. In some texts it even suggests the very mountains and valleys of the Isle of Skye itself were created by their footprints.

liopaí dearga fola   blood red lips.

tiomantas   commitment.

misneach   courage.

buanseasmhacht   resilience.

cathbharr   helmet, also battlefield.

fíor-fheiceáil   true seeing.

neart laoch   hero strength, strength of heroes, warrior strength.

conradh anam   soul contract.

scáth   shadow.

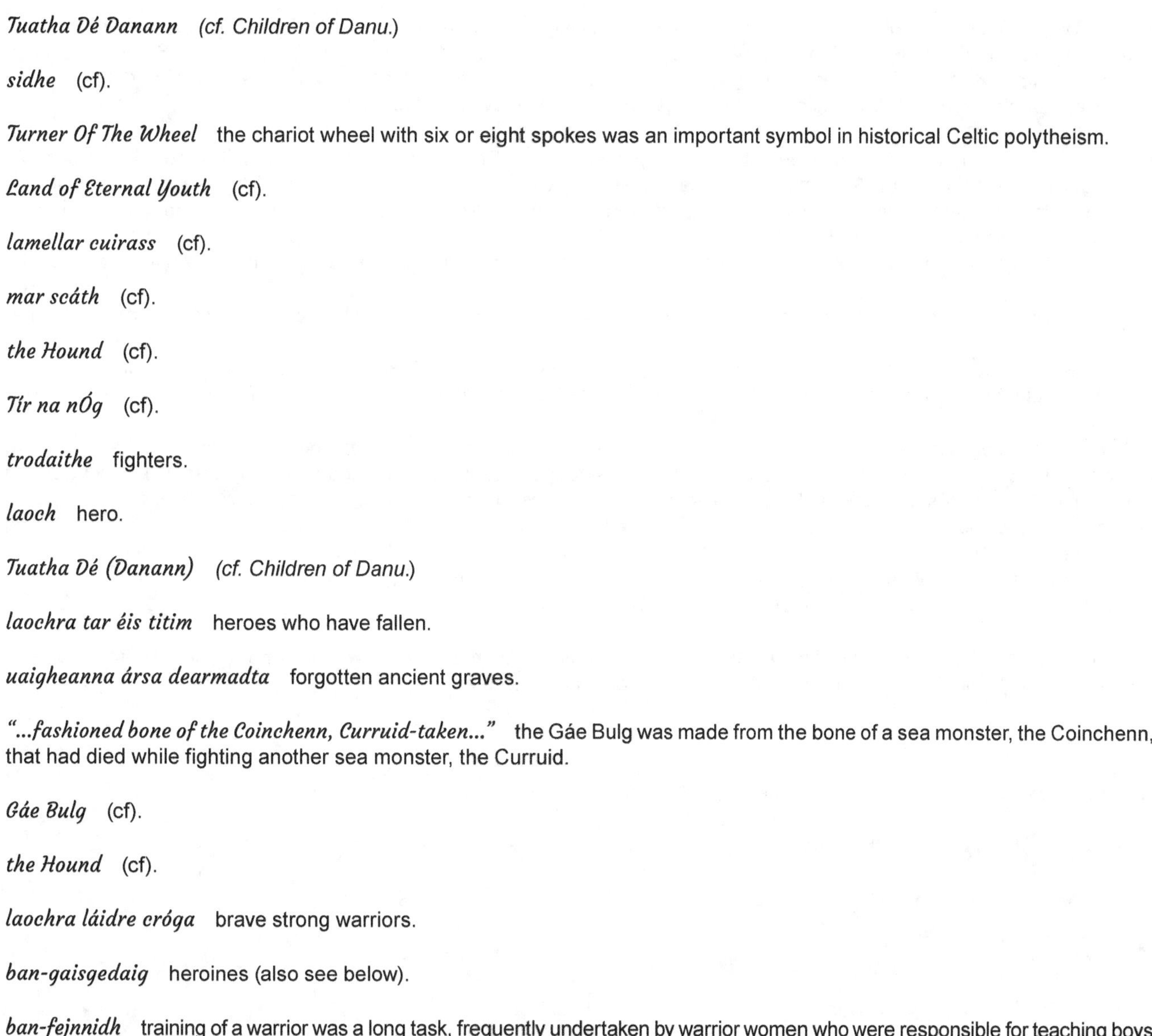

Tuatha Dé Danann   (cf. Children of Danu.)

sidhe   (cf).

Turner Of The Wheel   the chariot wheel with six or eight spokes was an important symbol in historical Celtic polytheism.

Land of Eternal Youth   (cf).

lamellar cuirass   (cf).

mar scáth   (cf).

the Hound   (cf).

Tír na nÓg   (cf).

trodaithe   fighters.

laoch   hero.

Tuatha Dé (Danann)   (cf. Children of Danu.)

laochra tar éis titim   heroes who have fallen.

uaigheanna ársa dearmadta   forgotten ancient graves.

"...fashioned bone of the Coinchenn, Curruid-taken..."   the Gáe Bulg was made from the bone of a sea monster, the Coinchenn, that had died while fighting another sea monster, the Curruid.

Gáe Bulg   (cf).

the Hound   (cf).

laochra láidre cróga   brave strong warriors.

ban-gaisgedaig   heroines (also see below).

ban-fejnnidh   training of a warrior was a long task, frequently undertaken by warrior women who were responsible for teaching boys the arts of combat and of love. Specific titles were given to these classes of female warriors such as BAN-GAISGEDAIG (BAN-meaning woman and a derivative of GAS which means young warrior) and BAN-FEJNNIDH (which combines BAN with FEINNIDH meaning 'band of warriors') so it seems they were classed according to age and experience, possibly starting their training as very young girls.

Ana   In Irish mythology, Anu (or Ana, sometimes given as Anann or Anand) is a goddess. She may be a goddess in her own right, or an alternate name for Danu.

Brigid   Brigid, meaning 'exalted one', is a goddess of pre-Christian Ireland. She appears in Irish mythology as a member of the Tuatha Dé Danann, the daughter of the Dagda and wife of Bres, with whom she had a son named Ruadán. She is associated with the spring season, fertility, healing, poetry and smithcraft. Brigid was "the goddess whom poets adored" and that she had two sisters: Brigid the healer and Brigid the smith. This suggests she may have been a triple deity.

Epona   Epona is unique in that she was not renamed or married to a Roman husband—she came to Rome as herself and blended quite smoothly into the Roman military. She is the only known Celtic deity to have been embraced in her original form by the Empire, with little adjustment made to her list of attributes. In Gallo-Roman religion, Epona was a protector of horses, donkeys, and mules. She was particularly a goddess of fertility, as shown by her attributes of a patera, cornucopia, ears of grain and the presence of foals in some sculptures. She and her horses might also have been leaders of the soul in the after-life ride.

Eriu   Eriu was a goddess of ancient Ireland. She is often seen as a personification of the land of Ireland itself, as it was after her that this small island was ultimately named. The name Eriu comes from Old Irish, which can probably be translated as something along the lines of *fullness, bounty, or abundance*. This gives the name of *Ireland* itself the meaning "land of abundance." Eriu was the daughter of Delbáeth and Ernmas, father and mother respectively, both of the tribe of the Tuatha Dé Danann.

Mórrígan   the Mórrígan or Mórrígan, also known as Morrígu, is a figure from Irish mythology. The name is Mór-Ríoghain in Modern Irish, and it has been translated as "great queen" or "phantom queen". The Mórrígan is mainly associated with war and fate, especially with foretelling doom, death or victory in battle. In this role she often appears as a crow, the badb. She incites warriors to battle and can help bring about victory over their enemies. The Mórrígan encourages warriors to do brave deeds, strikes fear into their enemies, and is portrayed washing the bloodstained clothes of those fated to die. She is most frequently seen as a goddess of battle and war and has also been seen as a manifestation of the earth- and sovereignty-goddess, chiefly representing the goddess's role as guardian of the territory and its people.

Cailleach   Cailleach is a common word in both Scottish and Irish Gaelic meaning "old woman" or "hag",derived from Caillech, a term meaning "veiled one" in Old Gaelic. Also means 'woman who uses magic'.

Fejnnidh   (cf).

trodaithe cumhachta   literally 'power fighters'.

Immrama na Anam   the 'death journey' to the Otherworld.

fear nó bean   'man or woman'.

Tír na nÓg   (cf).

laochra misniúla   courageous warriors.

sciatháin na n-éin   shieldmaidens.

naimhde anaithnid   unknown enemies.

Hy Braesil   (cf).

Dun Scaith   (cf).

Oweynagat   Oweynagat or the 'Cave of Cats' (or 'Cath', meaning battle) has to be one of the more unusual and unique sites in Ireland. The cave features a souterrain with a lintel supporting the entrance but then leads into a naturally formed cave. Oweynagat features heavily in Irish mythology, mainly because of its placement near Queen Medb's fort which was at the center of the ancient Connaught capital of 'Cruachan'. The cave was said to be the actual birthplace of Queen Medb herself. The cave continued to be known as a place of power, acting as a portal to the other-world - its power was extremely pronounced near Samhain, as this was when the veil between the worlds lessened.

Mórrígan   (cf).

Ellén Trechend   the Ellén Trechend is a three-headed monster referred to in Irish mythology. It is mentioned in the text Cath Maige Mucrama (The Battle of Mag Mucrima) as having emerged from the cave of Cruachan (Rathcroghan, County Roscommon) and laid Ireland waste until it was killed by the Ulaid poet and hero Amergin, Its name is difficult to interpret: trechend means "three-headed", but ellén is an obscure word. One translator interprets it as a "swarm of three-headed creatures"

Amergin   Amergin Glúingel ("white knees") (also spelled Amhairghin Glúngheal) or Glúnmar ("big knee") is a bard, druid and judge for the Milesians in the Irish Mythological Cycle. A number of poems attributed to Amergin are part of the Milesian mythology.

Brú na Bóinne   Brú na Bóinne, which means the 'palace' or the 'mansion' of the Boyne, refers to the area within the bend of the River Boyne which contains one of the world's most important prehistoric landscapes. The archaeological landscape within Brú na Bóinne is dominated by the three well-known large passage tombs, Knowth, Newgrange and Dowth, built some 5,000 years ago in the Neolithic or Late Stone Age. An additional ninety monuments have been recorded in the area giving rise to one of the most significant archaeological complexes in terms of scale and density of monuments and the material evidence that accompanies them. The Brú na Bóinne tombs, in particular Knowth, contain the largest assemblage of megalithic art in Western Europe. Brú na Bóinne was inscribed as a World Heritage Site in December 1993 in recognition of its outstanding universal value. The scale of passage tomb construction, the important concentration of megalithic art as well as the range of sites and the long continuity of activity were cited as reasons for the site's inscription.

áes sídhe   the "People of the Sídhe" (another name for the Tuatha Dé Danann).

Eochid son of Erc   Eochaid (modern spelling: Eochaidh), son of Erc, son of Rinnal, of the Fir Bolg became High King of Ireland when he overthrew Fodbgen. He was the first king to establish a system of justice in Ireland. No rain fell during his reign, only dew, and there was a harvest every year. His wife was the Goddess Tailtiu. Eochaid named his capital after her (modern Teltown, County Meath) and held a festival there every August. He ruled for ten years, until the Fir Bolg were defeated by the Tuatha Dé Danann in the first Battle of Magh Tuiredh. During the fighting Eochaid was overcome by thirst, but the druids of the Tuatha Dé hid all sources of water from him with their magic. As he searched for water, he was found and killed by the Mórrígan on the strand at Beltra Co. Sligo. According to tradition, he was buried under Eochy's Cairn.

Fir Bolg   the Fir Bolg (also spelt Firbolg and Fir Bholg) are the fourth group of people to settle in Ireland. They are descended from the Muintir Nemid, an earlier group who abandoned Ireland and went to different parts of Europe. Those who went to Greece became the Fir Bolg and eventually returned to the now-uninhabited Ireland. After ruling it for some time, they are overthrown by the invading Tuatha Dé Danann.

Nuada Airgeadlámh   in Irish mythology, Nuada or Nuadu (modern spelling: Nuadha), known by the epithet Airgetlám (Airgeadlámh, meaning "silver hand/arm"), was the first king of the Tuatha Dé Danann. He is also called Nechtan, Nuadu Necht and Elcmar, and is the husband of Boann. He is mostly known from the tale in which he loses his arm or hand in battle, and thus his kingship, but regains it after being magically healed by Dian Cécht. Nuada is thought to have been a god.

Dian Cécht   in Irish mythology, Dian Cécht (also known as Cainte or Canta) was the god of healing, the healer for the Tuatha Dé Danann.

Breas   Breas became King of the Tuatha De Danann when Nuadu was wounded in battle against the Fir Bolgs. He ruled unjustly and broke with the tradition of providing entertainment for his subjects. His rule as King of the Tuatha De Danann was oppressive. He connived with the Formorians, exacting taxes from his people. He made slaves of the Daghda, God of Wisdom, and Oghma the poet. He humiliated them by making them carry loads of firewood.

Fomóire   the Fomorians (Old Irish: Fomóire, Modern Irish: Fomhóraigh or Fomhóire) are a supernatural race in Irish mythology. They are often portrayed as hostile and monstrous beings who come from under the sea or the earth. Later, they were portrayed as giants and sea raiders. They are enemies of Ireland's first settlers and opponents of the Tuatha Dé Danann. However, their relationship with the Tuath Dé is complex and some of their members intermarry and have children. The Fomorians have thus been likened to the jötnar of Norse mythology. The Fomorians seem to have been gods who represent the harmful or destructive powers of nature; personifications of chaos, darkness, death, blight and drought. The Tuath Dé, in contrast, seem to represent the gods of growth and civilization.

Milesian   the Milesians were the final race to settle in Ireland. They represent the Irish people. The Milesians are Gaels who sail to Ireland from Iberia (Hispania) after spending hundreds of years travelling the earth. When they land in Ireland they contend with the Tuatha Dé Danann, who represent the pagan gods. The two groups agree to divide Ireland between them: the Milesians take the world above, while the Tuath Dé take the world below (i.e. the Otherworld).

féth fíada   cloak of concealment.

chun d'iontaobhas a chur i dom   to put your trust in me.

claimhteoireacht   swordsmanship.

seanchaí   The seanchaí were the storytellers of Ireland; the word means 'bearer of old lore'. These storytellers were a major source of entertainment before the spread of the written word, or the coming of film, radio and television. People would gather round the fire and the seanchaí would enthral them. Some of these storytellers travelled from town to town, and many renowned seanchaí came from the travelling community.

Mothaím uaim thú, Anamchara. Beidh cónaí ort i mo chuimhne croí go deo   I miss you, Soul friend. You will abide in my heart memory forever.

Aoife

Notes

After completing 'Scáthach' I knew that I couldn't leave my take on her story as a stand-alone, and the idea of creating a trilogy was born - 'Aoife' is the natural extension of 'Scáthach', her perspective on their relationship as Scáthach's twin sister and her version of events as it unfolds over time, and the third piece about the man who kind of comes between them for a time, Cú Chulainn.

As with the creation of 'Scáthach', extensive research was involved with 'Aoife', but a lot of the groundwork had already been done - the historical/mythological/imagined setting (Scáthach's pre-incarnate embodiment, her role as a trainer of warriors, her ascent to divinity, her "charge" to continue and train warriors/warrioresses of the mind and body), references to Ard-Greimne, their father, to 'the Hound' Cú Chulainn, the Otherworld, sluagh, Old Sligachan Bridge, and more, all assume the reader has previously read 'Scáthach' and its/her glossary. There are also several references to and a number of lines directly taken from 'Scáthach' that a savvy reader will notice, used to link the poems and its characters' stories together.

Info: Celtic and Old Irish peoples believed in reincarnation, knowing that this life was not their only life, and that, depending on how they'd spent their time here on this embodiment, they could come back as anything from an animal of various forms to an object of nature, possibly even as another human.

It is also true that one of the things the Celts and early Irish people feared was the idea of the 'sky falling on their heads' - possibly a racial memory of natural disasters happening after meteorite showers or post-volcanic ashen skies (my ideas) interpreted as negative divinely wrought consequences, the heavens falling, as it were. I have Aoife refer to the "...night sky falling..." as 'heaven*less*' because of her fear of and animosity towards Scáthach, which by extension she applies to divinity/the Otherworld in general.

The mute swan is a native swan to Ireland, and 'pen' is the term for a female swan.

Stories of (the other) Aoife

Aoife (The Bright One) was the daughter of Ailill of Aran, foster daughter to Bodhbh Dearg. the King of the Tuatha Dé Danann, and younger sister to Aobh, who was the first wife of Lir of SídhFionnachaidh. After Lir's wife died giving birth to twin boys, Aoife was offered as a second wife to console him. At first, Aoife was happy. She loved her four stepchildren and showered her affections on them. And her new husband was so besotted with his children that he wanted them all to sleep in the same room, so he could see them last thing at night and first thing in the morning when he opened his eyes. But Aoife became jealous of Lir's affections for his children. And as time passed her jealousy got the better of her. She planned a trip that fooled the children into thinking they were going to visit their step grandfather, Bodhbh. Aoife's plan was to kill the children along the way. But, she could not bring herself to wield her sword on the innocent children. Instead she cast a spell with her magic wand which turned the children of Lir into swans. She left them with their human sense and reason, their voices and their Irish. Fionnuala, the eldest and only girl, begged and pleaded for the spell to be reversed. And Aoife did feel some remorse at this stage, but it was too late. She did not have the power to reverse the spell. Instead she placed a limit on it, saying that it would last until a noble woman from the south married a noble man from the north.

When Bodhbh discovered Aoife's terrible deed, he changed her into a demon that was banished to the four winds forever. And some people say you can still hear her voice on a stormy night, sighing and sobbing above the sound of the wind.

Cú Chulainn

Glossary (in order of appearance)

Pieces of text adapted from the following sources (in no particular order):

The Prophecy of Scáthach: https://members.tripod.com/tuan_o_greenfields/prophecy.html
The Combat of Ferdiad and Cú Chulainn: http://adminstaff.vassar.edu/sttaylor/Cooley/Ferdiad.html
The Sickbed of Cú Chulainn - Bard Mythologies: https://bardmythologies.com/the-sickbed-of-cuchulainn/
Old Irish wisdom attributed to Aldfrith of Northumbria:
    https://archive.org/details/oldirishwisdomat00aldfuoft/page/n3/mode/2up?view=theater
The Slaying of Loch Son of Mofemis: http://adminstaff.vassar.edu/sttaylor/Cooley/LochMor.html
Irish Sagas: Aided Óenfir Aífe: https://iso.ucc.ie/Aided-aife/Aided-aife-text.html
The Tain Reading Guide:
    https://www.penguinrandomhouse.com/books/302034/the-tain-by-ciaran-carson/9780140455304/readers-guide/
The Curse of Macha - Bard mythologies: https://bardmythologies.com/the-curse-of-macha/
The Great Defeat on the Plain of Muirthemne before Cuchulainn's Death:
    https://sejh.pagesperso-orange.fr/keltia/version-en/deathcu2.html
The Tragic Death of Connla: https://www.maryjones.us/ctexts/aoife.html
The Irish Goddress of Herbs and Healing: Airmed - Claudia Merrill:
    https://www.claudiamerrill.com/blog/the-irish-goddess-airmed
Celtic Myth and Legend: The Gaelic Gods: Chapter V: The Gods of the Gaels:
    https://www.sacred-texts.com/neu/celt/cml/cml09.htm
Cú Chulainn - Wikipedia:
    https://en.wikipedia.org/wiki/C%C3%BA_Chulainn#Appearance http://www.feri.com/lurkingbear/fiona/Barabal.html
Mórrígan - http://gotireland.com/2013/10/30/irish-faerie-folk-of-yore-and-yesterday-the-morrigan/
https://www.academia.edu/15486900/The_Role_of_the_Morrigan_in_the_Cath_Maige_Tuired_Incitement_Battle_Ma
    gic_and_Prophecy

Cú Chulainn   (cf).

corse   (cf).

gombeen   a gombeen is an old Irish insult/word that's used to describe someone shady, or someone that's a bit of a del-boy/ wheeler-dealer-looking-to-make-a-quick-profit.

sluagh   (cf).

dobhar-chú   a creature of Irish folklore and a cryptid. Dobhar-chú is roughly translated into "water hound." It resembles both a dog and an otter though sometimes is described as a half dog, half fish. It lives in water and has fur with protective properties.

fetch   based in Irish folklore, a fetch is a supernatural double or an apparition of a living person. The sighting of a fetch is regarded as an omen, usually for impending death.

for what goes around comes around   refers to the fact that, according to some sources, the first animal that Cú Chulainn killed while still the boy Setanta was an otter. It fell back into the water at what was later named 'Lochan An Claiomh' (Lake of the Sword).

... the turning of the Wheel...   ie, fate (cf., the Turner Of The Wheel)

Scáthach   (cf).

my father,/he of the daystar   (cf., Lugh)

the Dagda   (Irish: An Dagda) was an important god in Irish mythology. One of the Tuatha Dé Danann, the Dagda is portrayed as a father-figure, king, and druid. He is associated with fertility, agriculture, manliness and strength, as well as magic, druidry and wisdom. He can control life and death, the weather and crops, as well as time and the seasons.

lorg mór   the Dadga's magic staff (or mace or club) that kills with one of its ends and brings back life with its other.

An Breisleach Mor   the region where Cú Chulainn made his last stand is known as "The Great Carnage", while the field in which this stone stands is called the Field of Slaughter.

Clogh an Fear Mor   the 'Stone of the Big Man' - also called Cú Chulainn's Stone, the Pierced Standing Stone, Cloghafarmore, Clochafarmore, or Clochfearmore, stands tall and proud in the north part of Rathiddy Townland. The historic standing stone is in the very centre of an area known in the Táin Bó Cúailnge as 'An Breisleach Mor' (c.f.)

plain of Muirtheimne   the plain of Mag Muirthemne (now in County Louth), area frequented by Cú Chulainn as the boy, Sétanta, and also the area of his final days.

three-legged bloodied motif marking my past, my present, my future   indirect references to both the symbols of triskelion alchemy (cf). and the Druidic symbol for the 'Awen' (cf).

roc catha   magical battle chants

vertigo naewithstanding, 'Give me what I want and no-one gets hurt   line references/adapted from the song 'Vertigo ' by U2.

Tír na nÓg   (cf).

riastrad   (cf).

Úathach   (cf).

the shadow's stone   refers to Dún Scáith, 'Fortress of Shadows', Scáthach's castle (cf).

pivoting bridge   one of the many obstacles on the way into Dún Scáith, also known as the 'bridge of leaping', it was an enchanted bridge, low at each end, and high in the middle, and whenever someone stepped on it, it would buck like a wild horse, trying to shake them off. It could narrow itself to the width of a hair or shorten itself to the length of an inch, and it would do all it could to shake a newcomer off. Cú Chulainn surpassed it by doing his famed 'salmon leap' onto the middle of the bridge, followed by another great leap off the other end of the bridge.

salmon-leap   Cú Chulainn's 'salmon leap' was of legendary status - he could leap to incredible heights, clearing fortress walls and battlefields like a salmon clearing a waterfall.

downward-turned lids darkened rustic with half cut crease her mystery   a number of texts mention Úathach as having 'white fingers, black eyebrows', some that she had white hair and black eyebrows - 'half cut crease' is an eye makeup style that, coupled with shading of the eyebrows, seemed to somehow explain her 'look'.

colg   a small thrusting sword (similar to the Roman *spatha*).

Cochar Croibne   not long after Cú Chulainn had arrived at Dún Scáith to become Scáthach's pupil he accidentally broke one of Uathach's fingers, and Úathach's suitor, Cochar Croibhe, challenged him to single combat, despite Úathach's protests. Cú Chulainn killed him and became Uathach's lover.

a mother's pleasure   Scáthach offered Úathach to Cú Chulainn to take as his without a 'bride price' (dowry).

Forgall   (cf).

his daughter   ie, Emer (cf).

friendship of her thighs   (cf).

Aoife   (cf).

Scáthach   (cf).

the Shadow, She-Witch, etc   references to Scáthach.

bandraíodóir   (cf).

my her our only son   refers to Connla, son of Cú Chulainn and Aoife (cf).

Breas   (cf).

Aoife   (cf).

Scáthach   (cf).

conception ... as convoluted as it was contentious   there are a number of versions of the story of Cú Chulainn's miraculous birth - I chose to use the earliest version of *Compert C(h)on Culainn* ("The Conception of Cú Chulainn"): his mother Deichtre (or Deichtine) is the daughter and charioteer of Conchobar mac Nessa, king of Ulster, and she accompanies him as he and the nobles of Ulaid hunt a flock of magical birds. As snow begins to fall, they seek shelter in a nearby house. As the host's wife goes into labour, Deichtre assists in the birth of a baby boy, while a mare gives birth to twin colts. The next morning, the men of Ulaid find themselves at the Brug na Bóinde or Brú na Bóinne, the neolithic mound at Newgrange (cf.) - the house and its occupants have disappeared, but the child and the colts remain. Deichtre takes the boy home and begins raising him as her own, but the boy falls ill and dies. The god Lugh appears to her and tells her he was their host that night, and that he has put his child in her womb, and to name him Sétanta. Her pregnancy turns into a scandal as she is betrothed to Sualtam mac Róich, and the Ulaid-men suspect Conchobar of being the father, so she aborts the child and goes to her husband's bed "virgin-whole". She then conceives a son with Sualtam, whom she names Sétanta.

Deichtre   Cú Chulainn's mortal mother (cf).

Ulaid king   ie, Conchobar mac Nessa, king of Ulaid in Cú Chulainn's time. He ruled from Emain Macha (near Armagh). According to legend, particularly in the Ulster Cycle of Irish mythology, the ancient territory of Ulaid spanned the whole of the modern province of Ulster, excluding County Cavan, but including County Louth. Its southern border was said to stretch from the River Drowes in the west to the River Boyne in the east. Ulaid (Old Irish), or Ulaidh (Modern Irish). Ulaid ceased to exist after its conquest in the late 12th century by the Anglo-Norman knight, John de Courcy, and was replaced with the Earldom of Ulster.

river's bend sidhe   (sidhe (cf.) refers specifically to Brug na Bóinde/Brú na Bóinne - see above).

leanbh   literally, "my child", an Irish affectionate term of endearment.

Lugh   (cf., reference *"betrayed your father's adherence to oath, truth, and law.."* in **Scáthach** glossary.)

Ollamh Érenn   the Ollamh Érenn or Chief Ollam of Ireland was a professional title of Gaelic Ireland, used here as an honorary title for Lugh.

Sétanta   (cf).

Conchobar king   (cf).

Sualtam mac Róich   Cú Chulainn's mortal father, and wife of Deichtre.

spark of the Light of the seed of me...   refers to Cú Chulainn's Otherworldly conception by Lugh.

Triskelion unity   derived from the Greek word "Triskeles" meaning "three legs", the Triskele or Triple Spiral is a complex ancient Celtic symbol. Often referred to by many as a Triskelion, its earliest creation dates back to the Neolithic era, as it can be seen at the entrance of Newgrange, Ireland. It is a symbol that consists of three interlocked spirals, and is one of the oldest Irish Celtic symbols in existence, best known to represent the three worlds; the celestial, physical, and spiritual. Other trinity connections associated with the triskele are life-death-rebirth, past-present-future, earth-water-sky, and creation-protection-destruction.

Each one deals with some aspect of personal growth, human development, and spiritual progress. One theory posits that the triskele represents reincarnation, as it consists of one continuous line that could be analogous to the unbroken movement of time. In this context, it represents the process of constantly moving forward to reach a state of understanding and enlightenment. Another theory states that at the Newgrange monument, the triskele is meant to symbolize pregnancy as the structure has a distinct womb-like appearance and the sun spirals in its movements every three months, with the symbol's three spirals representing nine months in total.

Otherwordly to/from the Otherworld (cf).

Conchobar, himself promoted... when Conchobar was seven, Fergus mac Róich was king of Ulster and fell in love with Conchobar's mother, Ness. She agrees to become his wife, on one condition: that Fergus allows Conchobar to be king for a year, so his children will be called the sons of a king (under Medieval Irish law inheritance passed through the male line, and only those who had a king as a male-line ancestor were eligible for kingship).The nobles of Ulster advise Fergus that this will not affect his standing with them, as the boy will be king in name only, so he agrees. But Conchobar, advised by his mother, ruled so well that by the end of the year it was decided he should be king permanently.

Sétanta to Hound to Hero Cú Chulainn's story in a nutshell.

Sencha Sencha mac Ailella, acting as an important judge and notable poet during the reign of Conchobar mac Nessa, volunteered to foster Cú Chulainn, but was only an educator. Sencha helped establish peace between the men of Ulaid.

Blaí Briugu Blaí Briugu (Blaí the Landholder or Hospitaller), another of Cú Chulainn's foster fathers, was wealthy and kept a hostel, and had a geasa (cf.) which required him to sleep with any woman who stayed there unaccompanied, which itself became the cause of his undoing: when Brig Bretach, wife of Celtchar, stayed there on her own, he slept with her, and for that Celtchar killed him (events not featured in this poem).

geasa (cf).

Fergus mac Róich Fergus mac Róich (son of Ró-ech or "great horse") was another of Cú Chulainn's foster fathers. He was formerly the king of Ulaid, but was tricked out of the kingship and betrayed by Conchobar mac Nessa (cf.),, and, therefore, became the ally and lover of Conchobar's enemy, queen Medb of Connacht (cf.),and joined her expedition against Ulaid in the Táin Bó Cúailnge (see below).The name Fergus (later Irish, 'Fearghus') means "man-strength" or "virility", and Fergus is described as being of enormous size and sexual potency, which led him into many a precarious situation, related in the story of the Táin Bó Flidhais (events not featured in this poem).

- Táin Bó Cúailnge ("the driving-off of cows of Cooley"), commonly known as The Cattle Raid of Cooley, or just The Táin, an epic from early Irish literature often called "The Irish Iliad". The Táin tells of a war against Ulster by Queen Medb of Connacht and her husband King Ailill, who intend to steal the stud bull, Donn Cuailnge. Due to a curse upon the King and warriors of Ulster, to suffer labour pains for nine days and nine nights (cf., Macha), the invaders are opposed only by teenaged Cú Chulainn. The Táin has had an enormous influence on Irish literature and culture. It is often considered Ireland's national epic.

Amergin (Amergin mac Eccit) (cf).

Findchóem sister of the Ulster king Conchobar mac Nessa, she was the wife of the poet Amergin, the mother of Conall Cernach, and the wet-nurse of Cú Chulainn.

Conall   son of Amregin and Findchoem, his parents' marriage was barren, until Findchoem visited a druid and was advised to drink from a certain well. She took a drink from the well, swallowing a worm with it, and became pregnant. Her brother, Cet mac Mágach (not featured in this poem), a Connachtman, protected his sister until she gave birth to a son, Conall. Druids came to initiate the child into their religion, and prophesied that he would kill more than half of the men of Connacht, and that he would always have a Connachtman's head on his belt. Cet took the child, put him under his heel and tried to break his neck, but only damaged it, leaving Conall with a crooked neck.

woodbine   Honeysuckle., or (Irish) Féithleann. Other names for honeysuckle include Irish vine, woodbine, fairy trumpets, honeybind, trumpet flowers, goats leaf and sweet suckle. The old name Woodbine describes the twisting, binding nature of the honeysuckle through the hedgerows. It was believed that if honeysuckle grew around the entrance to the home it prevented a witch from entering. In other places it's believed that grown around the doors it will bring good luck. If it grows well in your garden, then you will be protected from evil. In Ireland honeysuckle was believed to have a power against bad spirits, and it was used in a drink to cure the effects of the evil eye, as well as having a variety of other uses. Reference: http://irishhedgerows.weebly.com/flora.html

Dordmair, daughter of Domnall Maeltemel   Cú Chulainn's first female warrior trainer where he and two of his companions went '... to learn warfare and great feats". Reference: https://sejh.pagesperso-orange.fr/keltia/version-en/cu-training.html

Domnall Maeltemel   father of Dordmair, known as 'the soldiery'.

scáth dragan   literally 'shadow dragon', reference to Scáthach (cf).

wolfhound   refers to the Irish wolfhound, Canis lupus familiaris.

Coire Goirath   first of three 'Celtic chakras' - the cauldron of warming or incubation, located in the pelvis, it represents physical health, physical movement, and life force.

Coire Emmae   second of three 'Celtic chakras' - the cauldron of vocation or motion, located at the centre of the chest, in the area of the heart.

Coire Sois   third of three 'Celtic chakras' - the cauldron of wisdom or inspiration, located in the centre of the head. Reference for 'Celtic chakras': celtic chakras | Seven intentions

riastrad   (cf).

energy spent with and without breath   ie, aerobic and anaerobic.

Ulaid   (cf).

Lugh   (cf).

Amergin   (cf).

Turner of the Wheel   (cf).

Otherworld   (cf).

Dún Scáith   (cf).

seats of life   ie, heads (cf,, **Scáthach**)

Forgall   (cf).

Emer   (cf).

Aoife   (cf).

Emer   (cf).

ask the prophetess   ie, Scáthach.

Connla   (cf).

riastrad   (cf).

Ulaid   (cf).

Aoife   (cf).

Gáe Bulg   (cf).

Shadow-Witch   refers to Scáthach (cf).

Ferdiád   son of Damán, son of Dáire, of the Fir Domnann, was a warrior of Connacht in the Ulster Cycle of Irish mythology. In the *Táin Bó Cúailnge,* Ferdiád finds himself on the side of the war opposite to that taken by his best friend and foster-brother, Cú Chulainn (cf.), with whom he, too, had trained under Scáthach (cf.). He and Cú Chulainn are equal in all martial feats, with two exceptions: the Gáe Bulg (cf.), which Scáthach has taught only Cú Chulainn to use; and Ferdiád's horny skin, which no weapon can pierce. When Ailill (cf.) and Medb (cf.), king and queen of Connacht, invade Ulaid to steal the bull Donn Cúailnge, their progress is held up by Cú Chulainn, who demands single combat. After Cú Chulainn has defeated a series of Connacht champions, Medb sends for Ferdiád, but he only agrees to fight Cú Chulainn after Findabair (cf.), Ailill and Medb's daughter, has seductively plied him with alcohol, and Medb has variously bribed, shamed and goaded him to do so. They fight in the ford for three days, first fighting with 8 swords, darts, and spears, then fighting with "throwing-spears" and lances, and finally moving on to "heavy, hard-smiting swords." It is on the third day that Ferdiád starts to gain the upper hand. At this point, Cú Chulainn calls to his charioteer, Laeg, for the Gáe Bulg, which he floats down the river to him. Cú Chulainn throws a light spear at Ferdiád's chest, causing him to raise his shield, and then picks up the Gáe Bulg between his toes and thrusts it through his anus, upon which the barbs spread throughout his body, killing him - it is then removed from Ferdiád's body by Laeg (cf.), and Cú Chulainn mourns Ferdiád's death, praising his strength and bravery.

just as the souls of the dead...   . in Ireland there was a belief that the souls of the dead departed westwards over the sea with the setting sun.

Cathbad   Cathbad, or Cathbhadh (modern spelling), is the chief druid in the court of King Conchobar mac Nessa in the Ulster Cycle of Irish Mythology.

Manannán mac Lir   (cf).

Connla   (cf).

Tech Duinn   Donn ("the dark one", from Proto-Celtic 'Dhuosnos') was an ancestor of the Gaels and is believed to have been a god of the dead. Donn is said to have dwelt in Tech Duinn (the "house of Donn", or "house of the dark one"), where the souls of the dead gathered before travelling to their final destination in the Otherworld, or before being reincarnated. It is commonly identified with Bull Rock, an islet off the western tip of the Beara Peninsula. Bull Rock resembles a dolmen or portal tomb as it has a natural tunnel through it, allowing the sea to pass under it as if through a portal.

Hy Breasil   (cf).

Dagda   (cf).

Cermait...   Cermait (modern spelling: Cearmaid or "Kermit") of the Tuatha Dé Danann was a son of the Dagda and brother of Aed and Aengus.He was killed by Lugh after he had an affair with one of Lugh's wives, Buach. The Dagda cried tears of blood for his son, and later, while traveling with his son's body in the east, revived Cermait with His healing staff. Cermait's three sons, Mac Cuill, Mac Cecht and Mac Gréine, avenged his death, and went on to become joint High Kings of Ireland.

for already was my father Otherworld-bound   according to a poem of the dindsenchas*, Lugh was responsible for the death of Breas - Lugh killed him in revenge, but Cermait's sons (see above) killed Lugh in return, spearing him through the foot then drowning him in Loch Lugborta in County Westmeath. He had ruled for forty years.

Scáthach   (cf).

imbas forosnai   (cf).

Fedelm   (cf).

Medb   (cf., Queen Medb)

banfhili   (cf).

the fourfold cloaks worn upon the circle of life   the 'four stars of destiny' (source: *The Little Book of Celtic Wisdom*, John and Caitlin Mattheus, Element Books Limited, 1993, p11).

Otherworld   (cf).

Scáthach   (cf).

drakania   (cf).

Cú Chulainn   (cf).

baintside   (cf).

thy suire's ecstacy   suire, also known as murdúchann, merrows, or (Gaelic) muir-gheilt, samhghubha, muidhuachán, were sea-nymphs similar to the sirens from Greek mythology - I use the word here as a synonym for 'siren' meaning enchantress or femme fatale, referring to Scáthach. While the term 'siren' refers to a creature half bird and half woman who lured sailors to destruction by the sweetness of her song, according to the 'Book of Invasions' (English for the Lebor Gabála Érenn (literally "The Book of the Taking of Ireland"), a collection of poems and prose narratives in the Irish language intended to be a history of Ireland and the Irish peoples from the creation of the world to the Middle Ages.), these siren-like creatures were encountered by the legendary ancestors of the Irish (either Goidels or Milesians). These beings are said to appear as human from the waist up but have the body of a fish from the waist down, and have a gentle, modest, affectionate and benevolent disposition.They would seem to have been around for millennia, because, according to the bardic chroniclers, when the Milesians first landed on Irish shores the suire played around them on their passage. Female merrows were considered very beautiful, whereas the mermen in their true forms were ugly, another reason why merrow women sought out human men. What is known of them is that while immersed in the waters their hips are scaled, and those curves end in a long and flat-finned tail of varying and often beautiful coloration. They can swim near as swift as a lean-built porpoise, but rarely reach such speeds for anything but joy's sake, the merfolk having no natural predators in their waters, able to both outstrip and outsmart even the Sea Serpents of legend, or so it is said. When merfolk find themselves on land, their scales gradually recede, their long tails forming a pair of long and usually delicate legs. References: http://ynysseamaiderp.blogspot.com/p/merrows.html

https://www.alternatewars.com/Mythology/Irish_FL_Lageniensis.htm

dòigh nàdair   the way of nature. Reference: https://forest-therapy-scotland.com/doigh-nadair-the-way-of-nature/

golden eagles, hen harriers...   all birds listed are native birds of prey found in Ireland.

Dún Scáith   (cf).

Duncan   father of Scáthach 's children (surname unknown).

Emer   (cf).

plain of Muirthemne   (cf).

Sétanta   (cf).

Cathbad   (cf).

harpoon of mortal pain and death   Gáe Bulg (cf).

Scáthach   (cf).

Medb   (cf).

cailleach piseog   (cf).

Emer   (cf).

Lulochta Logo   Emer's father Forgall's holding.

Scibor, Ibor and Cat   Emer's brothers.

Fial   Emer's elder sister.

so spared the ignominy...   this line refers to her avoiding the public shame her brother's would have felt being left standing where others had fallen, and also to the shame she possibly would have felt knowing that Cú Chulainn had chosen Emer, despite her offering him her elder sister, and that as the elder of the two she, Fial, should have been married off first (that had been Forgall's plan all along).

Forgall   (cf).

every ford from Ath Scenmenn at Ailbine to the Boann at Breg...   after escaping with Emer, Cú Chulainn was pursued by Forgall's retinue - he killed Scenmenn [allay of Forgall] and ... one hundred more at Glondath... he reached the place called Rae Bán, or the White Plain. There he broke the followers in half ... and gave the new name of Crufit [sic,] to the place, the Sod of Blood. The remaining pursuers followed until the Boann River, at ... Ath Imfoit, where he ... turned and charged them. So it was that Cúchalainn killed one hundred men at every ford from Ath Scenmenn at Ailbine to the Boann at Breg. Reference: http://www.askaboutireland.ie/reading-room/life-society/irish-language-legends/cuchulainn-and-emer/the-union-of-cuc hulainn-a/

Rae Bán, the Plain of White, renamed from that on by I, Crufoit, the Sod of Blood   see note above.

first forcing lawful due   Conchobar retained the right to be the first to sleep with every new wife.

after gathering in all the herds of all the beasts around Sliab Fuait   to 'attempt to cool his passion' (ie, to calm him down over his right of 'first forcing'), Conchobar commanded Cú Chulainn outside to gather '... all the herds of all the beasts around Sliab Fuait...', but it didn't work - only Cathbad's suggestion of he and Fergus lying between Emer and Conchobar appeased both men ,and meant they each, and Emer, kept their, and her, honour. Reference: http://ams2-aai-web-1.anu.net/reading-room/life-society/irish-language-legends/cuchulainn-and-emer/the-union-of-cu chulainn-a/

sons of Calatin   (cf).

Cú Chulainn   (cf).

Maireann croí éadrom i bhfad   literally 'a light heart lives long'. (Irish).

claimhteoireacht   (cf).

Lugh of the Long Arm   (cf).

mistress of shade   Scáthach (cf).

Scáthach   (cf).

Connla   (cf).

beyond the ninth wave   (cf).

Medb   (cf).

Dark Queen of Connacht   refers to Medb (cf.). Connacht (also spelt Connaught) is one of the provinces of Ireland, in the west of Ireland. Until the ninth century it consisted of several independent major Gaelic kingdoms (Lúighne, Uí Maine, and Iar Connacht).

Macha's labour-pain curse against the men of Uliad   (see https://bardmythologies.com/the-curse-of-macha/ for further information) basically, Macha was forced to run a race against the horses of King Conchobar of Uliad whilst heavily pregnant and suffering labour pains - she wins, collapses to the ground and gives birth to stillborn twins, cursing the fighting men of Uliad thus: as soon as he was old enough to grow a beard, each fighting man of Ulaid would come under the curse for coming not to her aid, that in their hours of greatest need they will feel the pangs of labour for nine days and nine nights, the curse itself to last for nine generations.

though through my youth and my chin wast her deceit undone   Cú Chulainn was exempted from suffering the pangs of the curse because he was not yet old enough to grow a beard and be considered a man.

suire   (cf).

the Mórrígan   (cf).

Medb   (cf).

Ailill   Ailill (Ailell, Oilioll) is a male name, meaning "elf" in Old Irish. It is a prominent name in Irish mythology, as for Ailill mac Máta, King of Connacht and husband of Queen Medb (cf.) Ailill was a popular given name in medieval Ireland, meaning something like "beauty".

he her man of service   in ancient Ireland, whoever owned and brought more wealth and/or property into the marriage, man or woman, was the ruler of the household. If a woman was in possession of greater wealth than her husband, he was called *fer fognama* ("man of service" or "man without power over a wife"). I use it also referring to her lack of sexual permissiveness, assuming she took control in their marital bed, as well as in the bedrooms of her multiple promiscuous affairs.

quean   archaic noun meaning an impudent or badly behaved girl or woman, a prostitute.

malicious enough to murder another from resent   Medb, later queen of Connacht, was the first of Conchobar's many wives - she bore him a son called Amalgad, but soon left him (Conchobar). Medb's sister Eithne later conceived a son by him, but Medb murdered her by drowning her in a stream - Eithne's son Furbaide is delivered by posthumous Caesarian section.

she who intoxicates   Maeve (anglicised spelling of Medb) is a girl's name of Irish origin meaning "she who intoxicates".

Scáthach   (cf).

mistress of shadow   Scáthach (cf).

Ferdiad   (cf).

Fergus   (cf).

his shame of sword of wood and sex the cause   at one point during the Táin the Connacht army separated, with Ailill leading one section, and Medb and Fergus leading the other. Ailill was suspicious, and sent his charioteer to spy on them. The charioteer found Fergus and Medb having sex, and, unnoticed, stole Fergus' sword, which Ailill kept safe as proof. Fergus made himself a dummy sword of wood to hide his loss. Cúchulainn held up the army's progress by fighting a series of champions in single combat. Fergus was sent to face him, but as foster-father and foster-son, neither wanted to fight the other, and, in any case, Fergus had no sword. Cúchulainn agreed to yield on this occasion, on the condition that Fergus yield to him the next time they meet.

Ferdiad   (cf).

Scáthach   (cf).

Medb   (cf).

Ferdiad   (cf).

her mentor Goddess   ie, the Mórrígan.

Tech Duinn   (cf).

Donn   (cf., *Tech Duinn* reference above)

Otherworld   (cf).

Tír na nÓg   (cf).

Cú Chulainn   (cf).

Scáthach ni Uanaind   (cf).

my fall at thy hand wrongly augured so...   as part of her convincing Ferdiad to fight Cú Chulainn, Medb gave Ferdiad the false prediction of his victory.

she of wealth and cunning whom no spouse could bridle   ie, Medb.

Smith's Hound   ie, Cú Chulainn (cf).

Findabair of the champions, Queen of western Ériu, daughter of Ailill and Medb   Findabair or Finnabair was a daughter of Ailill and Queen Medb of Connacht in Irish mythology. The meaning of the name is "white phantom" (etymologically cognate with Gwenhwyfar, the original Welsh form of Guinevere). Findabair's hand is offered to a succession of warriors in exchange for their sparring with Cú Chulainn. Ultimately, her beauty and charms serve as the driving force behind the deaths of hundreds of men, even compelling Ferdiad to fight Cú Chulainn in single combat, leading to his death.

Ferdiad   (cf).

once proffered...   at one point, Medb parleys a truce with Cú Chulainn that he not attack her army by night but rather engage in one-on-one combat each day with a warrior - Findabair is offered to Cú Chulainn when no warrior can be found willing to fight him. After he accepts, she is taken to him by a fool dressed as the king, not by Ailill himself. Upon discovering this, Cú Chulainn kills the fool and puts a pillar through him and a pillar through Findabair's tunic, thus leaving two stones in that location, thereafter called the Fool's Stone and Finnabair's Stone.

queen of Cruachan   (cf).

the son of Daman mac Darè   Ferdiad (cf).

the Hound   (cf).

Cruachan's heroes   fighting men from the ancient capital of Connacht.

Ferdiad   (cf).

Hound from Emain Macha, Hound formed of all colours, Hound of Culann, the Border-hound, the War-hound   (cf).

Tuatha Dé Danann   (cf).

claideb   (cf).

this Hound   (cf).

Ferdiad   (cf).

boccanach and the bananach   (cf). 'the puckfaced Fays' and 'the whitefaced Fays'.

Aoife   (cf).

shadowed sister   ie, Scáthach (cf).

Dolb and Indolb   faerie friends of Cú Chulainn, reputedly Tuatha Dé Danann.

my Danaan with cowls unseen   as faerie folk, they (Dolb and Indol) were often considered invisible to mortal's eyes.

my deceit   ie, assistance by Dolb and Indolb.

thy armoured advantage   Ferdiad wears a type of horn skin of twice molten iron armour that no weapon may pierce, as well as a 'huge, goodly flag the size of a millstone'. (I took the idea of a 'horned skin' literally, having it made of chitin, like crustacean shell.)

Gáe Bulg   (cf).

Ferdiad son of Daman son of Darè   (cf).

men of Domnann   the Fir Domnann were a people named in Irish legendary history. The name Fir Domnann is based on the root *dumno-*, which means both 'deep' and 'the world'.

Danann   (cf).

Láeg's rebukes of revive   (cf., *Láeg*) Cú Chulainn gave permission to Láeg to rebuke and satirize him if he had fallen in combat and needed his fervour arousing by way of being shamed and ridiculed.

Ferdiad   (cf).

fidchell   fidchell (also spelled fidhcheall, fidceall, fitchneal or fithchill in Irish or gwyddbwyll in Welsh) was an ancient Celtic board game. The name in both Irish and Welsh is a compound translating to "wood sense"; the fact that the compound is identical in both languages demonstrates that the name is of extreme antiquity. The game is occasionally claimed to be a predecessor of the modern game chess. The game was played between two people who moved pieces across a board; the board shared its name with the game played upon it. The name has evolved into ficheall, the Irish word for chess; the similar gwyddbwyll is the name for chess in modern Welsh.

Cú Chulainn   (cf).

my father's wood wisdom gift   legend has it that fidchell was invented by Lugh.

spear of mortal pain and death   (cf).

Cú Chulainn   (cf).

Gáe Bulg   (cf).

Láeg   (cf). Láeg, or Lóeg, son of Riangabar, is the charioteer and constant companion of the hero Cú Chulainn in the Ulster Cycle of Irish mythology. His horses are Liath Macha and Dub Sainglend. Cú Chulainn sends Láeg to the Otherworld with Lí Ban, sister to Fand, and he brings back bountiful descriptions of the Otherworld in the tale *Serglige Con Culainn* (The Sickbed of Cúchulainn). In the tale of Cú Chulainn's death he is killed by Lugaid Cú Roi with a spear intended for Cú Chulainn.

Cú Chulainn   (cf).

the Shadow's gift   Cú Chulainn was the only one Scáthach taught the secrets of her Gáe Bulg to.

Medb   (cf).

Scáthach's cursed gift   Gáe Bulg (cf).

Ferdiad   (cf).

anas   Irish for anus.

Ferdiad   (cf).

Scáthach ni Uanaind   (cf).

colg and claideb   (cf).

Dún Scáith   (cf).

Ferdiad   (cf).

Connacht queen bitch   reference to Medb (cf).

ogam   ogam (Old Irish; ogham in Modern Irish) is an Early Medieval alphabet used primarily to write the early Irish language.

recall of the haunting lingua-touch of a drink of oblivion preceding impenetrable darkness...   here Cú Chulainn is referring to being given a 'drink of forgetfulness' by Cathbad (cf.) after his tryst with Fand (see below). His recollections begin as disparate images then become more detailed, clearer memories..

flock of white birds... none?   Cú Chulainn is with other men in Muirtheimne (cf.), hunting birds by the water. A number of the men kill two birds for their wives, so the women may wear feathers on each shoulder of their gowns. When all the women but Emer have birds, Cú Chulainn becomes determined to kill the largest, most beautiful birds who come '*winging in*' for her, but his aim is off for the first time ever and he only clips one of the birds on the wing. The birds, '*linked by red gold chain*', are clearly from the Otherworld, and although he was advised to leave them alone, Cú Chulainn had not - frustrated because of his misses he moodily stalks off and lays down by a nearby dolmen and falls asleep. In his dream-space the birds, one wounded, come to him as women of the sidhe (cf.) and whip and beat him into relative unconsciousness. For a full year he lays in bed and his wounds do not heal.

the balm of Emer's touch   Cú Chulainn is revived by Emer who sings songs of healing and reminds him of his feats, etc, to help bring him up from his torpor. He then tells her of his vision and his desire to aid Fand's plight. She convinces him to take Láeg with him.

the bird-women, one suire, wife to... the sea, but waves face away (unclear) from her   the two bird-women's names are Fand ('*one siren*') and Lí Ban ('*the other faerie*'), both from the Otherworld. Fand is wife to Manannán mac Lir (cf.), god of the sea - the 'waves face away from her' refers to his anger at her enrapture (and later affair) with Cú Chulainn.

'twas they put the cursed sickness into me   after casting a sling stone at them and wounding one (Fand) in the wing Cú Chulainn falls unconscious and feverish beside a standing stone. The two approach him in his delirium and attack him, beating him with

horsewhips so severely he lies in sickness for nearly a year until Lí Ban returns and agrees to cure him if he agrees to go to the Otherworld and assist Fand in battle ('a *plea for mine sword strength…*').

a plea for my sword strength,//whispers of healing and betrothal   Lí Ban promised she'd heal Cú Chulainn's sickness and give him Fand as a wife if he would help her husband, Labraid the Quicksword, in a coming battle against impossible odds on the fairy Plain of Light. Cúchulainn was rightly cautious of dealing with the sidhe (cf.), so he sent Láeg first to take a look, following the faerie/birds after he (Cú Chulainn) awoke. Láeg travelled with them, returned at last to tell Cú Chulainn both that the Plain was real and that Fand was enchantingly beautiful ('…*reporting confirmation of -?*'). With that, Cú Chulainn agreed to go to the battle.

Láeg   (cf).

overwhelming brightness   refers to the Plain of Light.

a king and champions toppled; snatches of naked skin, etc   the battle is successful, and Fand and Cú Chulainn join together and consummate their love…

strand of Baile   sight of reckoning of Emer and Fand, their (Cú Chulainn and Fand's) attempted eloping stopped only after Emer confronts the 'new lovers' with a troop of women armed with knives, though both women then recognise the other's unselfish love and request he take the other (seeing how besotted Cú Chulainn was with Fand she offers him to her, but as she (Fand) was already married and seeing the love Emer had for Cú Chulainn, she (Fand) relents and returns to her husband).

Emer   (cf).

suire   (cf).

wail of lament smothered by wave of shaken sea-sprayed cloak   as Cú Chulainn and Fand are both heartbroken, she asks Manannán to shake his cloak of mist between her and Cú Chulainn, ensuring that they will never meet again. Combined with Cathbad's 'drink of forgetfulness' (cf).

a tincture of drowsiness, shadow-laced   when Aofie approached Dún Scáith looking to do battle, Scáthach, fearful of Cú Chulainn's safety if he fought her sister, gave him a sleeping potion to keep him from the fight - but a potion that would put most people to sleep for twenty-four hours only knocked him out for an hour. The '*remnant scent of fear*' refers to an aftertaste of the fear or concern he sensed in Scáthach at the time.

begat the boy-child, etc   Connla (cf).

the brush of bloodied wine upon my lips… a mother's plea ignored   (cf., reference *"betrayed by thrice bloodied wine of Deichtre that would not unturn…"*).

the piquancy of roasted meat… ne'er returneth I to capacity hence…   (cf., reference *geasa*) after being tricked into breaking his geasa by the Mórrígan in tripled form appearing as three old hags and eating dog meat, Cú Chulainn's strength is depleted.

geasa   (cf).

Mórrígan   (cf).

Lugaid Cú Roí   (cf).

son of a different dog   Lugaid Cú Roí is the son of Cú Roí mac Dáire of Munster (cf.), whose name means "hound of the plain/field",[1] or more specifically, "hound of the battlefield".

in league with the sons and daughters of Calatin   (cf).

king-felling spear   "What will fall by this spear, O sons of Calatin?" asked Lugaid. "A king will fall by that spear," said the sons of Calatin.// Then Lugaid flung the spear at Cu Chulainn's chariot, and it reached the charioteer, Láeg mac Riangabra, and all his bowels came forth on the cushion of the chariot [king of charioteers].//Now Erc cast the spear at Cu Chulainn, and it lighted on his horse, the Gray of Macha. Cu Chulainn snatched out the spear. And each of them bade the other farewell. [king of horses]// Then Lugaid flung the spear and struck Cu Chulainn, and his bowels came forth on the cushion of the chariot…[king of men].. Reference: http://www.ancienttexts.org/library/celtic/ctexts/cuchulain3.html

Cú Chulainn   (cf).

… would have none save Láeg my charioteer deride me thereof…   in the text entitled 'Comrac Fir dead inso' (English translation: 'The Combat of Fediad and Cú Chulainn'), Cú Chulainn gives permission to Láeg to do exactly that with these words: 'And, therefore, if defeat be my lot this day, do thou prick me on and taunt me and speak evil to me, so that the more my spirit and anger shall rise in me....' (reference: The Combat of Ferdiad and Cú Chulainn: http://adminstaff.vassar.edu/sttaylor/Cooley/Ferdiad.html).

Sétanta   (cf).

iománaíocht   Old Irish term for the sport of hurling, an outdoor game of ancient Gaelic origin, played by men. One of Ireland's native Gaelic games.

clash of ash, bas, heel and toe…   two hurleys (cf.) colliding is colloquially known as "the clash of the ash", a poetic description that has come to be used as a romantic or poetic synonym for the game itself. The face of the hurley is called the bas, and is the area used to strike the ball. At the same end, the "heel" of the hurley is the area to the left of the band and at the hurley's edge. It is used to give height to a ball struck on the ground. The rounded area to the right of the band is the "toe" of the hurley, used in the roll lift or jab lift techniques which allow a player to gain legal possession of a ball into the hand from the ground.

provethed mineself with same camán and sliothar against Culann's watch-hound…   a hurley or hurl or hurling stick (Irish: camán) is a wooden stick used in the Irish sports of hurling and camogie. It typically measures between 45 and 96 cm (18 to 38 inches) long with a flattened, curved bas at the end. A sliothar is the hard leather-covered ball used in the game. When Setanta was rushed at by Culann's hound he raised his hurley and thwacked his sliothar at it with great force - his aim was perfect, the ball ripping into its mouth and through its body, killing it instantly.

geasa   (cf).

Fergus   (cf).

Medb   (cf).

sparing said dark queen when with woman's pangs I didst findeth her... as the final battle of the Táin Bó Cúailnge began Cú Chulainn stayed on the sidelines, recuperating from his wounds, until he saw Fergus advancing. He entered the fray and confronted Fergus, who kept his side of an earlier made bargain and yielded to him, pulling his forces off the field. Connacht's other allies panicked and Medb was forced to retreat. At this inopportune moment, she got her period, and, although Fergus formed a guard around her, Cú Chulainn broke through as she was dealing with it and had her at his mercy. However, he spared her because he did not think it right to kill women, and guarded her retreat back to Connacht as far as Athlone.

didst woundeth I single woman... the Mórrígan... etc before one combat a beautiful young woman came to Cú Chulainn, claiming to be the daughter of a king, and offered him her love, but he refused her. The woman revealed herself as the Mórrígan, and in revenge for this slight, she attacked him in various animal forms while he was engaged in combat against Lóch mac Mofemis. As an eel, she tripped him in the ford, but he broke her ribs. As a wolf, she stampeded cattle across the ford, but he blinded her eye with a sling stone. Finally, she appeared as a heifer at the head of the stampede, but he broke her leg with another sling stone. After Cú Chulainn finally defeated Lóch, the Mórrígan appeared to him as an old woman milking a cow, with the same injuries he had given her in her animal forms. She gave him three drinks of milk, and with each drink he blessed her, healing her wounds. bodach   a trickster or bogeyman figure in Gaelic folklore and mythology. In Irish legend, the bodach ('old man') is paired with the Caillech (hag, old woman).

daughter of Aed Ernmas...   an Irish mother goddess, mentioned in Lebor Gabála Érenn and "Cath Maige Tuired" as one of the Tuatha Dé Danann. Her daughters include the trinity of eponymous Irish goddesses Ériu, Banba and Fódla, the trinity of war goddesses the Badb, Macha and Anann (who is also called the Mórrígan), and also a trinity of sons, Glonn, Gnim, and Coscar. Her other sons are Fiacha and Ollom.Ernmas was killed during the first battle of Mag Tuired and is called a "she-farmer" in the Lebor Gabála Érenn.

I have not the time for women's backsides   line adapted from Mackillop, 336 - reference: https://www.worldhistory.org/The_Morrigan/

"my newly-bearded form thought worthy of hurting by Lóch, son of Mofemis..."   when first asked by Medb and Ailill to fight with Cú Chulainn, Lóch esteemed it "a task of no honour nor becoming to "attack a tender, young, smooth-chinned, beardless boy" but was later duped into doing so when Cú Chulainn was himself tricked into donning a false beard by Medb;s 'woman-bands' when he was told "no brave warrior in the camp thinks it seemly to come fight with thee, and thou beardless". When Lóch then engaged with Cú Chulainn in combat, the Mórrígan sought to undo him "what time he would be in sore distress when engaged in battle and combat with a goodly warrior", as she had vowed during the earlier Cattle-raid of Regomaina. Reference: http://adminstaff.vassar.edu/sttaylor/Cooley/LochMor.html

Lóch, son of Mofemis   Loch Mor ('the Great') son of Mofemis

Hound   (cf).

Lóch   (cf).

Gáe Bulg   (cf).

cailleach   literally means "old woman, hag" in Irish and Scottish Gaelic, also 'veiled one' in Old Gaelic. In Gaelic mythology she/it is a divine hag and ancestor, associated with the creation of the landscape and with the weather, especially storms and winter.

Cú Roí   (full name: Cú Roí mac Dáire) Cú Roí plays an important role in the 8th-century tale Fled Bricrenn (Bricriu's Feast). The trickster Bricriu incites the heroes Cú Chulainn, Conall Cernach and Lóegaire Búadach to compete for the champion's portion at a feast, and Cú Roí is one of those who judged among them. Like all the other judges, he chooses Cú Chulainn, but Conall and Lóegaire refuse to accept his verdict ('... mine topping of feats refuted...'). When the three heroes return to Ulster, Cú Roí appears to each in the guise of a hideous churl (bachlach) and challenges them to behead him, then allow him to return and behead them. Only Cú Chulainn is brave and honourable enough to submit himself to the churl's axe, so he is declared champion. This story is related to the "beheading game" motif appearing in many later works in Arthurian literature - most famously the 14th-century English poem Sir Gawain and the Green Knight, although closer correspondences are to be found in Diu Crône and La Mule sans frein, both of which feature a revolving fortress like Cú Roi's.

tongue-poisoned feast   the Feast of Bricriu (cf., below) Bricriu is a Celtic boy or man's name meaning 'the poison tongued'.

my later taking of his salmon-appled head...   Cú Roi was not an easy man to kill because his soul rested within an apple in the stomach of a salmon living in a stream in the Slieve mountains.

plucking of the wrong flower   refers to Bláthnat, a maiden abducted and married by Cú Roí', later rescued by Cúchulainn, who kills her husband, but who is in turn murdered by one of Cú Roí's loyal servants (see below). It is an Irish feminine name meaning "little flower" from the Irish word blath "flower" combined with a diminutive suffix.

redress for my shaming milkstreamed betokening   Cú Roí joined Cú Chulainn on a raid on Inis Fer Falga (probably the Isle of Man), in return for his choice of the spoils. They steal treasure, and abduct Blathnát, daughter of the island's king, who loves Cú Chulainn. But when asked to choose his share, Cú Roí chose Blathnát. Cú Chulainn tried to stop him taking her, but Cú Roí cut his hair and drove him into the ground up to his armpits before escaping, taking Blathnát with him to his castle in The Otherworld kingdom of Cathair Chonroi, a forbidding and lonely place on top of a high peak in the Slieve Mis mountains, made impenetrable because Cú Roí used spells and magic to confound his enemies by causing the castle to whirl around at night, and it was unable to be discovered by those who sought to do him harm (Blathnát invites Cú Chulainn inside, thereby nullifying that effect).) Cú Roí could only be killed in certain contrived circumstances (cf.), which Blathnát discovered by way of constantly flattering - taking an opportunity when most of Cú Roí's men were absent from the fort, she gave a signal to Cú Chulainn by pouring milk into the Fionnghlaise ('white stream', now the Derrymore River), which flowed out of the entrance to the castle, letting him know that Cú Roí was asleep.

lopping stroke of he forthcoming   Cú Chulainn stormed the fort, killing Cú Roí while he slept, and carried off Bláthnat.

her ending hidden by spell of illusion and caused not by these hands but by damned poet's thwarting   as Cú Roí's men returned up the valley Bláthnat placed a spell which made the valley walls dance in front of their eyes (walkers who ascend Caherconree via the Derrymore River valley to this day can still see this effect, which is caused by an optical illusion). However, Ferchertne, Cú Roí's poet, enraged at the betrayal of his lord, grabbed Blathnát and leapt off a cliff, killing her and himself while Cú Chulainn watched in horror ('*the bachlach's revenge a blight left in mine memory's wake*').

bachlach   Old Irish term meaning clown, churl, labourer, serf, bondman.

his son to cast my final piercing   refers to Lugaid Cú Roi (cf.), son of Cú Roí mac Dáire (cf).

one time found I sucking from another woman's woundedness shot slung from mine hand... charred and blackened wakes...   refers to the story, Aided Derbforgaill ("The Death of Derbforgaill"), where the Scandinavian princess Derbforgaill, whom Cú Chulainn rescues from being sacrificed to the Fomorians in lieu of her paying a tribute comes to Ireland with her handmaid in the form of a pair of swans seeking Cú Chulainn, with whom she has fallen in love. Cú Chulainn and his foster-son Lugaid Riab nDerg see the swans, and Cú Chulainn shoots Derbforgaill down with his sling. The slingstone penetrates her womb, and to save her life Cú Chulainn has to suck it from her side, but since he has tasted her blood he cannot marry her. Instead, he gives her to Lugaid, and they marry and have children. One day in deep winter, the men of Ulster make pillars of snow, and the women compete to see who can urinate the deepest into the pillar and prove herself the most desirable to men. Derbforgaill's urine reaches the ground, and the other women, out of jealousy, attack and mutilate her. Lugaid notices that the snow on the roof of her house has not melted, and realises she is close to death. He and Cú Chulainn rush to the house, but Derbforgaill dies shortly after they arrive, and Lugaid dies of grief. Cú Chulainn avenges them by demolishing the house with the women inside, killing 150 of them.

Fomorii   Fomorian (cf).

geasa   (cf).

Áine   Áine was the wife of Laoghaire Lorc, the high king of Ireland. When her husband was killed by his jealous brother, Áine protected her young son, and raised him to be a great king. Laoghaire Lorc's brother, Cobhthach, was jealous, and killed him. He then poisoned Laoghaire's son, Aillil. He saw Aillil's young son Labhraidh as being no threat, and showed his control over the child by gruesomely feeding him the heart of his father and his grandfather. Labhraidh's mother, Áine, was made to watch while this occurred, held by two strong men to prevent her from doing anything to help her son. She was broken hearted, and the child was so traumatised by this incident that he was struck dumb. She then cherished her dumb child, making sure that he received an education fit for a king, and also making sure that nobody discounted him as a person because of his affliction. He became so learned under her attentions that he became known as "Labhraidh Ollamh". Eventually, as he grew older, he got over the trauma and began to speak again. Cobhthach was jealous of Labhraidh, as he was perceived to be more generous than Cobhthach. And now that speech had returned to him, and that he was an educated man, Cobhthach began to realise that Labhraidh might be a threat to him. Áine advised him to go into exile until he was ready to come back. When he was old enough to seek revenge, he attacked Lenister and won. He then sent a message to Cobhthach telling him that he would be satisfied with the kingship of Leinster, and invited Cobhthach to a feast. The feast was to be held in a magnificent building made entirely of iron. Cobhthach did not trust Labhraidh and decided to bring with him his entire armed retinue. When he arrived for the feast he was suspicious, and refused to enter. He sent in half his men, and when nothing happened to them, he was somewhat mollified. Áine saw that he was still reluctant to enter the building, and realised that her son's plan was about to fall apart. She decided to take matters into her own hands. She whispered to her son "I am nearly dead anyway, regain your honour through me", and walked straight into the building before he could stop her. Seeing this, Cobhthach believed it was safe to enter. As soon as the last man stepped inside Labhraidh closed the great iron doors, fastened great chains around the entire building and, weeping for his mother, placed faggots all around the building to be set alight. The burning faggots transformed the building into a giant oven. Áine died exultantly, knowing that her husband had been avenged, and that her son had achieved the birthright of which he had been robbed.

westward my glance craving such from Lugh...   the Otherworld, abode of gods, certain heroes and ancestors, was always considered to be situated over the sea to the west, although entrances to it could be found in the mountain passes, passage chambers, mounds, sites of standing stones, faerie rings, even caves, waterfalls, certain trees, other significant features of nature, and more.

Lugh   (cf).

to remedy split fatal stone...   the Lia Fáil, meaning Stone of Destiny (or also "Speaking Stone" to account for its oracular legend), is a stone at the Inauguration Mound on the Hill of Tara in County Meath, Ireland, which served as the coronation stone for the High Kings of Ireland. It is also known as the Coronation Stone of Tara. According to legend, the Lia Fáil was thought to be magical: when the rightful High King of Ireland put his feet on it, the stone was said to roar in joy. The stone is also credited with the power to rejuvenate the king and also to endow him with a long reign. According to Lebor Gabála Érenn, Cú Chulainn split it with his sword when it failed to cry out under his protégé, Lugaid Riab nDerg – from then on it never cried out again, except many years later under Conn of the Hundred Battles.

Lugaid Riab nDerg   (cf).

Derbforgaill   (cf).

the Shadow's prophecies   ie, prophecies of Scáthach (cf).

Connla   (cf).

Cú Chulainn   (cf).

Tír Tairngire   (cf).

shadow queen   Scáthach

bandraíodóir   (cf).

what use men in Alba know my name and in the winter night pity my wail   line adapted from The Prophecy of Scáthach https://members.tripod.com/tuan_o_greenfields/prophecy.html Historically, the term 'Alba' refers to Britain as a whole and is ultimately based on the Indo-European root for "white". It later came to be used by Gaelic speakers in the form of Alba (dative Albainn, genitive Albann, now obsolete) as the name given to the former kingdom of the Picts.

Cú Chulainn, Sétanta, the Shadow's man-bitch   (cf).

Lugh   (cf).

An Dagda   (cf).

Tuatha Dé   (cf).

Scáthach   (cf).

Cú Chulainn   (cf).

fáelán   means "little wolf", derived from Gaelic *fáel* "wolf" combined with a diminutive suffix (also was the name of a later Irish saint who did missionary work in Scotland).

the War Hound   nickname referring to Cú Chulainn (cf).

not unlike the double beams of golden sun//illuminating earthen floor and upright stone...   refers to the Winter Solstice sunrise event at Newgrange, where the sun shines into the long passage on the shortest days of the year and illuminates the central chamber - it is the most heralded event in the Irish cultural calendar, and is a famous example of ancient astronomy in action in modern times. At dawn on Winter Solstice every year, just after 9am, the sun begins to rise across the Boyne Valley from Newgrange over a hill known locally as Red Mountain. Given the right weather conditions, the event is spectacular. At four and a half minutes past nine, the light from the rising sun strikes the front of Newgrange, and enters into the passage through the roofbox which was specially designed to capture the rays of the sun. For the following 14 minutes, the beam of light stretches into the passage of Newgrange and on into the central chamber, where, in Neolithic times, it illuminated the rear stone of the central recess of the chamber. With simple stone technology, these wonderful people captured a very significant astronomical and calendrical moment in the most spectacular way: the sunlight appears to be split into two beams – a higher beam and a lower beam. This is in fact true, the lower beam being formed by the doorway to the passage. It is the light which enters through the roofbox, however, which reaches the central chamber.

in the womb of the moon   refers to the unique feature of Newgrange where the passage is built on a slight gradient. Because of this gradient the sun beam, penetrating in a horizontal line when it appears over the hills to the south, shines straight into the back chamber rather than illuminating the passageway itself. Stone R21, at the entrance to the chamber, juts into the passage almost interrupting the light beam and is carved with six horizontal grooves. Precession has caused the sun to change its position on the horizon a small but significant distance so that instead of lighting up the farthest back chamber as it would have when the monument was built it now shines on the stone with the triple spiral engraved on it on the right/east side of the chamber. Newgrange is known as a brugh, or brú, which is occasionally translated as 'mansion', but the old Irish word for 'womb' is Brú, and so Brú na Bóinne may be more correctly translated as 'Womb of the Moon,' or 'Womb of the Bright Cow.

conception-place of mineself   Newgrange is said to be the place where the great mythical hero Cú Chulainn was conceived by his mother Deichtre - his spiritual father, Lugh, visited Deichtre in a dream while she stayed at the Brugh—Newgrange. Reference: https://www.authenticvacations.com/newgrange-20-intriguing-facts/

final mortal resting place for my father of the long arm after drowning   Lugh met his own end after his wife Buach took Cermait, son of the Dagda, as a lover. Upon discovering this affair, Lugh had Cermait killed and washed his hands of the incident. Cermait's three sons, however, were very much alive, and swore vengeance upon the king. After capturing Lugh, they drowned him in a lake, thus giving it the name Loch Lugborta. Lugh had ruled for forty years, and his death marked the beginning of the end for the Tuatha Dé Danann. Legend has it that Lugh and his mystical family were buried at Newgrange (cf). Dagda Mór and his three sons are also believed to be entombed at this holy temple. Reference: https://www.gaia.com/article/irelands-newgrange-tomb-a-megalithic-hub-of-mystical-curiosity

Ferdiad   (cf).

"Scáthach's foretelling..."   re, the Prophecy of Scáthach, https://members.tripod.com/tuan_o_greenfields/prophecy.html (doesn't directly mention Ferdiad, except by inference ('there are bitter wounds to bear" - my interpretation of that line)).

immrama   (cf).

beyond the ninth wave   (cf).

white horses of Manannán mac Lir   refers to the waves of the sea (*Manannán mac Lir* - cf.).

momentarily spancilled   refers to the practice of "spancilling," which was to use a short rope to tie an animal's left fore-leg to its right hind leg, thereby hobbling the animal and stopping it from wandering too far. Used here to refer to the waves of the sea being calmed by Manannán mac Lir.

Tech Duinn   (cf).

Hy Breasil   (cf).

echtrae   generally, echtrae was the Old Irish word for "adventure" (literally meaning an "outing". Though Echtrai (plural) often involve a journey to an otherworld, the exact destination or journey can vary - voyages take place by sea in Echtrae Conli; in a journey underneath a lake in Echtrae Laegairi; or into a fairy mound (Sidhe) in Echtrae Nerai, alternatively the story may not included such a journey but instead involve an interaction with otherworldly beings: in Echtrae Nerai, set on Samhain, the hero Nera sees prophetic visions whilst in the presence of a hanged man, whilst in Echtra Mac nEchach Muid-medóin, the hero Níall gains the sovereignty of Ireland by kissing a hag guarding a well.

though longer the years in the making   time happens at a different pace in the Otherworld: sometimes the hero returns after what he believes is a short time, only to find that all his companions are dead and he has actually been away for hundreds of years; sometimes the hero sets out on a quest, and a magic mist descends upon him/her. He may find himself before an unusual palace and enter to find a warrior or a beautiful woman who makes him/her welcome, and after strange adventures the hero may return successfully. However, even when the mortal manages to return to his/her own time and place, they are forever changed by his contact with the Otherworld.

shadow-cursed spear   refers to the *Gáe Bulg* (cf).

Connla   (cf). text automatically following adapted from The Tragic Death of Connla, reference: https://www.maryjones.us/ctexts/aoife.html

Ulaid   (cf).

Aoife's revenge   (cf).

the Shadow   re, Scáthach (cf).

heeded my woman's sooth   ie, Emer's. Refers to lines: "Do not go down!" said she. "It is a son of thine that is down there. Do not murder thy only son! It is not fair fight nor wise to rise up against thy son. Turn to me! Hear my voice! My advice is good. Let Cu Chulainn hear it! I know what name he will tell, if the boy down there is Connla, the only son of Aife," said Emer.//Then said Cú Chulainn: "Forbear, woman! Even though it were he who is there," said he, "I would kill him for the honor of Ulster." - cf., The Tragic Death of Connla https://www.maryjones.us/ctexts/aoife.html

"Agus crosaim thú"   Irish cursing was a potent art. They could rebound on their casters, unless they quickly cancelled their maledictions with a blessing formula such as 'agus crosaim thú' in Gaelic or its English translation: 'I cross you'. I have Cú Chulainn use the same words to rebound the hexes and predictions put upon him by Aoife and Scáthach. Reference: http://poorit.com/site/celtic-word-for-magic-428eed

Amergin   (cf).

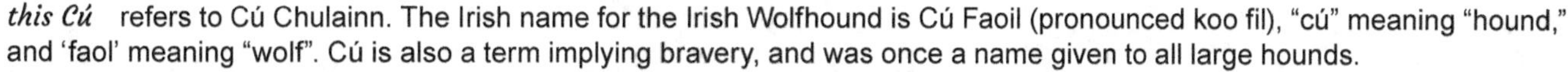

this Cú   refers to Cú Chulainn. The Irish name for the Irish Wolfhound is Cú Faoil (pronounced koo fil), "cú" meaning "hound," and 'faol' meaning "wolf". Cú is also a term implying bravery, and was once a name given to all large hounds.

Cú Chulainn   (cf).

Scáthach   (cf).

Cú Chulainn   (cf).

banfhili   (cf).

imbas forosnai   (cf).

Cruachan's heroes   refers to the men of Cruachan, the ancient capital of the kingdom of (Connaught Connacht) in Ireland.

Cú Chulainn.   (cf).

Scáthach ni Uanaind   (cf).

Cú Chulainn   (cf).

proud son of the sun   refers to him being the son of Lugh (cf).

Hound of Ulaid   ie, Cú Chulainn, Hound of Ulster.

Well of Sláine   the tale of the Well of Sláine takes place after the Battle of Mag Tuired (see below) - in this tale, Airmed (cf., below), along with her father and brothers, built a well to bring the slain warriors back to life after battle. The well was filled with healing herbs, and Airmed and the other healers sang an incantation over the waters to create an enchantment that could restore life when the warriors were dipped into it. The well was eventually abandoned, as the enemies of the Tuatha Dé Danann filled it up with stones so that it couldn't be used for healing. The legend goes that the site is still guarded by Dian Cécht (cf.) and his sons to this day.

(- the Battle of Mag Tuired   also spelled Moytura, a mythical plain in Ireland, was the scene of two important battles, neither featuring in this poem apart from references to the Well of Sláine itself, and particular individual characters (eg, Airmed, Lugh, Dian Cécht, Nuada, Balor, Mórrígan, etc). For further information regarding the two battles see https://en.wikipedia.org/wiki/Cath_Maige_Tuired.)

síoraíocht   (cf).

géilleadh deiridh   (cf).

ninefold elements...   reference: The Little Book of Celtic Wisdom. John and Caitlan Matthews, p9.

Tír na nÓg   (cf).

geasa   (cf).

Ériu   (cf).

Liam Macha   (cf).

the candour of Niamh, she who to refuse most irked wast)   Niamh (cf.) was a close and trusted friend of Cú Chulainn.

Ériu   (cf).

Badb   after their magically brewed sounds of war outside Emain Macha failed to draw Cú Chulainn out thanks to he being kept in the dark from hearing it by Conchobar, who, having heard of the plan concocted by the vengeful sons and daughters of the deceased sorcerer, feared he may well lose his champion to their druidic and sorcerous ways as revenge for the death of their father, kept him engaged with sports and feats for three days and nights, one of the daughters of Calatin shapeshifted into the appearance of Niamh (a trusted friend) and deceived him, urging him to pick up his arms as he was needed in the fray that eventually led to his death. Cú Chulainn lost his trust in all women as a result, even after Niamh tells him the truth, that *'not for the globe's gold nor the whole world's wealth had she e'er given I* [ie, Cú Chulainn*] that leave'*, but that it was Badb who had actually done so. In the mythology of Ireland her name means 'crow' in Old Irish, and in Modern Irish she is called Badhbh which means 'vulture'. The name literally means, in later Irish, 'scolding old hag' or witch, as well as 'scold crow' or 'skald crow' who appears on the battlefield . She was also a member of the fearsome Mórrígan, the triple goddess of death and prophecy. Often, Badb took the form of an old woman. It's unclear if Badb, the daughter of Calatin, is one and the same with Badb, the aspect of the Mórrígan, but for the purposes of this poem I took her as such.

thrice-cursed Calatin   (cf).

Cathbad   (cf).

Emer-mine   Emer (cf).

bodkin   short knife with a thin blade.

yellow-haired fairy woman washing my spoils   as Cú Chulainn rides to meet his enemies, he encounters the Mórrígan in the guise of a hag washing his bloody armour in a ford, an omen of his death. This line of text was adapted from stanza 28 of The Great Defeat on the Plain of Muirthemne before Cuchulainn's Death: 'Again he was on Emania's green, where Ulster's chiefs' and chieftains' daughters dolefully waiting for him raised piteous cries of grief. Last of all, Cathbad alone followed him ; nor as yet were they a great way from the fort when at the entrance into the Ford of Washing on Emania's plain they chanced upon a maiden, slender and white of her body, yellow of her hair. In grief and tribulation she on the ford's extreme brink ever washed and wrung crimson bloody spoils. "Little Cu," Cathbad asked, "seest thou not yonder sight? She is Badb's daughter that with woe and mourning washes thy gear, because she signifies thy fall and thy destruction by Meave's great hosting and by incantations of Calatin's children. Hence it is, my gentle foster-son, that thou shouldst refrain."...' Reference: https://sejh.pagesperso-orange.fr/keltia/version-en/deathcu2.html

Emania's green   'Emania' is the Latinized name for Emain Macha, or the palace of Emain - 'Emaina's green' refers to the plains around Emain Macha (Old Irish name for Navan Fort - an ancient ceremonial monument near Armagh, Northern Ireland.)

roasted deceit of crones three, embodiments of Her, the Morrigna, Badb, Macha, Nemain... the 'roasted deceit' refers to when Cú Chulainn was tricked into eating cooked dog meat by the three crones, breaking his own geasa, he unable to refuse their offering because in early Ireland there was a powerful general taboo against refusing hospitality, causing him to become spiritually (and physically) weakened for the fights ahead of him. In some texts there was only one crone, others three. The Morrigna (cf.) refers to the Mórrígan as a 'triple goddess' - one of Her most prominent aspects was Her nature as a triple goddess of war. In many stories, she appeared as both an individual and as three goddesses acting under a single name, depending on the literary source. In some cases, the daughters of Ernmas, Badb, Macha, and Anand were named as the Mórrígan, with Nemain or Fea sometimes replacing one of the goddesses in the triad. Elsewhere, the Mórrígan was listed as a sister of Badb and Macha, with Anand simply serving as an alternate name for the goddess. This inconsistency likely represented early Irish scholars' attempts to resolve a number of conflicting oral traditions. Reference: https://mythopedia.com/celtic-mythology/gods/morrigan/

thrice bloodied wine of my mother's cup (cf).

imbas forosnai (cf).

hooded shadow witch herself ie, *Scáthach (cf).*

Sétanta-come-Cú Chulainn (cf).

bone-fire original term for 'bonfire'.

Conchobar (cf).

Muirtheimne's plain (cf).

the Wheel's turning (cf., the Turner of the Wheel.)

Cathbad's call to take arms one day at Emain Macha, Cú Chulainn, still only a boy and known by his birth name, Sétanta overhears Cathbad teaching his pupils. One asks him what that day is auspicious for, and Cathbad replies that any warrior who takes arms that day will have everlasting fame. Cú Chulainn, though only seven years old, goes to Conchobar and asks for arms. None of the weapons given to him withstand his strength, until Conchobar gives him his own weapons. But when Cathbad sees this he grieves, because he had not finished his prophecy—the warrior who took arms that day would be famous, but his life would be short.

Scáthach's hex... (cf., The Prophecy of Scáthach https://members.tripod.com/tuan_o_greenfields/prophecy.html).

Plain of Muirtheimne (cf).

shining beings to come up from their mounds ie, áes sídhe (cf.), banished by the Milesians to reside forever underground.

the Dagda and His shaft (cf).

Dian Cécht (cf).

Airmed   goddess of healing, a member of the Tuatha dé Danann, daughter of Dian Cécht and the sister of Miach, an alchemist. She is mentioned in the Irish text Cath Maige Tuired as the one who assisted in healing during the second Battle of Maige Tuired.

lorg mór   (cf).

silvered hand for Nuada   'Nuadu's hand was cut off in the first battle of Mag Tuired - Sreng mac Sengainn (not featured in this poem) struck it from him. So, with Credne the brazier (not featured in this poem) helping him, Dian Cécht the physician put on him a silver hand that moved as well as any other hand.' - Cath Maig Tuired, trans. By Elizabeth A. Gray.

reclaimed first king of the children of Danu whose death paved for my father the way   Nuada was the first king of the Tuatha dé Danann (children of Danu), but, as the law of the time (which Nuada himself had written) dictated the king need be of whole mind and body, or 'wholly intact', and, having lost his hand in the first battle of Mag Tuired, he succeeded his throne to Breas (cf.), whose seven-year rule was marred with hunger and dissent. Once his 'new' prosthetic hand had been created by Dian Cécht and Goibniu, he and his brothers staged a coup and reclaimed the throne. In the final battle of Mag Tuired, however, Balor decapitated Nuada, and Lugh became king in his stead.

though prefereth I guts rewove of flesh and sinew...   indirect reference to the skill of Miach (see note following).

Miach of his father's spite no more, fourth cut of jealousy the cause   text found in the Cath Maige Tuired (The Second Battle of Mag Tuired), translated by Elizabeth A. Gray,: 33. Now Nuadu was being treated, and Dian Cécht put a silver hand on him which had the movement of any other hand. But his son Miach did not like that. He went to the hand and said "joint to joint of it, and sinew to sinew"; and he healed it in nine days and nights. The first three days he carried it against his side, and it became covered with skin. The second three days he carried it against his chest. The third three days he would cast white wisps of black bulrushes after they had been blackened in a fire.//34. Dian Cécht did not like that cure. He hurled a sword at the crown of his son's head and cut his skin to the flesh. The young man healed it by means of his skill. He struck him again and cut his flesh until he reached the bone. The young man healed it by the same means. He struck the third blow and reached the membrane of his brain. The young man healed this too by the same means. Then he struck the fourth blow and cut out the brain, so that Miach died; and Dian Cécht said that no physician could heal him of that blow.
Reference: https://www.sacred-texts.com/neu/cmt/cmteng.htm

the daughter, she of incant and herb   refers to Airmed (cf.) My use of the words 'incant and herb' refers to her singing chants over the water to activate its healing properties and save the wounded men at Sláigne's Well (also spelt 'Sláine's Well' - cf.), and to her knowledge of 'all the herbs on earth' and 'all the cures for every ailment under the sun' - she was a master druid, and it was she who imbued the Well of Slaine with its potent, curative power with her incantations and the many herbs she gathered and ground from the nearby plain Lusmag, or 'herb-plain'.
Reference: https://www.claudiamerrill.com/blog/the-irish-goddess-airmed

Awen-blessed   referred to as the flowing spirit, or the Celtic notion of indescribable wisdom, Druids believed in the ability of the Awen to spark creative inspiration and aesthetic powers among artists, as a source of instinctive knowledge, and, as implied in The Book of Taliesin, as an infusion from the divine (reference: https://en.wikipedia.org/wiki/Taliesin) because it awakens energy from the environment and transfers it into the mind, body, and soul. The word Awen derives from the Indo-European root -uel, meaning 'to blow', and has the same root as the word awel meaning 'breeze' in Welsh and 'wind' or 'gale' in Cornish. The three lines of the Arwen symbol relate to earth, sea and air; body, mind and spirit; or love, wisdom and truth.

for didst not her tears of grieving herbs produce...   in the mythology, her father Dian Cécht became jealous of his children's ability to heal: when King Nuada's arm was severed from his body in battle, he called upon Dian Cecht as his Chief Physician. Dian Cecht wanted to replace the King's arm with a new limb he fashioned from silver; however, Miach had a different plan. Miach was able to create an arm from flesh, and Airmed used her healing knowledge to bring the arm to life. Their father became so enraged that he murdered Miach and buried him on the battlefield (see note above *Miach of his father's spite no more, fourth cut of jealousy the cause*). Airmed rushed to the grave and was so distraught that from her tears 365 herbs grew. She then spread her cloak across the herbs to gather them up. Dian Cécht also became enraged by this and mixed them all up, casting them across the earth. This is why they say to this day nobody knows all the herbs and their healing properties, only those that are touched by Awen or intuitive knowledge can know. Reference: https://www.claudiamerrill.com/blog/the-irish-goddess-airmed

sláine   deliberately spelt this way to reference the Well of Sláine (cf).

Tir na nÓg (cf).

co-walker   Irish and Scottish folkloric figure. Just before or after someone died, an exact replica was often seen walking about. A woman on her deathbed might be seen in the woods, or someone recently deceased at their own wake. These co-walkers were sometimes described as twin souls freed, with the approach of death, but they were also spoken of as faeries, disguised as the person who stood on the edge of the Otherworld. It was important never to speak to these shades or faeries who would ultimately depart and not be seen again, though it is unclear whether the danger was considered to be to the deceased or the living.

síoraíocht   (cf).

my family's bean-sídhe   (cf., *baintside*) families often had a particular bean-sídhe that became 'attached' to them. See also notes: *leannán sídhe* and below. 'Bean-sidhe' means 'woman of the burial mounds'. Because banshees are probably one of Ireland's more well-known ghost-like spirits I wanted to somehow weave one into this work, but still make it 'believable' - after much research I found out about Clíodhna (see below), but then had to find a point in Cú Chulainn's history or ancestry that would serve as a realistic way to explain why/how she would've attached one to his bloodline in the first place - again, after extensive research, I found a way...

itself birthed into being and attached to my bloodline as payback long ago by Clíodhna, queen of sidheog   in Irish mythology, Clíodhna is a Queen of the Banshees of the Tuatha Dé Danann. Clíodhna is another of the beautiful feminine Irish goddesses whose responsibility was the Celtic Otherworld, and so she is associated with light and happiness - she was a goddess of love and beauty There is a colder edge to her character,however, and she is often depicted as stealing or causing the death of mortals, not necessarily from malice, but more out of cold disregard for insignificant mortal life. It is said that she used to employ her beauty in order to seduce men and to lure them to their deaths by the sea-shore. This is supposedly what gave rise to the old Irish superstition that it is unlucky to see a woman before you put to sea. She is said to have drowned in the harbour of Glandore, and the noise of the waves entering cliff caves near that spot has since been called Tonn Clíodhna, or Clíodhna's wave, also used to refer to the ninth, and largest, wave of every set. Its noise is loud and sudden and is said to foretell the death of a king or noble man in Ulster (Uliad). Clíodhna also foretold that, because of the way she was treated by mortals, a great wave sent by her would one day engulf all of Munster. In this poem, I have Clíodhna, as their queen, be responsible for the creation/'birth' of all bean sidhe (baintside, or banshees), in part because of her anger towards Manannán mac Lir for his taking of her away from her mortal lover, Ciabhán, the very reason she left the Otherworld in the first place, and at Dian Cécht for his killing of Méiche, the child born from the union of An Dagda and the Mórrígan, she (Clíodhna) having been looking forward to watching from afar the 'fell filth' that would have ensued had it/he (Méiche) survived, and, Dian Cécht being the great grandfather of Cú Chulainn, 'attaching' a bean sidhe (banshee) to his bloodline out of spite.

turneth her beauty sour didst she and redress becometh her satisfaction from loss of sport and swain 'sport' refers to Clíodhna's 'voyeuristic witnessing' to mortal happenings, her indifference to their/our affairs meaning she'd look on but rarely interfere - I surmised her 'loss' of such 'pleasure' and her loss of 'swain',came from her being taken from her mortal lover, and being so angry at her father for doing so, no matter his intention (see above), the primary catalyst for her actually becoming the queen of the sidheog in the first place.

Dian Cécht's thwarting... Dian Cécht once saved Ireland from the risk of being depopulated by three serpents. Dagda, the father of the gods, and his wife, the Mórrígan (Goddess of War, Death and Rebirth), had a child that was so evil in its appearance that Dian Cécht passed the motion that the child should be killed in infancy. On doing so, he opened the infants' heart to find three serpents inside that would de-populate Ireland when they would fully grow. He destroyed the serpents by burning them and casting their ashes into a river that boiled, killing every creature within it. The river became known as the River Barrow, the second longest river in Ireland after the River Shannon. https://surroundedbyselcouth.tumblr.com/post/169088550465/athe-metrical-dindshenchas-poem-13-berba-the

Méiche the only son of the Mórrígan, conceived in tryst with An Dagda (see previous note).

scion of the juice of the Mórrígan and the spunk of the Dadga ie, Méiche (cf).

Ériu (cf).

scattered in silent river, neither barrow nor mound safety, tomb without walls nor roof-tree its watery grave, seething and boiling to rags all things living therein indirect reference to the River Barrow, Ireland's second longest river. The Irish hydronym *Bhearú* has been derived from the Proto-Celtic *boru-* ("boil, brew"), and the river's name is associated with the legendary deeds of Dian Cécht who slew three serpents found in the heart of The Mórrígan's infant son and threw them into the Barrow, thus causing it to boil. Alternate spellings exist, including 'Berbae' or 'Berba' - in the previous few lines of this poem, referring to the 'fell filth', etc, that would've come about had Méiche lived, I use adapted sections of the text of poem 13 of The Metrical Dindshenchas, 'Berba'. Reference: https://surroundedbyselcouth.tumblr.com/post/169088550465/athe-metrical-dindshenchas-poem-13-berba-the

bean-sidhe (cf).

fertile Father and His raven bitch ie, An Dagdqa and the Mórrígan (cf).

still enraged at Manannán Mac Lir for his taking of her from her Ciabhán's side with incantation of the ninth wave Clíodhna left the otherworldly island of Tir Tairngire ("the land of promise") to be with her mortal lover, Ciabhán, but she was taken by a wave as she slept by her lover's side due to the incantations of Manannán mac Lir, dragged out to sea and drowned. See also note *beyond the ninth wave* in **Scáthach**. As both guardian of the Otherworld and Clíodhna's father, I surmised that Manannán Mac Lir had two very good reasons for taking Clíodhna away from Ciabhán - one, because he was mortal and the entrance to the Otherworld needed to be protected from mortal knowledge, and, as Clíodhna had made the extraordinary choice to leave it behind for love, being so enamoured she may have easily given that secret away in conversation with her beloved; and two, as her father and a deity, he wanted her to take up with another from their world (ie, the Otherworld), not a mortal, and he must've known that reasoning with her to change her mind was futile.

her vitriol still heard in every breaking wave thundering from the sea cf., 'Clíodhna's wave' in note *itself birthed into being and attached to mine bloodline as payback long ago by Clíodhna, queen of sidheog every drowned sailor lured towards her lovesong*   Clíodhna is said to have lured sailors to the sea-shore where they would drown, unconcerned as she was with the fate of mere mortals. Reference: https://www.ireland-information.com/irish-mythology/cliodhna-irish-legend.html

harbouring of my blood-line, Dal Duana-come-Lugh   Cían managed to save one of his three children from Balor by bringing him to a little boat he had hidden away, fleeing with fire and storm from the boiling oceans hard at his heels - he delivered the child to Manannán Mac Lir to raise, and the boy, then known as Dal Duana, became in time Lugh, king of the Tuatha Dé Danann. Reference: https://emeraldisle.ie/balor-of-the-evil-eye

the sun who held the light of this Cú Chulainn in his Otherworldly seed   ie, Lugh (cf).

Dian Cécht   (cf).

Tailtiu, last queen of the Fir Bolg   Tailtiu was the wife of Eochaid mac Eirc, last Fir Bolg High King of Ireland, who named his capital after her (Teltown, between Navan and Kells). She survived the invasion of the Tuatha Dé Danann and became the foster mother of Lugh. Tailtiu cleared a great forest in order for the Irish to plant the first fields, but this feat exhausted her and when she was finished, she laid down at her castle and died. The Lughnasadh games were actually the funeral games held by Lugh in her honour.

Áenach Tailteann   games founded by Lugh Lámhfhada, the Ollamh Érenn (master craftsman or doctor of the sciences), as a mourning ceremony for the death of his foster-mother Tailtiu. Lugh buried Tailtiu underneath a mound in an area that took her name and was later called Tailteann in County Meath. The event was held during the last fortnight of July and culminated with the celebration of Lughnasadh, or Lammas Eve (1 August). The ancient Áenach had three functions: honoring the dead, proclaiming laws, and funeral games and festivities to entertain. The first function took between one and three days depending on the importance of the deceased. Guests would sing mourning chants called the Guba, after which druids would improvise Cepógs, songs in memory of the dead. The dead would then be burnt on a funeral pyre. The second function would then be carried out during a universal truce by the Ollamh Érenn, giving out laws to the people via bards and druids and culminating in the igniting of another massive fire. The custom of rejoicing after a funeral was then enshrined in the Cuiteach Fuait, games of mental and physical ability. Games included the long jump, high jump, running, hurling, spear throwing, boxing, contests in swordfighting, archery, wrestling, swimming, and chariot and horse racing. They also included competitions in strategy, singing, dancing and story-telling, along with crafts competitions for goldsmiths, jewellers, weavers and armourers. Along with ensuring a meritocracy, the games would also feature a mass arranged marriage, where couples met for the first time and were given up to a year and a day to divorce on the hills of separation· In later medieval times, the games were revived and called the Tailten Fair, consisting of contests of strength and skill, horse races, religious celebrations, and a traditional time for couples to contract "Handfasting" trial marriages. "Taillten marriages" were legal up until the 13th century.

Cían   (cf).

Eithne   (cf).

one whose name meant death/the father of evil eye, Fomor king, Balor of the Mighty Blows   in Irish mythology, Balor, or Balar, was a leader of the Fomorians (cf). He is often described as a giant with a large eye that wreaked destruction when opened. Balor takes part in the Battle of Mag Tuired, and is primarily known from the tale in which he is killed by his grandson, Lugh of the Tuatha Dé Danann. He has been interpreted as a personification of the scorching sun.

Cían's serving-girl employment on desolate bandit isle where eaten meat uncooked his artifice   once he'd gained entry into Túr Mór, Cían pretended to be a serving-girl in order to get close to Eithne. 'Bandit isle' refers to it being the isle breached by Biróg and Cían. Use of the line 'where meat uncooked...' refers to the horrid state of the conditions within which Balor had imprisoned his daughter.

held counsel with ocean's master by night his guile   ie, he had meetings with Manannán Mac Lir to arrange saving the children via the sea.

Eithne's liberation from lifelong loneliness his shrewd maneuver   she had been imprisoned in the tower atop Túr Mór her whole life, and Cían's skillful coming to her was her liberation from her torment.

my dream-seen grandfather's face her deliverance   although never having seen any men before, Eithne had multiple visions of Cían before he came to her tower.

their tryst in crystal tower atop Túr Mór pregnant with consequence   Lugh was conceived in a secret liaison between Cían and Eithne at Túr Mór ('great tower'), part of Dún Bhaloir, 'the Anvil' part of Balor's Fort on Tory Island (Irish: Toraigh), inine miles of the coast of Co Donegal.

attempted drowning of leanbh three at Balor's behest further cause of this family's darkened fortune   I decided this event in Cú Chulainn's family history was another reason why Clíodhna maintained her vitriol towards him, the attempt at filicide somehow furthering her malice, the thought of someone trying to kill a child perhaps reminding her of her loss, she craving to have borne and reared a child for Ciabán.

fear of druidic prophecy his argument, fear of druidic devices borne of smoke-plumed spell of death the fuel, though it to no avail, his covet his undoing   when Balor was a boy, passing by a house he heard the druids of the Formorians chanting from inside. He knew that they were preparing spells of death and destruction to use in upcoming battles against the Tuatha Dé Danann, and he knew that one was never supposed to look in on druids during their work. But with the window open a crack and the temptation too great to resist, he peeped in, just for a moment. When he looked, a plume of smoke from the druids' spells shot out and hit him in the eye - he cried out in pain, and the druids all came running. They realized that the spell of death they had been making had gone into Balor's eye, and anyone he looked at with that eye from then on would die. Thereafter, Balor kept his eye closed among his own people, but whenever he went into battle he had only to open it and look upon his enemies for them to fall dead before him. Reference: https://en.wikipedia.org/wiki/Balor
On that same day in Balor's youth, he was told of a prophecy by his father's druid which filled him with terror: he was warned that he would be murdered by his own grandson. Because of his fear of their prediction, when she was born Balor imprisoned his beautiful daughter, Ethniu, in a crystal tower on the headlands of Tory Island, leaving twelve female companions, or druidesses, to watch over her.
At that time, a magical cow known as Glas Gaibhnenn was owned by Cían, a lord of land, a man of the Tuatha Dé Danann, and Balor highly coveted and later stole it, leading it to Glas Gaibhnenn, his remote fortress on Tory Island. Cian sought revenge on Balor for the theft of his cow - he persuaded a *filidh*, or sorceress, of the Tuatha Dé Danann, called Biróg, to help him. Biróg told Cían that, as Balor forbade any man visiting Eithne in her tower prison, the only way to gain access to Balor's daughter was to dress in the guise of a woman, as twelve female companions guarded the maiden night and day. Biróg smuggled Cían past the twelve female companion attendants so he could seduce Eithne. Biróg and Cían left the next morning. Eithne remembered nothing of Cían because Biróg used her magic to wipe the memory of him from the poor maiden's mind. Eithne bore triplets after her romantic encounter with Cían, but Balor found the three infant boys and became so angry that he sacrificed the poor children by throwing them into the sea. Biróg rescued one of the babies and carried him to Goibniu the smith (cf.) to be fostered.

The boy was Lugh, the "fair-haired", and he grew to be a skilled warrior and champion of the Tuatha Dé Danann. Legends said Lugh was so beautiful and radiant that no mortal could look upon him and live, much like his son, Cú Chulainn. Because of his many skills, Nuada, the leader of the Tuatha Dé Danann, and the other gods of the same, asked Lugh for his help in a war against the Fomorians. The supernatural spear which Lugh owned together with the many talents he possessed as a warrior allowed him to eventually become the leader of the Tuatha Dé Danann, when, during the second battle of Magh Tuireadh (cf.), Nuada was killed during the battle. Lugh assumed the position of head chieftain after Nuada's death.
Lugh saw Balor during the fighting on the battlefield and used his slingshot to destroy Balor's evil eye, thus fulfilling the prophecy.
Reference: https://celtsandmyths.tumblr.com/post/182944610665/balor-of-the-evil-eye-in-celtic-mythology

Balor used the fear generated by the prophecy of his own death as his excuse to imprison Eithne, and I also reason that another part of that fear came from his experience as a boy when he defied the druidic prohibition on watching them create their magic, due to the pain and suffering he experienced as a result.

one child thus surviving   ie, Lugh (cf).

his own grandson   ie, Lugh (cf).

Clíodhna   (cf).

Lugh of the long arm   (cf).

prophecy so unravelled   (cf). (ie, prophecy that Balor would be slain by his own grandson.)

Clíodhna   (cf).

Biróg's claim of leannán sídhe   Biróg, or Biroge of the Mountain, Birog), in Irish folklore, is the leannan sídhe or the female familiar spirit of Cian who aids him in the folktale about his wooing of Balor's daughter Eithne. Leannán sídhe are usually depicted as a beautiful woman of the Aos Sí ("people of the barrows") who takes a human lover. Lovers of the leannán sídhe are said to live brief, though highly inspired, lives. The name comes from the Gaelic words for a sweetheart, lover, or concubine and the term for inhabitants of fairy mounds (fairy)

Cian   (cf).

corses   (cf).

lament of beauty taken   (cf).

as did falleth she so far from shapely, comely allure and status   (cf.) I surmised that by choosing to leave the Otherworld and then becoming queen of the sidheog after losing Ciabhán, Clíodhna had forfeited the right to remain known as the Goddess of Love and Beauty.

her own birds' curing calls, kingfisher, blue tit, bullfinch   as the goddess of love and beauty, Clíodhna was surrounded by three magical birds - kingfisher, blue tit, bullfinch - whose fabulous songs could cure all ills. Those who heard the songs were lulled into a deep sleep and when they awoke found that their sickness had been cured. I decided that not even her own birds of healing could reach her when she drowned. Reference: https://www.ireland-information.com/irish-mythology/cliodhna-irish-legend.html

caoine   from Old Irish caíne ("gentleness, pleasantness, beauty"), from caín ("fine, good, fair, beautiful; soft, smooth; soft, gentle; fine, clement"). In Ireland and parts of Scotland, a traditional part of mourning is the keening woman (bean chaointe), who wails a lament—in Irish: Caoineadh. 'Caoin' means "to weep, to wail". This keening woman may in some cases be a professional, and the best keeners would be in high demand. Irish legend speaks of a lament being sung by a fairy woman, or banshee/bean sidhe/baintside. She would sing it when a family member died or was about to die, even if the person had died far away and news of their death had not yet come. In those cases, her wailing would be the first warning the household had of the death. The banshee was also a predictor of death. If someone was about to enter a situation where it is unlikely they will come out alive, she would warn people by screaming or wailing, giving rise to a banshee also being known as a wailing woman.

voicing ... my very fall by Medb's great hosting and by incantations of Calatin's children   (cf).

king-slayer spear   Lugaid Cú Roi had three magical spears made, and it was prophesied that a king would fall by each of them.

son of the battlefield hound   ie, Lugaid Cú Roi, son of Cú Roi (cf).

Loeg mac Riangabra, king of charioteers   (cf).

Grey of Macha, king of horses   (cf).

dobhar-chú   (cf).

Scáthach   (cf).

Conchobar's champion of the Red Branch Knights   ie, Cú Chulainn. The Red Branch Knights were an elite group of warriors who served as the king's personal bodyguard as well as defending Ulaid (Ulster) from other provinces. The name *Red Branch* comes from the name of the assembly hall in Emain Macha. It was called "*Craebh Ruadh*" in Irish Gaelic.

Uliad   (cf).

only warrior exempted from birth-pang curse of she of the speed of wind   refers to the curse of Macha (cf.) - because of his youth, Cú Chulainn was exempted from the effects of Macha's curse (see note following). The 'speed of wind' refers to the speed Macha ran whilst heavily pregnant.

only my beardlessness my saviour ... without mine holding of Medb's forces at bay   at the age of seventeen, Cú Chulainn single-handedly defended Ulaid (Ulster) from the army of Connacht in the Táin Bó Cúailnge. Cú Chulainn allowed Medb (cf.) to take Ulaid by surprise because he was with a woman when he should have been watching the border. The men of Ulaid were disabled by a curse that caused them to suffer from labour pains (cf.), so it became up to Cú Chulainn to stop Medb's army from advancing further. He did so by invoking the right of single combat at fords. He defeated champion after champion in a standoff that lasted for months.

met with death in birthing faux   for failing to use their strength to defend her in her time of need, Macha declared that their strength would become useless to them. Whenever they needed it most, their strength would desert them, and for nine days and nine nights, they would endure the pains of a woman in childbirth - hence 'birthing faux'. (cf).

men of Ériu   (cf).

Emain Macha   (cf).

no more the provoking of their husband's wrath   Cú Chulainn was said to be so handsome and beautiful the men of Ulaid worried that, without a wife of his own, he would steal their wives and ruin their daughters.

War Hound   one of Cú Chulainn's nicknames (cf).

colg   (cf).

claideb   (cf).

men of Ériu   men of Ireland (cf).

swedge   informal Scottish for a fight or a brawl (noun), or to right or brawl (verb).

rammy   Scottish term for a general fight, a "free for all", a scuffle, a violent disturbance or commotion (Gsw.).

my father   referring to Lugh (cf).

riastrad   (cf).

welkin   literary noun referring to the sky or heaven.

"My father..."   referring to Lugh (cf.) specifically, but this piece of text ("My father - of need?") mimics Jesus's last words on the cross, highlighting the similarities between His and Cú Chulainn's plights (dying/sublimating and passing into myth and legend after three days on their respective 'crosses' (Cú Chulainn's being the Stone of the Big Man, 'Clogh an Fear Mor' (cf)).

roar of agony and excruciation of Macha's final exertion   (cf).

Áine's last whispered prayer before her martyred immolation   (cf.) I envisaged her saying a silent prayer to her gods as she walked into the conflagration, for her own soul and for her son's promised revenge.

géilleadh deiridh   (cf).

Forgall   (cf).

Úathach   (cf).

Aoife   (cf).

Scáthach   (cf).

Ferdiad   (cf).

Connla   (cf).

Emer   (cf).

Ériu   (cf.) land and goddess combined

one of sisters three   Ériu was one of three sisters, the other two are likewise considered sovereign goddesses of Ireland, however, neither Banba nor Fódla are as well known or respected as Ériu (see note *gaveth she…* below).

Milesians   inhabitants of Ireland following the Tuatha Dé Danann. The descendants of Milesians are said to be the monarchs and leading families of early Ireland.

the Tuatha Dè fading, so passing the fifth age of the world   the Tuatha Dé were the fifth peoples to inhabit/conquer Ireland. The tribe of the Fomorians were on the scene long before any other races came to Ireland. However, the Fomors lived mainly in the sea (Irish: Fomhóire, means 'from the sea'). The first outside race to invade Ireland was the race of the Partholon - very little is known of them, but after 300 years of struggle against the Fomors, the Partholons died of an epidemic. Next came the race of Nemed who also suffered from an epidemic. This time, though, some of the Nemedians survived, only to be oppressed by the Fomors. Later came colonizers from Spain or Greece called the Fir Bolgs. They were actually three tribes; men of Domnu, men of Gaillion, and men of Bolg. They intermarried with the Fomors and held the country until the arrival of the Tuatha Dé Danann. They were followed by the Milesians, then came the Irish Celts, then the Picts (from Roman 'pictii', meaning painted.) Various other waves of races/peoples followed after...

their queen's names inshrined upon the very sod itself, Banba, Fódla, Ériu   (cf).

their husbands grandsons of the Dadga, sons of sun, hazel, and plough   during the time of the Milesian Invasion, the sister-goddesses were respectively married to the three Danaan kings of the Tuatha Dé Danann, Mac Grené ('Son of the Sun'), Mac Cuill ('Son of Hazel') and Mac Cécht ('Son of the Plough'). The three Danann kings were grandsons of the Dagda, god of life and death and chief of the Tuatha Dé Danann. Reference: https://www.ancientpages.com/2019/02/15/eriu-powerful-irish-goddess-and-sacred-uisneach-hill-where-she-and-god-l ugh-are-buried/

Ériu hath more the mantle worn, for 'twas with calm utterance she words of power and draíocht spake/gaveth she injury for the insult to Donn mac Miled for his slur, sentence of death enacted, he drowning his fate   one of the reasons Ériu was more widely known, and the reason Ireland is named after her, is from one of her better-known legends that speaks of the invasion of the Milesians, and how Ériu and her sisters stood against the invaders and demanded they leave. "One, Donn mac Miled, replied to her demand with insults, and Eriu calmly sentenced him to death; he drowned shortly thereafter." Thus Ireland was named after her, later written as Erin, and she became a popular symbol for Romantic Ireland in countless stories and poems thereafter. Reference: https://irishstudies.sunygeneseoenglish.org/eriu-mebd/

draíocht   Irish term, whose literal translation is (1) druidic art, druidism, and (2) , witchcraft, magic or charm, enchantment, is a 'power' or 'talent' attributed to the Tuatha Dé Danann, and specifically Ériu, in their/her ability to overcome the Fir Bolg.

Medb   (cf).

Connla   (cf).

her water spear   ie, the *Gáe Bulg* (cf).

dòigh nàdair   (cf).

mistress of shade   (ie, Scáthach - cf.)

Scáthach's salute   refers to lines from the prophecy of Scáthach (cf).
Reference: https://members.tripod.com/tuan_o_greenfields/prophecy.html

my father's satisfaction   ie., Lugh's blessing (cf).

Setanta   (cf).

Turner of the Wheel   (cf).

sidhe   (cf).

my father's chain   (ie, the stars of the Milky Way - cf.)

embosomed by Danu   (cf., note: *Children of Danu*) the Irish mother goddess Danu was the ancestor from which all Tuatha Dé Danann claimed descent. Despite her importance to Irish mythology and though She was the mother goddess and namesake of the Tuatha Dé Danann tribe, much about her remains shrouded in mystery. Danu was the source of the tribe's common heritage, as well as its nobility, unity, and power. As a goddess of sovereignty and power, Danu would grant gifts to rulers and those of noble birth. Though such gifts varied in value and substance, it is nevertheless clear that the kings, chiefs, and Ollam of the Tuatha Dé Danann all drew their power from her. The Tuatha Dé Danann were creative, crafty, and skilled; it has been theorized that Danu was the source of such talents. As a mother goddess, Danu was also believed to have suckled many of the gods (hence 'embosomed') and instilled in them a sense of wisdom. She was an ancient deity, and made no appearances in the larger Celtic mythos. Though scholars have frequently sought answers regarding this mysterious matriarch, few definitive details have been found - many scholars believed Danu to be a representation of the Danube River. Given the migratory nature of the Tuatha Dé Danann, it has been speculated that she was a wind or earth and river goddess as well. All things in Ireland depended upon her blessings. Her connection to the earth also tied her to the fairies, fairy mounds, and the many standing stones and dolmens of Ireland.

proclaimed worthy of the hero's portions for my feats   refers to events that occurred at Bricriu's Feast (cf.) where the troublemaker Bricriu once incited three heroes, Cú Chulainn, Conall Cernach and Lóegaire Búadach, to compete for the champion's portion at his feast. In every test that was set Cú Chulainn came out on top, but neither Conall nor Lóegaire would accept the result. Cú Roí mac Dáire of Munster settled it by visiting each in the guise of a hideous churl and challenging them to behead him, then allow him to return and behead them in return. Conall and Lóegaire both behead Cú Roí, who picked up his head and left, but when the time came for him to return they fled. Only Cú Chulainn was brave and honourable enough to submit himself to Cú Roí's axe; Cú Roí spared him and he was declared champion.

floating in my spirit-chariot above Emain Macha   (ine adapted from text from The Death of Cú Chulainn http://www.ancienttexts.org/library/celtic/ctexts/cuchulain3.html) Emain Macha was the traditional seat of the kings of Ulster and the capital of the Ulstermen (Ulaid). It has been identified as the present Navan Fort, an enclosure approximately two miles west of the city of Armagh. The Irish name of Navan Fort is Eamhain Mhacha, from Old Irish Emain Macha. The second element refers to the goddess Macha, for whom nearby Armagh (Ard Mhacha) is also named - the name Eamhain Mhacha has been interpreted as "Macha's twins" or "Macha's brooch", referring to the curse of Macha (cf., Macha's labour-pain curse against the men of Uliad). It was the centre around which clustered the romantic tales of the Red Branch Knights of the king of Uliad, Conchobar mac Nessa, of which as a boy Setanta sought out and joined, and as Cú Chulainn was one of their champions.

Reul Near, Reul Deas, Reul Niar, Reul Tuath   stars of the East, South, West, North, known as the Four Stars of Destiny (source: (source: *The Little Book of Celtic Wisdom*, John and Caitlin Mattheus, Element Books Limited, 1993, p11).

knotted triad leaves of the trinities, the three-legged whorls of triskelion alchemy   (cf., triskelion)

the places where the sun sets and the ages of the moon   references lines from the "Song of Amergin".

shadow witch's prophecy of me   cf., the prophecy of Scáthach. Reference: *https://members.tripod.com/tuan_o_greenfields/prophecy.html*

my father   Lugh (cf).

Hy Breasil   (cf).

mistress of shade   Scáthach (cf).

my Cú   Cú Chulainn (cf).

Medb   (cf).

She, darkest raven of death's despair and blood's foreboding, the Morrígu Herself   (cf., the Mórrígan)

'twas kings three didst fall by the spear...   refers to the deaths of the three 'kings' by the three magical spears fashioned by Lugaid Cú Roi - Cú Chulainn's charioteer, his main horse, and, of course, himself.

Lugaid   (cf).

Láeg mac Riangabra, king of charioteers   (cf).

Gray of Macha, king of horses   (cf).

Sétanta-come- Cú Chulainn   (cf).

níos fearr déanach ná riamh   better late than never (Irish-English)

Lugh   (cf).

the light of the sun within me   reference to Lugh (cf).

Tír na nÓg   (cf).

Ériu   (cf).

Turner of the Wheel   (cf).

síoraíocht   (cf).

entwined in the branches and reaching night sky of the tracks of the snow-killed calf across the raven blackness   refers to the mythological story of 'Deirdre of the Sorrows', also sometimes called "The Tragical Death of the Sons of Uisneach". References: https://bardmythologies.com/deirdre-of-the-sorrows/ https://mythicalireland.com/MI/blog/astronomy-and-the-sky/the-milky-way-the-twining-branches-of-deirdre-and-her-lov er-naoise/

the snow-killed calf   specifically refers to the moment when Deirdre witnessed a calf being slaughtered and a raven came out to peck at the blood spilt upon the snow, and instead of being upset at the sight she fell in love with the three colours black, white, and red, and swore she would 'only give her love to a man with hair as black as a raven, skin as white as snow, and cheeks as red as blood' - who her nurse, Leabharcham, informed her could only be the nephew of King Conchobar mac Nessa of Ulster and a son of Uisneach, Noíse. The rest of her/their story is convoluted, but results in their tragic deaths (see above). The 'tracks' across the 'raven blackness' are the stars of the Milky Way across the night sky (see also the note *the white cow's hooves spanning the darkening sky below*), the use of the word '*raven*' referring to both the raven in the above legend and, for me, another appearance of the twister of fates Herself, the Mórrígan.

Uliad   (cf).

Cú Chulainn   (cf).

Connla   (cf).

Ferdiad   (cf).

Aoife   (cf).

Mórrígan   (cf).

Medb   (cf).

luna wolven   a luna wolf is another term for the alpha female in the pack, which is the counterpart of the alpha male. She is the main female, and the rest of the group will also provide help and guidance for the luna wolf, and will protect her against enemies and her pups when she is pregnant.

teardrop of beauty   refers to Fand ("tear", "teardrop of beauty") or Fann ("weak, helpless person'") was an otherworldly woman in Irish mythology. The two forms of her name are not phonetic variants, but two different words of different meaning.

drinking not from mine mother's cups   (cf. note: "*betrayed by thrice bloodied wine of Deichtre that would not unturn...*".)

Emer's six gifts so suitable   the qualities prized by the ancient Celts: beauty, chastity, sweet speech, needlework, voice and wisdom, which Emer was said to possess to perfection.
Reference: https://bardmythologies.com/cuchulainn-the-wooing-of-emer/

friendship of the Shadow's thighs   refers to Scáthach and his laying and sleeping with her.

Forgall's broken bond   (cf., note: *Forgall.*)

Bláthnat's fall forced   (cf. note: *redress for mine shaming milkstreamed betokening.*)

Beltane fires   (cf).

Turner of the Wheel   (cf).

echtrai plural of echtra or echtrae   (cf).

the cauldrons inside of)   (cf).

Ériu   (cf).

Eochaid Ollathair   Eochaid or Eochaidh (earlier Eochu or Eocho, sometimes Anglicised as Eochy, Achaius or Haughey) is a popular medieval Irish and Scottish Gaelic name deriving from Old Irish *ech*, horse, borne by a variety of historical and legendary figures, including the Dadga.

upended His Coire ansic's undried oatmeal broth   magical cauldron from the Tuatha Dé city of Murias known as The Un-Dry, the food from which was sure to satiate any host - it was said to be bottomless, and from it no man left unsatisfied. It was said to have a ladle so big that two people could fit in it.

this Hound   Cú Chulainn (cf).

Scáthach ni Uanaind, Warrior Maid, She-Witch   (cf).

this Hound   Cú Chulainn (cf).

Scáthach   (cf).

na cruinne ar fad   Irish for 'the whole universe'.

síoraíocht   (cf).

Díadacht   (cf).

dòigh nàdair   (cf).

Mórrígan   (cf).

scald-crow   tradition remains that the scald crow (a subspecies of the carrion crow, Corvus corone cornix, that has a grey body and black head, wings, and tail) is often seen as an omen of death.

Badb Catha   the Badb Catha, literally meaning "battle crow," was a figure in Irish mythology described as a demoness or a war and crow goddess who frequented battlefields, delighted with the deaths that occurred there. She was one of the three aspects of the Mórrígan. She would often take the form of a screaming raven or crow, striking fear into those who heard her, and could also be heard as a voice among the corpses on a battlefield. Battlefields themselves were sometimes referred to as "the gardens of the Badb". Linked to the Mórrígan, Badb, as an evil personality, frequented battle fields before and after the slaughter. In this role, Badb was known as *badhbh chaointe* who presaged death as a 'weeping' or 'keening' crow. Badb was identified with the *bean-sidhe* (cf., note: *baintsidhe*) or banshee, in her function of pre-empting death to certain families. The bean-sidhe was a phantom, a spectre, or female fairy, who is also commemorated in County Kerry at Lisabe, or Badb's fort. The term *bodh* or *badh* originally meant rage, fury, or violence, which eventually came to signify a fairy, witch or goddess.

spaewife   (cf).

Táin   (cf).

dream or enchanted vision upon Grellach Dolluid   refers to sections of text from 'The Cattle-Raid of Regamna, The Yellow Book of Lecan', a prelude to the Táin Bó Cúailnge where Cú Chulainn encounters the Mórrígan riding in a chariot pulled by a one-legged horse with the pole of the chariot passing through its body to its forehead and accompanied by 'great man' with a red cloak and a staff of hazel driving a forlorn-looking cow before him - after discourse and then when challenged they disappear, only a black bird left in their place.Cú Chulainn denies Her power over him, telling Her that "If only I had known it was you, not thus should we have separated." The Mórrígan then declares She is the "... guarding of thy death - that I am, and I shall be...", and that "this clay-land shall be called dolluid (of evil,)" and it has been the Grellach Dolluid ever since.
Reference: http://www.ancienttexts.org/library/celtic/ctexts/regamna.html

if I had known 'twas She in form of hag with tripple-teated cow I'd not have healed Her...   (cf).

Scáthach   (cf).

this Hound   Cú Chulainn (cf).

áes sídhe   (cf).

battles of Maige Tuired   (cf).

who cried portends of doom and rained down fire and blood upon the Fir Bolg on behalf of Her own   There are various stories of Mórrígan, some are contradictory or change depending on the source. However, the Mórrígan (and Her sisters/aspects Badb and Macha) is/are first seen in the Battle of Mag Tuired between the Tuatha Dé Danann (who invaded Ireland) and their followers and the indigenous Fir Bolgs. Before the battle erupted, the Mórrígan cried out doom and used sorcery against the Fir Bolg to rain down fire and blood so that they could not move for three days and nights. (adapted from text: 'It was then that Badb and Macha and Mórrígan went to the Knoll of the Taking of the Hostages, and to the Hill of Summoning of Hosts at Tara, and sent forth magic showers of sorcery and compact clouds of mist and a furious rain of fire, with a downpour of red blood from the air on the warriors' heads; and they allowed the Fir Bolg neither rest nor stay for three days and nights. 'A poor thing,' said the Fir Bolg, 'is the sorcery of our sorcerers that they cannot protect us from the sorcery of the Tuatha Dé,' 'But we will protect you,' said Fathach, Gnathach, Ingnathach, and Cesard, the sorcerers of the Fir Bolg; and they stayed the sorcery of the Tuatha Dé.') Reference: https://loraobrien.ie/first-battle-of-moytura-cath-muige-tuired-cunga/

Fir Bolg   (cf).

Fomorian   (cf).

breasts heaving   indirect reference to the *Dá Chích na Morrígna* ("two breasts of the Mórrígan"), a pair of hills in County Meath.

the Otherworld   (cf).

the Dagda   (cf).

the Unius   a river of Connacht where the Mórrígan was washing herself when the Dagda returned from the camp of the Fomori and coupled with Her. The foot of the Unius was called the Ford of Destruction since the second battle of Magh Tuiread. Méiche (cf.) came from their union.

two handfuls of Indech's blood...   after killing him with magic, Mórrígan gave to the gathered host Indech's "blood in her two palms" Refererence: https://www.academia.edu/15486900/The_Role_of_the_Morrigan_in_the_Cath_Maige_Tuired_Incitement_Battle_Ma gic_and_Prophecy

Indech   Indech mac De Domnann, king of the Fomori (cf.) in the tale of the second battle of Mag Tuiredh (cf.).

Ford of Destruction   refers to the Ford of Unsen at the foot of the Unius river (cf.), named such because of the magical injury done there to the Indech (cf.).

Fomorian   (cf).

Méiche's snakes Her abortion   (cf).

Clíodhna   (cf).

masts of Macha...   term refers to severed heads left on a battlefield ('harvest of Macha'). Further, the ground was considered sacred after the battle, as the soldiers would leave until the next day so Mórrígan could gather the souls of the slain undisturbed. Reference: http://goddessschool.com/projects/AvalonRaine/TheMorrigan.html

Táin   (cf).

Ériu   (cf).

bairdne   'bardic craft, bardic composition, bardic metre' in early Irish.

the spear that spoils and wages battle, the boar of valour, the powerful ox   text adapted from the Song of Amergin.

war-hound of Culann   ie, Cú Chulainn - it was killing Culann's fierce guard dog that gave rise to the boy Setanta thereafter being known as Cú Chulainn (ie, 'Culann's Hound).

truly do we suffer deaths three...   text directly following adapted from quote by David Eagleham, "Metamorphosis", Sum: Forty Tales from the Afterlives, 2009

corvid crow-woman   refers to the Mórrígan. *Emer* (cf).

Aoife   (cf).

Scáthach   (cf).

Connla   (cf).

Ferdiad   (cf).

Úathach   (cf).

Deichtre   (cf).

Bláthnat   (cf).

Cathbad   (cf).

Ériu   (cf).

Tír Na nÓg   (cf).

sidhe mounds   (cf., *sidhe*)

Fae   a type of mythical being or legendary creature ((also *fay, fae, fey, fair folk*, or *faerie*) found in the folklore of multiple European cultures (including Celtic, Slavic, German, English, and French folklore), a form of spirit, often described as metaphysical, supernatural, or preternatural. Here referring to both beings/spirits of the underground-bound Tuatha Dé Danann and faeries in general. Point of interest: 'fae' means 'from' in Scottish.

Ulaid   (cf).

this Hound   Cú Chulainn (cf).

Turner of the Wheel   (cf).

my father's chain   Lugh's sling rod, named "Lugh's Chain", was the rainbow and the Milky Way.

the white cow's hooves spanning the darkening sky   in Irish mythology, the main name of the Milky Way was Bealach na Bó Finne — Way of the White Cow. It was regarded as a heavenly reflection of the sacred River Boyne, which is described as "the Great Silver Yoke" and the "White Marrow of Fedlimid," names which could equally apply to the Milky Way.

Lugaid Cú Roi   (cf).

sons and daughters of Calatin   (cf).

this great Táin   (cf).

naught but a fair man facing his foes in the starlit ford of night   references a line from the Táin Bó Cúailnge (cf.), I also use it as a suggestion of the internal struggles Cú Chulainn faces at the final crossing place (ford) between the worlds. It also opens up for discussion Ireland's myths/ mythological heroes' astronomical connection. Reference: https://mythicalireland.com/MI/blog/astronomy-and-the-sky/lugh-of-the-long-arm-carries-the-sun-on-the-summer-solsti ce/

the great mering   the dividing line between two kingdoms, in this context meaning the dividing line between the world of flesh and blood and the Otherworld.

Turner of the Wheel   (cf).

my Father   (cf).

An Dagda   (cf).

···

Connla

Glossary (in order of appearence)

child of the child of light   Connla was the son of Cú Chulainn and Aoife (cf)

the son of a son of the sun god   Cú Chulainn was the son of Lugh (cf)

Lugh of the Long Arm   (cf)

she of radiant joy and beauty   Aoife(cf)

my home above the sea   Dún Scáith (cf)

Aoife   (cf)

the Hound   (cf)

Conchobar   (cf)

Aunt Scáth   (cf)

Dún Scáith   (cf)

Scáthach   (cf)

cailleach feasa   (cf)

Turner of the Wheel   (cf)

stars of my grandfather's chain   ie, the Milky Way in the night sky, referred to as 'Lugh's Chain'.

Scáthach   (cf).

Aunt Scáth   (cf).

Scythian skills   several Irish texts, notably the Book of Invasions, claim that the Irish originated in Scythia. Although there was no actual ancient land by that name there was a migratory group in eastern Europe called the Scythians - noted for their horsemanship and their impressive gold, they may have interacted with the Celts in their original homeland in central Europe, as suggested by the similarity of swirling La Téne art and some Scythian patterns. There also might have been some connection to Scythia in reference to Scáthach as it was nicknamed the 'land of witches' (ref: Scythia - Land of Witches by Christopher Penczak, 'Shaman witchcraft'), mentioned in Scáthach (https://thejourneyofaurora.wordpress.com/2019/12/02/scathach/). Some sources speculate that both Scáthach and Aoife were 'daughters of the 'king of Scythia'.

deamhans   god, Irish Gaelic for 'god, goddess, or divine power' (originally from *daemon* - Latin, and, before that, the Greek word, δαίμων, meaning the same.

coire goirath   (cf., also http://www.summerlands.com/crossroads/library/threecau.htm)

stramash   (cf).

sluagh   (cf)

Aoife of legend and myth before her who laments her own jealousies still   (cf, **Stories of (the other) Aoife**)

Lir   Lir of SídhFionnachaidh (cf, **Stories of (the other) Aoife**)

Fionnuala   eldest and only daughter of Aobh, the first wife of Lir of SídhFionnachaidh

Mother and the other Aoife   differentiates between the two Aoifes. (cf).

my Aoife   referring to his mother (cf).

neither Mother nor Scáthach, nor even Úathach   (cf).

Úathach   (cf)

gift without bride-price,/Aunt Scáth's attempt to pacify him   (cf).

he broke any whispered pledges... as soon as Aoife appeared...   (cf).

Úathach/Aoife/... sword between Scáthach's breasts...   (cf).

whilst under Scáthach's tutelage... used Úathach for a time ... used Scáthach's knowledge ... to further his own cause   (cf).

split her suitor twain, took his position as her man   (cf)

skulked back to Emer   (cf)

... the unravelling of her revengeance, Scáthach's pique...   (cf).

... whilst under Scáthach's tutelage... to further his own cause   sources differ in the length of time Cú Chulainn trained with Scáthach, some say a year and a day, others up to seven years in all (for this trilogy I chose the former).

Dún Scáith   (cf)

Aunt Scáth's darkened domain ie, Dún Scáith   (cf).

Emer   (cf).

Scáthach and Úathach   (cf).

Ulaid   (cf).

Cú Chulainn   (cf).

the Wheel   (cf).

Fae   (cf)

vates   In modern English, the nouns *vates* (/ˈveɪtiːz/) and *ovate* (UK: /ˈɒvət, ˈoʊveɪt/, US: /ˈoʊveɪt/), are used as technical terms for ancient Celtic bards, prophets and philosophers. The terms correspond to a Proto-Celtic word which can be reconstructed as *wātis.They are sometimes also used as English equivalents to later Celtic terms such as Irish *fáith* "prophet, seer".

spae (I'm looking at you, Aunt Scáth)   (cf).

the Wheel   (cf).

Few survived Aunt Scáth's teachings   (cf).

windows to his soul   eyes

his seven pupils   Cú Chulainn was said to have seven pupils in each eye (Reference: The most elaborate description of his appearance comes later in the Táin: "And certainly the youth Cúchulainn mac Sualdaim was handsome as he came to show his form to the armies. You would think he had three distinct heads of hair—brown at the base, blood-red in the middle, and a crown of golden yellow. This hair was settled strikingly into three coils on the cleft at the back of his head. Each long loose-flowing strand hung down in shining splendour over his shoulders, deep-gold and beautiful and fine as a thread of gold. A hundred neat red-gold curls shone darkly on his neck, and his head was covered with a hundred crimson threads matted with gems. He had four dimples in each cheek—yellow, green, crimson and blue—and seven bright pupils, eye-jewels, in each kingly eye. Each foot had seven toes and each hand seven fingers, the nails with the grip of a hawk's claw or a gryphon's clench." - Thomas Kinsella (translator), *The Táin*, Oxford University Press, 1969, pp. 156–158).

son of both 'Cú Chulainn and… Aoife'   (cf).

cursed belly spear   the Gáe Bulg (also Gáe Bulga, Gáe Bolg, Gáe Bolga), meaning "spear of mortal pain/death", "gapped/notched spear", or "belly spear", was the name of the spear of Cúchulainn in the Ulster Cycle of Irish mythology. It was given to him by his martial arts teacher, the warrior woman Scáthach, and its technique was taught only to him. (cf)

the one feat Scáthach taught not to this boy   (cf)

riastrad   (cf)

your and Scáthach's mentoring   (cf).

Aunt Scáth's secrets of invincibility and sorcery   (cf).

Otherworldly   (cf)

colg   (cf)

claideb   (cf)

camán   wooden stick used to hit the ball in hurley

sparra   long, narrow battle axe (also called a 'sparth')

scian   'knife' in Irish

ferocities of you and Aunt Scáth'   refers to Aoife and Aunt Scáthach   (cf).

Ard-Greimne, maternal grandfather mine   (cf)

crucible of Aunt Scáth's initiations and... Mother's affection   (cf).

Gae Bulg   (cf).

Aoife of beforetimes   (cf).

Dún Scáith   (cf).

pounding, foam-flecked froth of Manannán's wild herd   ie, waves of the sea crashing against the shore

sluagh   (cf).

Cet   son of Duncan and Scáthach

Cuar   son of Duncan and Scáthach

secret and elusive cousins training solely under Scáthach's tutelage   (cf).

Culann's Hound   (cf).

culmination of Mother's and Aunt Scáth's thirst for satisfaction   (cf).

Connla   (cf).

just as Aunt Scáth discarded Duncan   (cf).

Aunt Scáth   (cf).

scars of Aunt Scáth's sundering   (cf).

raven mistress   the Mórrígan (cf)

queen of crows   the Mórrígan (cf)

Aunt Scáth's homage only casual but cursory   because of her eldritch origins snd her observations of the world, epoch, mythology, and lineage she had chosen to infiltrate before 'incarnating', Scáthach was aware of the Mórrígan's far reaching and almost timeless influence and the populace's veneration of Her, and she kept up a casual and cursory adherence to such mostly for appearance's sake, though she also knew She could be a powerful ally, if required.

seat of my life   head

Èirinn   Ireland

Cú Chulainn   (cf).

bound to the whims of Mother and Aunt Scáth   (cf).

Red Branch champions   in the Ulster Cycle of Irish mythology the Red Branch (from Old Irish *Cróeb Ruad* 'dull red branch', alternatively from Old Irish *Cróeb Derg* 'bright red branch') was the name of two or three royal houses of the king of Ulaid (Ulster), Conchobar mac Nessa (cf) at his capital Emain Macha (Navan Fort, near Armagh)

Uliad   (cf).

Hound of Ulaid   (cf)

she of radiance, beauty, and joy   Aoife (cf)

Scáthach ni Uanaind   (cf)

Ard-Greimne of Lethra   (cf)

Aunt Scáth, you taught the art of no distraction   (cf).

sparra   (cf).

Aunt Scáth's maleficence   (cf).

"Here is my son for you, men of Ulaid"   line adapted from https://www.maryjones.us/ctexts/aoife.html

Tech Duinn   (cf)

ar an tslí   Irish for 'en route' Reference: https://www.libraryireland.com/SocialHistoryAncientIreland/I-III-9.php)

the Otherworld   (cf)

Aunt Scáth's bitter accord   (cf).

beyond the ninth wave   (cf)

Úathach

Glossary (in order of appearance)

Máthair   Old Irish for mother.

Dún Scáith   (cf).

Scáthach ni Uanaind   (cf)

cailleach feasa   (cf).

cailleach piseog   (cf).

cailleach an chlaíomh   witch of the sword

bandraíodóir   (cf)

bród sotalach iomarcach   Old Irish for 'excessive, arrogant pride'.

liopaí dearga fola   blood red lips.

géilleadh deiridh   ultimate surrender.

claimhteoireacht   swordmanship

Máthair   (cf).

ceannlann   armour (cf).

Máthair   (cf).

Lasair, Ingean Bhuidhe, Latiaran   (cf).

Cet and Cuar   (cf).

Iomaíocht   competition.

mian leis an bhfeoil   (cf).

Warrior Maid, She-Witch, She Who Strikes Fear   (cf).

cioch   (cf).

aoibh   (cf).

súile suirí   flirting eyes

Cú Chulainn, the Hound of Uliad   (cf).

flah   to show off or boast

Bridge of Leaping   (cf).

lasair náire   'flame of shame'

áer Áer   is traditionally translated as 'satire' and has been the focus of a certain amount of attention in mediaeval Irish studies in recent times. DIL (10) defines áer as '(a) cutting, incising; (b) act of satirising, lampooning, defaming'. It also refers to the word *rind/rindad* 'cut, cutting' for comparison, and this Dillon (1953a, 82, note on l.10) translates as 'point' which in turn equates with the modern Irish word *rinn*, meaning 'point, tip', i.e., *rinn sleá, rinn claímh* 'point of spear, point of sword' (Ó Dónaill, 1977, 1001). Thus *áer* has affinities with *rind*(ad). Binchy (1941, 69) describes *áer* as a 'formidable weapon with which members of the poetic orders (*grád fhiled*) enforced claims either on their own behalf or on behalf of other persons who employed them...To satirise a person without lawful ground is a delict which entitles the victim to recover the full amount of his honour-price as a penalty'. <u>Satirical Narrative in Early Irish Literature</u>, p4

Máthair   (cf).

coire goirath   (cf).

Máthair   (cf).

Cochar Croibne   (cf).

suire   (cf, 'thy suire's ecstacy')

son of a sun god   (cf).

Cochar   (cf).

Cú Chulain   (cf).

Máthair   (cf).

in cenaind n-gárechtig   the fair-headed boisterous one

in míarlig míepertaig   the evil-counselling, evil-speaking one

sclábhaí airnéise   (cf).

Máthair   (cf).

the Hound   (cf).

leannán cuileáilte   discarded lover.

mallacht   curses the Wheel (cf).

the Wheel   (cf).

the Hound   (cf).

claideb   (cf).

Auntie Aoife   (cf).

Máthair   (cf).

friendship of my thighs   (cf).

windows of my soul   (cf).

rape of trade   (cf).

claimhteoireacht   (cf).

Máthair   (cf).

Cú Chulain   (cf).

mar dhea   an ironic insertion similar to 'As if!', 'Yeah, right!', or a sarcastic 'Indeed…' or 'Supposedly', has been described as an 'expression of sardonic disbelief or dissent used to drive home the untruthfulness of some assertion, supposition, or pretence, similar to but infinitely stronger than the English 'forsooth'.

gáe bulga   (cf, '… the belly spear…')

Bridge of Leaping   (cf).

Glenn of Peril   (cf).

drank the faerie's waters   (cf).

Máthair   (cf).

caellich piseog   (cf).

banfhili   (cf).

Cú Chulainn is to falter soon   (cf).

Plain of Muirtheimne   (cf).

dobhar-chú   (cf).

Cochar Croibne   (cf).

the Hound   (cf).

the Wheel   (cf).

Máthair   (cf).

'... clansmen of white bronze... of life's edge'   refers to plays involved in the game of *fidchell* (cf).

imbas forosnai   (cf).

Máthair   (cf).

Mórrígan   (cf).

bandraíodóir   (cf).

imbas forosnai   (cf).

spaewife   (cf).

Máthair   (cf).

banfhili   (cf).

Fedelm   (cf).

cailleach piseog   (cf).

Emer   (cf).

Queen Medb   (cf).

Phantom Queen   the Mórrígan (cf).

Aoife's only son by the father   (cf).

Connla   (cf).

the bone of the Coinchenn   (cf, '... the belly spear...')

Ferdiad   (cf).

riastrad   (cf).

the rabid Hound   (cf, Cú Chulainn)

geasa   (cf).

Dún Scáith   (cf)

Máthair   (cf)

Ban-righinn Scáthach   literally Irish for 'shadow queen'.

longer lasting than the dying breath of the lung's of any bloodied eagle   refers to a method of ritual execution as detailed in late Skaldic poetry, mostly attributed to the Vikings. I refer to its use by '... *Badb witches of the Drunes...*' as mentioned in *pdfcoffee.com_d20-slaine-the-rpg-of-celtic-heroes-pdf-free.pdf*, p37.

Máthair   (cf).

stramash   (cf).

Máthair   (cf).

Ban-righinn Scáthach   (cf).

géilleadh deiridh   (cf).

mar scáth   (cf).

Máthair   (cf).

Hy Breasil   (cf).

Mothaím uaim thú, Máthair   I miss you, mother.

rúin adh   (cf).

Lig di, a mahdraí!   'Let her be, you dogs!'

Fognad dúib ág is ernbas!   'May danger and death follow you all!'

Marhadh fáisg ort!   'The squeezeband of death on you!' (This is based on an item made from any material used to keep the mouths of corpses shut that was tied around the jaw and head - basically wishing death on the person/s.

'Narab marthain duit!   'May you not remain alive!' (literally, 'may not be/remaining in existence/to you' ('don't exist for you').

mallachts   curses.

Máthair   (cf).

Úathach   (cf).

Máthair   (cf).

Dún Scáith   (cf).

Mothaím uaim thú, Máthair   (cf).

Úathach the Unassailable   one of Úathach's titles as both a warrior princess and as a goddess.

Ban-righinn Scáthach ni Uanaind   (cf).

Ard-Greimne of Lethra   (cf).

woad designs   (cf).

He of the Silver Hand   (cf, *Nuada Airgeadlámh*).

people of Danu   (cf, *Children of Danu*).

the Sword of Light, Claíomh Solais   *Claíomh Solais* (also: Claimh Solais, Cliamh Soluis, and Claidheamh Soluis) was the sword of Nuada of the Silver Hand, the first ruler of the Tuatha Dé Danann, who lost his hand (or arm, it's still up for debate) in the first Battle of Magh Tuireadh. One of the Four Treasures (or Jewels) of the Tuatha Dé Danann, Claimh Solais was sometimes described as Nuadu's Cainnel (a glowing bright torch). Once unsheathed, no enemy could survive its wrath. To quote from Celtic scholar Whitley Stokes' 1891 translation of the *Cath Maige Tuired* (*The Second Battle of Moytura*): "Out of Findias was brought the Sword of Nuada. When it was drawn from its deadly sheath, no one ever escaped from it, and it was irresistible." Claimh Solais is the first in a long folkloric tradition of glowing swords, which includes Cruaidín Catutchenn (Cú Chulainn's sword). <u>The 20 Most Legendary Weapons From Irish Mythology - IrishMyths</u>

Gáe Bulg's twin   (cf, *Gáe Bulg*. Úathach's possession of the Nuada's sword, and Scáthach's retrieval of it from a cache of artefacts of the people of Danu is entirely my creation - it just felt right that she (Úathach) would possess a powerful sword of legendary status, and the *Claíomh Solais* seemed the perfect choice).

trodaithe cumhachta of truth   (cf).

the Otherworld   (cf).

Máthair   (cf).

claimhteoireacht   (cf).

roc catha   (cf).

enech   Old Irish term meaning 'face' - ie, honour and reputation.

Airmed's herbs and her healing bath of sound   (cf)

Lugh of the Long Arm   (cf).

raven queen   refers to the Mórrígan (cf).

Cú Chulainn, Sétanta, Máthai, Aoife   (cf).

the Wheel   (cf).

echtrae   *(cf)*.

immrama   *(cf)*.

'... the mering wall beyond the ninth wave'   (cf).

the Summerland   Another term for Tír na nÓg, the Summerlands were not a place of eternal reward or punishment, but rather another stage of existence, a realm of the ancestors and the divine. There, souls rested, reflected, learnt from its experiences of its previous life, and prepared for its eventual rebirth.

the Otherworld   (cf).

claiomhs   (cf).

Ban-righinn Scáthach, Máthair   (cf).

your great Wrath   line adapted from 'Scáthach's Prayer', text found at blueroebuck.com/scathach.html

'*... not even the hands of Dian Cécht could heal...*'   Indirect reference to both Dian Cécht and the prosthetic silver hand he constructed for Nuada Airgeadlámh (cf).

Máthair   (cf).

bairdne   (cf).

Máthair   (cf).

claíomh   (cf).

'*Filleann an feall ar an bhfeallaire*'   Irish for, 'The bad deed returns on the bad-deed doer'.

Otherworldly   (cf).

the Goddess of Death, Herself, Ban-ríghinn Scáthach, She Who Strikes Fear, the Dark Goddess, the Warrior Maid, the She Witch   all terms for Scáthach (cf).

cailleach feasa, cailleach piseog, cailleach an chlaíomh   (cf).

Bandraíodóir   (cf).

Máthair   (cf).

Tír na nÓg   (cf).

mar scáth   (cf).

Áine   (cf).

Claimhteoireacht   (cf).

Máthair   (cf).

enech   (cf).

sarhaed   honour-price, a monetary value based on one's *enech* that defines the maximum amount they can be liable for in an oath or business deal, as well as reflecting the price that would be owed their kin if they are illegally killed or otherwise injured (physically or in terms of loss of honour).

gríosach   embers

Cú Chulainn   (cf).

sciath mhaighdean   (cf).

Úathach the Terrible   another of Úathach's titles as both a warrior princess and as a goddess.

'... forever the Maiden Goddess for no seed shall be planted in the womb of me that survives beyond the morning after, all praise to woman's ways and heart kissed gold without measure sprung from Airmed's tears of grief...'   Refers indirectly to *laserwort*, also once known as *silphium*, an ancient herb used by the Romans and many others as a 'morning after pill'. It seed or fruit was relatively heart-shaped, and it was so sought after it was considered to be worth its weight in gold, and I included it as one of the 365 healing herbs ('... all the healing herbs of the world...') that sprung from the earth covering Her brother Miach's body (cf). References for *silphium* https://en.wikipedia.org/wiki/Silphium and https://ecotonemagazine.org/poetry/extinction-laserpicium/ .

dòigh nàdair   (cf; the way of nature. Reference: https://forest-therapy-scotland.com/doigh-nadair-the-way-of-nature/)

Tír na nÓg   (cf).

síoraíocht   (cf).

géilleadh deiridh   (cf).

claimhteoireacht   (cf).

crann na haithne, crann-nathair   (cf).

Mothaím uaim thú, Máthair. Beidh cónaí ort i mo chuimhne croí go deo
(I miss you, Mother. You will abide in my heart memory forever.)

....

Emer

Glossary (in order of appearance)

Hound   (cf).

sluagh   (cf).

thy father's long arm   reference to Lugh, one of His names being 'Lugh of the Long Arm' (cf).

Bealach na Bó Finne,   the Way of the White Cow (cf).

Plain of Muirthemne   (cf).

Airmed   (cf).

Tuatha Dé Danann   (cf).
Line referenced from '*... the Druids, lifting up their hands to heaven, and pouring forth dreadful imprecations, scared our soldiers by the unfamiliar sight, so that, as if their limbs were paralysed, they stood motionless, and exposed to wounds.*' The quote "*the Druids, lifting up their hands to heaven, and pouring forth dreadful imprecations, scared our soldiers by the unfamiliar sight, so that, as if their limbs were paralysed, they stood motionless, and exposed to wounds*" is from *The Annals by Roman historian Cornelius Tacitus*. The quote describes the Roman conquest of Anglesey and the terrifying sight of the Druids performing rituals that scared the Roman soldiers.

battles of Mag Tuired   cf, note under *Well of Sláine* (cf).

riastrad   (cf).

laoch misniúil   Old Irish for brave warrior

Uliad   (cf).

Alba   (cf).

Ériu   (cf).

féth fíada   (Old Irish: féth fíada, féth fiada, feth fiadha, fé fíada, faeth fiadha) is a magical mist or veil in Irish mythology, which members of the Tuatha Dé Danann use to enshroud themselves, rendering their presence invisible to human eyesight.

coire emmae   (cf).

Connla   (cf).

Aoife's only son   (cf).

Sétanta   (cf).

roc catha   (cf).

Ferdiad   (cf).

Scáthach   (cf).

the fashioned bone of the Coinchenn, Curruid-taken / her belly spear, the Gáe Bulg   (cf).

the Hound   (cf).

Ferdiad   (cf).

Cathbad's spell of illusion liberation   (cf).

Manannán mac Lir   (cf).

Tech Duinn, the house of the dark one   (cf).

Hy Breasil   (cf).

fingal   crime of kin-slaying

corpdíre   body-fine

Conchobar   (cf).

... as had Elatha of the Otherworld when he knew Bres as his own and averted such a course...   In *The Second Battle of Mag Tuired*, Bres is the son of Ériu and her Otherworld lover, Elatha, who leaves a ring for the son she will bear him. Father and son eventually meet, but combat between them is avoided when Elatha sees the ring and recognises Bres.

Connla   (cf).

Aoife   (cf).

Scáthach   (cf).

e Cú Chulainn   (cf).

eagna na laochra   warrior's wisdom

Tír na nÓg   (cf).

cétmuinter   'chief wife' - ie, first wife, the only kind of marriage acceptable to her as a woman of high status (*A Woman's Words, Emer and female speech in the Ulster Cycle*, University of Toronto Press Incorporated 1997, pp 37-38, 49)

Lugaid Mac Nois, son of Nos, son of Alamac   (cf).

Muirthemne's Plain   (cf).

riastrad   (cf).

cathchriss   (*'thy tunics, apron, and cathchriss of tanned and hardened leather having failed thee at the last......'*) Cú Chulainn's armour consisted of twenty-seven tunics [*cneslenti*] worn next to his skin, waxed, board like, compact, which were bound with strings and ropes and thongs close to his fair skin. Over that outside he put his hero's battle girdle [*cathchriss*] of hard leather, tough and tanned, made from the best part of seven ox-hides of yearlings, which covered him from the thin part of his side to the thick part of his arm-pit; he used to wear it to repel spears (*gai*) and points (*rend*) and darts (*iaernn*)and lances (*sleg*) and arrows (*saiget*), for they glanced from it as if they had struck against stone or rock or horn. Then he put on his apron (*fuathbroic*) of filmy silk with its border of variegated white gold, against the soft lower part of his body. Outside his apron of filmy silk he put on his dark apron *(dond{f}uathbroic)*of pliable brown leather made from the choicest part of four yearling ox-hides with his battle-girdle (cf.) of cows' skins about it.

Scáthach   (cf).

Medb   (cf).

Sétanta-come-Cú Chulainn   (cf).

sliotar   (cf).

Claimhteoireacht   (cf).

warriors of the Red Branch   (cf).

loving arms of thy Father's embrace   reference to Lugh of the Long Arm (cf).

Mórrígan   (cf).

Muirthemne Plain   (cf).

men in Alba   (cf).

Cruachan's heroes   (cf).

Scáthach   (cf).

She of Shadow   refers to Scáthach (cf).

the Dagda to resurrect thy broken form with His lorg mór   (cf).

Aoife and Úathach   (cf).

the Dagda, Himself   (cf).

sons and daughters of Calatin   (cf).

Lugaid Cú Roi   (cf).

mighty wave of Medb's armies   (cf).

the Scald Crow, Herself, the Mórrígan   (cf).

bairdne tales   (cf).

seanchaí, bearers of old lore   (cf).

Turner of the Wheel   (cf).

the Shadow   (cf).

cétmuinter   (cf).

enech   (cf).

Ériu   (cf).

... thrice-bloodied wine of Deichtre that would not unturn...   (cf).

dobhar-chú   (cf).

turning of the Wheel   (cf).

Connla   (cf).

Ferdiad's bed of blood   (cf).

Aofie's scorn   (cf).

Mórrígan and Medb   (cf).

teardrop of beauty   (cf).

Emer's six gifts so suitable   (cf).

friendship of the Shadow's thighs   (cf).

Forgall my father's broken bond   (cf).

Bláthnat's fall forced   (cf).

burning of the jealous bitches   refers to the story, Aided Derbforgaill ("The Death of Derbforgaill"). See note in **Cú Chulainn**: *one time found I sucking from another woman's woundedness shot slung from mine hand... charred and blackened wakes...* (cf).

nae matter the death of the hound...   refers to Culann's hound.

Beltane fires   (cf).

the Dagda   (cf).

dóigh nádair, the way of nature   (cf).

to refill thy cauldron's broth   (cf).

cétmuinter   (cf).

Mothaím uaim thú, Anamchara./Beidh cónaí ort i mo chuimhne croí go deo   (I miss you, Soul friend. You will abide in my heart memory fore'er)   (cf).